THE HORROR AT LAVENDER EDGE

*Supernatural terror in
1970s London*

Christopher Henderson

Shadowtime Publishing

eBook ISBN-13: 978-0-9541995-8-6
Paperback ISBN-13: 978-1-9160805-1-5
First published 2019. Second paperback edition published 2022.

Cover designed by 100 Covers.

Shadowtime Publishing

*In memory of John ('The Castellan')
Smyth. If there is a life beyond this one,
I hope you have found a place where
streams of whiskey are flowing.*

There's a ragged hole in the world that we know,
And it's calling me home from the end of the
show.

CRYSTAL STARCRUISER ('BACK IN THE
BEYOND', 1971)

CONTENTS

CHAPTER 1

They weren't alone. That had been clear the moment they arrived. Whatever lingered here was powerful, strong enough to have bristled the edge of his mind as he opened the door, and at that first hint he had slammed down his shutters. It was too dangerous to risk exposure before he had to.

Where was it?

Even with the lights full on, the auditorium was gloomy. Pools of shadow lay everywhere: lurking below them at the foot of these steps, behind the whispering tinsel ribbons of the stage curtains, under every row of stained red velvet seating. And the substance that haunted this place needn't be concealed in the darkness, or hiding in the silence that crouched around them. It could be anywhere, kept at bay only as long as his mental barrier held.

Why the hell did he put himself through this?

He clicked the switch and the house lights died. Carefully, his eyes adjusting, he sat on the step and felt around for the microphone. When he lifted it to his mouth and spoke, his voice was steady. Mostly.

'Commencing Session Four, Pyramus theatre, Old Compton Street. Our location is now the back of the auditorium. Harry Undine recording.'

Two or three hundred cushioned seats soaked up his words. The hush thickened. He was as ready as he was going to get.

Undine took a long, deep breath, and let it out slowly, trying to calm his thumping heart as he allowed his mind to ease open, just a fraction, just far enough for only the topmost skim of impressions to filter in, and …

… nothing happened.

He slumped with relief.

He raised the microphone again. 'It's now the morning of Tuesday the twelfth of October, 1971. The time is just coming up to around oh-three-hundred hours. I think. Also present is Doctor Ray Buckley. We are about to – oh, bloody hell!'

Undine stumbled to his feet, sweeping glowing ash and the dropped cigarette from his trouser leg. As he flicked the burning tip into the dark, his heel caught the edge of the step, and he lost his balance, sitting again with a spine-jarring thud. The impact jolted the microphone from his fingers, and it fell to the greasy carpet.

Ray chuckled. 'And we'll leave Session Four there, I think.' He switched on his torch, stopped the tape recorder, and retrieved the mike from where it had rolled. 'You alright?'

Undine dusted his trousers, and made sure his thoughts were composed before the torch beam caught him. 'Yeah.'

He found his cigarette. Dead. He scowled and tossed it under the nearest row of chairs.

'Well, we might as well join the others.' Ray handed the second torch to Undine. 'If there were any ghosts up here, I reckon you've scared them away.'

Undine's short laugh was purely for his friend's benefit. He locked the tape recorder into its carrying case and gave the darkened auditorium a last appraising look.

Pulling a walkie-talkie from his holdall, Ray thumbed the switch. 'Ray to Archie. All quiet up here. We're on our way down to you now. Over.'

Static scratched the air, roughening the soft Scottish reply. 'Okay. We're just about set up down here. See you in a few moments. Over.'

Downstairs. Yeah, that's where it would be. Nerves building once more, twisting his stomach, Undine followed Ray down the steps to where a black-painted door waited to swallow them.

❊　　❊　　❊

Damp misery permeated the concrete corridor, and it was unrelieved by the old advertising posters sellotaped to the walls. The women featured in assorted stages of undress were already largely forgotten performers here, at one of Soho's less-than-glamorous venues.

Ray's torch played across them. 'Blimey.'

'Don't look too close, Sunny. You'll go blind.' Undine walked on, brushing a strand of cobweb from his hair. It seemed the cleaners were no keener than he was to spend time down here.

Voices seeped around the corner. A moment later, the corridor revealed Professor Archibald James, ex-archaeologist and now head of the London office of the Corsi Institute, in subdued conversation with the manager. Bob? Bill? Something like that.

Whatever his name was, his brown hair was girlishly long, and greasy with the sleaze of working here. At least he wasn't a hippy. Bloody Sixties flotsam, still hoping that flowers, love and a conman's mystical claptrap could solve the world's problems. Soppy nutters with no clue about the forces they dabbled with. The Beatles had a lot to answer for.

'Ah,' said Archie. 'Here they are. No luck upstairs then?'

'Sweet F.A.,' said Undine.

Archie nodded. 'Well, no matter. Robert and I have everything prepared down here. We're ready whenever you are.'

'The Gents?' Ray grinned. 'Hardly the classiest spooks you've got!'

Robert shrugged. 'Weren't always a toilet. Used to be just the basement.'

Someone had propped the Gents door open with an ancient fire bucket. It was full of sand and fag butts. Undine glanced inside the room and saw that Archie had already set up his 'Octopus' machine. He walked in, nervous as he sensed a pushing at his defences: thoughts of the door slamming shut and trapping him forever in dense blackness, to starve and to rot…. He stopped. His fingers ached, the nails tingling.

'Okay,' said Archie, and Undine heard the note of approval in his tone. The Professor reached into the pocket of his tweed jacket, his watery blue eyes fixed on Undine. 'Let's start right where you are now, shall we?'

'Fine by me.' Undine willed himself to appear calm as he accepted the pendulum Archie passed to him despite knowing he didn't need it. A solid clunk rang from dirty tiles as Ray pushed home the cable connecting tape recorder to Octopus; he tapped the microphone.

'Testing. One, two. One, two.'

Satisfied that the needles on both machines were responding as they should, Ray passed the mike to Archie.

Undine cleared his throat as Archie recorded a brief statement of the session number, time and location, and Ray took up position behind the camera tripod.

Robert watched, running fingers through his lank hair. 'What do you want me to do?'

'Oh, just make yourself comfortable,' said Archie. 'But do keep your eyes and ears open, if you could. One can never have too many potential witnesses on these occasions.'

'Take a seat over there if you like.' Undine nodded towards the stalls that lined the opposite wall. 'Anything does happen, at least you'll be in the right place.'

'Yeah. I'll stand over here, ta,' said Robert, moving back out into the corridor.

Archie murmured absent assent. He knelt in front of the heavy, grey metal box that housed the main body of the Octopus, checking its readiness. Cables snaked across the stained floor from an assortment of gadgets arrayed around the room, carrying their findings back to the box. A large roll of paper dominated the top, rotating smoothly and enabling eight delicate arms, each tipped with a different-coloured pen, to leave jagged traces according to the information that came in.

'Humidity levels seem interesting,' said Archie. 'Magnetics too. Gentlemen, I think we're ready.'

Undine swallowed hard and slowed his breathing, staring at the useless pendulum as, gingerly, he relaxed the hold on his mind.

Shadows shifted. Undine closed his eyes,

and let a taste of the room's impressions filter through.

A great weight of emotion filled the surrounding air.

He allowed the tiniest tendril of his opening consciousness to reach into the room.

Yeah, there was something down here. Not very far away at all. It was –

Here! He recoiled, his pulse pounding in the hollow below his Adam's apple.

Careful, he cautioned himself. You can do this.

He took another deep breath. Held it. Exhaled, letting out anxiety as he released his thoughts again, accepting the presence. Probing the boundary, wrapping understanding around the shape of it.

Another, watchful, part of Undine's mind now felt the keen sharpness of Archie's intellect, studying him, and the spiky warmth of Ray's cynical amusement. He ignored them and kept his eyes shut, keeping his facial expression as neutral as he could.

He'd been correct. Whatever this was in here with them, it had power. More power than anything he had encountered before while working with the Institute team. It wasn't reacting to him though, thank Christ. Not yet. Perhaps this was an opportunity to learn more about his so-called 'gift'.

Undine dared to press a little deeper. Still

no reaction. As long as he didn't push too hard, maybe he could –

He pierced a membrane.

Surface tension broke, and all at once a pressure front of darkness was roaring out, bursting over Undine, drenching him.

'Something's up.' Ray's voice.

Undine's lungs boiled with viscous black despair. It flooded his insides, surging up and into his mouth. Loss and resentment stabbed his brain, and a terrible sound was rising all around him like a tidal wave.

'Is everything okay?'

He recognized Archie's Highland burr, but it came from so far away, on the other side of a thickness of reality. Behind –

… broken nails clawing at a locked door – bloodied fingers, skin scraped raw to the bone – a dying man fuelled by a final surge of panic …

Undine's body rebelled. He staggered towards the stalls, compelled to purge himself of the foulness filling him, and somewhere over his shoulder a camera clicked.

❊   ❊   ❊

Archie pulled the wheel around and the old three-tonner yawed left, bouncing off the pavement as it escaped the dingy Soho backstreets. The morning sky shone a crisp, pale blue. Shop shutters rattled open and office workers streamed desk-ward over the pavements as the team's lorry slid into the traffic on Charing Cross Road. Sunlight poured through the passenger window, turning Ray into a skeletal silhouette, and the searing brightness of his halo would have brought tears to Undine's eyes had those tears not already been there.

With disgust, Undine realized he was on the verge of crying. Nothing to do with the dazzling light: this was an after-effect of the emotional echoes that had swamped him at the theatre. Residue like that almost always left him a weepy mess, which was bad enough if you happened to be a teenage girl but inexcusable in a man who'd turned 30 several months ago. A profound shudder rose from the ache that filled his chest, and he bit back a sudden eruption of self-directed anger as he discreetly wiped moisture from his eyes, disguising the move by coughing into his hands.

Bloody hell, his mouth tasted filthy. His skin was grubby too, and his hair itched.

'How're you feeling?' asked Ray.

Undine rubbed his stomach, pretending to soothe the food poisoning cramps he'd invented to hide the truth. With the three men squashed together in the cab, his arm had little room to move.

He faked a tight smile. 'Still playing up. Be glad to get back.'

Archie gave the sluggish steering wheel

another mighty tug, wrestling the unwieldy vehicle to the right this time. The sun slid in front of them, blazing through the windscreen as they rumbled and squeaked along Holborn. Archie hunched forward, squinting into the glare. His eyesight wasn't up to this. As sick as he felt, Undine started to wish he hadn't relinquished his usual role as driver. Christ, even Ray would be preferable to the old man – and Ray couldn't tell a crankshaft from a spare tyre.

The lorry lurched. Undine's neck ached. He would never get used to sleeping bags. Not that he'd got any sleep. He had spent the last few hours staring towards the ceiling that loomed unseen in the murk above the Pyramus's stage, too afraid to let down his guard even for an instant. He'd wanted to go home, but Archie had insisted they stay as long as possible.

'Don't worry,' said Ray. 'Plenty of bog roll back at the Warehouse.'

'Oh aye,' said Archie. 'We'll soon put the spring back in your step! Strong, sweet tea, that's what you need. All of us. Wake us up before the debriefing. And then, if memory serves, there's a very fine single malt in my desk. I believe our success calls for a wee celebration.'

Ray snorted. 'Success? What exactly do you think happened? That a ghost tried to possess Undine's bowels?'

'Oh, I'm fairly sure something occurred.'

'Such as?'

'We were getting some very interesting readings. I'll want to go over the tracings as soon as we can. And we certainly need to find out what our indisposed friend here picked up.'

'Sorry, Archie,' said Undine, forcing a bonhomie he did not feel. 'All I "picked up" was a message that the curry house I went to yesterday should be condemned.'

Ray chuckled. 'No argument from me! If Undine's cast-iron gut couldn't handle the spices, the place should be shut down for the public good!'

They bounced over another pothole that Archie hadn't spotted, squeezing a further groan from Undine.

'So it was pure coincidence, was it?' said Archie. 'Perhaps you could remind me, Dr Buckley: whereabouts in the Pyramus is it that people tend to report anomalous experiences?'

Undine knew the answer now. He would know it even if Archie hadn't finally revealed the results of his background research after letting Undine go in blind.

'I know, I know,' replied Ray. 'The Gents. But –'

'And where precisely were we when the Octopus started to register unusual activity?'

Ray sighed.

'The 1930s!' announced Archie. He spoke as if he were back in his old lecture hall. 'The Pyramus theatre in Old Compton Street, after standing derelict for a decade, has been brought dirt-cheap by one Mr Godwin, and is being remodelled. One afternoon, in the midst of a fierce storm, a tramp steals past the workmen and creeps down into the depths of the building in search of shelter.'

A bitterness came to Undine's mouth.

Archie recited his notes from memory, almost verbatim. Clearly enjoying himself, he rolled his r's and fell back into the lilting Scottish rhythms he had used when performing for his students. 'Safe, dry and warm, the tramp falls asleep, lulled by the distant banging of hammers. Unknown to him, however, this is to be the last day of work. For that same evening, the workmen leave for the final time, locking the doors behind them, and unwittingly making a prisoner of the poor, sleeping tramp.'

'It's classic folklore!' scoffed Ray.

Archie was undeterred. 'He awakes to find himself alone in the dark, empty underground room. There are no windows, no other exits, only the one weighty and very locked door. It is almost a fortnight before the theatre's owner returns from a trip abroad, looks around the building to check the workmen have done their jobs correctly, and – last of all – makes his way down to the basement where he unlocks that door, opens it, and sees –'

Undine did his best not to hear. He focused on the black tarmac slipping by beneath them. At the deep, shadowed ruts and cracked white lines as they approached, then vanished into the past. Memories churned, threatening to bring back the nausea.

'- with dried blood, his nails ripped out, and his fingers worn to the bone. There are marks gouged into the wood on the inside of the door, where he tried for days to claw his way out. To escape what had become his tomb.'

The lorry heaved south onto Tower Bridge. Across the river and to their left, old warehouses loomed over the Thames, which lay thick and motionless, its green waters dull despite the sunlight.

'And, ever since,' continued Archie, 'there have been reports of visitors to that establishment, when they are not distracted by the lascivious goings-on on stage, feeling uncomfortable in what is now the gentlemen's toilet. The very same place where our unfortunate vagrant met his end.'

'Feeling uncomfortable?' repeated Ray. 'I'm not surprised! What are some of the things people say they've experienced down there?' He pulled out a tatty notebook. 'I jotted down what you told us. Here we go. "Strange smells" – there's a shock. "A sense they're not alone, that maybe they are being watched." Well, it *is* Soho. There's a pretty good chance someone really was there, peeping at them!'

'Ah, there's more to it than that, as you very well know. I have several accounts – consistent accounts – of witnesses who say they were overcome by the urge to escape that room. Who felt trapped, desperate to get out.'

Undine shivered.

'And more than one member of staff has resigned after hearing an eerie, scratching, scraping sound down there, long after the last patron has departed.'

'I should go into business if I were you, Archie. Selling mousetraps to your contacts. You'd make a fortune getting rid of their weird noises!'

Archie smiled. 'Well, let's wait to see what the Octopus recorded, shall we? Always follow the evidence, that's what I say. It's a good job I went to see Robert this afternoon. We'd have missed all the fun otherwise.'

Undine grunted. 'It's a good job the rest of us didn't have plans for last night.'

'Oh yeah?' Ray smirked, eager for details. 'Had a bird lined up, did you?'

Undine said nothing. Let his friend think what he wanted. Sunny was still too young to understand the attraction of solitude. To be alone, with nothing more energetic to do than read a book or listen to a record. Perhaps try out a new recipe.

Their schedule had changed late yesterday. The Pyramus stayed closed on Monday evenings, and the Institute had previously obtained permission to set up their equipment and monitor the venue until around midnight. But yesterday afternoon, when Archie visited the place to get the lie of the land ahead of their investigation, he had somehow smooth-talked the manager into staying with them overnight, giving them an extra few hours there. It must be that accent, Undine thought. It could slip under your defences if you let down your guard.

A stray thought drifted up from his subconscious. It flared for a moment, then died before he could identify it.

At last, they turned onto the familiar cobbles of Shad Thames. Tall brick warehouses stretched away down the narrow street, as they had for the past hundred years, although only one or two of the buildings still fulfilled their intended purpose. These days, a changing world forced ships to unload goods farther east, away from London's heart, and this once-bustling area on the south bank of the river had been sliding downhill for a long time.

Not all the warehouses were abandoned, though. Rent was cheap, and the open, rambling building coming into view was in many ways ideal for the Institute's needs.

'Home sweet home,' said Ray.

Archie looked at Undine. 'If you're up to it, I'd like to interview you straight away. Get your memories on tape while the episode is still fresh in your mind.'

'You're having a laugh,' said Undine. 'I'm

done for the day.'

He checked his wristwatch. Almost half nine. He'd been on the go since arriving at the Warehouse yesterday morning, a little over 24 hours ago.

'I'll give you and Sunny here a hand lugging in the bags, but after that I've a date with a comfy mattress. Besides, nothing happened back there.'

'That's what I've been trying to tell him,' said Ray.

'Nevertheless,' said Archie, 'it wouldn't hurt for you to describe whatever you can remember up until the point where you became ... unwell. You never know. Even the smallest detail, correlated with the sensor data, might be revealing.'

The old three-tonner grumbled the last few feet over the cobbles.

'Sorry.' Undine turned to look out of the window.

Archie gave the softest of sighs. 'Okay then. We'll take it up tomorrow. I suppose we could all do with a rest. Let's get everything safely stowed away and call it a day, hmm?'

'Suits me,' said Ray, stifling a yawn.

With a crunch, Archie shifted into a lower gear and encouraged the lorry into their parking spot. It shuddered to a halt, attracting the attention of a young woman seated on a low wall outside their building.

Undine felt that annoying niggle again, as

if he had forgotten something. He dismissed it as another after-effect of earlier, and took out his Embassies. He lit one, drew the smoke deep inside, and offered the pack to Ray.

'Cheers, mate.'

'Archie?'

'Oh, not for me. Thanks all the same.' Archie patted his breast pocket, where his faithful pipe nestled.

'Cor!' Ray exhaled smoke with a whistle of appreciation. 'She's a bit of alright, isn't she?'

The woman had stood up and was peering in their direction, one hand shading her eyes from the sun. She was a little on the short side for Undine's taste, with blonde hair cut into a shaggy style that he supposed must be fashionable. Dark blue bell-bottomed jeans hugged her slim waist.

Ray sat up straighter. He nudged Undine.

'Here we go! She's coming over! Be cool.' He fidgeted, taking another quick puff of his cigarette. 'Blimey, that jumper's tight.'

'I can't say I recognize her,' said Archie. 'Oh dear. She doesn't look too jolly now, does she?'

Archie rolled down his window. Cold air swirled into the cab's ripe interior.

Boots clattered onto the footplate and then a face was peering inside. Hazel eyes, heavy with too much mascara, blazed as they studied the three tired men.

'Is one of you called Undine?'

CHAPTER 2

A warm fug of smoke and stale sweat oozed from the lorry. Her first impulse was to pull away, step back down to the cobbles, and wait for the trio to get out. Instead, Jo Cross tightened her grip on the roof and stood her ground.

With practised eyes, she sized up the tired faces gawping at her. Three of them. All men, naturally. The eldest by some way sat in the driver's seat, just a few inches from her: a tweed-clad academic type who looked as if he rarely ventured beyond the realm of dust and books. He was well-built though, despite his years. Likely to have been quite the outdoorsman in his younger days.

The youngest was in his mid-twenties, same as her. Or possibly a year or two older. He sat on the far side: a skinny, awkward-looking bloke whose blushing face was too narrow for his enormous nose. His clothes were dreadful: he appeared to be wearing several different, clashing outfits at the same time.

With some difficulty, she dragged her gaze from the fashion crime-scene to check out the third man, squashed between his companions. Shadowed, deep-set eyes in a rugged face. Blunt features that might be handsome enough – if he lost a pound or two. Good suit though. Dark, decent tailoring. There was some style there, hidden though it was under the crumples and ash stains.

'Well?' she prompted after nobody replied.

A light came on in Dark Suit's eyes, coupled with an expression of dismay that was swiftly caught and controlled.

'Oh, pissing hell.'

'I take it you're Undine.'

'In the flesh, sweetheart. Hang on.'

Doors opened and the men stepped out with varying degrees of reluctance. Jo hopped down to face them. Tweedy gave her an uncertain but pleasant smile. His skinny companion nodded an eager greeting but kept his distance, hovering like a naughty schoolboy. Last to exit was Undine. He walked towards her, pulling on a black trench coat, which he probably thought made him look like Michael Caine's character in that awful 'Get Carter' film her ex had taken her to a few months ago. It didn't, although it did suit him in a rough and ready kind of way. He halted, looking her up and down.

'You 'phoned yesterday,' he said. It wasn't a

question.

'And you told me Professor James would meet me at nine o'clock.' She pulled up her sleeve, raised herself to her full five-and-a-half (nearly) feet, and pushed her watch up into Undine's face.

'I've been sitting out here in the cold for over half an hour, waiting for someone to turn up.'

'Yeah. Sorry about that, love. Business. You're right, though. It is a bit parky.' He nodded at her leather jacket. 'You should zip up.'

❈   ❈   ❈

'Sorry again, my dear.' Professor James opened the door. 'Ladies first. Normally, I would have been here to meet you, but our plans changed at the last minute yesterday.'

Jo walked inside. The Professor's words flattened and hollowed as he entered after her. 'So I'm afraid I didn't get the message that you had called.'

The interior of the old warehouse was vast, dingy, and – from the sound – largely empty. On the far wall, large, gently arched windows comprised of countless small panes did little to let in the daylight, and Jo was grateful to hear the snap of a light switch.

Bulbs glowed to life, unshaded, strung from the high ceiling. Hardly pretty, but at least she wouldn't trip over all the cables she could now see strewn around.

'No harm done, I guess,' she said.

'Good, good. Well, this way.'

The Professor led her across the floor. It was concrete: cold and damp. As the bulbs brightened, the brick walls proved to be painted a dismal sage colour above a thick band of darker forest green. Jo followed him past cast-iron columns, painted with the same thick band of dark green at the base but this time with cream above, and under an arch which was only just tall enough for him to pass through without ducking. He headed for a flight of stairs in the far corner.

'What's that smell?' she asked.

'Oh, I believe they used to store spices here.'

She sniffed again, appreciating the aroma more now that she knew what it was. All these years later and those scents still infused the brickwork. What must it have been like, back in its heyday?

Professor James started up the steps. Jo walked after him, conscious of Undine and his friend close behind her as they lugged bulky canvas holdalls and plastic cases upstairs. Doubtless enjoying the view. At the top, the Professor ushered her into an office, where the floor had been made a little more inviting by the judicious use of rugs.

The skinny one deposited his bags in a corner. He scurried to a sideboard, where there was a kettle and an assortment of mugs of differing sizes and colours.

'Fancy a coffee?'

'I'd prefer tea, to be honest. If you have any.'

He flashed a smile, keen to please. 'No problem. Milk and sugar?'

'Just milk, thanks.'

'Archie?'

'Oh, whatever you're having will be fine.' Professor James waved a hand at the mismatched chairs scattered around the room. Liberated, perhaps, from different offices that had gone out of business over the years. 'Do take a seat, Miss. Wherever you like.'

Despite her impatience, Jo had to admit his accent was lovely. Real old Highlands. Rich and warm and full of gentle strength.

'Thank you, Professor.' She chose the closest chair.

'Archie. Please.' He took his own seat, behind an impressive wooden desk.

'Okay. Archie.' She leaned forward and shook his hand. 'I'm Jo. Jo Cross.'

'A pleasure.' He gestured at the one trying not to scald himself as he sloshed water from the kettle. 'That's Doctor Ray Buckley. And Undine you've already met, of course.'

'Yes.'

'Coffee for me, Sunny.' Undine dropped one of his cases to the floor, then lifted the other, bulkier case onto the desk. He took more care with that one. The thud told her it was heavy.

Undine yawned. 'Two sugars.' He stared at Jo and his shoulders slumped. 'Best make it strong.'

Jo ignored him and addressed Archie. 'Looks like you had an eventful night.' She indicated the cases and gave him her most disarming smile. 'Anywhere interesting?'

'Indeed!' Archie popped the latches on the case Undine had placed in front of him, and opened the lid to reveal a grey metal box. There was a clack as he released a catch, and then he was pulling out a chunky roll of paper, covered with scratchy, multi-coloured lines.

His eyes blazed with youthful excitement. 'I know it doesn't look like much, but we might just have proved the existence of ghoul zones!'

'I'm sorry?'

'His pet project.' Ray handed her a mug of tea. The mug was chipped, but less so than those he gave the others. It probably passed for their best china.

'Archie is quite the Lethbridge devotee,' continued Ray. 'He believes that ghosts – or, rather, what people generally think of as ghosts – can be explained as recordings. Certain events – angry, violent events, say – are supposedly imprinted on the environment in some exotic manner yet to be defined, forming what folk like Archie call "ghoul zones".'

'Okay,' said Jo, sensing the scepticism in Ray's tone but not knowing how to take it.

'And when the right person comes along,

they interact with the zone in such a way – again, yet to be defined – that they trigger the recording and see what seems to be a ghost.'

'Is that true?'

'It's what I hope to show.' Archie offered an amused, long-suffering smile. 'Not everyone agrees.'

'What sort of person is the "right person"?' she ventured.

'Ah, now there's a fascinating question.'

Archie's eyes strayed towards Undine as if expecting him to contribute. The dark-suited man only blew on his coffee.

'But this machine,' asked Jo, 'can detect these zones?'

Ray scoffed.

Archie was unruffled. 'Let's just say we've been getting some very intriguing results.'

He was clearly keen to tell her more, and so she asked how the machine worked, listening quietly as he answered, giving room for the old man's enthusiasm and letting him wax lyrical about what he called his 'Octopus'. Archie had invented the contraption himself, she learned, or at least had it constructed according to his design. Its key feature was the way it combined inputs from various probes that measured a range of environmental factors including magnetism, humidity and temperature. There was also something about the way a location reacted to sound, with the Octopus playing

24

adjustable audio frequencies into a chosen area and listening to the result. The entire spectrum of collected information was recorded as multiple traces onto a single roll of paper, which must be the coloured lines that jittered and jagged along the paper Archie was now showing her.

'Everything is automatically time-stamped too,' he beamed. 'See? So every factor can be correlated.'

'Archie,' said Undine. 'You're boring our guest.'

'Hm?'

'Not at all,' said Jo.

'This isn't why she came here though.' Undine glared at her. 'Is it?'

She held his gaze. The coffee must have re-animated him because he bore less resemblance to a warmed-over zombie now.

'You're right,' she said. 'The fact is, guys, I need your help to get rid of a ghost.'

✻　　✻　　✻

'Sorry, love,' said Undine. 'You've got the wrong people.'

Jo opened her mouth, but Undine continued before she could say anything.

'Look, I apologize for not passing your message to Archie. We had a lot going on and your call slipped my mind. It happens. And I'm sorry for your wasted journey but, like I said, you've got the wrong people.'

He stepped towards her, hand rising to take her by the shoulder and guide her out.

Jo stayed where she was.

'You don't believe in ghosts?' she asked.

Undine rolled his eyes.

Jo looked to Archie for support. The Professor had taken out a pipe and was methodically pressing tobacco into the bowl.

'It's a little more complicated, my dear. The question shouldn't be whether one believes in ghosts but rather what one believes ghosts to be.'

Jo frowned. 'I don't understand.'

Ray took his cue. 'Put it this way.' He took off his ugly jacket, giving full view of an even more tasteless shirt, and hung it over the back of his chair. 'When you think of a ghost, I imagine you're thinking in terms of a spirit, aren't you? The soul of a deceased person either returned to our world or maybe trapped here. Something along those lines, yeah?'

'That's what ghosts are, aren't they?'

'Possibly,' said Archie.

'No,' said Ray.

Archie chuckled softly. He struck a match.

'So what are they?' asked Jo.

Sweet-smelling smoke blossomed into the air.

'Well,' said Archie, 'my suspicion – and, despite my colleague's scepticism, it's an opinion that's becoming more widely accepted – is that what we're dealing with can be better understood as recordings – or the "ghoul zones" I was speaking of. My aim is to study them, a task made difficult, unfortunately, by their apparent rarity. The last thing I would wish to do is, as you phrase it, get rid of one!'

He leaned back in his chair. 'On the other hand, if you would permit me to arrange a proper investigation of your "ghost", I would be delighted to assist. Perhaps we might schedule something for next week?'

'Next week?'

'Aye. And in the meantime, try not to worry. The unknown is frightening, but the main thing to remember is that these recordings cannot hurt you.'

Archie puffed on his pipe.

Undine lifted his mug to his mouth and found it empty. He grunted and lit a cigarette, blowing the thin smoke to the ceiling where it mingled with Archie's growing, aromatic cloud.

Ray scraped his seat closer to Jo's and produced his own packet of cigarettes, offering her one. She shook her head.

Ray's eyes expressed sympathy. 'Sorry. I'd love to help you, but –'

'You don't believe in ghosts either?' Jo was incredulous. The Corsi Institute was not what she had expected.

'I believe in ghost *stories*,' Ray replied,

stressing the final word as if that both explained things and made them better. It did neither.

'My focus is on the psychosocial aspect of the supernatural.' Ray licked his lips. 'The strange stories people share, and the psychology involved.' His hands became more mobile. 'The perceptual and cognitive factors at play, how witnesses process often-ambiguous stimuli, and how their beliefs factor into their experiences.'

He paused, like someone waiting for a round of applause. 'How experience and belief interact?'

'You've lost me,' said Jo.

'He likes poking around inside people's heads,' said Undine. 'And he collects fairy stories.'

'There's more to it than that.' Ray looked crestfallen.

'Indeed there is,' scolded Archie. 'There are many ways to approach this subject matter, my dear, and the only firm truth is that none of us really knows all the facts for sure.' He turned to each of his companions in turn. 'We could all of us do with keeping a more open mind from time to time, and remember that, in all honesty, we do not know all the answers. And therein lies the fascination.'

'Well said, boss,' said Ray.

Undine's expression was harder to read.

Archie pulled out a desk drawer and removed a diary. A scrap of paper poked out, acting as a bookmark, and he opened the book at the indicated page. The sound he uttered led Jo to guess he had just found Undine's note regarding her appointment.

He rested his pipe on an ashtray, turned over a handful of blank pages, and unscrewed his fountain pen. 'Let's see. It will take us a few days to go through the data we collected last night....'

'This morning,' muttered Undine.

'But we should be free after, say, next Wednesday. Would that suit you, Miss Cross? May I schedule you in for next Thursday?'

'I don't believe this!' She'd had enough, and it took all her effort to remain seated. 'I know you must be tired after whatever you were up to last night.' She looked at Archie. 'And I realize you really just want to lock yourself away with your roll of paper and read whatever weird story those scribbles tell you, but this is more important. A friend of mine desperately needs your help. Her house is haunted.'

Archie started to object to the phrase. She cut him short.

'I don't care what scientific mumbo-jumbo you'd rather use. The plain fact is, her house is haunted, and she's at her wits' end. There's something going on, something terrifying, and I don't care what you want to call it. A ghost, a ghoulie zone, a spirit, a demon or the Devil himself! She needs help and you're supposed to be the experts. I thought you'd be interested, but none of you can even be bothered to listen.'

Jo took a deep breath, annoyed with herself for losing her temper.

Of the three men, Archie at least had the manners to look abashed. She imagined he was used to a calmer, more measured form of academic dispute.

It was Ray who broke the silence.

'Sorry.' He hesitated, fumbling for words. 'The thing is, we get a lot of inquiries like this. People – well-meaning people – asking for help. They want exorcisms, to rid their homes of unwanted "presences", that sort of thing. But we're scientists.' An adolescent whine crept into his voice. 'What we do, it isn't about getting rid of phenomena. We want to document them. To further mankind's knowledge of this world.'

'And, perhaps, the next.' Archie's soft Scottish accent spread oil on the rough waters, and Jo felt herself calming, her anger ebbing into the space between them.

'Perhaps,' said Ray with a small smile.

Undine stubbed out his cigarette. 'You want an exorcism? Try the local Spiritualist church. They're into all that nonsense.'

Before she knew what she was doing, Jo was on her feet and fighting the urge to march across to the arrogant dark-suited figure and knee him where it would hurt. Her fingernails bit into her palms as she reminded herself she needed these people's help.

'Okay,' she said, drawing the word out. 'As I mentioned, I do appreciate how tired you must all be after your little adventure, so I'm going to leave now and let you get some rest. But I'll be back tomorrow. Maybe then you'll have the courtesy to actually listen to what I have to tell you.'

She turned and strode to the door. Ray made to follow her.

'Don't bother,' she told him. 'I know the way. Remember: tomorrow afternoon. You don't have anything in your diary for then, so you'd better make a note before it slips anyone's mind.'

With that, Jo marched out of the office. She thought about slamming the door behind her, but left it open instead so they could watch her walk away.

CHAPTER 3

'Think she'll be back?' Ray glanced at the clock yet again. Almost two p.m.

Undine snorted. 'Little Miss Exorcism? If she's got any sense, she'll have done what I said. Gone to see the church mob, get them to wave their incense around a bit.'

He hoped she had. Part of him did want to help their previous day's visitor, but something about her set his alarm bells ringing. He didn't trust her, although he couldn't explain why, but more than that was the impression that, in some obscure way, she represented danger. She had definitely got into his head. Last night's Rat Pack adventure – a wonderful dream of an evening on the tiles with Frank, Dean and Sammy – had evaporated around three this morning when he'd started awake to crumpled sheets, damp with sweat.

'Reckon I have a chance with her?'

Ray's question pulled Undine from his

reverie. He looked at his friend with new interest. 'I thought I could smell aftershave.' Ray had made a special effort with his clothes today as well. He appeared to have covered himself with glue and run blindfolded through the bargain basement of a department store. 'Sunny, I can honestly say you'll catch her eye.'

'Would one of you young bucks mind passing me the solder?' asked Archie.

Undine spotted a spool in the toolbox at his feet. He handed it across. Tiny screwdrivers, needle-nosed pliers, and a myriad delicate tools he had no names for littered Archie's desk. In the centre squatted the Octopus, its grey metal case removed and its innards undergoing a form of surgery.

Archie tutted. 'I appear to be missing the amplifier leads. They must still be in the lorry.'

'I'll check,' said Ray. He hurried out, whistling a cheerful tune as his footsteps bounded down the stairs.

Archie unplugged a handful of wires, reached deep into the box's guts, and tugged.

'Everything okay?' asked Undine.

The Professor extricated a green plastic card and squinted at it. Its surface was spidered with silver tracery and what were presumably electronic components, although the technology was beyond Undine. 'Oh, fine, fine. Just needs a few adjustments. The soldering iron?'

Undine took it from the desk and slapped it

into Archie's waiting palm.

For the next few minutes, Archie worked with intense concentration. Undine watched, impatient for the Professor to finish fiddling with his gadget and move on to analysing the machine's readings from last night. Would they finally yield the clues he sought? The sensations in the Gents had been unusually strong, and he didn't want to have put himself through that pain for nothing.

Not that he was ready yet to admit it had happened.

Archie continued his tinkering, and Undine tried to make sense of the tangle of wires and metal and plastic. But the fierce flare at the tip of the soldering iron was painful to watch. He rubbed his tired eyes.

From below came the sound of the door closing, then footsteps climbing the staircase.

They stopped in the doorway.

'Did you find it?' asked Archie, his head still buried in his machine.

'Oh yes.'

Ray sounded chirpy. Undine took his hands from his eyes and turned around.

The moment he saw the figure standing next to Ray, cold terror seized him. Icy tendrils shot into his veins, and he staggered. The room's corners thickened, swelled, and spread towards him, and then they were smothering him.

The world went dim – and was gone.

✳   ✳   ✳

Voices.

There was hard pressure at the back of his skull. His head was resting against the wall. He remembered the thud of it hitting.

Archie glanced in his direction. The Professor was still seated at his desk. Likewise, Ray had not moved an inch, and neither had their visitor. Undine couldn't have been out more than a moment.

Ray was laughing. 'Do you often have that effect on men?'

Undine's wooziness started to clear. He must be even more tired than he'd realized, or perhaps it was another lingering after-effect from the theatre. Their visitor was just the blonde from yesterday, who had swapped her tight jumper for a flowery blue blouse.

She gave Ray a pleasant smile, then turned to Archie. Her hazel eyes were bright beneath her heavy mascara. 'Hello again. It's Archie, isn't it? WPC Cross. I hope I've caught you at a better time.'

The Professor put down his tools. 'Oh, you're a policewoman? I'm sorry, I didn't realize.'

He started to stand, but she told him not to worry and leaned down to offer a handshake. Archie took her hand with enthusiasm.

Undine noticed she had left the top buttons

of her blouse undone, and he helped himself to a peek. 'Not your usual uniform, I take it?'

He lifted his eyes to meet hers and saw irritation flare in them. She held her position for a beat, then slowly raised herself upright, bending from the waist with an athlete's grace.

'Plain clothes,' she said. 'Mr …?'

'Undine.'

'Oh, yes. That's right. Just Undine?'

'Just Undine.'

Her eyes narrowed.

Ray clapped his hands together. 'Tea, wasn't it? I was about to make a cuppa anyway so it's no hassle. Without sugar?'

The policewoman flashed him another smile. 'Thanks, Ray. That'd be lovely.'

'Biscuit?'

'If you're having one.'

Ray beamed. 'Be right back.'

Archie decided to stand after all. He smoothed the creases from his jacket. 'I really didn't realize. How may we assist you, Constable?' He frowned. 'It is "Constable", is it? I can't say I've ever had to address a policewoman before.'

'"Jo" is fine.'

'Aye, well. We're always happy to help the police. If you had said….'

'You didn't give me much of a chance!' But the humour dancing in her voice took the sting out of her criticism. She peered down into the splayed entrails of the grey box. 'Ooh! Isn't this what you were telling me about yesterday? It looks complicated. What're you up to?'

'Just some running repairs,' said Archie. 'A never-ending task! The equipment is a wee bit on the delicate side for field work, you see. There are always a few knocks and bumps to contend with.'

'May I?' Jo reached for one of the thin green cards scattered around the desk.

'By all means. Though take care not to touch the metal parts. Hold it by the edge, like this.'

Jo took the card and turned it over with careful fingers. 'What is it?'

'A PCB,' said Archie. 'A printed circuit board. The brain of the Octopus.'

'Wow. What does it do?'

Despite his misgivings, Undine's mouth twitched as Archie chattered away. She'd certainly got him going. Nothing pleased the Professor more than an excuse to show off his contraption.

'I don't see any moving parts,' said Jo, studying the board again. 'How do these work?'

'It's all in the pathways.' Archie traced a pattern in the air with the stem of his unlit pipe. 'Essentially, the pathways guide the electricity. They tell the electrons where to go and which components to activate.'

'Like guiding them through a maze?'

'If you like. I picture it more as a road network, with a system of routes and traffic lights to control the flow of traffic.'

'That is so clever.'

Jo handed the board back to him, and he laid it next to the soldering iron.

'You repair them yourself?'

'Oh aye, indeed. Each is unique, you see. Bespoke. One couldn't simply buy these in a shop.'

'So you make them yourself too?'

'Ah, not quite. But they are engineered according to my own design.'

Jo cooed with wonder. 'That's amazing.'

Archie was positively glowing by now. Undine lit an Embassy to hide his reluctant admiration. She was a piece of work, this blonde.

The door opened, pushed by Ray's backside as he reversed into the room carrying a mug and a plate of biscuits. He handed the drink to Jo, and cleared room on the desk for the plate. 'Help yourself to biccies. I hope these are alright for you. They're all we had.'

'They're perfect, Ray, thanks. Are you not having anything?'

Ray looked at his empty hands. 'Oh. I forgot.'

'Cool, Sunny,' said Undine. 'Very cool.' He took a digestive.

'So,' said Archie. 'How can we help you, Jo?'

Her open, friendly expression wavered. Undine saw it, but her indecision was gone in an instant and when she answered, she was all smiles again.

'Professor James – Archie – you gave your contact details to my sergeant last year. Dave Hawkins? At Fair Green police station in Mitcham.'

Archie tried to remember.

'In south London,' she prompted. 'Out near Wimbledon?'

'I expect you're right. We left our details with stations all over London, asked them to keep them on file. It was the Institute's idea. A person who happens to experience something strange and troubling, they reasoned, might well go to the police to ask for help. But the police, as you'll be aware, would be unequipped to give that help, so might welcome our outside expertise and call us in to consult. A decent enough idea, I thought. Not that it produced much in the way of results.'

'Well, it's why I'm here,' said Jo.

Undine knew how eager Archie had been for this day to arrive, but his unease was growing stronger by the second. Time to step in.

'Sorry, sweetheart but as we told you yesterday, we're not exorcists. If the Spiritualists turned you down then I suggest you find a priest.'

A shadow passed across Jo's features. 'I already tried. They couldn't help.'

Ray pulled up a chair for Jo. She sat, and he pulled up another for himself, placing it close to her. 'What happened?' he asked.

'Not much. Nothing at all, really.' She looked

from Ray to Archie, and back again, ignoring Undine. 'I had a word with a vicar – he's a family friend; my parents have known him for years – and he agreed to visit the house. The house where all this is going on, that is. That was last week. He did his thing, whatever they do: holy water, prayers, blessing the place. I guess you'll know the procedure better than I do.'

Archie had taken out his notebook. 'Without success, I take it?'

'From what I was told, nothing happened while he was there. He did his bit, then he left. And an hour or so later, everything started up again exactly as before.'

'What sort of activity would that be?'

'You mean the weird stuff? Only little things at first. The lady who lives there told me how she would get these creepy feelings, like there was somebody in the house watching her. I put it down to grief at first. Her husband had died not too long before. But then were there other incidents.'

Ray leaned forward, stopping just short of taking her hand. 'Such as?'

'Cold draughts, for one thing, even though all the windows were locked up tight. I couldn't work out where they were coming from. And little ornaments going missing and then turning up in the strangest places. Even places she knew she'd checked before. Then there was trouble with the lights.'

A change came over her as she spoke. She seemed smaller, more vulnerable, and genuinely worried for the lady she was talking about. Undine squashed down the guilt nibbling at him.

Archie scratched away at his notebook. 'How long has this been going on?'

'Only a couple of weeks,' Jo replied. 'That said, I made a few informal enquiries around the area, chatted to neighbours and so on, and it seems there have been stories about the house for a long time.'

'I see.' Archie sat a little straighter, and Undine knew exactly what the Scot was about to ask. For some reason, the question scared him: it felt like being trapped in a car that was out of control and heading for a crash.

'Has anything happened recently that might have affected the structure?'

'What do you mean?'

'Oh, any nearby building work, for example?'

'I don't know about nearby but, since you mention it, there is work being done inside the house itself.' Her hazel eyes flashed. 'You've got some idea what this is, haven't you?'

She was quick. She'd make a decent detective one day.

Archie's reply was cautious. 'Let's just say it's suggestive.'

If they carried on down this path it would soon be too late to turn back. Undine cleared his throat. 'Archie, we've still got the Pyramus

41

results to go through. You said it yourself: there's a mass of data there, and we need to analyse it while the details are still fresh. We don't have the time to get involved in anything else right now.'

'Yeah, but nothing happened at the theatre,' said Ray. He reached for a biscuit. 'Unless I'm missing something?'

Undine felt Archie's keen gaze. He considered his position.

'No,' he said at last. 'You're right. Nothing happened.'

'Okay then.' Archie returned his attention to Jo. 'I'm sorry, my dear. You were saying: what manner of building work is it?'

'Just some decorating, as far as I know. Mind you, it's all on hold for the moment. The guys she hired to do the job did a runner before it was finished.'

'Did they, now? Hence the police involvement?'

Jo was puzzled for a moment. 'Hm? Oh, no. I didn't mean it like that. They scarpered after they got spooked. When the faces appeared.'

Faces. The word crashed over Undine. It drenched him in meaning, but the meaning evaporated before he could make sense of it.

Jo was still talking.

'They appear in the walls, apparently. Every now and again.' She sounded apologetic, embarrassed by what she had to tell them. 'They were just marks on the wallpaper to start with.

Mrs Wyndham – she's the one who lives there – she thought it was the builders at first, mucking about. But they swore blind it was nothing to do with them. They looked like patches of dirt or damp or something to begin with, but then it was like they began to come into focus and…. Well, they became faces.'

A noticeable shiver passed through Jo. Undine, annoyed with himself, felt it too. Even Archie seemed troubled.

Ray, on the other hand, appeared intrigued. Excited, even. 'Hold on. Which police station did you say you're from?'

'Fair Green,' said Jo. 'In Mitcham.'

'And this house you're talking about. Does it have a name?'

'It's called Lavender Edge.'

Ray scraped his chair back and stood, laughing. 'I don't believe it!'

Archie tamped tobacco into the bowl of his pipe. 'I take it you know something about this?'

'Do I ever! I grew up in Morden.' Ray turned to Jo, and added: 'Not far from the Tube station?'

She nodded to show she knew where he meant.

'Morden's right next to Mitcham,' he explained for the benefit of the others. 'Anyway, when I was about 12 years old, I found this book. Great British ghost stories – you know the type of thing – and it had a whole section in there on Lavender Edge!'

He shook his head, smiling. 'I'd been to the library, and on my way out I saw a table piled up with books for sale. Ones they were getting rid of to make room on the shelves. I had a rummage through and there was this book. The moment I saw it, I knew I wanted it, so I took it to the desk to ask how much it cost.' He grinned at Jo. 'I was worried I wouldn't be able to afford it because I only had a couple of coins on me, just enough for a bag of sweets and the bus back. But the librarian said he couldn't sell it to me because it wasn't one of theirs.'

A slight crease appeared between his eyes. 'I didn't know whether he meant I could take it or not, and then this old guy waiting in the queue behind me kind of bent forward and whispered to me to keep the book. He told me I should accept it as "a gift from the Cosmos". It was an odd thing to say, which I guess is why I remember it, but that's what I did, and the book turned out to be amazing.'

'What was it called?' asked Jo.

'Wish I could remember that as clearly! I'd love to read it again, especially now, but my parents must have chucked it out at some point. But that Mitcham story freaked me out as a kid!'

He smiled ruefully. 'Every time I saw wallpaper, I'd see faces in the pattern. I was convinced for ages they were the faces from Lavender Edge, coming to get me!'

Undine could not help glancing at the

Warehouse walls, glad they were painted rather than wallpapered.

Archie struck a match, and brought flame to tobacco. With gentle concentration, he drew on the mouthpiece. At last, he asked: 'Did your book offer any explanation for what causes these faces?

Ray shook his head. 'No. Nobody could explain them. At least, not back then. And I might be wrong but as far as I'm aware nobody has ever carried out a proper investigation of those reports.'

He paused, but Archie left the bait untouched. His watery blue eyes seemed to be contemplating his pipe.

'Obviously, there's the folklore,' Ray continued. 'That the faces are the spirits of people murdered on the site years ago. Or the house is possessed by demons or what have you. But as to the scientific explanation – perhaps old drawings that leached into the plaster and stained the wallpaper, or maybe just random marks people misinterpret because of the tales....'

Another huge grin broke across his long, skinny features. He couldn't hold it in any longer.

'Flipping hell, though! The Faces of Lavender Edge. I can't believe it. It was that story, more than anything else, that got me interested in folklore in the first place!'

'I take it you didn't actually see any

phenomena with your own eyes,' said Undine, addressing Jo.

She glared up at him, defiant. 'Actually,' she repeated, 'I did.'

'No way!' said Ray. The 12-year-old who had found that book was clearly still alive inside the man. At 28, Ray was only a few years younger than Undine, but the gap between the two of them often felt greater.

Archie leaned back in his chair, the perfume of pipe smoke rising around him. 'Well, my dear, you seem to have won yourself an audience. Before we go any further, I think we should make an official record of your testimony.'

For the first time, Jo appeared uncomfortable. 'There's not much more I can tell you myself. It's Mrs Wyndham you need to speak to.'

'Plenty of time for that,' said Archie.

'There's nothing to be concerned about,' said Ray. 'It's only to get your version of what happened on record. People often remember events in different ways, so we like to interview each witness separately.'

Jo raised an eyebrow. 'I do know something about how to interview witnesses.'

'I didn't mean –'

She laughed, cutting him short. 'It's alright. No offence taken. Honestly, though, there's just not much I can tell you.'

Nevertheless, she took her own small

notebook from her handbag. 'I went to the house twice,' she said, checking what she had written there. 'The first time on the evening of Monday the thirtieth of August. About six weeks ago. We – my colleague and I – were asked to go there by a man who came up to us in the street. We never found out who he was, and Mrs Wyndham didn't know either, although I think she had her suspicions. She didn't want to invite us in, and we didn't have any grounds to look further into it, so we went away.'

Undine wondered what he could do this moment to make the policewoman go away.

'Our second visit was one week later, on Tuesday the seventh of September. That was after Mrs Wyndham herself invited us back. Or begged us, would be more accurate. And that time, I did see … something.'

She frowned. 'I know I did. We all did. But the details.... They're not there. I've tried to remember. I've been trying ever since it happened, but it's like trying to remember a dream. Or a nightmare. The more I think about it, the more it all melts away.'

Archie tapped his pipe. 'What do you think?' The question was intended for Ray.

'Repressed memories?'

Archie gave a slow nod.

'Or it really was nothing but a dream,' said Undine.

Jo's back stiffened, but she kept it turned to

him and did not respond.

'You know how we could find out,' said Ray.

'Aye.'

Jo looked from Ray to Archie, and back again. 'Why are you staring at me like that?'

CHAPTER 4

Professor Archie James slotted the microphone into its looped metal stand and balanced it upright on the chair. It would be near enough to pick up everything Jo said.

Undine took the free end of the cable, and plugged it in. He slotted a fresh reel into the Grundig, switched on the power, and waited for the indicator panel to glow orange. He gave the microphone a couple of taps with his finger. The needle flickered in time to the magnified echoes of his touch. Satisfied, he pushed the buttons to start the machine recording, watched the spools revolve, and ensured the tape was transferring correctly. Finally, he confirmed the counter numbers were moving.

'We're good.'

Jo wriggled into the old sofa in an effort to make herself more comfortable. The fabric had been itchy against her neck and so Ray had taken off his jacket and rolled it into a pillow for her.

She pressed her head against it, and closed her eyes.

'Try to relax,' said Undine.

'Easy for you to say. I've never done this before. Any funny business and the lot of you are getting locked up. Got that?'

Ray smirked at Undine. Jo had zipped her brown leather jacket up as high as it would go but its fitted cut still drew attention to her slim body. Undine just wanted this over with. He stepped away and let Archie take over at the microphone.

'You're perfectly safe,' the Professor reassured her in a warm Highland murmur. 'All that's about to happen is that you'll feel very relaxed and dreamy. I'll help you to allow your memories to rise up, all by themselves, to a place where you can see them. Just let them come, all very natural, and describe whatever comes to you.'

'Okay,' said Jo.

'Good. Now, we're going to breathe in. Nice and deep and slow. And hold it. And now let it out, and as you breathe out, imagine all your cares leaving your body. Good. Now, breathe in. And you're allowing light and calmness to fill your lungs, and you can feel it spreading all the way through your limbs, and out to the tips of your fingers and your toes….'

Undine had watched Archie hypnotize dozens of witnesses, yet he still marvelled at how quickly the Professor could guide someone into a light hypnotic trance. In half a minute, Jo's features had softened, and she was breathing deeply and easily. She looked younger than before, less sure of herself. He again felt an urge to help her, but the throttling swirl of doubt and fear held him back.

'You wanted to tell us about Lavender Edge,' said Archie.

Jo's breathing quickened.

Archie kept his tone low and soothing and, gradually, she calmed.

'Tell me how you became involved.'

For a moment, Undine thought she hadn't heard. He was about to call a halt to proceedings when she replied, her words slurred and drowsy.

'Our shift's going to be over soon. We've left Ravensbury Park. We're heading north. We're starting back to the station.'

❊   ❊   ❊

Her feet ached but she didn't mind. It was good to get out of the station for a change, instead of another dull day of shuffling papers. She'd have preferred a different partner, though.

PC Dick Condie shoved the sneering teenager against the wall.

'You're wasting your time, filth.' The words were spat in an accent Jo associated with Belfast.

'Shut yer face, Eamon,' said Dick, living up to his name. As usual.

51

Jo kept her face a stern mask, watching Dick empty his suspect's pockets onto the pavement. Yes, it was good to get out of the station for a couple of hours, but she was ready to go back now. She'd joined the Force to help people, not to harass them like this.

She could almost feel the disapproving stares of strangers behind her, sitting in the slow-moving traffic and watching the unexpected show on their way home from work. She tried to put them out of her mind, to concentrate on the job – and jumped when a gnarled hand clutched her arm.

'Excuse me, Constable.'

Jo whirled around, annoyed she had let herself be startled like that.

'Please,' said the elderly man who had touched her. 'Your help is needed.'

('What does he look like?'

Jo muttered, uneasy: 'I don't know. I can't see his face.')

The old man's eyes pulled her in. Behind his spectacles, they burned with desperate longing, imploring her to listen. He was speaking, but his voice was inside her head. It filled her reality, informing her where she had to go, where she was needed, right now, right this instant.

Yes. She had to help. This was why she had joined. This was her chance to make a difference.

'Little scrote.'

Dick strutted back towards her, having released his catch into the wild. She watched the teenager scamper away.

'Hurry up, Dick. We need to –'

She stopped, puzzled. The old man had gone.

(*'Look around. Can you see the old man?'*

'He's not there. I don't understand where he's gone. Dick can't see him either. He's laughing at me.')

'Well, go on then, WPC Cross. This is where your mystery man told us to go. Knock on the flaming door!'

Jo reached for the knocker, wondering why she had hesitated. Time was getting on, and the wind was picking up as it whipped down from a darkening sky. They should have been back at the station by now. That's what Dick really wanted, of course, but she wasn't going to let him push her around. She set her face, lifted the iron ring and rapped with authority.

Seconds fell away, and by the time she heard a chain rattle she was losing her nerve again. She didn't like this house. It was much older than the other houses on Rivermead Path, and in poor repair, but that wasn't the reason. The plain fact was that the big, old building with its dark, crumbling brickwork and blank windows gave her the creeps.

'Who's there?'

A woman's voice. Elderly but determined,

and more upper-class than she would have expected for the area.

'It's the police, madam. We received a report you might need assistance.'

The tall wooden door creaked open a few inches until a security chain stopped it. The gap revealed a redoubtable-looking woman with steel-grey hair set like a helmet.

'Assistance? What nonsense.'

('*What does she say has been happening at the house?*'

'*Nothing. She's very insistent. All a load of stuff and nonsense, she says. She claims people are trying to stop her redecorating her own home.*'

'*Does she say why?*'

'*I don't know. Dick is urging us to leave. Says the man in the street was wasting our time. I think he's wrong. Something is going on here. The woman's name is Mrs Wyndham. I want to help her, but she's telling me to go.*'

'*What happens next?*'

'*We go. We have no choice.*')

❋   ❋   ❋

Archie eased himself to his feet. He left the tape recorder humming and squeaking beside Jo and motioned for Ray and Undine to join him at the far side of the room.

'The old man is an interesting detail,' he

whispered. 'It reminds me of those studies of "crisis apparitions".'

Undine knew what he was referring to. He had read the same reports of deceased persons appearing to the living at or shortly after the moment of death. Like pretty much everything that fell under the Corsi Institute's purview, there was perpetual dispute that the idea was supported by any factual evidence.

'I'd like to know who he was,' said Archie. 'Our policewoman said the old lady's husband died not so long before this happened. Perhaps there's a connection?'

'That's a bit of a leap,' said Undine.

Ray nodded. 'Got to say I agree, Archie. Sorry. You're always reminding us to follow the evidence, not to twist the facts to fit the theory.'

'Aye, well, it's something to bear in mind.' Archie referred to his notebook. 'I think we've covered the first night now. Let's move on to what happened the following week, after Mrs Wyndham invited them back.'

*   *   *

Jo waited on the gloomy front step, still hearing the echo of her knock in the empty silence. Please, God, she thought, make Dick behave himself.

He'd been a bloody nightmare this last week, creeping around behind her at the station, making spooky 'whooo' noises, and shambling in her wake like a monster in one of those Hammer films. Plus of course he had told everyone about her 'funny feeling' that had made her drag him along to the 'haunted house'. It was the last thing she needed. It was hard enough for a woman to get taken seriously in this job.

The chain scraped, the door creaked back, and Mrs Wyndham ushered them inside with quick, urgent gestures.

The poor woman looked awful. Even worse than this morning when she had turned up at the front desk, asking to see the young WPC from the week before. Jo had wanted to accompany her home straight away, but Sergeant Hawkins had had a female suspect in custody and needed Jo to babysit the prisoner's children while her house was searched.

Jo followed Mrs Wyndham through a long, narrow hall where white dust sheets draped unseen furniture. At the far end, beyond an ornate grandfather clock from which the sheets had been pulled back to reveal its face, a door opened into what the old lady described as the drawing room. The large space would once have been stylish, but now the fabrics and wallpaper were faded.

Dick seemed unusually subdued.

They sat, Jo sinking into the deep-cushioned armchair. For a moment, it appeared as if Mrs Wyndham was regretting her decision to ask them here, as if she were about to apologize and ask them to leave instead.

Then the dam broke, and her words poured out.

('What did she tell you?'

'Strange things have been happening here. The builders.'

'What about the builders?'

'They complain how cold it is where they're working. Problems with the electric. One of them lost some tools. Said he left them on the floor but when he went back they weren't there anymore. Mrs Wyndham thinks they're making it up. Or she used to think that.'

'She doesn't now?'

Jo shifted uncomfortably on the sofa. 'There's an odd smell. It's like…. It makes me think of bumper cars.'

Archie looked to Ray and Undine. 'Ozone?' he mouthed. Ray nodded. Undine said nothing.

'Are the builders working in the house now?' asked Archie.

'No. They left yesterday. They quit. Everything's a mess upstairs, she says.'

'How long had they been working there before they quit?'

Jo did not respond.

'Jo?'

'She says they started last week. Monday morning.'

Ray checked a calendar. 'Monday the sixth of September. Hang on, isn't that the same date –?'

Archie nodded. 'Aye, that's the day she said the old man urged her to go to the house.'

He returned his attention to Jo. 'The builders. What made them leave?'

'Mrs Wyndham says one of them screamed. He was shouting about seeing faces in the walls. They ran downstairs. Won't come back. After they left, things got much worse. They.... Oh! What was that?')

Jo struggled out of the deep cushions and rushed towards the table. It looked antique, with elegantly curved legs that sang of a different era, but the style wasn't what had grabbed her attention.

'Did you see that?' she asked.

She guessed Dick had. He was staring at the corner where the table had stood moments before, his face pale in the dusty light.

'It moved,' said Jo. 'I swear it just slid out from this corner, about an inch.'

Mrs Wyndham made no comment.

Jo dropped to her knees and felt around for strings in case someone had used something like cotton, invisible against the shadows, to pull the table. But who, and why?

She found nothing.

Standing again, she lifted the table by one edge. The frame was delicate and remarkably light, but it would have taken a considerable blast of wind to propel the table over this thick carpet. Jo knew there had been no such gust but, even so, she crossed to each of the room's two large bay windows and ran her hands over the frames to check. There was not the slightest suggestion of a draught.

'Did you see it?' she demanded of her colleague.

Dick refused to reply.

Jo started to walk back to the table. She kept her eyes locked on it, untrusting.

Halfway there, she froze. The weird fairground smell was back, stronger this time. The hairs on her arms tingled. Then her surroundings lurched, and an unseen weight was spilling into the room, filling the air. As she tried desperately to decide what to do, a loud knock cracked from the ceiling.

From upstairs.

From the room the builders had been working in.

Her heart hammered. Her uniform no longer felt like the suit of armour it usually did. She took hold of the strap of her handbag and tugged it straighter.

'Who else is in the house?' she asked.

'Nobody but us,' said Mrs Wyndham.

Jo crept to the door and looked out into the hallway. Empty.

Dick had not moved.

'Come on!' she hissed.

Reluctantly, he climbed out of his armchair and joined her, casting occasional suspicious glances back at the table.

Jo stole out of the room and to the foot of the staircase. The air around her seemed to vibrate. She peered up past the carved stair post, almost certain she could hear quiet scratching and thumping sounds coming from the landing at the top, but it was difficult to be sure over the sound of her own breathing, so she held her breath. The sounds continued.

She started up the stairs, one soft step at a time.

Mrs Wyndham came behind her. Dick chose to be Tail-end Charlie.

At the landing, the air crackled with energy.

All the doors up here were open. Without a word, Mrs Wyndham pointed to one doorway, and Jo crept towards it, until she was close enough to look around the corner.

✳   ✳   ✳

On the sofa, Jo moaned. The muscles in her limbs tensed. Her head rolled to the left, then snatched to the right as her mind rejected memories she did not want to face.

Ray turned to Archie with an expression of questioning concern.

Archie pulled a face. 'Aye. I think that will

have to do for now. Jo, I want you to focus on my voice. Let everything else fall away.'

Jo whimpered with terror.

'You've left the house,' said Archie, 'and you're floating through a beautiful summer afternoon. You are as light as a butterfly, and come to rest on your back in a meadow. The grass is soft beneath you, and you are enveloped in the scent of flowers being carried on a gentle breeze. The sunlight is warm and relaxing on your skin. And very slowly, you feel yourself begin to wake from the most wonderful and refreshing sleep. Okay, Jo, in just a moment I'm going to count backwards from ten, and I want you to –'

Jo gasped, and jerked into full wakefulness.

Ray pushed a glass of water into her trembling hands.

'It's alright. You're fine.'

Undine's hands were as unsteady as hers. The way Jo had described those vibrations in the air, the sense of a building pressure, had struck a chord with him. He lit another cigarette, turning his back on the others to hide the shaking in his fingers. From the sound of it, Lavender Edge genuinely was 'haunted' – whatever that clumsy word signified. Potentially, the place held answers that might help him, and although the thought of going there made him anxious, he was used to feeling that way about haunted houses. So why did the prospect of visiting this particular example fill him with such dread?

Jo swung her legs off the sofa. 'Did it work?'

'You did great,' said Ray.

'Indeed,' said Archie. 'Very interesting. Very interesting indeed.'

'But I still don't remember what I saw up there, in that room.'

The Professor tapped his pipe against his chin. 'No. Whatever it was must have distressed you a great deal. Try not to be concerned, though. Your memories will come out in time. In the wash, as it were. But you've told us enough to persuade me.'

Jo's eyes brightened. 'You'll help?'

'You expect us to believe that load of old bollocks?'

Undine's words were out before he knew he was going to speak, a primal defensive urge throwing them into the conversation.

Archie stared at him, his eyebrows halfway up his forehead. Ray blushed. Jo glared.

Undine groped for some way to justify his comment. 'Pardon my language. Ladies present, and all that. But, hypnosis – it's hardly reliable, is it? Come on, Archie, don't give me that look. You've made your own reservations about hypnosis clear enough in the past. So have you, Sunny. Her story could have come from anywhere. Maybe her boyfriend takes her to too many horror films. All that spookiness seeping into her subconscious while they're busy making out on the back seat –'

'Hey!'

'And how can we be sure she really was hypnotized in any case? She might have been spinning a yarn to –'

Jo leapt to her feet. 'What the hell is your problem?'

'Okay, that's enough.' Archie pushed his chair back, walked around the desk, and inserted himself between Undine and Jo. Regardless of his advanced years and normally mild, academic demeanour, the elderly Highlander had a powerful physical presence, and was as tall as Undine himself.

'Dr Buckley, would you mind taking care of our guest for a few minutes?'

Ray put an arm around Jo's shoulders and guided her in the direction of the next room. Jo shook herself free and opened the door for herself. Ray closed the door behind them.

At once, the room felt very quiet. Undine avoided Archie's piercing eyes.

The Professor spoke first. 'How's your stomach?'

Undine shrugged. 'Fine.' He drew on his cigarette, and blew the smoke out of the corner of his mouth.

'You weren't feeling quite the ticket the other night.'

Archie was probing. Undine knew how those pale blue eyes, so deceptively dreamy, hid an intelligence sharp enough to ambush the unwary. Not for the first time, he wondered how much Archie had already guessed about his 'ability'. And, again not for the first time, he considered coming clean and telling the Professor everything. Would life be simpler then? With the two of them working in partnership, would Undine be more likely to find the answers he sought?

Probably. Except it wasn't so simple. Even though Undine admired and even liked the older man, when it came down to it, Archie would always be a scientist first. There was no way Undine would ever let himself become someone's guinea pig, with all his frailties and sensitivity (that vile bloody word!) exposed for the world to see.

'Like I said, I had a stomach cramp.'

'Ah,' said Archie.

Undine did his best to fake an easy-going smile. 'Okay, I admit it. I'm still knackered after the theatre. Utterly shagged out, if I'm honest. And I guess I'm a little disappointed too, because the investigation didn't pan out as we'd hoped.'

The Professor said nothing for several seconds, hoping Undine would add more, but at last he conceded. 'Aye, it's a shame we didn't find more, but who knows? Perhaps our trusty Octopus will yet prove to hold an interesting tale.'

He looked down at his beloved machine, in bits below him. 'I'm afraid, however, we're going to have to postpone repairs for a little while.'

Damn it. 'We're going to investigate her haunted house, aren't we?'

'I think we have to. I do appreciate your reservations, but I found WPC Cross's testimony compelling. Prima facie, it warrants at least an exploratory visit.' He smiled. 'Not to mention that young Ray would be most put out were we to turn down the opportunity to look into his favourite bedtime story.'

Archie paused for a moment before adding: 'Of course, if you're still under the weather, you needn't go with us. I'm sure we'd all understand.'

Was Archie manipulating him? It was tough to be certain. The Scot would have made an excellent poker player.

Undine took a final drag on his Embassy, exhaled heavily, and stubbed out the cigarette in a chunky porcelain ashtray, long ago liberated from a local pub.

'Don't worry about me. But I still think it's a complete waste of our time.'

'Good lad. Then that's settled.'

Archie called Ray and Jo back into his office, and gathered them all around his desk. From the depths of a drawer he produced four cut-glass tumblers and a bottle of deep amber liquid.

'A toast,' he declared, pouring them each a generous measure. 'Mind you don't spill any. What you have there is Lagavulin, single-malted nectar of the Hebridean gods.'

Undine put the tumbler to his nose and breathed in the rich, smoky aroma. It evoked the roar of a bonfire on a wintry night.

Archie raised his glass. 'Gentlemen, and lady. To the pursuit of knowledge, and to our next adventure. To Lavender Edge!'

For the first time since her arrival at the Warehouse yesterday morning, Undine saw a genuine smile appear on Jo's face. It dimpled her cheeks and gave her a mischievous, elfin air as she lifted her glass, thanked them all, and took a tentative sip of the fiery liquid.

Undine drank too, his thoughts turning inwards and his worries souring the whisky's taste.

CHAPTER 5

The police station was coming up on the right. Jo turned her face away, staring into the near-side mirror at the shrinking reflections of familiar shops until the station was behind them, and she could relax a little because Undine was still driving and showing no signs of stopping.

She dared to look through the windscreen again. Mitcham's decorative clock-tower was ahead. Sergeant Hawkins had once told her it commemorated Queen Victoria's Diamond Jubilee and was built on the site of the old village pump. No reason not to believe him: he had worked at Fair Green for donkey's years. Beside the clock stood a low, timber-framed building, which wouldn't have been out of place in a Tudor garden but which actually housed public toilets, while on the other side of the road a small expanse of well-trimmed grass framed neat little flowerbeds. Technically, this was still south London, but that was only because the ever-expanding city now sprawled into Surrey. Even under gloomy skies like these, Mitcham was a pretty town, retaining more than a trace of its bygone charm. Not that Undine would have noticed.

The traffic lights turned red.

'You'll need to go straight on,' she told him.

Undine heaved the lorry into the correct lane. He didn't speak. He'd barely spoken since the Warehouse, but that suited her fine. They squealed to a halt. The cab lurched forward, and collapsed back, and she wondered how Archie and Ray were coping in the back on those hard wooden benches. The vehicle was clearly Army surplus, and not designed for comfort.

Light drizzle spattered the glass. Undine switched the wipers on. The lights turned green.

'It's not far now.'

His only response was a grunt. Was he sulking? Well, tough. She'd gone out of her way to prove to them this was serious. She'd even let these people hypnotize her! They had agreed to come.

They passed the old Cricket Green (maybe the oldest in the world, according to Hawkins) and soon the road rose over a railway line. A little further on, on the right, she could see the spot where the old man had accosted her and Dick Condie. She thought of pointing out the location to Undine, but decided not to bother.

'Take the next left.'

She checked her watch. Nearly three p.m. The old lady had expected them to arrive hours ago, but Archie had been determined to bring his electronic thingamajig and there had been an issue with one of its 'circuit boards'. Some sort of blockage on one of the pathways the electricity was supposed to follow, apparently. Despite his assurances otherwise, he had been unable to fix it and in the end they had left the machine behind.

They swung into Rivermead Path. Undine turned on the headlights. It was only October, but the evenings were drawing in and dark clouds, combined with the trees crowding overhead, kept out the thin afternoon light.

Undine parked where she told him, then jumped down from the cab and strode to the rear of the lorry where she heard him pull back the tarpaulin cover. Jo opened her own door and gauged the distance to the pavement below. 'Thanks for nothing.' She clambered down, keeping a tight grip on the door frame. No, the Army didn't do comfort, and neither did they design vehicles with boots like these in mind.

As she reached the ground, Ray walked around from the back, struggling with a bulging canvas holdall. She was pleased to note he still wore the jacket she had encouraged him to change into this morning.

'You sure about this?' he asked, fussing at the lapels with his free hand.

'Trust me. You look terrific.'

That was an exaggeration, but it was definitely an improvement on his earlier ensemble. Thank God they kept spare clothes in their offices in case they needed to change after long nights in dusty, dirty locations.

Archie joined them, carrying a holdall of his own, followed by Undine who was burdened with yet another holdall in addition to the bulky plastic case she knew contained the tape recorder.

'Can I help you with any bags?' she asked.

'No, thank you, dear. That's everything now.' The Professor studied their surroundings, picking out a large house, older than its neighbours, set back from the road behind a high wall of grimy, time-worn bricks.

Jo confirmed his guess. 'That's the one.'

'Well, then. I suppose you had best introduce us.'

Ray, still puffed with pleasure from her compliment, gawped at the house like a boy at a sweet counter. Undine, on the other hand, seemed…. Jo couldn't read his expression exactly, but he wasn't thrilled.

Just wait until you get inside, she thought as she led them through the gate. Then you'll understand why I need you here.

❋   ❋   ❋

'Now, these ones I discovered last week.'

Mrs Wyndham handed Archie the two halves of a broken dish, passing them to him with a reverence more typically reserved for saintly relics. Her hands shook, either from age or from strained nerves – or both.

'They were on the kitchen floor. It's tiled, you see.'

Archie turned the crockery over in his hands.

'Had it been inside the drawer?' prompted Jo. 'Like the others?'

Mrs Wyndham nodded. 'Yes. The drawer was still closed when I found these.'

'It's not the first time that's happened.' Jo was keen for Archie to grasp the full implication of everything he was being told.

Undine stood on the far side of the drawing room, looking out of one of the two bay windows, although Jo doubted he could see anything other than his own reflection against the murk beyond the glass. That window, she remembered from her earlier visits, looked out onto the path that ran beside the house, connecting the property's front and rear gardens. The second bay held French windows, which, when opened, led through to a small, glass-panelled conservatory she assumed had been added to the house at a later date. The conservatory, in turn, opened into the back garden.

Archie handed back the broken dish. He

retained his air of polite interest, but Jo was growing anxious. The house felt so peaceful this afternoon, not at all the conditions she had led the researchers to expect.

Even Ray's enthusiasm was fading. The young man paced up and down the hall between this room and the front door, listening and watching and finding nothing.

She couldn't understand it. The air was light. Clean. Over the past two hours there had been no hint of that electric tinge to the atmosphere, that tantalizing, enervating sense of something about to happen. Right now, except for its size, its lost grandeur, and the shrouded white evidence of building work put on indefinite hold, Lavender Edge felt just like any other house.

From the hall came the sedate, solid ticking of a grandfather clock. As the conversation died, the ticking settled over them like sleep.

Mrs Wyndham placed the pieces of dish into the cardboard box beside her on the sofa. Her movements were deliberate, as controlled as the steel-grey hair set firm around her head. The elderly lady was holding it together, but much more stress and she might well crack. And when she did, she could fall apart as readily as her crockery.

'I never asked you,' said Jo, 'why is the road called Rivermead? I don't remember any river outside.'

Mrs Wyndham looked up from the box. She

spotted Undine, still standing at the window with his back to everyone, and her lips pursed. He hadn't uttered a word since his initial hello.

'A river?' she said. 'Oh, yes. There was one once. See over there, on the wall?'

Jo stood and walked across to the small framed watercolour hanging there. The colours were bleached by time, but she recognized the house as Lavender Edge, in an older, more rural setting with no neighbouring buildings in sight. A narrow stream ran through the mid-ground, beside a dirt track; beyond that, vast fields of what must be lavender stretched away under a wide sky towards a distant, flat horizon.

Ray wandered into the room to see the painting.

'A river?' Archie jotted that into his notebook. 'Did you know there are theories that running water is a factor in certain types of haunting? There are some who believe the ionization effect creates a form of recording medium. That, under the correct circumstances, such a field might retain an imprint, as it were, of events.'

'There are also some who believe that to be a right old load of nonsense.' Ray gave the old lady a cheery wink.

'Indeed,' she said. Mrs Wyndham's smile was faint and short-lived.

'It looks very different,' said Jo. 'The surroundings, I mean. How long has the house stood here?'

'Since the middle of the eighteenth century. It was built by one of my late husband's ancestors.'

'So it's been in the family a fair while, then,' said Ray.

'Yes.' Mrs Wyndham clearly considered his comment redundant. A muscle twitched by her right eye. Then she softened. 'Forgive me. The past few weeks have been a strain. Yes, the house has, as you say, been in the family for a number of generations. Ronald, my late husband, would have been able to tell you more. Local history was something of a hobby for him.' A thought occurred to her. 'He amassed quite a collection of documents. I would be pleased to search for them, should you feel they might be pertinent. It might take me a few days.'

'That would be marvellous,' said Archie.

'Good,' said Mrs Wyndham.

The ticking of the clock grew loud again.

'Good,' she repeated.

Undine finally turned to face the room.

'Alright if I take a look upstairs?' he asked.

*　　*　　*

Mrs Wyndham led them up the staircase. Undine followed her, and Jo, behind him, wondered how much his Chelsea boots had cost. A decent bob or two, she reckoned. They were clean, unlike his crumpled black suit, which appeared to be the same one he had worn yesterday. He hadn't bothered changing clothes. A smear of ash streaked the back of his left trouser leg.

They crowded together on the landing, which also felt different to before. The last time Jo had stood here, on this spot, looking towards that door, she.... She tried to tease the memory out, but the details remained frustratingly out of reach. Something had happened in that room, but what?

'This way, please'. Mrs Wyndham held her head high as she crossed to the bedroom door, but she hesitated before turning the handle. Then she pushed the door open and, staying on the threshold, reached inside to switch on the light.

Undine sauntered in past her, acting nonchalant but not quite pulling it off.

The room was a mess. Its plan echoed the drawing room immediately below, with the same arrangement of two bay windows: one to their left looking out over the rear garden and the other directly ahead overlooking the path along the side of the house. To Jo's right, as she walked inside, a hole had been knocked into the dividing wall. The damage was around a foot-and-a-half in diameter, with wooden splinters and cracked plaster showing at the ragged perimeter where the torn wallpaper ended. Protective sheets and workmen's tools lay around the floor, their edges blurred by drifts of white dust.

From behind, on the landing, came the sound of another door opening. A few moments later, it closed again, and Archie walked in to join them at the hole. 'It doesn't go all the way through to the next room.' He sounded thoughtful. 'There must be quite a gap between the walls.'

Ray placed his hands against the wallpaper, then leaned in for a closer examination until his enormous nose was practically pressed to the surface. 'Is this where the faces manifested?'

'It is,' said Mrs Wyndham.

The wallpaper was tasteful, if old-fashioned, and had obviously been hanging for many years; what must once have been bursts of yellow among vibrant greens and delicate blushes of rose had faded into the predominantly beige background, giving the whole something of the air of an ancient sepia photograph. Jo traced the printed floral design, picking out petals and stems and the curving sweep of what she was sure her mother would call acanthus leaves, and saw nothing out of the ordinary. She took a step nearer, and her foot knocked against a hammer abandoned by the workmen. What could have made them flee that way? Had they seen the same thing she had – whatever that had been?

As if reading her thoughts, Archie asked Mrs Wyndham to describe again what the builders claimed had happened in this room. Her reply added nothing to the details Jo had given before and which Mrs Wyndham had confirmed downstairs.

'You should really ask them yourself,' concluded the elderly lady.

Archie smiled. 'Aye, we will. Perhaps you would pass me their telephone number before we leave?'

Jo reached into her handbag. 'I've got it right here.' She handed over a sheet of paper bearing the number and an address in her neat, precise handwriting. 'I've tried phoning them a couple of times, but no joy getting through yet.'

'You don't mind it I take a few pics up here, do you?' Ray was already unzipping the bag he had brought upstairs with him.

'By all means,' said Mrs Wyndham. She stepped to the side to give him a clearer view.

Archie did the same. 'I'm curious to know everyone's impressions. What about you, Undine? How does this room feel to you?'

The dark-suited figure appeared to be listening to something – or perhaps *for* something. All Jo could hear was the ticking from downstairs and the rustle of their own movements. Then Undine turned around, and she was startled by how serious he looked. The last time she had seen anyone as intently focused as that, she had been with a team of Flying Squad officers as they prepared to storm the house of an armed bank robber. Those men had been facing down the possibility of a shotgun. She couldn't imagine what Undine was so worried about.

They waited in silence for several seconds until at last he shrugged. 'Feels fine to me.'

There was a flash of light, and as an after-image of Undine's head danced before her, Jo heard a camera being wound forward.

'How about you, Ray?' asked Archie.

'I swear, I'll never understand why you bother asking us that. You know me and Undine are about as psychic as a pair of bricks!'

Gentle laughter passed between the two men, and Jo suddenly saw beneath their veneer of polite professionalism. They weren't taking this seriously! Having seen the house for themselves, they probably put everything she'd told them down to the overactive imagination of a doddery old woman.

'It's not usually this quiet,' she said. She looked to Mrs Wyndham to back her up, but the elderly lady was staring at the hole in the wall. Her face was blank, almost shell-shocked. Surely the researchers could see she needed help?

Maybe Archie did sense something of the sort. As he looked at Mrs Wyndham, Jo got the impression his detached scepticism loosened a notch or two.

'Aye, well,' he said. 'Perhaps it's a blessing that events have calmed down for now. We all need a holiday once in a while. Is there anybody you could stay with for a few days? Any children possibly?'

A sad smile touched Mrs Wyndham's lips. 'No, no children. Poor Ronald always wanted a son, but it wasn't to be.'

'Ever thought about moving?' asked Undine. 'Sell up and move into somewhere a bit more modern? Should get a good price for this old pile.'

'Certainly not! This "old pile" has been in the family for a long time. I will tell you the same thing I told that dreadful Mr Erskine after Ronald passed away: Lavender Edge is my home. Nobody or nothing will drive me away.'

Jo was familiar with this part of the story. Erskine was a snake: a local property developer, who – after learning of Ronald Wyndham's death in April – kept calling at the house, offering to help the grieving widow. Thankfully, Mrs Wyndham saw through him. He'd only wanted her to sell the house to him, so that he could knock it down and put up two, or even three, smaller homes on the site. Earning himself a huge profit in the process, of course. Just thinking about it made her blood boil.

She flinched as a second camera flash lit the room. Ray winked a good-natured apology to her, took a long look at the wall with the hole, and walked out onto the landing to take more photographs. He ran out of film, and set about changing the roll.

'Have you reached any conclusions yet, Professor James?' Mrs Wyndham's irritation with Undine had fired her up again, and her eyes glittered with controlled determination.

'Just Archie, please.'

'Very well. Thank you, and you may call me Margaret.' Her words were friendly, but Jo was reminded of the headmistress at her middle school. As much as she had come to empathize with Mrs Wyndham, she would hate to get on the wrong side of the old lady's undoubtedly volatile temper. 'You must have formed some opinion by now?'

Archie hesitated. 'Well,' he began, choosing his words with care, 'what you've told me so far does appear to fit a general pattern of phenomena. There are definitely cases in the literature where physical disturbances such as building work are considered by some to have triggered anomalous activity.'

'So you have dealt with similar situations before.'

'Oh, yes.'

'And you have been able to stop them.'

It was less a question than a challenge. Jo bit her lip, hoping Archie was not about to launch into a version of Ray's speech at the Warehouse, about how the duty of a scientist was to document, not destroy, phenomena. Mrs Wyndham would not take at all kindly to that approach.

But Archie phrased his response with diplomatic grace. 'Perhaps it would reassure you to know that the type of activity you describe, once triggered, tends to burn itself out relatively quickly. You say it began around six weeks ago. That's already rather a long time. Aye, there's good reason to believe the worst is already over.'

Undine opened his mouth as if to interject. Then he seemed to change his mind, and returned his attention to the wall.

'I see.' Mrs Wyndham's lips tightened, then – as Archie continued in smooth, melodic tones – they relaxed, and the gleam in her eyes dimmed.

'We are involved with another ongoing investigation just now, Margaret. So, as events here appear calm for the moment, I propose we arrange to visit you again in a week or two to find out how matters are progressing. In the meantime, it would help us greatly were you to keep a journal record of anything else that occurs. If anything does.'

'A journal. Yes. Of course.' Spoken with cool English civility, but Jo heard the defeat in her tone.

A moment later, Archie was walking through the door. Undine, with a final, troubled look at the hole in the wall, followed him to the landing, where Ray was packing away the last of his camera equipment.

Was that it? After all that work to convince them to come here?

'Hey!' Jo ran after them. 'Where the hell do you think you're going?'

CHAPTER 6

'Bloody woman!'

Undine wiped drizzle from his neck and peered through the chilly dusk, searching for the shop he'd noticed when parking the lorry. If only that jumped-up little policewoman hadn't stuck her oar in! He could be home again by now, warm and dry in his kitchen, and savouring the delicious aromas of spices sizzling in oil. Instead, he was cold and damp, with a belly heavy with leftover roast beef sandwiches and weak tea, facing another miserable night in yet another strange house.

He spotted the shop. It stood on the corner almost directly opposite Lavender Edge, and looked to be the sort of general store that sold newspapers, tobacco, sweets, and just about anything else that might turn a bob or two. Turning up the collar of his trench coat, Undine jogged across the empty road.

Archie had given in too easily. Faced with

Jo's indignation, and coupled with the renewed determination of the old battle-axe who owned the house, the Professor had conceded that he might have been premature in his decision. Most of the activity in Lavender Edge occurred at night, it seemed, and so Archie would stay a few hours longer before reaching any final conclusions. Which meant Undine and Ray would be staying too.

The change to his plans – again! – was bad enough. To make things worse, the policewoman had been correct. There really was something inside the old house, and it was still active, despite Archie's suggestion otherwise. Undine had been uncomfortable from the moment he'd arrived, as if he could sense a wild animal lurking in the shadows, studying those who had intruded upon its territory. It had been present in the room downstairs, but hidden, keeping its distance even when Undine dared to open his mental shutters a fraction and reach out a little further into the house. Its calculating lack of reaction, although welcome in one way, troubled him, and his concern had only deepened upon entering the room upstairs. That hole in the wall bothered him most. It wasn't that he had sensed anything inside, because he hadn't; it was because he was horribly sure he should have.

He hopped over a puddle and onto the pavement, and examined the building on the corner. A word – 'Oldroyd's' – appeared above the windows in cracked and peeling lettering of a style that looked more Victorian than twentieth-century. The store owner's name? Possibly. The original Oldroyd would be long dead by now, but perhaps the shop represented a family business, passed down from one generation to the next. Given that it was already gone seven, Undine half expected the place to be closed, but when he pushed the door it opened, and an unseen bell jangled overhead.

He walked inside. Evening air blew in with him, lifting dust and disturbing such a thick mustiness of old paper and over-boiled cabbage that he was glad his sense of smell was dulled by years of smoking. He shut the door, and a weighty stillness reclaimed the interior. There was no sign of the owner, a man Mrs Wyndham painted in less than glowing colours. He was always prying, she said; always wanting to know everything going on in the neighbourhood. Undine, who valued his own privacy, despised gossip.

In front of him was a counter, empty apart from a hefty, battleship-grey cash-register. Magazines and newspapers hung from a wall-mounted rack on his right, the headlines concerning some argument over recent internment laws in Northern Ireland. Things were a bloody mess over there. The lower rungs held what appeared to be local history publications. Clearly the work of amateurs, they sported the spongy mauve print of Banda machine production, and were little more than thin sheaves of paper, stapled together in a haphazard manner. The closest featured a striking illustration on its cover: an intricate maze pattern reminiscent of a photograph Undine had seen before. Of a prehistoric carving somewhere? Irritatingly, the publication bore no title, no author name, and no clue as to what the maze signified, but he wasn't here for reading matter. He turned away from the rack and headed left, deeper into the shop, past shelves piled high with packets of crisps, chocolate bars, and a leering display of plastic masks: a Frankenstein monster, a Mummy, Dracula....

'May I help you?'

Undine turned. An elderly, frail-looking man now stood at the cash-register. Undine hadn't heard him enter, but the ribbons that curtained a doorway behind him were swaying. Long-limbed, with thinning, straw-coloured hair, the man wore a shabby pinstriped suit that might once have been brown.

'I'm looking for batteries,' said Undine.

'Batteries, eh?' The man's voice was reedy, but he spoke in clipped tones with a kind of forgotten authority. 'Let's see.' He turned to a long series of shallow wooden drawers, and after a moment's consideration, pulled one out. 'What type are you after?'

'Like these, if you have them.' Undine took

a dead battery from his pocket. It was from his torch, which had started to falter half an hour earlier, not long after the house lights themselves died. When Mrs Wyndham had mentioned that such disruptions to the power supply were another symptom of whatever plagued her home, that policewoman – Jo – had immediately looked out of a window and confirmed that it wasn't a general power cut because lights remained on in the neighbouring houses. Undine's only contribution had been to flick the useless light switch up and down, and to swear.

'About a dozen, I reckon,' said Undine. 'To be on the safe side.' The Institute would reimburse him, and it wouldn't hurt to get a few spares for Archie and Ray, who used the same make of torch. 'Oh, and a couple of candles too.'

The shopkeeper reached into his breast pocket and extracted a pair of spectacles. They were ancient things, with delicate wire frames that he fastened over his prominent ears. A crack jagged through the left lens, although he seemed either ignorant of or unbothered by this as he studied Undine.

'Up to anything interesting?'

Undine shrugged. 'This and that.'

'Hm. Working over the road, are you? In the old place.'

'The old place?'

'Lavender Edge.'

Undine sighed. It would be too much work to avoid this nosey git's questions. Quicker to answer him and get going. 'That's right. Just helping the lady who lives there sort out a few things.'

The shopkeeper leaned backward, clutching his lapels and peering down his nose through his lenses. 'Are you indeed? Hm.' For several long seconds, he stood inspecting Undine. At last, he nodded. 'Yes. Yes, I think you must be. You took your time.'

'I'm sorry?'

'No need to be sorry, young man. You're here now.' He deposited a handful of batteries on the wooden surface. 'These are all I have in stock. Now, candles you said?'

With a cracking of knees, he disappeared behind the counter. He continued talking, and Undine strained to catch his muffled words.

'She's hired some builders, did you know?'

'Just a spot of redecoration. From what I've seen it's probably a good idea.'

'It most certainly is not!'

The spectacled face popped up again, birdlike in its abrupt twitchiness.

Undine cursed under his breath, remembering something else Mrs Wyndham had mentioned a few hours ago: that the 'crazy old man at the shop' had turned up on her doorstep just minutes after the builders arrived for their first day's work, demanding to know her plans, and insisting that there must be no damage to the historic building.

Maybe the guy was some sort of eccentric local history buff. He had that look.

'Some sites should not be interfered with!' The shopkeeper stood, and placed four candles down between them, one at a time, at right angles to the counter edge. He adjusted them until the gaps between each were equal. 'Do you know what a "thin place" is?'

'You've lost me.'

'Hm. Few folk do nowadays. At a thin place, the membrane between this reality and another is at its weakest.' His eyes gleamed hard and black, like those of a crow. He fixed them on Undine. 'Most people do not see. They close their minds to the cosmos.'

Oh, hell. The absence of long hair had fooled him at first, but Undine saw it now. A pissing hippy! Give it a minute or two and this old fool would be chanting and waving around sticks of LSD-infused incense. Or did you have to be young to be a hippy? Maybe he was one of their 'gurus' or whatever the hell they called themselves.

Anxious to be gone, Undine scooped up the batteries and divided them among his coat pockets. He tucked the candles into the inside pockets of his suit jacket to protect them from the drizzle. 'How much do I owe you?'

The shopkeeper gazed at Undine for another

few seconds. Then he seemed to reach a decision. He rang up the items, took Undine's coins, and counted out his change with painstaking care.

'There we go, sir,' he smiled. 'Sorry that took so long. I'll never get used to this new decimal money.'

Undine pulled his collar back up. The unseen bell jangled again as he opened the door and stepped into the rain. After the musty stillness inside, the cold, fresh air came as a relief.

Before the door closed behind him, the shopkeeper called out a final warning. 'Remember what I said! There can be no alterations to that house. It was built as it was for good reason.'

CHAPTER 7

The ticking was driving her crazy. Even through the closed bedroom door, she felt the slow, steady, thudding knocks from the hall downstairs. And between them, nothing but dusty silence.

Jo huddled deeper into her jacket, although the thin leather did little to keep out the chill seeping into the room from outside. She wriggled, trying to get more comfortable. The floorboards were bare and hard, and the dust sheet she sat on was even thinner than her jacket. She thought again about sitting on the blanket Mrs Wyndham had loaned her, but that was spread across her lap and was currently the only thing keeping her legs warm.

The three men from the Corsi Institute were coping better. They were old hands at this, who had come prepared with their own blankets – brought in from the lorry – and vacuum flasks they had refilled with Mrs Wyndham's tea. They did this kind of thing all the time, although presumably most of their investigations were less boring than this. Hard to see the attraction otherwise.

In fact, it was hard to see anything at all. Jo's companions showed as little more than masses of darkness against a slightly lighter darkness, and she could identify them only by remembering where each had been when they blew out their candle. That was Ray sitting cross-legged, a few feet to her right, furtively shuffling his weight from one buttock to the other. Beyond him, the dark mass representing Archie was smaller than it ought to be, and the wrong shape. Maybe he was slumped forward, his head hanging down. Was he asleep? Further away, out to her left, was Undine: tense, motionless, and soundless.

She could smell the heat of their bodies, and the stale tobacco odour oozing out of their clothes. Also the lingering aroma of wax and candle smoke. The researchers conducted these vigils in the dark, Ray had explained, because that made it easier to notice any 'low-level light anomalies'.

Rain spattered against the window. The big tape recorder hummed. Archie's breathing became heavier, and cloth rustled as Ray shuffled around again. But, underneath the solid ticking of the clock, the house itself made no sound at all. No cracking of water pipes, no creaking from wooden beams as the old building settled, nothing. It was horrible. The house might have been holding its breath, watching them, waiting to see what they would do.

Jo shook the thought away. The darkness was playing tricks on her.

Then again, of the four people in this room, she was the only one who knew – truly knew – that Lavender Edge was haunted. She needed to keep her wits about her. Don't let the situation get to you, but don't underestimate the potential either.

At least Mrs Wyndham might be getting a decent night's sleep for once. After a lengthy chat with Archie, who turned out to be quite the charmer when necessary, the elderly lady had agreed to let Jo and the researchers stay in her home overnight. On one strict condition: that she herself would be going to bed, and they would not disturb her unless for a genuine emergency. Jo suspected Mrs Wyndham was secretly pleased to have company in the house; all the same, it was trusting of her to allow strangers to stay, even if she did believe there was a police officer chaperoning them.

Guilt soured her musings. She hated having to lie to the old lady, even though it was for a good reason. Mrs Wyndham needed their help, and the Corsi team needed that proved to them – so why in God's name did tonight have to be the one occasion when this damned house felt normal?

She turned again to the idea she'd been toying with for the past half-hour, wondering if she should say something.

A heavy clunk shattered the silence. Jo heard a sharp inhalation from Archie's direction, and she was instantly alert, but the others were stretching, taking deep breaths, and showing no concern. The sound had just been the team's tape recorder, automatically switching off as the spool ran out.

Ray clicked on his torch. He found his matches, lit a candle, and handed the stick to Archie. As everyone lit their own candles from the flame, Ray rustled in a small pile of sweets and oddments by his feet, and slipped something into his mouth.

In the dancing light, Archie examined his watch. 'Almost midnight. I think we could all do with a wee break, eh?'

'Not half,' said Ray, clambering upright and massaging cramp from his calf muscles.

Jo stood as well, stiff from the cold that had soaked into her backside. She slipped her hands into the back pockets of her jeans, grateful for the warmth from her palms.

Across the room, Undine lit a cigarette from his candle. The glow flickered over his blunt features, throwing his thoughtful eyes into even deeper shadows than usual.

'Just our luck, huh?' said Jo, trying to lighten

the glum mood. 'We had to pick the one night all the ghosts go on holiday.'

Ray gave a half-hearted smile.

She changed tack. 'Look, it's not usually like this, I swear. Mrs Wyndham told you the truth. She's terrified of what's been happening here. And I've seen things myself, don't forget.'

'Oh, it's not that we don't believe you,' said Archie. 'Sometimes the fish are biting and sometimes they're not. But a wise fisherman knows better than to stand in dead water.'

He was clearly planning to leave soon. Perhaps her idea was a stupid one, but what did she have to lose?

'I've been thinking,' she said. 'The other morning, what you told me about "ghoul zones": you seemed to be saying that hauntings are like recordings. Like maybe events can be imprinted onto their surroundings.'

'Aye,' said Archie. 'I think that might well be the case.'

'Well, if a ghost is a recording, why do we need to hang around waiting until it just happens to start playing? Isn't there something we could do to trigger it?'

Archie pulled out his pipe and, with infuriating calm, began to pack tobacco into the bowl. Jo fought the impulse to hurry him.

'I would imagine that's a possibility,' he said at last. 'If' – and he jabbed the stem of his pipe into the air – 'we knew what the trigger mechanism might be.' He put a match to the bowl, drawing the tobacco into life. 'I'm afraid we're a long way off from knowing that yet.'

'Actually,' said Ray, sucking on his sweet. 'I've been thinking too. Not had much else to do for the last few hours!'

He wandered across to the hole in the wall. It looked bigger in the candlelight.

'Look, for the sake of argument, let's assume that people really have experienced weird phenomena here. You know I'm generally sceptical about this stuff, but stories have circulated about this house for years, on and off. There's likely to be something behind them, whatever it is.'

Archie tilted his head, listening but not committing himself one way or the other.

'Well, again for the sake of argument, let's say the recent resurgence in "activity" is somehow linked to this building work.' Ray gestured towards the hole.

'Seems pretty obvious to me,' said Jo. 'It started the same day!'

'Perhaps,' said Archie cautiously.

'Okay,' said Ray. 'So, in terms of the theories favoured by our esteemed Professor James, the implication would be that the builders disturbed something. That the work, in some manner, reactivated a form of energy stored within these walls.'

'You don't believe that,' said Undine. He

approached Ray, but his eyes did not look away from the hole. The candlelight deepened the lines in his furrowed brow.

Ray gave a good-natured shrug. 'Not really. You ask me, the building work probably damaged the plumbing and the electrics. That might explain most of the strange noises, as well as tonight's power cut.'

'And the table?' Jo had been warming to the skinny scientist with the awful clothes, but his casual dismissal felt like a personal attack. 'I saw it move myself! And I wasn't the only one.'

The cold that had soaked in from the floor shuddered through her as a memory began to surface. For a moment, she almost had the details: the other part of what had happened to her that night, right here in this room. Then they were gone, leaving only a bad taste in her mind.

'Might the workmen have damaged the floors too?' asked Ray. 'Before we go, we should check whether they're level. But the point I'm trying to make is that we've been sitting here in the dark, literally, just waiting for something to happen of its own accord. Obviously, that's not working, so Jo's right. We should try something more active. Try to provoke the phenomena ourselves.'

Archie drew on his pipe. 'What do you propose?'

Ray switched his torch back on and played light over the torn wallpaper, cracked plaster, and broken brickwork framing the hole in the wall. 'What if there's something inside there?'

His eyes twinkled with boyish enthusiasm. 'Those old stories about the faces at Lavender Edge – a lot of them speculated that people had died here, you know. That their spirits had got trapped in the walls.'

He broke off a ragged piece of plaster and crumbled it between finger and thumb. 'What if there was some truth to those tales? Like, maybe someone was murdered here at some point, and the killer bricked up their corpse in the wall.'

'And, what, now they haunt the place?' Jo was surprised to hear such an idea from Ray, and not keen on the thought there might be a skeleton hidden just a few feet away.

He chuckled. 'I was thinking more along the lines of folklore. That the stories are folk memories – corrupted ones – of a real event in the past.' He rubbed plaster dust from his fingers. 'But I try to keep an open mind. Archie's ideas feel pretty far-out to me, but I reckon we should test them if we can. Do something to the wall ourselves to replicate what the builders were up to, and see whether we can re-trigger whatever spooked them. I mean, wouldn't that be the scientific, experimental approach?'

Archie gazed at the hole, tapping his pipe against his chin.

Undine cleared his throat. 'I don't know about this, Sunny.'

'Nothing else is going on,' said Ray. 'What's

the worst that could happen?'

Undine appeared about to argue, then changed his mind and stared instead at the hole.

'We'd have to be quiet,' said Archie. 'Margaret's asleep, don't forget.'

Mrs Wyndham's bedroom was only a short distance away, across the landing. There were, however, two closed doors between them and her.

The tweed-jacketed Professor walked up to the hole and inspected the edges. 'Aye. Perhaps we could peel this back a bit without too much noise.'

Undine took a sudden step away from the wall. His head was cocked, listening, but Jo heard only the pattering rain and the interminable ticking of the grandfather clock downstairs. Undine shambled around the room until he moved behind her and passed out of view.

She turned back to Archie. 'Believe me, she's put up with a lot worse over the last few weeks. As long as you don't start swinging hammers around, I doubt she'd even hear you.'

'The old witch is lying to you! You're wasting your time!'

The whisper was harsh enough to make Jo jump. It had come from directly behind her, spat almost into her ear. She shot Undine a vicious glare over her shoulder.

'Nice one,' said Ray. 'Okay, pass us the other torches, would you? This'll be easier if we can see what we're doing.'

Overhead, the lightbulb stuttered and popped into life. The power had come back on, at last.

Ray grinned. 'As if by magic.'

Jo glanced towards the light switch, near the door. She had checked the switch herself when the electricity failed, and remembered snapping it up and down a few times, but surely she'd left it up, in the 'off' position? She always did that, for safety.

But the switch was definitely down.

Dark wisps of smoke curled into the air as the team snuffed out their candles for the second time. In the electric bulb's yellow spill, the hole looked smaller. Ray leaned forward, blew into the void, and jerked back coughing amid a cloud of plaster dust.

What was that?

Jo waved her hands to shush Ray's spluttering. 'Did you hear that?' The sound had been brief: a sort of faint scrabbling that seemed to come from inside the hole.

Ray shook his head.

'You need to leave,' Undine whispered into her ear.

She whirled around, ready to slap him, but he was farther away than she had expected. He feigned a puzzled innocence, shaking his head to ask what she was accusing him of. She spun away in disgust, and heard the scrabbling again.

It was soft but there was no mistaking now that the sound came from inside the wall.

Nobody reacted.

'Seriously, don't you guys hear that?'

Ray's eyes were watering as he tried to clear dust from his throat. Archie dribbled cold tea from his flask into a plastic mug and handed it to the younger man. Undine, unsurprisingly, showed no inclination to do anything at all.

It was up to her then, skeleton or not. She pushed Ray away from the hole, and closed her fingers around a chunk of plaster. Using both hands, she prised it towards her. It came away easily. She peeled a flap of wallpaper from the surface, ripped it away, and it fluttered to the floor. She crumbled off another inch or two of plaster, then another, exposing more of the brickwork.

The scrabbling was louder now, but she still couldn't see what was causing it.

She quashed the fleeting fear of what might happen if this, now, what she was doing, triggered the ghost or energy or whatever the hell had scared away the workmen. So what if it did? Wasn't that what they'd wanted? And if these pig-headed idiots actually saw it for themselves, they might finally decide to help!

More plaster came away.

Jo gripped one of the narrow bricks and tugged. It took only a little effort to work it loose. One of the men moved closer, and she was aware of his breath on her neck. She tried to pass the brick back to him, but whoever was there refused to take it.

'That's enough,' he whispered. His hand took her upper arm. 'Come away from there.'

She recognized the voice. That damned Undine!

She let the brick drop, and it hit the floor with a hollow thunk. Plaster dust filled her mouth and nostrils, and she coughed and snorted, gulping for air, but she wasn't about to stop now.

The hand pulled again, more insistent this time. With a grunt of irritation, she twisted away, grabbing another brick, and then another, dropping them behind her, careless now of the noise they made.

Something was there, in the too-deep space behind the bricks. But not bone. It felt like wood. A thick wooden beam, standing vertical. Another cough escaped her. It wafted away concealing dust, and she thought she glimpsed some sort of lump embedded in the wood.

Undine's hand was on her again. She wrenched free, and pivoted to her left so that her shadow no longer blocked her view inside. Light from the room fell past her, into the cavity.

She reached in, straining.

Her fingertips touched the surface. Just out of reach.

She forced herself further inside. A finger brushed against what felt like rock. It was roughly the size of a clenched fist, and, yes, it was embedded in the wood. Feeble light bounced off fine white granules, and showed a dark, narrow outline.

With an outstretched fingernail, she scraped dust from that outline, revealing a slight gap around the outside of the stone. She thrust deeper, touching the stone's edge, grasping, slipping, trying to work it loose. It was heavy. She jiggled it, pulled at it. Her breathing came in gasps. Her heart raced and her shoulder hurt where she pressed against the broken wall, but she needed to release what was there, to bring it out, into the light....

It came out!

She clutched the stone to her in triumph. Leather rasped against brick as she re-emerged into the room, clasping her prize to her like someone who had unearthed a Fabergé egg.

Undine was still there. With an outburst of spite that surprised her, she pushed backwards, hard and fast, hoping the impact would barge him over, but she encountered only air and nearly lost her balance.

'Get your hands off me!' she warned as she turned to face him.

But Undine was several feet away. His hands were on his stomach, his arms tight to his chest. His eyes were screwed shut, and he looked, if anything, constipated.

Closest to her was Ray. He gave her a

confused smile. 'Nobody's touching you.'

'What have you found there?' asked Archie.

The bulb overhead flickered. A long, low creaking soughed through the room, as if a massive weight were coming to rest on protesting floorboards. From the landing, on the other side of the closed door, water pipes rattled. It was utterly different to the deathly hush that had so frustrated her earlier. And something else had changed, although for a few moments she was unsure what.

Archie came closer. 'May I?'

She let him take the stone from her, wondering why the object had held such importance a moment ago. The Scot turned it over in his big hands, feeling the dark surface. He raised the stone to his mouth and blew on it sharply, twice.

She realized what else was different about the house. The ticking had stopped.

'Fascinating,' murmured Archie.

Undine groaned. Ray reached him as he bent double. 'What's up, mate?'

The air in the room was warmer. Thicker. It throbbed, and it tingled. Jo smelled that crackling tang she associated with bumper cars at the fairground, and another creak rose around them. She imagined the floor bowing beneath her feet.

Oh, God. Not again.

Someone's walkie-talkie hissed a burst of

static, and the room went black. Glass tinkled: the sound of the lightbulb smashing onto the ground in front of her.

Undine was saying something. Or, rather, words were pushing out of him, seemingly against his will. Jo didn't want to hear them. Somehow, she already knew what they would be. She had no conscious recollection of what had happened in this room last time, but memories were stirring.

... *In the walls* ...

'Walls,' moaned Undine. 'They're in the walls.'

Torchlight shafted through the dark, swinging wildly to find Undine's teeth bared in a grimace. Then Ray was holding his friend, keeping the light on Undine's face as if he thought the brightness alone might wash away his pain. 'It's alright, mate,' he was saying. 'You're okay.'

A ripple passed through the room.

And was gone.

The air was back to normal, the burnt electric tang only a scent memory, and the clock downstairs was ticking.

Jo's training kicked in. Control the situation: that's what they'd taught her. She saw Undine's torch, took it, and thumbed it on. She looked for Archie, and found him on the floor next to one of the team's equipment bags, with his feet tangled in a rucked-up section of dust sheet. He was obviously shocked, but he was conscious and moving, so she turned to check on the others. Undine was picking himself up, refusing to meet Ray's inquiring gaze. She went to him in case he needed medical aid, but he shooed her away.

The door opened. Light poured in from the landing.

'It's happening again, isn't it?' Mrs Wyndham's voice conveyed an awful mixture of fear and weary resignation.

Jo wondered how to respond.

Then she heard movement behind her, and a stifled cry from Archie.

CHAPTER 8

'Any news?' Jo stood back as Ray unlocked the Warehouse door.

'Doc thinks it was a simple fracture.' He gestured for her to enter first. 'Archie's not sure how it happened, just that he lost his balance and fell. Must have caught his foot in that sheet. Anyway, Undine's gone to pick him up.'

They crossed the empty floor in silence. This was her fault. Archie was no spring chicken, and he would have trouble coping with a broken arm for the next few weeks.

At the bottom of the stairs, Ray stopped and stared at her. 'How are you feeling?'

Jo wasn't sure how to answer. Not counting her parents, it was a long time since someone had expressed concern for her well-being. There was a perception among the general public that police officers formed close bonds with one another, but having someone taking the piss out of you, whether to your face or behind your back, didn't qualify as friendship. Not in her eyes anyway. Maybe it was different for men.

'Okay,' she said. 'I guess.'

Cold October daylight struggled to penetrate the small glass windowpanes. The light, weak though it was, was enough to make her fear of only a few hours ago seem unreal, like the ebbing memory of a nightmare.

'You sure? You had a bit of a weird turn back at that house.'

She attempted a laugh, hoping it sounded more convincing to Ray than to her own ears. 'I think we all did.'

They reached the first floor and Ray invited her into his office. She draped her leather jacket over the back of the nearest chair, and stretched, cracking the muscles in her neck and shoulders. It had been a long night. After Ray and Undine had taken Archie to A and E, Jo had stayed with Mrs Wyndham, sitting in the drawing room and fortifying themselves with brandy from the drinks cabinet until the old woman assured her she was quite capable of looking after herself. With that, Mrs Wyndham had gone back to bed. Jo, meanwhile, lacking transport because the men had driven off in the lorry, was left to spend a tense night alone on the sofa. Following the excitement upstairs, the house had lapsed into silence, punctuated by the solid, steady ticking of the grandfather clock, but sleep – what little came to her – had been light and restless.

She sucked in a lungful of oxygen and told herself she was awake and alert. 'What's the plan then, Dr Buckley?'

Ray surfaced from wherever his own thoughts had taken him. His skinny, guileless face broadcast the fact he had no idea what to do next.

He looked so lost that Jo felt a wave of fondness towards the awkward young man. 'I mean, where do we go from here? I don't know the technical terms you scientists would use but it seems to me we're over the first hurdle. At least we know now we're dealing with something real, don't we?'

'I guess so.' Ray shook off whatever had been troubling him and made an effort to pull himself together.

'So?'

He thought for a moment. 'I suppose we could start going through the data. Everything's still in the back of the lorry. We were knackered when we got back, couldn't face lugging it all in.'

'Great.' Jo stood, eager to begin.

'It's in quite a mess. We just chucked it all in because we wanted to get to the hospital.'

That was a point: if Undine was away fetching the Professor, how come she had seen the team's lorry parked in front of the Warehouse only a few minutes ago?

She asked Ray.

He pulled open a cupboard door, revealing

a clothes rail hung with garments. 'He got the bus.' Reaching inside without paying attention, he took an orange-and-tan checked jacket off its hanger. It was hideous. Her opinion must have showed in her expression because, with one arm already in a sleeve, Ray hesitated.

'What do you reckon?'

'With that shirt? Maybe something blue?'

'Huh. Okay.'

He rummaged along the rail, pulled out a dark blue blazer, and held it up for her approval.

'Better,' she smiled.

✽   ✽   ✽

A chill wind whipped through the valley between the towering, dilapidated warehouses. It carried the washed-out stink of seaweed and rubbish, and the mournful cries of hungry gulls: reminders that the sluggish waters of the River Thames lay just on the other side of the Institute's offices.

Jo accepted Ray's hand and let him pull her up into the back of the drab green lorry. He wasn't kidding. This was a mess.

They gathered together blankets, notebooks and torches from the wooden struts that constituted a floor, and stuffed them into bags. Ray examined the walkie-talkies, confirming each was still working, while Jo looked beneath the side benches for a screw-on plastic cup that had gone missing from one of the Thermos flasks. There was no sign of it, and she suspected it was still lying on a dust sheet in that bedroom at Lavender Edge. The wind rippled the tarpaulin, briefly raising the rear flaps.

'Pass me that, would you?' said Ray.

He was holding a reel he had prised off the tape recorder, and Jo followed his gaze towards an empty cardboard packet. She handed it to him.

'Cheers.'

He dropped the reel into the packet, labelled the outside and gave it back to her to put into her holdall. When he had locked the recorder into its carrying case, he stood, and gave their surroundings a final quick inspection. 'Reckon that's the lot.'

A few minutes later, they were climbing the steps back to his office.

'You been doing this a long time?' asked Jo.

'A while, yeah. Depends. I've been studying the subject pretty much my whole life. Working with the boys, only a couple of years. Just with Archie at first. Started while I was doing my doctorate.'

'In the supernatural?'

Ray chuckled. 'Psychology. Specifically, my thesis was on ways in which "time slip" experiences might be explained as errors in cognitive processing.'

'Impressive,' said Jo, uncertain that was the

right word.

'Guaranteed to get you a good job!' Ray joked. 'I was lucky, though. I landed on my feet when I met Archie.'

'What are "time slips" then?'

'They're pretty rare, but they're when someone finds themselves temporarily – if you'll pardon the pun! – in the wrong time period. Or that's what they believe, at any rate.' He shrugged. 'They usually think they've slipped back into the past, although there are reports of people supposedly travelling into the future for a short while. There's a famous case happened in 1901, when a couple of English ladies visiting Versailles palace in France apparently wandered around the place as it had been during the time of Marie Antoinette!'

'Seriously? That can really happen?'

'Oh, I shouldn't think so.'

Ray put down the case and his two holdalls, and took a moment to catch his breath. He shouldn't be carrying so much at once. Was he trying to impress her?

'Funny thing is,' said Ray, 'I've never been much of a believer in the paranormal. Not since I was a boy anyway. It's just that I love the folklore side of it.'

'So last night must have made you question a few things, eh?'

A crease appeared between Ray's eyes. 'How do you mean?'

'With everything that happened. The lightbulb and the noises, and that horrible sensation in the air. We all felt it.'

'Well, yes. But when you stop to think about it, what did actually happen?'

That wasn't what she'd expected him to say.

'Fear's a peculiar thing,' said Ray. 'In the right circumstances, it's like a contagion. It colours your perceptions, but if you step back and reconsider events calmly and rationally, what are you left with?'

Jo started to reply, and discovered she didn't know what she wanted to say.

'But, well, what about your rude friend?' she asked at last.

Ray considered his words before replying. 'I asked him about that. He didn't want to talk about it.'

'Well, *something* happened to him,' insisted Jo. 'You saw it as well as I did. That was more than just someone getting a little spooked. And that stuff he said – about how "they" were inside the walls – I swear I knew exactly what he was going to say before he said it! You can't dismiss that.'

Ray shrugged again. She guessed he thought the gesture made him look cool, but it came across as condescending. Her next question emerged sounding ruder than intended.

'What's that supposed to mean?'

'Déjà vu.' Ray seemed unaware how smug he sounded. 'Once you start to study how memory works, you realize it's nothing at all the way most people think it is. Memories aren't reliable, for one thing, and they can play odd tricks on you if you're not careful.'

What the hell was he trying to say? She knew what had happened! She'd been there!

Realizing that her fists were clenched, she relaxed her hands – but it was no wonder she was frustrated. After last night, she had been certain these damned researchers would acknowledge that something was happening in Mrs Wyndham's house.

'Still,' said Ray, 'we'll have a clearer idea of the facts soon, after we cross-reference our accounts.' He smiled ruefully. 'Shame the recorder had stopped by that point. We should have changed tapes right after the session was over, and kept recording. Remind me next time, will you?'

So at least there was going to be a next time. Somewhat mollified, she picked up the holdall she'd brought up the stairs. It weighed a ton. 'Where do you want this?'

'That one's Archie's. Best leave it in his office for now. It's that one over there.'

Jo was already on her way. 'I remember.' She dragged the bag through. The surface of Archie's desk was cluttered with tools, wires, and assorted electronic bits and pieces. Although the Professor had reassembled most of his Octopus gadget since the other day, it seemed he'd had to abandon one of the fragile green circuit boards partway through working on it. Not wanting to disturb anything, Jo slid the holdall under the desk, tucking it well back so Archie wouldn't trip over the handle when he returned.

Back in Ray's office, she found him folding blankets into a neat pile.

'Must be interesting work though.' She kept her voice light and her impatience under control. 'Even for an unbeliever.'

'Wouldn't swap it for anything.'

He shoved the blankets into the cupboard, lifting them onto a shelf above his kaleidoscopic array of suits. Jo would have given them a good wash first, because of all the dust in them. She decided not to mention it. Instead, she asked: 'Even after last night?'

'Of course.' Ray looked as if she'd just asked whether birds could fly. 'Last night was fascinating! I can't wait to compare everyone's accounts. Which we're all going to need to write up as soon as possible, you know, while the details are fresh in our minds. You as well.'

His eyes sparkled. 'I especially want to know what you saw inside the cavity. But don't tell me! Not yet. Can't risk biasing my own account.'

Jo shook her head, what was left of her irritation melting into amused bemusement. Dealing with scientists was going to take some getting used to.

Ray wiped his dusty palms on the back of his

trousers.

'So,' said Jo, 'how would someone get into investigating this sort of stuff? If they wanted to?'

That got his attention. 'You interested?'

'I might be.' She turned the idea over, examining how it felt. Last night had been frightening, she couldn't deny that. The more she considered it, however, the more appealing she found the thought of helping people in Mrs Wyndham's situation. Who else could they turn to? Certainly not the police. She had seen first-hand how that worked out.

'Yeah,' she said. 'Yeah, maybe.'

Ray's answering grin grew so wide it threatened to split his narrow head in two. 'Catching crooks not exciting enough for you?'

She thought about telling him the truth. But this wasn't the time. Not yet.

'Must be satisfying,' she said, 'being able to help people the way you do.'

'I suppose so. Not thought about that side of it, to be honest.'

'That, Doctor Buckley, is why your Institute would benefit from a feminine touch.'

'No argument here.' Ray perched himself on the edge of his desk and offered her a cigarette. She shook her head. Watching him light his fag, and now that he was wearing the blazer, he was better-looking than she had realized at their first meeting.

'You'd also be getting the benefit of my own investigative training,' Jo added. 'You know we're going to need to interview Mrs Wyndham's builders, to get their side of the story. I could talk to them for you. They teach us a thing or two about interviewing people at Peel House, you know.'

Ray breathed out smoke. His eyes, suddenly insightful, analysed her. 'The police aren't keen on helping Mrs Wyndham, are they?'

'No.' Jo fought down a rush of temper at the memory. 'As far as they're concerned, she's just some dotty old woman who needs carting off to the closest loony bin.'

'Yet you're still taking care of her.'

Jo wondered how she should respond, but was saved by the sound of a door slamming shut below them. A few seconds later, heavy footsteps thudded up the staircase. They reached the top, and a tall figure swept past the doorway in a swirl of black trench coat, only to disappear into the next room without a word of greeting.

Ray hurried out, like a puppy rushing to greet his returning master. With less enthusiasm, Jo followed.

They found Undine collapsed in his chair, swigging from a silver hip flask. She smelled cheap Scotch.

'What's she doing here?' said Undine.

'We bought the gear in,' said Ray. 'Your stuff's in my office. We're ready to get going when you are.' He paused. 'Archie not with you?'

'They're keeping him in. Observation. Because of his age.' Undine glared at Jo. The accusation was clear. 'They say he had a nasty shock.'

'How's his arm?' she asked.

Undine ignored her.

'We were just about to write our reports,' said Ray. 'No time like the present.'

Undine took another slug from his flask.

Jo folded her arms. 'You felt it, didn't you?'

'No idea what you're talking about.'

'Oh, come on! All that business with "They're in the walls"? You looked like you were about to have a heart attack!'

'I'm surprised you noticed anyone else,' said Undine. 'What with your little hissy-fit, trying to rip the place apart with your bare hands. It's always the same with women. Drama and hysteria.'

'Don't change the subject.'

'My friend's in hospital, in case you've forgotten.'

'How is that my fault?'

He pulled a face.

The urge to drive her fist into the exasperating bastard's nose was strong. Jo swung away from his desk and fixed her eyes on the pale green wall, sucking in calming breaths.

For Christ's sake, don't blow this now.

'Easy, mate,' said Ray. 'It was an accident. And

she's right, to be fair: something did happen to you.'

Undine scoffed.

'But we shouldn't be discussing this. Not before we write down what we remember. Shall we get started?'

From somewhere, Ray produced notepads and pens, and he offered them to Jo and Undine. She knew his intention had much to do with smoothing things over, but the report-writing was good practice. It wasn't a million miles from techniques the police had taught her.

She took one of the pens and a pad. 'Okay. So, what sort of thing did you need me to write?'

'Not you,' said Undine.

'Excuse me?'

Undine stood, and the smells of whisky and stale tobacco billowed up with him. His bloodshot eyes glowered from shadowed hollows. He looked as if he hadn't had a decent night's sleep in weeks, or possibly years.

'Archie's going to be out of action for at least the next few days,' he said, 'so I'm taking charge. And I say this whole nonsense with Mrs Wind-up and her wallpaper faces is a waste of Institute resources. So here's the plan. I'm going out for some breakfast, and when I get back I'm going to phone what's-his-name at the Pyramus and arrange for us to do some proper work there. You up for that, Sunny?'

Jo began to protest.

But Ray was speaking at the same time. 'Ah, okay. If you really think so. And Jo too? We were just talking about how useful it would be to have her on board, and –'

Undine snorted. 'Not a chance.'

He rounded on Jo.

'Now get your arse out of my office, darling. You've done more than enough damage.'

CHAPTER 9

He couldn't risk the old bat spotting the lorry. As Undine pulled away from the traffic lights, he kept a wary eye on the Friday afternoon shoppers and saw plenty of elderly ladies moving through the herd, wrapped in overcoats and headscarves and brandishing wheeled shopping bags; so far as he could see, however, Mrs Wyndham was not among them.

The cricket pitch slipped past. He passed a couple of pubs that he remembered seeing the day before, and a few more shops, then the busy part of town was behind him and the road was dropping as he neared the railway station. Rivermead Path came up on his left, but he drove on and over another small bridge with water running beneath, then heaved the beast of a lorry around to the right, into what the sign identified as Wandle Road. Named, presumably, for the river that ran through south London.

There was a grinding crunch as he messed up

the gear change.

'Get stuffed.'

His head ached from lack of sleep and the stress of the argument with Ray. Things had kicked off when Undine returned from the cafe. Clearly upset about the policewoman, the younger man had pestered Undine to explain those final few minutes at the house last night. He'd even set up the tape recorder and microphone, ready for Undine to dictate his account instead of writing it down the same as usual.

As much as Undine liked Ray, there were details he wasn't ready to share with anyone. All at once, he'd been unable to take the badgering a moment longer.

'Oh, why don't you just piss off after your girlfriend, Sunny? You've been drooling like a puppy ever since you clapped eyes on her.'

'That's not what this is about!'

Undine had often thought the skinny psychologist too timid for his own good, but this time Ray impressed him, making it plain he intended to pursue the Lavender Edge case with or without Undine's permission. A return visit to the Soho theatre would take at least a few days to arrange, and in the meantime Ray was going to interview Mrs Wyndham's builders, like it or not. Undine couldn't remember ever seeing Ray so determined about anything. It finally pushed him into the decision he'd been resisting.

'Okay, okay. Put a sock in it, Sunny. We're not really going back to Soho. We're sticking with Lavender Edge for now. See how it goes.'

'But you said –'

'That was for blondie's benefit.'

Ray looked so confused that Undine relented. 'Alright, I admit it. I lost my temper. I was wrong, and now I've changed my mind. Happy?'

A slow smile spread across Ray's thin face. 'Nice one! I'll let her know.'

He started towards the door before Undine could reply.

'No. Sorry, mate, but she's still out.'

'But –'

Undine shut him off. 'You saw her last night. The chaos she caused. She'd get in our way.'

He held back his deeper concern: that the impulsive policewoman had no idea of the danger involved. At least Ray approached situations with the calm rationality of a scientist, as did Archie. Not her. She was reckless, like a kid playing catch with an unexploded bomb.

Whatever Undine had sensed last night was powerful. He'd felt it even before walking through the front door. There was an oppressiveness about the old building, some presence that crouched within every inch of the dark brickwork and radiated from the blank windows that stared at him as he walked up the path. That sense of being studied – not by anyone in particular but by some intangible malevolence – had possessed an almost physical weight, and he had half-expected the others to feel it too. Although, judging by their reactions, they had felt nothing – until the end.

The details of those final minutes had dissolved like strands of nightmare, but – according to Ray – Undine had said something like 'they're in the wall'. Just thinking about the phrase now sent a shock of dread through Undine's nervous system, although he had no recollection of saying it, and no idea what it meant.

He saw a parking space and switched on his indicator.

There was no doubt that the same sort of mysterious and painful force that had burned him in the past was present at Lavender Edge – yet that was only a part of what he had sensed there. The rest of it, that oppressive presence, was something he had never encountered before, not even at the Soho theatre. The prospect of a closer encounter with it terrified him, but what if it could lead him to some of the answers he had been seeking for so long?

So, yes, despite his deep reservations, Undine would continue the investigation into what was happening at Lavender Edge, but no, WPC Cross would not be accompanying them. And now that she was out of the picture, and he was in charge, the Institute researchers would proceed slowly and carefully, taking the time to conduct proper background research of the location before anybody went blundering into that house again.

Which was why, without having told Ray where he was going, Undine was here now. He didn't want Ray with him; if Mrs Wyndham did happen to spot them, she would want them to go back to the house with her and Ray would be too soft to turn her down. So Undine had instructed him to do as he'd wanted and interview the frightened workmen: a couple of Irish brothers who operated as Doyle Construction Ltd out of an address in Garrett Lane, Tooting. It should keep him out of the way for a few hours.

He left the lorry in a side street and walked back down to the main road. In only a minute or so he was re-crossing the bridge over the Wandle. Wind rustled a nearby stand of trees, where a gate led through into grassland. The noticeboard read Ravensbury Park.

The name was familiar. It seemed that, by coincidence, he was following the same route WPC Cross and her colleague had taken that evening on their way back to the police station. He recognized the road names too as he came to them, and imagined the scene: PC Condie searching the young toerag's pockets, and the unknown man appearing to Cross and begging her to hurry to Lavender Edge.

He stopped, and looked through the traffic. Between the cars, he spotted the opening to

Rivermead Path a short distance away. This must be about where the constables had crossed, just as she had related. He thought about how her answers under hypnosis had added detail to her story without changing the basic structure, and felt confident she had told them the truth. Yet he didn't trust her. Whenever he thought of her, his mind reacted the same way his gut would warn him not to eat rancid meat.

And what the pissing hell had last night been about, trying to tear down the wall with her bare hands? Crazy cow.

He walked down Rivermead Path. Ahead, a group of boys shouted and laughed as they kicked an empty can between them along the pavement on their way home from school. They paid Undine no heed as he threaded his way through their game. Metal skittered across tarmac, then, with a hollow clatter, bounced off the mustard yellow door of a parked Hillman Avenger. Cries of dismay and blame rang out as Undine reached the corner shop.

It looked different in daylight, even with sunset fast approaching, but the ancient lettering above the door and windows assured him it was the same place: 'Oldroyd's'. If the shopkeeper were as nosey as Mrs Wyndham claimed, he should be a useful source of information about the area, especially if he had been working in this shop a long time. From his outburst yesterday, he certainly thought he knew something about Mrs Wyndham's house. Undine should have questioned him at the time and saved himself a journey today, but that was his own fault. He just hoped the old fool wouldn't start off on that hippy crap again because he really wasn't in the mood.

Across the road, the blank windows of Lavender Edge watched him push the door open.

The bell jangled as he stepped inside. As the sound shimmered away, a deep silence rolled in, until not even the boys' cries penetrated the dim interior.

'You're back.' The shopkeeper's eyes twinkled behind those wire-framed spectacles with their irritating, spider-cracked lens. Behind him, to the side of the ribbon-curtained doorway, the wall was decorated with Tarot cards, fastened in place with tarnished drawing pins.

Undine hadn't noticed those yesterday. He tried not to let his distaste for occult mumbo-jumbo appear too obvious.

'How did it go?' asked the shopkeeper in his clipped, reedy voice.

'So so.'

'Hm.' The shopkeeper smirked. 'And how may I help you today?'

Undine breathed in the musty air, with its whiff of boiled cabbage. 'This shop's been around a good while, by the look of it.'

The shopkeeper acknowledged the comment. 'Family business?'

'In a manner of speaking.'

'Which, going by the name outside, would make you Mr Oldroyd, right?'

A smile invited Undine to continue.

He'd take that as a yes, then. He gestured at the pamphlets on the rack next to him. 'Guess people around here enjoy local stories, eh? You must have picked up some juicy titbits yourself, over the years.'

'"Gossip", do you mean?'

Undine recalled Mrs Wyndham's disparaging comments. Was the shopkeeper toying with him?

'I was thinking more along the lines of local history.'

The twinkle in Oldroyd's eyes blazed brighter. 'Mitcham is very old, Mr …?'

'Undine.'

'Undine?' Oldroyd's mouth twitched in amusement. 'Yes, very old. Did you know there was an Anglo-Saxon settlement just to the north of here, Mr Undine?'

'My history's a bit rusty. Anglo-Saxon? How far back are we talking?'

'Oh, fifteen hundred years. Give or take. We have the Bidders to thank for much of what we know, of course. They excavated the burial ground.'

'Bidders?'

Oldroyd waved a dismissive hand. 'Prominent townsfolk.'

'Right. And let me guess – we're standing on the burial ground right now?'

Something which was not quite a smile twisted Oldroyd's pale lips. 'Not quite. Not here. Although the house in which you're interested does stand a little closer to those graves. Somewhere around the eastern perimeter of the old grounds, as far as the archaeologists were able to determine.'

'You're talking about Mrs Wyndham's place.'

'One of her husband's ancestors was responsible for the house, you know. Joseph Wyndham. Got into the calico bleaching business. He did rather well for himself, did young Joseph.'

'It looks old.'

'1746. That's when Lavender Edge was completed.'

Undine was surprised the old man could bring such detail to mind.

Now Oldroyd did smile. 'I have, as you say, been here a long time. One picks up these little facts.'

'I'm not complaining, Mr Oldroyd. It's all very helpful.' Undine opened a notebook. 'Do you mind?'

'Please do. Now, where was I?'

'You were saying when the house was built.'

'Ah yes. This might interest you. Joseph's choice of location ruffled one or two feathers. It entailed demolishing an older building, you see, one that already stood on the site. Only a ruin by then, but some things are better left unchanged. Unaltered, hm? Don't you agree?'

Undine shrugged and half-nodded.

It seemed to satisfy Oldroyd. 'But Joseph refused to be deterred, notwithstanding the vociferous objections against him. He gained his house. And, sadly, he came to regret it.'

Undine scribbled notes as Oldroyd continued.

'They say the disturbances began almost at once. His first workers ran off. He had the devil of a time finding enough men to finish building the place, but I suppose if you have enough money....'

'What sort of disturbances?'

Oldroyd leaned forward and rested his elbows on the scratched wooden counter. Long fingers came together in a steeple and his black, crow-like eyes fixed on Undine. 'It was to be expected. They damaged the Weall.'

'The warl?' Undine tried to replicate the old man's pronunciation. It was tricky, as if the sound of the syllable altered midway through, from the 'a' sound heard in words like cat and hat, to the longer 'a' of father or last. It sounded foreign. Or was it an Anglo-Saxon word?

The light in the shopkeeper's eyes grew fierce. 'The faces are back, aren't they?'

Undine found himself reluctant to answer directly. 'Oh yeah, I heard there was some story about faces. What are they?'

'I warned her. I did what I could to stop her.'

'Are they supposed to be ghosts or something?' Undine ended the question with an uncomfortable laugh to show he found the idea embarrassing.

Oldroyd stared at him like he was an idiot.

'Have you ever heard of a shaman, Mr Undine? Hm? Do you know what that word means?'

The question caught Undine off guard. Vague associations bubbled up from memory, and he tried his best to articulate them. 'Hippy crap. Lots of foreign Johnnies with bones through their noses. I don't know. Witch doctors? Dancing around fires chanting a lot of oogabooga mumbo-jumbo, stuff like that.'

Oldroyd lowered his gaze, as if he had anticipated better. 'I see. Nevertheless, you'll have to stop her.'

'That's not why we're –'

'You know what I'm talking about.'

Rapier-like menace ran through Oldroyd's words. His eyes lifted from the floor, locking back onto Undine's.

Something had changed. Oldroyd fizzed with energy. Some mania was building in him, gripping him, animating him, and an unexpected thought struck Undine. Might the shopkeeper be having an LSD flashback? He didn't really know what that meant, except that it was something bad that happened to hippies who took too many drugs, but whether the old man's demons were chemically induced or psychological, Undine suddenly felt vulnerable. He wished Archie were with him. Or even Ray.

'Lavender Edge is a thin place, Mr Undine.'

Not this bollocks again! Undine stepped back, and accidentally knocked the magazine rack. It wobbled, and he instinctively reached out to steady it. He caught sight again of the local history pamphlets. Maybe he could get what he needed from those: ideally the contact details for someone who could clue him in on the area's history but who didn't turn out to be a raving nutter.

Oldroyd raised the counter-top, removing the only barrier between them.

'You must stop her!' His command sounded horrible in that thin, piping voice.

Undine grabbed a couple of the pamphlets. He held them up, as if to ward off the shopkeeper.

'How much?' Bunching them into one hand, he fumbled inside his pocket with the other.

'It must be you!'

Undine took out his wallet and offered a pound note. Oldroyd ignored the money, reaching for him with long, claw-like fingers.

'Please!'

Bugger this.

Undine let the note drop to the floor, and turned. He pulled open the door, walked out through the jangling of the bell and hurried away, trench coat unbuttoned and flapping in the brisk air.

CHAPTER 10

Damn him! Jo stormed past glowing window displays, scarcely aware of those late-afternoon shoppers who got in her way. He wasn't the boss. What did he even contribute? Professor James was the one in charge, and clearly the brains of the outfit. Ray played a role too: the social scientist to provide a more sceptical viewpoint and counterbalance Archie's weird theories. But Undine? That arrogant arsehole wasn't even a scientist as far as she could tell.

So what was he? Going by his odd behaviour last night, he maybe fancied himself as a psychic, although she had seen more convincing performances at those dodgy seaside booths where crooks armed with crystal balls talked gullible punters into crossing their palms with silver. But there was something about him....

She blew past a young mother driving a pushchair. Ray had let her down too. Half an hour she'd stood waiting like a fool outside that stupid old warehouse after Undine threw her out, confident Ray would come after her and offer to patch things up. But no. Nothing.

All boys together. Same old story.

So she had made the lengthy bus journey from Tower Bridge all the way south to Mitcham. Two hours in the traffic, her temper reaching boiling point well before she arrived at Lavender Edge to reassure poor Mrs Wyndham that she would not be giving up on her, and to apologize for inviting such incompetent investigators into her home. Jo would find a new team, she promised, a better one.

And she would.

A bowler-hatted businessman chose the wrong moment to step through a door. Jo clattered into him and his hat came free, falling to the ground. Without pausing to say sorry, she grabbed the door before it closed, pushed it back open, and marched into Mitcham Public Library.

Halfway down the wide corridor, a wooden desk created a central island and two streams, one to the left for returning books and one to the right for checking them out. Two members of staff were on duty, and both looked up with disapproval at her approach. She needed to calm down. She closed her eyes for a moment, took a breath, then stepped up to the desk.

The librarian – a pinch-faced woman in her forties with spectacles that made her resemble an angry owl – arranged her thin lips into a smile.

'Good afternoon.'

Jo gave a fake smile of her own. 'Hi. I'm looking for a directory of local …'

What was the proper word? Scientists? Ghost-hunters? Weirdos?

'Services,' she decided. 'Or maybe businesses?'

The librarian did not react.

'And possibly universities?'

'One moment.' The librarian moved to the end of her desk, taking steps so tiny that from Jo's position her torso appeared to be floating. She opened the gate. 'This way,' she sniffed, and she set off into the body of the library without waiting for a reply.

Soon, Jo was sitting at a vast table surfaced in cracked green leather, dwarfed by a pile of reference volumes. Her stomach growled but she ignored it. She had a lot to go through and time was marching on.

She took down the topmost book, and got to work.

Useless. Jo stretched the aching muscles in her neck and shoulders, and rolled her head. She pushed aside the last of the volumes, reluctant to do what she would now have to.

As she stood, her chair knocked the table leg, bringing an annoyed glance from the intense young man seated opposite who had spent the past half-hour filling dozens of sheets of paper with crabbed handwritten notes. She raised her eyebrows in apology and crept back to the main desk.

The owl-faced woman was crouched almost out of sight, filing returned books into unseen slots on her side of the wooden island. Jo waited until those eyes peered across the desktop at her.

'Hi,' she whispered. 'Me again.'

The librarian's torso levitated to its normal height. 'Did you find what you needed?'

'I'm afraid not.' Jo hesitated. She knew what she wanted to ask for – and after the last few weeks, she knew beyond doubt that the supernatural was real – but this was still awkward. Then she remembered how distraught Mrs Wyndham had been an hour or so ago, and it strengthened her resolve.

'I need to find some information on psychical researchers. Groups who investigate the supernatural. Would you have anything like that?'

The librarian's expression did not change. Neither did she say anything.

'Please?'

Any personal judgement was masked by the woman's professional exterior. She signalled to Jo to follow her and floated once more into the body of the library, this time leading Jo deeper, past one stack of books after another until they stood in an alcove beneath a high window. It seemed a little dimmer here, a little dustier than the other areas. Or was that her imagination?

'You might find what you need here.'

Jo thanked the librarian and waited for her to glide away before she began to study the bookshelves. An accusing label at eye level read 'Occult', and she felt the heat of curious stares as she scanned the titles before her: 'Phantoms and Folklore', 'Black Magic in the Atomic Age', 'Visitation from Venus'.... She wondered about the book Ray remembered reading as a boy, whether the library might hold a copy, but she didn't know its name, and it didn't matter now anyway. It wouldn't have what she needed.

The most promising title here belonged to a book on 'The Science of Séances'. She took it down and, to her delight, found an appendix listing contact details for the organizations referred to in the various chapters. Even better, two were in London. She took her notebook from her handbag and jotted down the addresses and telephone numbers.

The next book she tried turned out to describe ghostly encounters in North America. No good.

Material swished close to the back of her head. She looked around and found a scruffy young man, most likely a student, trying to see past her to the shelves. He was dishy, despite his crumpled clothing, and she danced aside to allow him to reach what he wanted from the neighbouring section on religion. His hushed thank you was almost playfully intimate. Then he noticed what was in her hand, and his friendly smile melted into pitying condescension.

Her cheeks burning red, Jo snatched another title at random from the shelf and buried herself in the corner where two stacks met, so nobody could see her face.

The new book turned out to be a collection of London ghost stories, each tale dating from the twentieth century and each, according to the lurid cover, 'true'. Nothing in the table of contents offered what she was hoping to find – a list of research groups for readers to contact if interested – but as she skimmed the index her attention snagged on a familiar name.

James, Professor Archibald.

She flipped at once to the relevant page and discovered a short entry on what the author referred to as 'The Flower Girl of Harson Avenue.' The story was set in Streatham, no more than a few miles from this library, and it began in 1936 when eight-year-old 'Elsie' (the author had withheld her real name) had been playing outside her house in the aforementioned Harson Avenue. For some reason never determined, she had run out into the road and straight into the path of a car. Over the years following this accident (presumably a fatal accident, although the author failed to make that clear) a number of drivers had crashed near the same spot, and afterwards each claimed to have swerved to avoid a young girl who suddenly ran out in front of them. There was never any sign of the child when the worried driver left their vehicle to look for her, yet they all agreed on her description: she had been wearing a dress patterned with blue and yellow flowers – a dress just like that worn by little Elsie on that tragic day.

The writer went on to list the dates of accidents near that spot since 1936. Jo was more concerned with finding the reference to Archie. She reached the very bottom of the page before she found the entry for an incident just two years ago, in 1969. The final word on the page was 'Professor'.

She turned over.

This was it. A certain Professor Archibald James had begun to investigate this story after a double-decker bus crashed into a garden wall in Harson Avenue on the morning of 18 March 1969. True to form, the bus driver claimed afterwards that he had swerved to avoid a young girl who seemingly vanished after the accident. At the time of writing, it was the most recent manifestation of the presumed ghost.

Two photographs took up the rest of the page, the top one a reproduction of a press image showing the aftermath of the crash. The bus driver could be seen sitting on the pavement, smoking, with the nearside front of his vehicle embedded in the remains of a low stone wall. Below this, the lower photograph showed Archie. The images were grainy, but Jo recognized the old Highlander readily enough as he posed for the camera in his tweeds, looking thoughtful with his pipe clamped between his teeth. A skinny figure stood beside him, facing away from the photographer, and even in black-and-white that explosion of mismatched clothes could only have been sported by Ray. She could not see their annoying colleague though.

There was a caption, with Archie's name and describing him as a psychical investigator with the Corsi Institute, a private body which funded research in many countries around the world. And that was all. There was nothing else about his or the Institute's involvement – and, Jo reminded herself, nothing at all that would help her find a better team of investigators.

She was about to shut the book when something struck her about the first photograph. Holding the page up to the fading afternoon light, she squinted at the driver sitting on the pavement, London Transport cap in one hand, cigarette in the other. Surely she must be imagining it.

She looked even more closely.

He really did look like Undine.

* * *

The caption gave the photograph's source as the 'South London News' for the week ending 21 March 1969. Jo returned to the desk, where the librarian made a show of adjusting her angry owl spectacles as she checked the clock before guiding Jo back to the reading table and asking her to wait. A few minutes later, she reappeared, carrying an enormous leather-bound volume, which proved to hold archived copies of the 'South London News' for the whole of 1969. It took up most of the table surface and Jo was pleased the intense young man opposite had left.

'We close at five,' the librarian commented as she floated away.

Jo checked her watch again. Just gone half past four.

She turned over the pages, entire editions at a time as she peeled back the weeks, looking for March. Paper crackled and rustled, and a dry scent rose around her.

It did not take long to find. There, on the front page of the 21 March edition, was the photograph she had already seen. Above it, the headline stated: 'BUS CRASH INJURES TWO, DEMOLISHES GARDEN WALL'. She read on:

'Mary Wilkins, 20, was taken to hospital on Tuesday morning after a bus crash in Harson Avenue.

'The driver was also slightly hurt when his bus, a No. 59 *en route* to Streatham Garage, swerved off the road close to the junction with the High Road and careered into the front garden belonging to Mr and Mrs Morrison.

'Mr Morrison, 51, who hurried home from the barbershop he owns nearby, expressed his anger over the destruction of his garden wall, but said that he was relieved his wife Vera, 52, had escaped unharmed.

'"She's a tough old bird," he told our reporter. "We've been through worse than this."

'Other neighbours were quick to offer help to the dazed passengers, although the driver, who was visibly shaken, refused any assistance and waved away everyone who approached him.

'Miss Wilkins, a telephonist at Archers & Stanley, had been descending the stairs at the time of the accident and was taken by ambulance to St James Hospital with a suspected broken wrist.

'The residents of Harson Avenue have become used to traffic accidents. Over the last ten years, no fewer than four separate incidents have been reported in which motor vehicles have come to grief in this unlucky stretch of road.

'One neighbour of Mr Morrison, who did not wish to be named, linked the recurring accidents with the local legend of a ghost girl, which is said to rush into the road ahead of oncoming vehicles, "spooking" motorists and causing them to crash.

'The phantom is rumoured to be the spirit of the tragic victim of an earlier accident here. Her apparition is claimed to be identifiable by her distinctive yellow and blue flowered dress in a style of long ago.

'Mr Harold Undine, 28, who was driving the bus, told police that he had indeed swerved to avoid a child but when our reporter asked him about the ghost, he replied that the child he saw had been wearing modern clothing.'

Yeah, right.

Jo made a speedy calculation: if Undine had been 28 in March of 1969, he would be around 30 now. 'Her' Undine looked a bit older than that – acted older too – but she felt sure it was the same person.

To her right, the lights went out.

She looked across and spotted the librarian drifting through the book stacks, flicking off light switches in those parts of the library that were now deserted.

Glancing through the rest of the article, Jo found it consisted of little more than an account of the traffic jam that built up in the high road, the crash having occurred during the morning rush hour. Neither Archie nor Ray was mentioned, but the Institute probably wouldn't have become involved in the case until after they'd learned of this accident. Perhaps from reading this very article.

She folded the newspapers back into position and closed the enormous cover. Her cheery goodbye to the librarian was met with an impassive look.

Mild embarrassment aside, she was glad she'd come. She had contact details now for a couple of different supernatural research bodies, and first thing tomorrow morning she would start to check them out.

She walked past the wooden island and opened the door into the rapidly darkening evening. Maybe there was also a way she could turn the unexpected information about Mr Undine to her advantage.

CHAPTER 11

Most evenings, Undine appreciated the vibrant mayhem of Brixton Market. In the midst of such constant eruption of life, any psychic echoes he might stray into should go unnoticed, the bustle and noise distracting him in the same way a whirlwind would keep away the stench of a rotting corpse. Usually, the chaos was welcome.

Not this evening.

Clutching his carrier bag tight to protect its contents from the dirty air, Undine turned into Coldharbour Lane and hurried in the direction of his bedsit. After the last few days and nights he needed a break, and he knew no better cure than cooking. Alwyn had done him proud. The bag contained diced chunks of best goat shoulder, and Undine was eager to try Gloria's latest recipe.

Thoughts of what lay ahead almost put what Archie would call a spring in his exhausted step. Plenty of chopped onion, fried with garlic and ginger; add a couple of chili peppers and a handful of curry leaves. Delicious. And the smells would be amazing!

Sid's bookshop was closed when he reached it. Yellow light seeped through its grimy windows.

The meat would need slow cooking. Maybe around three hours, which meant it would be a pretty late dinner tonight. Worth it, though – as long as he got started very soon. He jiggled his key from the lining of his pocket and was reaching for the side door when a loud knocking interrupted him. He looked around and saw Sid banging on a window with one hand. The other beckoned Undine into the shop.

Undine's heart, and his stomach, sank.

Sid re-locked the door the moment Undine was inside. 'How you doin', Mr U?' He licked his lips. 'I've got that book you was after.'

He scuttled off, vanishing into one of the many nooks not immediately apparent to the shop's casual visitors. A few seconds later, he reappeared, a slim hardback in one hand and a length of crinkled and torn brown paper in the other. 'Wrap it for you?'

'It's fine as it is,' said Undine.

Sid leered, and gave Undine the book. 'Guess it could be worse.' The words came in a cloud of stale breath, and he ran his fingers through lank, thinning hair.

Undine studied the cover. A slender brunette, her own tresses long and artfully arranged over her naked body, held a gleaming chalice in her lap as she sat on the edge of an altar which was draped with black cloth. The image was salacious, daring the reader to enter; it did not fit the book's dry title: 'Principles of Psychic Occultism'.

'Still weird though.' Behind the thick lenses of his glasses, Sid's magnified eyes ogled the girl. His tongue flicked around his lips again.

Weird it might be, but at least it was legal, unlike much of the 'specialist' literature Sid sourced for his clientele. He was an unsavoury character, although he could be relied upon for his discretion; moreover, having a landlord who owned and ran a bookshop came in handy when Undine wanted to find out more about esoteric and occasionally disreputable topics. Undine cast an eye over the labyrinth of groaning bookcases, the shelves crammed with thousands of titles. He'd planned to avoid any further worry about Lavender Edge tonight, but now that he was here....

'You wouldn't happen to have anything about London ghost stories, would you?'

Sid scratched his nose. 'Ner. Don't get much call for that stuff.'

'What about shamanism?' asked Undine, remembering Oldroyd's odd question some hours before.

'Dunno. What's that, then?' The tongue came out again.

'Get your mind out of the gutter, Sid. It's nothing smutty. It's –' Undine hesitated, realizing he didn't know enough to explain the word. 'Something to do with primitive religion. I think.'

'More weird stuff, eh?' Sid shrugged. 'I could try and find something for you. Probably take a few days?'

It wouldn't hurt to find out what Oldroyd had meant. 'Okay, yeah. Go on then.' Undine reached for his wallet. 'How much do I owe you?'

He handed over sufficient to pay for both the second-hand book and the rent he owed for his room upstairs, and headed to the exit. Only another few minutes and he'd be home.

'Hold on, Mr U!'

Undine swore under his breath. He stopped, and pivoted on his heel.

'No need to go back in the cold.' Sid took Undine through to the rear of the store and opened the door that accessed the building's interior stairwell. 'That'd be daft.'

Undine mumbled his thanks.

'Any time,' said Sid, giving the naked brunette one last look as Undine made his escape.

✻　　✻　　✻

Undine placed the book on his small table and tossed the pamphlets from Oldroyd's shop on top. They were curled from their journey inside his jacket, but he didn't care. He shook the drizzle from his trench coat, hung it on the back of the bedsit's single wooden chair, and took the bag of meat through to the cramped area he tried to think of as his kitchen.

Music. That's what he needed before anything else. Soothing sounds to wash away the day. He pondered Sinatra, then Frankie Laine, and eventually chose Dean Martin's 'Welcome to My World'. One of his later albums but doubtless destined to become a classic. When you considered what passed for music these days, this was in an altogether different class.

The orchestra swelled, buoying Dean's warm voice, and soon Undine was humming along to 'In the Chapel in the Moonlight'. He closed his eyes, and let the familiar strains work their magic. Here, in this dingy room, he could at last let down his guard. His home was no palace, but he knew for certain it was free of psychic impressions, and that made it priceless. Here was perhaps the only place he could fully relax in peace and solitude.

… *Have you ever heard of a shaman, Mr Undine?* …

The memory slipped between soaring violins. He tried to push it away, only for Oldroyd's reedy voice to sigh back into his head. He opened his eyes.

Bollocks.

It was going to bother him until he found out what a shaman actually was. Vague associations with primitive tribes and witch doctors were not enough, and cooking would have to wait a few minutes more.

On the floor, in a neat pile beside his LPs, was Undine's small personal library. He had amassed it over the past couple of years, and – other than cookbooks – the majority of titles were to do with psychical research, extra-sensory perception, and such subjects as mediums and séance-room phenomena. Some he had stumbled across in second-hand bookshops and jumble sales, but most he had specifically asked Sid to locate for him as he pursued various leads that had, for a while, appeared promising. Many of the books were heavy-going, academic texts, and could be difficult to follow, but Undine was nothing if not stubborn and would persevere until he gleaned a basic idea of what the author was saying.

To date, none of the books had given him the answers he sought.

He lifted half the pile onto the carpet and started to work one particular book out from the bottom of the remainder. As his library grew, a cheap set of bookshelves was becoming a necessity, and he really would need to get something sorted out one of these days. In the meantime, he carefully prised out the dictionary of occult terminology he was after.

There turned out to be only a brief entry

on what he wanted. The concept of a shaman (who might otherwise be known as a witch doctor or medicine man) was, he read, especially prevalent among peoples of northern Asia and North America, although it was not limited to those places. A shaman, it seemed, was someone regarded as an intermediary between the people of his community and a world of good or evil spirits; a solitary figure, whose abilities forced him to live apart from normal society, but who nevertheless held a position of honour as a 'walker between worlds'.

That was the lot. He supposed he had a clearer understanding of the expression now, if not why Oldroyd had used it. The old shopkeeper had used another peculiar phrase too. What was it? A 'thin place'? 'Thin location'? A thin something, at any rate. Undine peeled back a few more pages until he reached the T's. There was no entry for anything starting with 'Thin'.

His stomach rumbled, reminding him that he had had nothing to eat since that bacon roll at lunchtime. Time to get the meat started.

He re-stacked his books and returned to the kitchen area. After popping a frying pan on a gas ring, he unpinned a sheet of paper from the cupboard door and read again the recipe Gloria had slipped under his door last week. As he selected spices from the jars that filled most of the narrow shelves, he remembered the mouth-watering aromas that had blossomed from her room next door and hoped he would do her recipe justice.

His shoulder gave a twinge. He rolled his head, cracking the muscles in his neck. Last night had really....

He shook the thought away. Lavender Edge would wait until tomorrow. Tonight was for him alone.

There was a knock at the door.

'You home, mate?'

Sunny's voice. Anyone else and Undine would have ignored it, pretending afterwards to have fallen asleep if he needed an excuse, but this was unusual. He couldn't remember his friend ever calling around uninvited before.

He put down the spices and opened the door to reveal Ray and two bottles of Whitbread Pale Ale.

'Couldn't find any Watney's. Hope these'll do.'

Ray's mackintosh was blotched dark where rain had muted the garish orange hue. Undine gestured to him to take it off, and lifted his own coat, now nearly dry, from the chair. Checking that his friend's back was turned, he dropped the trench coat over his library, hiding it from view, then hung the mac on the chair before opening the bottles.

'Cool music,' said Ray, accepting a bottle as he looked around the tiny room. 'Uh oh! Gonna lose that if you're not careful.'

Undine followed his nod, to where a grey cat,

almost silver against the darkness, sat staring in through the 'kitchen' window, hopeful eyes huge and fixed on the carrier bag of diced meat. With a fond smile, Undine crossed to the refrigerator. He took out a bowl of scraps, emptied them onto the dish he kept under the sink, and opened the window a few inches.

'Not today, Frank,' he said, blocking the cat when it tried to come inside. He slid the dish onto the ledge. 'This is yours. You can have my leftovers tomorrow, if there are any.'

The stray took no notice. It was already eating.

When Undine turned back, he saw that Ray had found the corner shop's pamphlets. He was flicking through the one with the striking maze design on the cover.

'Didn't know you were into history,' said Ray. He picked up another, this one with a cricket match on the front, and flipped through it, turning to pages at random.

'Got them from that shop near Mrs Wyndham's.'

Undine took the pamphlet Ray had finished with and glanced through it himself for the first time. An article about the lavender industry in Mitcham, a history of the town's Vestry Hall, photographs of last year's May Queen ceremony. All written and produced by enthusiastic amateurs, by the look of it. Nothing in the contents appeared to mention mazes, which seemed odd.

'What did you buy 'em for?' asked Ray.

'No particular reason. Just thought they might have some information about the area.'

'Doesn't seem like it.'

'Well, it was just an idea.'

Ray took a long drink from his bottle. 'How are you doing anyway? Feeling any better?'

Ah, that explained the visit. Undine would have preferred to be left on his own, but part of him was touched by Ray's concern. The more so because the youngster must still be smarting over that business with the policewoman.

'I'm fine.' He finally took a sip of the Whitbread. It tasted better than he had feared.

'You never said what happened back there. At the house.'

Ray clearly wasn't going to let him off so easily.

'Truth is, Sunny,' started Undine, trying to decide what that truth was going to be, 'things have been getting on top of me a bit lately.' Inspiration struck. 'Bird trouble.'

Ray blinked. Then his face cracked into a wide smile and his shoulders sagged with relief. He nodded, a little too vigorously, too eager to appear a man of the world.

'Got you! Heh, I should have guessed! What's her name?'

'That would be telling.' Undine took another mouthful, swallowing it down with his guilt.

'You hungry?'

'Starving!' But Ray's enthusiasm vanished when he looked again at the jars of spice. 'But you know what I'm like with foreign food.'

Undine gave the diced goat a last, longing look. 'Don't worry about it. We can eat out.'

He turned off the gas ring and put the meat into the fridge. Out on the ledge, the cat was still eating.

'There's an almost decent caff not far away,' said Undine. 'Should suit you. Then you can tell me how you got on earlier.'

They drained their bottles and left them in Undine's sink.

In the corridor outside, Gloria's husband was finishing on the shared payphone. As he hung up the receiver, he beamed a greeting.

'Harry!'

'Evening, Peter. How's it going?'

'Good.' His rich Caribbean voice rolled out from his deep chest. 'It's all good. You tried that recipe yet?'

'Almost. Last-minute change of plans.' Undine raised his chin towards Ray. 'We're off to the Atlantic instead.'

Peter leaned close to Ray. 'You should let this man cook for you.' He lowered his voice to a confidential bass. 'He's better at it than he looks.'

'Young Raymond here has what you might call a delicate constitution,' said Undine.

Ray blushed, and smiled an apology.

Peter chuckled, the sound a warm rumble.

'We'll probably pop along to the Grave after,' said Undine. 'If you fancy joining us for a pint?'

Peter shook his head, his chuckle growing. 'Appreciate that, but I've got my own plans. With Gloria, if you know what I mean!'

Undine clapped him on the shoulder as he walked off, Ray following close on his heels.

'Don't forget to tell her how that recipe works out,' Peter called after him. 'She's already got a whole bunch of others waiting for you!'

Undine shouted back his thanks.

'Come on then, Sunny,' he said, leading the way down the staircase. 'Let's go get you something boring.'

CHAPTER 12

'Another two pints of Red when you're ready, Rita love.'

Undine cast an appreciative eye over the barmaid's figure as she stretched up to reach fresh glasses. Next to him, flowery beige tie loosened and askew, leaned Ray, his eyes bulging.

They took their drinks to a table away from the main throng and dropped into the beer-stained seats.

'What d'you say he called it again?' slurred Ray.

Undine balanced his cigarette in the dip of the overflowing ashtray, and took a mouthful of ale before striking a dramatic pose and enunciating his answer like a bad Shakespearean actor. 'A thin place.'

Ray whistled a few bars of what Undine guessed was the theme music of a spooky film or radio show. He was out of tune but nobody in The Old Grove Tavern – known to all and sundry as 'The Grave' – was paying attention, or would have cared if they were.

'Something like that anyway.' Undine laughed and retrieved his cigarette. Ruined plans or not, he was glad his friend had turned up at his door. The younger man was too insecure to come out and say it, but Undine realized now how upset he had been this morning. Best to put it all behind them. He reached forward and chinked their glasses together. Ray burped. It smelled of egg and chips.

Over food, they had talked about their afternoons. Undine had recounted his visit to Oldroyd's corner shop, focusing on the new information regarding the history of Lavender Edge while keeping to himself the shopkeeper's oblique references to shamanism and his baffling intimation that Undine should understand what that meant.

Ray, in turn, had described his attempts to interview the Doyle brothers. He had tried to telephone them at the number Jo had given, but one call after another had gone unanswered. He thought they might be away working on another building job.

'This was weird, though.' Ray shuffled to the edge of his soggy seat, and, bending so far forward that Undine feared he would topple to the carpet, groped through the inside pockets of his blazer. When those proved empty, he tried the outer pockets, and this time found what he was after. He pulled out a buff envelope, folded in two.

'I gave up on the phone, so I developed these instead.'

He uncreased the envelope and extracted a bundle of photographic prints. Undine recognized the shots as those taken in Lavender Edge, but even at first glance he could see something was wrong.

'Camera fault?'

Ray shook his head. 'Checked all that.' He lifted his glass and took a gulp. 'Camera's fine. So was the film stock, and the chemicals. Everything.'

Undine studied the prints. The views were identifiable – this one showed the wall the builders had started to demolish, and this showed the upstairs landing – but a bizarre warping affected the images, as if a playful god had decided to poke a finger into each scene and swirl reality into crazy loops of madness. He turned to the next photo. From the framing, Ray had been more interested here in taking a portrait of the policewoman than documenting the investigation. Her face appeared blurred, partly by movement, but the distortion ran deeper than that and her mascara-heavy eyes resembled whirlpools of black ink, hollows of utter darkness which threatened to pull the viewer through the paper and into an alien realm beyond.

Undine shuddered, tendrils of memory rising. Another thought occurred: why hadn't Ray shown him these photos a few hours ago? He'd obviously had them on him back at the bedsit. Perhaps he'd needed some Dutch courage first.

He placed the prints on the table, careful to avoid the beer spills, and reached again to the ashtray.

'What do you think caused it?'

'I don't know,' said Ray. 'Some sort of energy at the site, maybe. Magnetism? It's not exactly my field. Hopefully, Archie's gizmo will pick it up when we go back.' He glanced at Undine with a peculiar mix of longing and trepidation.

So that explained why he hadn't shown them before now. Ray was nervous. Of him. Of the way Undine would react to his suggestion.

He felt renewed guilt over their argument. 'We will go back,' Undine assured him. 'Soon.'

But not before they gained a better idea of what they'd be walking into. Until Archie rejoined them, Undine was in charge, and there would be no bloody policewoman hurrying them along, rushing them headlong into the unknown and disturbing who knew what forces lurked inside Lavender Edge. He remembered the way she had literally stuck her nose into that hole in the wall, and buried memories stirred again, threatening to writhe into his conscious mind.

'Okay, Sunny?'

Ray nodded, gazing at the stack of photos. His forlorn expression was more than Undine could stand. He stubbed out his cigarette and swallowed the dregs from his glass.

'Right. Another?'

Ray managed a smile. 'If you're buying.'

When they had arrived, the pub had been filled with office workers. The cheap suits had since given way to a more boisterous crowd of young Friday-night revellers, and Undine needed to elbow his way back from the bar, holding his breath against clouds of pungent aftershave and eye-watering perfume. And all the time he remained aware of the potentiality of emotional echoes as he navigated a psychic minefield of violence hidden beneath the hubbub. This would need to be his last pint, before the alcohol weakened his defences too much.

He got back to the table just as Ray, unaware Undine was behind him, was putting away the photo showing the policewoman. Poor sap. It was true what they said: no accounting for taste. Undine paused for a few diplomatic seconds, then strode past and banged Ray's beer down in front of him.

'There you go.' He collapsed into his seat. 'So, what plans for the weekend?'

The question seemed to stump Ray, and Undine wondered if his friend had even realized tomorrow was Saturday. Before any answer emerged, however, somebody else's words thundered above their heads.

'What the bloody hell d'ye think you're playing at?'

Archie towered over the seated pair, a tweed-clad mountain of fury. The big Highlander's right arm rested in a sling, the plaster cast just visible, and his accent had thickened with the anger that ruddied his face.

'I've just been to see Margaret Wyndham. Would one of you wee idiots care to enlighten me as to why the police have told her I'm no longer allowed to set foot in her house?'

✽   ✽   ✽

Undine handed Archie a double Scotch. The Highlander sniffed it, sipped, grimaced, and put it down. He waved the photographs at Undine.

'So, why aren't you there now?'

How much to tell him? Undine had never been certain how much Archie already knew, although he had long suspected the elderly Professor had a shrewd idea of what really lay behind the bus crash two years ago. His invitation to Undine at that time to join his team as a 'sorely needed' driver had always seemed contrived, and it was quite possible Archie was aware of Undine's 'gift' and of his need to learn how to control it. If so, maybe he would understand Undine's concerns over returning to that house. Or perhaps not. After all, not even Undine himself could say why the building affected him so badly.

Then there was Sunny to consider. After the accident, when Undine accepted Archie's invitation, he had let Ray believe he shared the younger man's scepticism towards the supernatural. It was easier than admitting the truth, and in those first few days and weeks, they had bonded over that lie. He couldn't betray their friendship now, especially not after this morning.

Archie stabbed one of the eerie photographs with a powerful finger from his uninjured hand. 'How many years have we been looking for evidence like this? I'll bet you a pound to a penny that the energy that did this is the same force postulated by Lethbridge. This is our proof! There's a ghoul zone at Lavender Edge, and it's active right now!'

He jabbed the photo twice more to emphasize the last two words.

Whatever Archie did or did not suspect about Undine's ability, the Scot was clearly intent on making them go back to the house.

'We have no way of knowing how long we have before the zone goes dormant. Hellfire, man, we don't even know *why* it has become active again now, except it might be connected to something the builders did. Dear God, this is our golden opportunity, gentlemen. And what do you choose to do with it? Go to the flaming pub!'

At this point, Ray would normally have played Devil's Advocate, challenging Archie's certainty that the photographs proved his theories were correct, but – as drunk as he was – the social scientist was smart enough to keep his mouth closed.

'Aye, it's a damned good job I discharged myself when I did. Stop you couple of clowns making this any worse. Mark my words. We are *not* going to miss out on this opportunity. And we *are* going to help Margaret.'

The Highlander glowered at Undine. 'And we are going to use every tool we have at our disposal. Do I make myself clear?'

Every tool? Was that a coded message?

The alcohol was not helping Undine think. He broke eye contact with Archie.

Meanwhile, Ray slowly processed Archie's outburst, and as his befuddled brain got to grips with the implications, his posture changed. He stopped cowering and sat up straighter. Undine guessed he was looking forward again to investigating the ghost story that had so captivated him as a boy.

Undine tried to inject a note of caution. 'I still think we should take this slowly. If you –'

Archie did not let him finish. 'No. It's my decision to make and I've made it. First thing tomorrow morning, you are going to personally apologize to WPC Cross. We've worked damned hard at gaining a reputation for the Institute and

I will not have our working relationship with the police jeopardized before it has even begun.'

How had he heard about that?

'I don't mind going to apologize,' offered Ray. 'If Undine has other plans.'

Archie shook his head. 'No. It needs to come from him.'

Disappointment spread across Ray's face, mingled with guilt. He must have told Archie about this morning's argument while Undine was at the bar ordering whisky.

'And you'd better flaming well grovel if that's what it takes. In Margaret's eyes, Jo Cross is the only one who's made any effort at all to help her these past weeks.' Archie took a breath. 'Now, Margaret is willing – in principle – for us to continue our investigation and return to her house tomorrow night, but the only person she fully trusts is that policewoman, and she is not prepared to let in anybody Cross says shouldn't be there.'

The fire in Archie's voice burned out, giving way to a regretful determination. 'Make this good, Undine. Or you needn't bother coming back to the Warehouse.'

What?! Was Archie being serious? Shocked into confusion, Undine considered his options. He wanted nothing further to do with WPC Jo Cross. She symbolized danger, and although he was unable to explain what he meant by that, the mere thought of being with her again inside

Lavender Edge churned his stomach. Moreover, he didn't trust her. Whatever it was and whatever her reasons, he felt sure she was hiding a secret from them.

Yet he had spent most of his life in constant fear, afraid of his unwanted ability, and of what he might be exposed to as he searched for ways in which to understand its nature and to free himself from its curse. It was only recently that he had truly begun to believe his work with Archie and Ray might eventually lead to answers. To walk away from the Institute now would be to give up on that hope, and to give in forever to the fear.

He saw Ray, sitting behind Archie, silently urging him to agree.

He had no choice. Not really.

'Okay,' he said.

Archie nodded. All at once, he looked tired. He couldn't have got much rest at the hospital.

Ray's skinny face split apart in a tipsy grin. 'Nice one. What'll I do?'

'You'll have interviewed the builders already, I suppose?' asked Archie.

'I tried phoning them a few times but there was no reply.' Ray's eagerness to resume the investigation almost overcame the slur in his speech. He stood with a wobble, scanning the walls for a phone. 'I'll try calling them again.'

Archie released a sigh of relief. 'Thank you. I doubt they'll be at their office on a Friday night, though. You can wait 'til Monday morning.'

He gave the photographs back to Ray.

'Aye then, I'm going home. And I suggest the pair of you do the same. We're in for a long night tomorrow.'

He gave Undine a lingering, meaningful look. Unsure quite what meaning was intended, Undine kept his misgivings to himself.

'Not going to finish your whisky before you go?' asked Ray.

Archie scowled at the half-empty glass. 'Ach, I wouldn't call that whisky,' he grumbled, although not without a trace of his old good humour.

Undine watched him leave, and tried not to show how scared he was of what would happen tomorrow.

CHAPTER 13

What an absolute waste of a morning! Eyes screwed shut and fingers pinching the bridge of her nose, Jo held in a scream of frustration.

When she opened her eyes again, the teenage girl sitting next to her glanced away, feigning sudden interest in an empty crisp packet on the bus floor. Why not? It wasn't as if the youngster had more important things to worry about. What would her plans be for this Saturday morning anyway? Shopping with friends on Oxford Street? Maybe off to meet a boyfriend for a precious few hours away from parental scrutiny? Jo thought of her own younger days, to the spoilt brat she'd been back then, and cringed. She still carried the burden of her past selfishness. Was that what drove her to play the Good Samaritan now?

The bus crept through Carshalton, its snail-like advance driving home her own lack of progress over the past couple of hours. She had already travelled to a dismal terraced house off the South Circular, where the now defunct Putney Spectral Investigations had turned out to consist of a pair of young lads who had only just left school when the author of 'The Science of Séances' came to interview them. Unfortunately for Jo, their shared obsession with psychic phenomena had been brief, ending at around the same time their acne cleared up and they discovered girls. They couldn't help.

From Putney, Jo had taken the train into Clapham Junction, then another back out into the southerly London Borough of Sutton to try the second of the two organizations on her list. The Cleansing of Spirit had been her preferred option because, unlike P.S.I., it was based not too far away from Mitcham, but it had proved to be an evangelical church, more interested in cleansing Jo of her suspected wickedness than in offering supernatural advice.

At least one of the Putney lads had given her a lead. She should try contacting a 'respectable' (so he assured her) body called the Society for Psychical Research, or S.P.R.

What was it with all these initials?

The bus lumbered on, crossing the border into the south of Mitcham. From her seat on the top deck, Jo wiped condensation from the window and recognized Ravensbury Park. As they passed Rivermead Path to the right, she peered down its length, trying to catch sight of

Mrs Wyndham's house. She couldn't see it.

Her original intention had been to alight here and tell the elderly lady she had found a new team to replace the mob who had let them down so badly. With that plan dead, she might as well stay on as far as the library. With luck, the owl-faced librarian would help her find a telephone number for this S.P.R., then she could head back to Mrs Wyndham's and give them a ring from there.

Nobody was playing on Cricket Green this morning. The bus rocked as a gaggle of stony-faced shoppers climbed on board, then it resumed its journey in the direction of Fair Green and the police station. Jo still found it odd how Mitcham had two greens – an 'upper' and a 'lower' one – so close to one another, but on her first day here, Sergeant Hawkins had oriented her on some of the area's quirks. The town's weird double centre was, or so he had been informed, the result of Mitcham's origin as two separate settlements, dating back many centuries, which had over hundreds of years grown and merged into one another.

Did the town's great age have any bearing on events at Lavender Edge? Maybe she should look into that, so she could mention it to the S.P.R. when she spoke to them. After all, ghosts tend to haunt old places, don't they?

Or do they? Professor James thought that ghosts were more like zones of strong emotional imprints. Well, even if that were true, maybe those zones built up over time. Or maybe the older a place is, the more chance there is that something once happened to create the sort of effect Archie envisioned. That made sense, didn't it?

The bus lurched, pulling in to the stop. Although she was seated on the far side, and mostly hidden by the girl, Jo shielded her face with her hand. She tried to make the move casual by pretending to scratch her left ear. This was the closest bus stop to the library, which she could see only 20 or so feet ahead on the opposite side of the road, but it was right outside Fair Green police station, and she didn't want to be spotted by anyone she knew. Better to get off at the next stop and walk back.

She waited for the driver to pull out before she stood and squeezed past the teenager.

❋ ❋ ❋

Jo pulled her leather jacket tighter, and raised the collar. The stiff wind tore into her hair, but she wasn't too worried. The shag cut she'd got a few weeks ago would be easy to sort out when she got indoors because she would only need to muss her fingers through it. It was a fantastic style. No wonder Jane Fonda liked it so much.

The traffic lights by Mitcham Public Library turned red, and another bus – this one a

Routemaster heading back towards Fair Green –
squealed to a halt. A flurry of movement drew
her police-honed attention to the rear window
of the upper deck, where a figure had leapt to
its feet and was forcing its way down through
passengers struggling to climb the steep stairs.
From their body language, they were none too
happy about it. The figure reached the bottom
just as the lights changed and the bus began
to accelerate, and the conductor tried to hold
whoever it was back. Then the conductor was
pushed away, and the passenger jumped down
from the moving platform in a flap of black coat.

Oh, God. What was he doing here?

Undine hit the pavement hard, the impact
jarring his cigarette from his mouth. It dropped
against his chest, and he swore as he batted
sparks away, smearing ash over his dark suit in
the process.

Passers-by gave looks of disinterested
disapproval, and Jo considered losing herself
among them. But Undine had seen her and was
walking her way. She stopped, folded her arms,
and lifted her chin.

'Quite the dramatic entrance.'

Undine puffed, hands on thighs as he
recovered his breath. His own jacket hung open,
revealing a straining shirt. Nothing that exercise
couldn't fix, but he appeared to be a man who
enjoyed his food a bit too much for his own good.
His wife (no, amend that, girlfriend: no wedding

ring) must be a decent cook. Or perhaps it was a beer belly.

Jo stepped around him. He followed. She was almost at the library steps when the newspaper article popped into her mind. What if Undine thought she was snooping on him? That was ridiculous: how would he know? But the thought was in her head now, and she knew she was acting nervous, and what if he picked up on that? She couldn't go in there with him.

Yet she couldn't just walk on because that would take her right past the front windows of the police station.

Undine wheezed. 'Glad I caught you. Was going to try to catch you at work. This is better. Private.'

'Private?' Jo moved aside, giving way to a clutch of carrier-bag toting women.

'In a manner of speaking.'

Her fists tightened. He was already trying her patience.

'What do you want, Undine?'

He took a deep breath. He clearly had something to say, but it seemed stuck in his throat.

'To apologize,' he said at last, through teeth that were only slightly gritted.

Her eyebrows shot up. Had she heard that right? 'Apologize?'

'Yes. I am very sorry for losing my rag yesterday. I wasn't feeling good and I was knackered, but that's no excuse for my unprofessional behaviour. So I'm apologizing.'

'Professor James?'

'Huh?'

'Was it Archie who put you up to this?'

Undine contemplated his answer for several seconds before replying. 'We did talk about it.' He shuffled his feet. 'But he was right. And he – that is, all of us – hope we can continue working together. If it's okay with you, we're ready to go back to that house this evening.'

Relief swept through her. She was no longer back at square one! Had it been anyone but Undine, she might have flung her arms around him.

She walked on a few paces to lead him away from the library, and as they came to a shop doorway, she sensed him flinch. For an instant, a shadow crossed his face, and, with a subtle motion, he veered away from the wall as if stepping around an obstacle only he could perceive.

And Jo recalled a hot July night. Thugs out looking for trouble, armed with chains and lengths of wood, had set upon a young Pakistani student walking home alone. A shocking, vicious assault. Hearing the cries, she, along with a half-dozen fellow constables, raced out of the station, she reaching the victim first and trying to staunch his bleeding as he lay on the ground, right on this spot, but despite her efforts he would die before he reached the hospital….

… *The imprint of violent emotions* …

Was it really possible?

'How is Professor James?' she asked.

'On the mend.' Undine sounded distracted.

'And Ray?'

'Ray's Ray.'

'Right.'

She bit back the urge to confront Undine with what she had read yesterday, and what she now believed he was hiding. There would be time for that later, once they had helped Mrs Wyndham. 'And you? You feeling better? You don't look great.'

'Hangover,' he said. 'I'll manage.'

They were almost opposite the police station now. Jo manoeuvred herself to the inside of the pavement, pleased for once that she was short because it let her hide behind Undine.

He halted, expecting her to cross the road. When she stayed where she was, he frowned.

'Not on duty today?'

'No,' she said. Which was true.

He waited for her to elaborate. It was a trick she had used herself often enough, and she returned his gaze until he rolled his eyes.

'Well, what about your colleague?' he asked. 'The one who went to the house with you. Since we're here, why don't we see if he's free? He might be able to tell us something useful.'

Jo doubted the appropriately named Dick had

ever been of any real use to anybody, but she kept that thought to herself. She shook her head. 'He won't be there. Same shifts as me.'

Undine's dark eyes narrowed. She held her breath. Please don't push this, she thought.

Something was definitely on his mind, but after another long second he broke eye contact and reached for his cigarettes.

She saw an opportunity to get away. 'Okay then. Well, I've some things I need to get on with now, but I'll be seeing Mrs Wyndham this afternoon.'

'You'll ask her about tonight, if we can come?'

'I'm sure it will be fine. She wants this all finished as quickly as possible, but yes, I'll check with her to make certain, and I'll let you know if there are any problems. Will I be able to phone you if I need?'

'You've still got the number?'

'Right here.' She patted her pocket, and the reassuring shape of her notebook.

'Someone will be at the Warehouse until around five, if you call before then.'

And if I do call, she thought, will my message get passed along this time?

'Good,' she said. 'Guess I'll see you tonight.'

Undine blew smoke from his nostrils and nodded.

Jo turned, and kept her head down as she hurried away. She could feel Undine standing there, watching her leave, a puzzled expression on his bleary, unshaven face. She was going in the wrong direction, but she knew the backstreets around here and could nip left down the next road and circle back around to the library that way. Hopefully, she'd no longer needed contact details for those other researchers, but it wouldn't hurt to hunt down their telephone number just in case. Anyway, it might be useful to take a peek at the library's local history collection while she was there, to find out just how old Mitcham was, and whether its past held any clues that might help them.

Afterwards, she could make the twenty-odd-minute walk to Lavender Edge to give Mrs Wyndham the good news, and that would leave her just enough time to pop home, get changed and grab something hot to eat.

Which she would need, because it looked now like she had an unexpectedly long night in front of her.

CHAPTER 14

A 'walker between worlds': part of his dictionary's definition of a shaman. The phrase came to mind as Undine followed Archie through the garden gate, leaving Rivermead Path and approaching the front door of Lavender Edge, damp gravel crunching underfoot.

Behind them, Ray did his best to keep up. He was burdened with half of Archie's gear as well as his own. Undine's hands were full too, one gripping the strap of his own heavy holdall and the other the handle of the case containing the Octopus's body. The machine had been rebuilt that afternoon by Ray, working under the Professor's watchful supervision.

Lightning flashed without a sound, illuminating the house's high, crumbling brick front. Then it was gone, replaced by darkness and the sliding after-image of large, blank windows regarding the three intruders as they neared.

Archie marched up onto the concrete step beneath the portico. He put down his holdall, started to raise his plastered right hand, remembered, and knocked on the door with his left hand instead. Far away, the sky rumbled.

Undine did not want to be here. He blinked away the retinal image of those windows, but the imprint of their blind gaze remained. Whatever he had sensed here the night before last, felt stronger now. That disturbed him, but not as much as the resurgent feeling that the impressions here differed from any he had received anywhere else. Those echoes at the Pyramus theatre, for example – that awful, lingering loss and terror and resentment – had been horrific, but they had not been undercut by this sense of … awareness.

It scared him. Archie's threat had done its job, and brought him here tonight, but this would be Undine's final visit to Lavender Edge. He did not know how he would wriggle out of the rest of the investigation without jeopardizing his position in the Institute, but he would find a way. He just needed to get through the next few hours first, and keep his defences up.

A crack of light widened as the door opened.

'Archie, how lovely to see you again.' Mrs Wyndham stepped back from the door. 'Do come in.'

The policewoman, Jo Cross, waited behind her, in the hallway. She was in plain clothes again. Didn't she ever wear a uniform?

'Good evening, Margaret,' said Archie. 'Thank you for inviting us back. You remember my colleagues? Doctor Buckley. Mr Undine.'

Ray went first, crossing the threshold as the sky whited out for a second time. The formidable old lady nodded him a greeting. She barely looked at Undine as he brought up the rear.

She closed the door. Thunder boomed outside. The storm was closing in.

'Do head straight through to the drawing room. Make yourselves comfortable. Archie, you'll find a small suitcase in there. My late husband's papers. You're welcome to borrow them.'

'Oh aye. His family history research. That will be very helpful.'

'Hi, Jo,' said Ray. 'What do you reckon?' He opened his arms, displaying the outfit he had wasted half the morning shopping for.

She pursed her lips in grudging approval. 'Yeah, okay. Not too bad. You might be getting the hang of this.'

Undine turned away from the pair of them. Nothing appeared to have changed inside the house since Thursday. The thudding ticks of the grandfather clock remained a beating heart under the tall, dust-shrouded outline at the end of the hall.

As Archie disappeared into the drawing room with Mrs Wyndham, Undine called after him.

'Where do you want the Octopus?'

The policewoman nodded acknowledgement of his presence. 'Undine.'

'Constable.'

Archie's voice drifted back, suggesting they set up in the upstairs room as before. That was where phenomena had been reported most often.

Great. After last time, that was the last place Undine wanted to revisit. But he had prepared as best he could, spending the afternoon at home and taking a short nap before rustling up a quick Spanish omelette. The goat meat, regrettably, was still in his fridge, but at least the eggs had been hot and filling and would keep his strength up. He took a deep, resigned breath. Showtime. 'Give us a hand, will you, Sunny?'

With Ray's help, Undine lumbered the equipment up the staircase and arranged the Octopus's magnetic, temperature, pressure, and other probes around the bedroom. They weren't too particular where they put the sensors because they knew Archie would want to fine-tune the placement anyway, but they checked the torches worked and tested the walkie-talkies, and Undine placed the tape recorder and microphone in the rough centre of the floor. All the while, he kept his back to the ominous hole in the wall and his thoughts away from what might lurk within the blackness.

'Don't know why you need to bother with all

that junk,' said Jo. 'Considering what you can do.'

'What did you say?'

Undine's question came out sharper than intended, and Jo started. She stood in the doorway, gazing with apprehension towards the hole. She turned to him, feigning baffled innocence.

'What did you just say?' he repeated.

'I didn't say anything.'

Before Undine could ask why she was lying, Archie walked in, deep in quiet conversation with Mrs Wyndham. He carried a small tartan suitcase. Ray handed him a walkie-talkie and gave a thumbs-up.

'Just about set, boss.'

'Good, good.' The big Scot cast a critical eye over the arrangement. He reached for the closest probe, moving it a fraction of an inch to the left. The next one he moved a touch to the right.

'Looking good, gentlemen. It's a shame we didn't have our trusty Octopus with us last time, eh? Well, fingers crossed we catch something tonight!'

Undine glanced back at the policewoman, but her attention was once again on the hole.

※　　※　　※

The shaman. A solitary figure. Able to act as an intermediary between the world of his community and a world of spirits. What exactly did that mean, a 'world of spirits'? A primitive way of describing those painful psychic echoes to which Undine was vulnerable? Which begged the question: did shamanic traditions teach ways to control such abilities? Was that what the shopkeeper had been hinting at?

Undine huddled into his blanket and struggled to discipline his drifting thoughts. There was danger here; he could not afford to let his defences slip. Seconds crawled by, one tormenting tick at a time. Windows rattled to spattering, gust-driven rain and – although there was no more lightning – a constant rumbling had enveloped the house for the past few hours.

The ceiling creaked again. The settling of an old house, or something more?

On the opposite side of the room, dimly illuminated by candlelight, Mrs Wyndham tensed.

'It's okay,' said Archie, patting her arm.

She nodded. Archie had reminded her earlier that they needed to find out what they were dealing with before they could get rid of it.

If it were possible to get rid of it. Undine wished Archie would make that small detail clearer to the old woman. He hoped the Professor was not putting ambition ahead of other concerns.

'He's risking us all,' muttered Ray from the shadows to his right.

It wasn't like Sunny to say things like that!

Undine tried to make eye contact with his friend, to show that he shared his concern, but the gloom made that impossible.

The night wore on, the strains of the past couple of days dragging at Undine as he grew ever more conscious that his concentration was faltering. He dug his fingernails into his palms, hoping the pain would cut through the fatigue washing over him. It was vital his mind stayed strong, that he kept his shutters up.

'You must have heard that!'

Mrs Wyndham's whisper was harsh, with a brittle edge. She would not be able to take much more. To tell the truth, he was surprised the old woman had stuck it out in this house for so long. Undoubtedly, she was made of strong stuff, but her stiff upper lip was starting to quiver. Weeks had passed since her plea for help, and her understandable impatience was leaking out as anger.

'I heard my name,' insisted Mrs Wyndham. She turned to the policewoman to back her up. 'Jo?'

'I'm not sure. I think I heard something, but....'

Mrs Wyndham let out a frustrated, trembling sigh. Ray tried to reassure her, explaining in his most calming, condescending tones that her mind might have been playing tricks, and how human nature automatically sought to impose sense on ambiguous sounds.

'I know what I heard!' she whispered back. 'I might be old, young man, but my faculties are quite as sharp as yours.'

'I don't like this,' murmured Jo.

Nor do I, thought Undine, maintaining a close watch on her silhouette in case she decided to interfere like last time.

A tremor passed through the floorboards. The effect of thunder, possibly, or perhaps a lorry passing nearby. Don't dwell on it. Stay focused.

To his left, Jo gasped.

'You alright?' asked Ray.

'Cold. Like a draught on the back of my neck.' She shivered. 'Can't you feel that?'

She was right. The air was no longer still. It almost tingled.

Was that movement by the hole? Undine looked to see, and the instant his eyes left her, Jo called out.

'Stand back! I'll deal with this!'

He snapped back to her. She hadn't moved. She was still seated, arms wrapped around her legs against the sharpening chill.

But any moment now, she would leap to her feet, as reckless as before. She wanted to try again to tear the wall apart!

Undine's heart pounded. Fury surged. She didn't belong here with them, not with her temperament. Her unpredictability put them all in peril! Especially him!

It was her fault they were here. And what

did that idiot Archie think he was doing, forcing them to return after being hurt himself last time? And that bloody fool Ray, blinded by his infatuation for a pretty blonde in a tight jumper!

The air throbbed. She was a liar. There was no chill. It was growing warmer, thicker. Sweat ran into his eyebrows. Fire raged. The skin of Undine's mind blistered in the fierce heat.

And that ozone tang was back, that scorched fairground bumper-car spikiness. Surely the others could smell it?

He looked around. Faces flickered in the candlelit murk, making them hard to read, but nobody reacted. No, they weren't feeling this, they weren't smelling the electricity in the air. Which implied....

It was already in his mind! His barriers had failed!

With that sickening realization came the awareness of something alien inside him. Panic swelled, and threatened to burst its own banks. The invader shifted, and Undine sensed cunning: an animal wariness and intelligence. Rigid with fear, he closed his eyes, shutting out the world as his thoughts tumbled. He dared not move. Any attempt to alert the others would shatter the fragile status quo, and Christ knew what would happen then!

In between those timeless moments, logic seeped in. It brought a nauseating clarity of thought. He had been afraid for years that the strange forces around him would one day breach his mental barriers. His hope had been to find a way to strengthen those defences, or discover some method either of protecting himself or ideally of purging himself altogether of his psychic 'gift', before it was too late. Well, now it *was* too late – but he was damned if he'd go down without a fight. If some uncivilized witchdoctor in a godforsaken land could learn to handle this psychic bollocks then so could he!

Undine relaxed the iron hold on his mind, and reached out instead with the sensitivity he had repressed for so long. The release, after all this time, was almost joyful. He let his feelings rush forward, keeping low, pre-emptively ducking beneath the expected counterpunch. Flames roared. They flared, scorching the interior of his mind. He tasted screams. He pushed on and through and then he was inside a howling misery of despair and pain; a hopeless pleading that was forever swirling within the walls of Lavender Edge. And Undine was in that vortex, and the vortex was in him, and the pain was an all-consuming cold tsunami of fire....

And he had made a terrible, terrible mistake. He couldn't take this!

Stumbling backwards, Undine groped blindly for an exit from his own thoughts, desperate to get away and slam the shutters down behind him, but he was trapped. Dry rivers of fire poured in through each of his senses. His mind was alight. His very sense of self was being devoured by crackling, roaring chaos as living flames crowded inside, forcing themselves into a fleshy vessel that no longer knew its identity. Heat squeezed deeper into a space that could not contain it.

Conflagration collapsed upon itself, creating an impossibly dense sphere of superheated madness – and now a different energy was emerging at its core, expanding in defiance of the endless inrush, swelling irresistibly against a building force that could never give way.

With a searing crack of white-hot insanity, reality split apart. A shattering explosion of psychic power ripped out from the centre of Undine's being, and the shockwave threw his eyelids open.

He sat.

A half-remembered external world trickled in through deadened optic and auditory nerves. Electric information came to rest against dulled synapses.

Light. Non-light. Sound.

Shapes.

People he had seen before, in the same positions they had been in an eternity ago.

They showed no reaction to his return.

Disoriented and drained and powerless to act, Undine sat and saw and heard.

❊　　❊　　❊

THE HORROR AT LAVENDER EDGE

'I'm getting something.' Ray shone his torch onto the top of the Octopus where a spiky trace was appearing on the rotating paper. 'The magnetics.'

Both bay windows banged in their wooden frames. Undine was aware of the frigid air that gusted across his ankles, but he could not react, even when the candles around the floor guttered out. Ray and Jo switched on torches at almost the same moment, but their beams did not dispel the shadows clinging to the damaged wall, and in those shadows hung a luminosity.

Had it been there before, invisible in the dim illumination?

'It's still active!' Archie's voice. Triumphant. 'Ray, are you getting this?'

In the younger man's torchlight, the arms atop the Octopus were going crazy, tracing frantic lines of ink.

'I see it,' said Ray. He cleared his throat and spoke shakily into the microphone. 'We are seeing a patch of light – more like a glow – on the wall close to where the builders were working. It's a whitish glow – not brilliant white – there are other colours, or suggestions of colour inside it – like a pearl. I think it's brighter than it was. Yes, I'm certain of it. It's quite clear now. Roughly circular, no clearly defined edge. Fading as you go out from the centre. I'd say it's about the diameter of a saucer.'

'It's getting bigger,' said Archie.

The icy air was gone. All around Undine was

warmth and a low-pitched humming buzz.

'Temperature's rising,' said Ray, looking at the readings. 'Picking up electromagnetics too. God, I can smell it!'

So could Undine. That dodgem tang. Now in the real world.

'I think this is what happened before.' There was fear in Jo's voice.

Darkness swam through the luminous patch, the floral pattern on the wallpaper coalescing into denser colours, resolving into shapes, resolving into –

'It's a face!' Ray, awestruck, sounded almost delighted.

Mrs Wyndham moaned in terror. Jo went to her.

The glow was the size of a human head, its intensity such that it stayed visible even as Ray played the light from his torch across it.

'Take a flaming picture!' said Archie.

Ray tossed his torch into Archie's lap, grabbed his camera and released the shutter. He wound the film on and took another shot, and then another.

'I don't believe this,' he said, half laughing as he stepped back to take a photograph from another angle.

The shifting shapes came into focus. The face was that of a man. Heavy brows under an impression of thinning hair cut ruthlessly short. An aquiline nose surmounting a thick moustache. The beige and sepia tones of the wallpaper gave the image a disturbing, almost flesh-like quality.

Undine heard Archie call out: 'Do you recognize him, WPC Cross? Could it be the same man who appeared to you before, who told you to come here?'

'I –' she started, staring at the features manifesting before them. 'Maybe. I don't know.'

Ray lifted his camera again, and was poised to take another photo when Mrs Wyndham screamed.

CHAPTER 15

'Margaret, wait!'

Jo hurried after Mrs Wyndham as she fled onto the landing. She crossed the threshold, and everything changed.

It was as if, the whole time they had sat in the bedroom, somebody had been pumping in air, more and more of it, the pressure increasing bar by bar until it began to crush them, and they had not even noticed. By contrast, the air out here was thin and still. It held no electric tang, the only scents being dust and the lingering aroma of the lamb casserole Mrs Wyndham had cooked that afternoon. Jo heard the distant drumming of rain against glass, and from below the steady tick-tock-tick of the shrouded grandfather clock.

She reached the distraught old lady. 'Let me make you a cup of tea.'

Mrs Wyndham shook her head, stifling a sob. 'Please. Just leave me alone. All of you.'

Archie's voice bubbled from the bedroom. He

no longer sounded frightened, but enthusiastic, shouting encouragement to Ray to take more photographs, while calling out detailed descriptions of what he was experiencing, presumably for the benefit of the tape recorder. By the sound of it, the ghostly image was fading back into the wallpaper. Ray's comments also sounded more thrilled now than scared. The other one, Undine, was keeping quiet.

Mrs Wyndham's skin looked pale as marble. Her gaze was directed inward. Was she in shock?

One of the men erupted into laughter. How dare they! Their behaviour was more than insensitive – it was disgusting, as bad as her police colleagues' had been!

'Absolutely fantastic!' exclaimed Archie.

Mrs Wyndham shuddered.

'They're only trying to help,' said Jo. Privately, what she wanted to do was march straight back in there and kick some respect into them, but her first duty should be to calm the elderly lady down. 'They just need to know what they're dealing with first. I guess it's like how a doctor needs to diagnose an illness before he can tell what medicine to prescribe.'

'You don't understand.' Mrs Wyndham's voice teetered on the verge of cracking.

'Understand what?'

'What we saw. In there.' Mrs Wyndham inclined her head towards the bedroom but refused to see inside. 'It looked like my Ronald.'

At the back of her mind, Jo was still thinking about Archie's suggestion, wondering if the unsettling visage on the wall had borne any resemblance to the strange man who'd spoken to her by Ravensbury Park. It took a moment to recollect where she had heard the name Ronald before. Then she remembered: Mrs Wyndham's late husband. He had died half a year ago.

She repressed a surge of excitement, annoyed with herself for reacting like one of those scientists. But could this be it? Was this the clue Archie needed to start making things right?

'You have to tell them!'

Mrs Wyndham did not respond.

'If this –' Jo groped for the right words to use. 'If what's happening has something to do with your husband's spirit…. Don't you see? If he's trapped in the house somehow, maybe that's what all this is about. We need to help him. To….'

To what? Move on? How did they describe this stuff, these Spiritualists or whatever they were called?

'Look, this is all beyond me,' she admitted, 'but Professor James is an expert in this subject. He'll know what to do.'

She prayed that was true.

Mrs Wyndham grimaced. 'No.' She appeared older suddenly. 'No. That was not my husband.'

'You just said –'

'No, dear. I said it *looked* like him. But it wasn't Ronald. It was wearing his face, but it wasn't him.'

Mrs Wyndham's eyes glistened with tears. Jo reached for her, but the elderly lady pulled away. She sniffed, and held herself straighter.

'I'm sorry, Constable. This has gone too far now. Thank you for what you have done but tomorrow morning I shall telephone Mr Erskine to advise him that I have changed my mind. He can buy this house. He's welcome to it.'

She re-stiffened her upper lip, and just about succeeded in controlling her voice.

'In the meantime, I should like you all to leave my home please.'

❈   ❈   ❈

He needed a cigarette. Badly. But that would mean reaching into his pocket, which might as well be a million miles away. Right now, simply remaining upright on this chair took everything Undine had.

Information trickled into his fried brain, as slow as sand through an hourglass.

Archie in energetic conversation with Ray. Talking about the face. Undine remembered the face. Dark shapes swimming in a blur of light. Coming together to form a proud nose, a moustache.

Archie had identified the face, he told Ray. He had seen it in photographs. In pictures shown to him by the old woman. Earlier. When Undine was upstairs, here, in this room, setting up the big grey box.

The machine.

The Octopus. It sat on the floor close to Ray. The arms on top were twitching. The pens were tracing multi-coloured tracks on the paper rolling beneath. Undine wondered if he should tell someone.

He looked at the wall. No face there now. Electric light shone in the room. Someone must have switched it on. He looked at the hole. Tattered edges framed a deep blackness that pulled at him like gravity.

The face was Ronald. That's what Archie was saying. Ronald had been Mrs Wyndham's husband, and that's why she was upset.

Ray laughed because he had seen one of the faces from his book.

Nobody had ever identified a face here before, said Archie. That made this important.

Ray agreed. There were stories that the faces were the spirits of people who had died here. There had been no evidence for that, though. Until now.

They might be recordings, said Archie. Echoes of people. Not spirits.

Undine's head hurt. What Archie and Ray were saying, it was not right. He wanted to tell them that. He thought it was more important than the important things they were telling each other.

But he was not himself. All he could do was watch and listen and hope the fuzziness went away.

* * *

'Margaret, please. You don't mean that.'

Jo knew how much Lavender Edge meant to Mrs Wyndham. Her husband had inherited the old house from his father, who had inherited it from his father before him, and so on back through the generations. After Ronald's death, she had vowed to take care of it to honour his memory. Her own relatives had all passed on long ago, so in a way this building was the only family she had left.

The old woman's lips whitened, blood forced out as they pressed together. She did not reply.

'You can't give up. Not now.'

A wrinkle of doubt appeared between Mrs Wyndham's eyes. Then her features tightened another notch. 'It doesn't matter. Enough is enough.' She marched past Jo and back into the bedroom where the researchers were still chattering.

Jo followed her inside. As soon as she entered, she felt that the pressure of a few minutes before had lifted. Even so, the atmosphere retained an edge, a charge of potential. Whatever was happening was not over.

'Gentlemen,' announced Mrs Wyndham. 'Thank you for trying to help but I must ask you all to leave.'

Archie whirled around.

'I am sorry, Professor James. I know you mean well, but this situation has gone on for too long. I can take it no longer.'

'Don't be hasty now. We're just starting to make some progress.'

Mrs Wyndham blinked away tears.

'For God's sake, show a little sensitivity, will you?' said Jo. 'This might be fun and games to you lot, but this is her home. Her life.'

Archie walked over and took the old lady's hand. 'Please, Margaret, listen to me. I understand why you feel this way. I recognized his face.' He nodded. 'I know it's upsetting but with this new information, we may be able to help you.'

Mrs Wyndham pulled her hand away.

Jo inserted herself between the pair, turned her back to the tweed-clad Scot, and faced Mrs Wyndham. 'It's okay,' she told her. 'You might be right about getting away from here, for a short while at least. You've been through so much.'

Mrs Wyndham looked less certain than before.

'You don't need to make any decisions now you might regret tomorrow,' said Jo.

'Aye, that's wise advice,' said Archie, moving forward. 'And there's no need to worry about the house. We'd look after the place for you.'

He placed a heavy hand on Jo's shoulder. She resisted the urge to shrug it off.

'And thanks to WPC Cross here, you'd even have the police looking after your home while you're away. There's not many who can say that.'

Jo squirmed inside but said nothing.

Mrs Wyndham raised her chin. 'Do as you will,' she said. 'I no longer consider this my home, and I shall be leaving as soon as I have packed a bag. Should you wish to stay here until the house is sold then you may do so. I no longer care.'

Jo watched her retreat from the room, and wondered whether she should go after her.

Archie released a deep sigh. It was sickening with satisfaction.

She ripped away from his grasp. 'Get your bloody hand off me!'

'Ah, it's probably for the best. She could certainly do with a few days' break, and it'll give us the space and time we need. Now that we know the phenomena are connected in some manner with her husband's death, we can start to find out what's causing them.'

He didn't care a jot about Mrs Wyndham's well-being! This was about his research, pure and simple, and now he wanted the whole house as a plaything so he could test his theories. Well, it would be a pleasure to burst his arrogant little bubble.

'It wasn't him,' she said.

Full of thoughts and plans, Archie seemed not to register her comment. It was Ray who responded.

'Huh?'

He looked so baffled it was comical. She nearly laughed. Everyone in this house was going mad!

Behind him, still sprawled on his chair like an idiot, Undine muttered away. She ignored him.

'It. Wasn't. Mr. Wyndham's. Face,' said Jo, speaking as she would to a child. She frowned, confusion clouding what had been so clear a moment ago. 'Or rather, it was – except something else was wearing his face.'

Undine stirred. 'Wearing his face,' he murmured.

'Don't you dare make fun of me!' she spat at Undine. 'You've been undermining me since the moment I asked for your lot's help!'

'Easy, Jo,' said Ray. Hurt showed all over his skinny, gormless face.

Archie wandered off. He knelt beside his ridiculous box of tricks, absorbed in the data tracings. The pens jiggered and jaggered, drawing their crazy, spiky mountain ranges.

'He's been lying to all of us,' Jo told Ray, pointing at Undine who was still too lazy to bother standing up. 'You must see that! Unless you're in on it as well – is that it?'

Ray stared back. Oh, for Heaven's sake, he

looked ready to blub!

She jabbed another accusing finger towards the unresponsive Undine. 'And why didn't that bastard tell Mrs Wyndham why he's here with you? Why won't he use his powers to help her?'

'Powers? I don't –'

'Oh, come on! He's one of those psychics or mediums or whatever the hell you people call them. It's obvious! You're as bad as the police were. You think you can get away with treating me like some stupid plonk!'

Ray's head shook from side to side. 'Archie?' he pleaded.

The Professor glanced up from his gadget, gazed at Ray for a moment, then returned to his readings.

Ray's bottom lip wobbled. He turned to Undine instead for back-up. 'Tell her she's wrong.'

But Undine was lost in his own thoughts. 'Wearing his face,' he repeated. 'Yeah. That makes more sense.'

'And you're supposed to be the psychology expert around here,' said Jo, taunting Ray. 'Can't even tell when your own mates are lying to you. He knows.' Indicating Archie. 'Him over there, pretending not to hear me.'

A long, low creak ran through the floorboards.

Ray backed away, his head down, shaking off the accusations. 'You're getting caught up in it,' he said. 'We all are.' He spoke more to himself than anyone else. She picked up snatches of his gobbledegook: how this was all so fascinating ... the construction of personal reality from environmental stimuli ... perceptions shaped by expectations and fears ... group forces moulding shared experience ... we see what we expect to see ... we fool ourselves....

'Oh no you don't,' came a Scottish rumble. 'You're not going to rationalize this all away, Dr Buckley. God damn it, man! Look at these!' Archie clambered to his feet. He clamped his uninjured hand on the back of Ray's neck and held the younger man down so that his forehead was no more than an inch above the revolving paper. 'See that! That is hard evidence!'

Jo turned back to Undine. She felt full of wild triumph and did not understand why. She wiped perspiration from her forehead. 'Now you,' she said. 'It's time to end this charade.'

Undine moaned. His eyes drifted in her direction. He looked drunk.

'You know what's really going on here, don't you?' said Jo. 'Spit it out, so we can do something to stop it!'

Undine drew in a shaky breath. His eyes could not quite focus on her. 'Don't need to answer your questions,' he said. He had to force each syllable out, but what he said next knocked her for six.

'You're not the police.'

Archie stopped talking. He turned his head.

Jo knew she needed to respond fast, to deny his accusation, but the words wouldn't come.

Archie let go of Ray. He walked towards her. 'What was that?'

'Not police.' Undine's head lolled forward, the effort too much.

'I already explained,' said Jo, flustered. 'I'm in plain clothes.'

'But you'll have some identification?' Archie stepped closer.

'Look,' she began. 'We're all here to help Mrs Wyndham –'

'You told me we would be assisting an official investigation.'

'You are.' God, why did this have to come up now? 'Sort of.'

It was so hot in here.

A thunderous crack tore through the air. Plaster dust shook free from the hole in the wall and billowed in tenuous clouds.

Undine groaned in pain, clutching his stomach. He lurched from his chair and staggered away to the landing.

'Look at the state of him,' said a nearby voice that was Ray's yet somehow was not. 'Hungover again.'

'Archie! You've got to see this!'

That was definitely Ray this time. He sat crouched on the floor, gawping at the Octopus.

'I'll not forget about this,' Archie told her as

he made to walk towards Ray and his machine. 'You have some explaining to do, lassie!'

The room yawed. Jo almost lost her balance.

Archie pulled Ray to his feet and ordered him to take more photographs. Then he was yelling into his walkie-talkie, his accent growing thicker by the word as he demanded Undine get his Sassenach arse back in here.

Jo stared around. Undine had disappeared.

Ray ambled by in a daze, camera dangling from loose hands as he took photos at random.

We've all gone insane, thought Jo.

Mrs Wyndham called from outside the room, her voice angry and distressed. She was leaving to stay with her friend Elsie. She swept past the doorway, wrapped in a coat and wearing a headscarf. There was a small brown suitcase in her hand. Only Jo took any notice of the elderly lady.

'You're meant to be helping her!' she cried to Archie.

The Professor laughed, rapt in front of his machine.

She grabbed one of the walkie-talkies and raced after the old lady. 'I'll deal with it myself then!' She ran onto the landing, nearly skidding as her foot met the dust sheet.

The entire house now felt stuffed with potential energy, the tang of ozone, and the maddening tick-tock-tick of the grandfather clock.

She saw Mrs Wyndham reach the bottom of the stairs.

CHAPTER 16

Not the way out. Undine stood at the edge of what must be a patio, and the way forward was a swamp of boggy lawn. Black shapes loomed around him, a deeper black than the night, rustling and hissing in the storm-driven rain and the stink of damp earth.

A door crashed shut behind him.

He spun towards the sound. Thunder exploded and a simultaneous flash lit up a conservatory he recognized. But it looked different. It took him several seconds to work out why: he had only seen that room from inside the house before. The swinging door smashed back into its frame with a brittle rattle of glass panes.

He remembered reaching the bottom of the staircase, had a clear recollection of his heel thudding hard into the carpeted hallway. His thinking was muddy and the explanation reluctant, but it came to him that he must have turned the wrong way. He should have turned right at the foot of the stairs. That would have taken him to the front door, which had presumably been his intention. The other direction, left, would have led him past the grandfather clock and into the drawing room. That's the way he must have come: through the drawing room, into the conservatory, and out here into the back garden.

Wind leached warmth from his wet clothes. His compulsion had been to get away, outside, to the road, and to keep running. He could still do that – except it would mean going back through the house.

Rain drenched his hair. It ran down his face. The sensation of it trickled into the blasted earth of his mind, where it revived and encouraged thought and memory. Memory of what he had felt in the house. He had encountered what Archie called 'ghoul zones' before – those psychic shadows that haunted sites of violence, distress, despair; turbulent echoes of loss, hatred, abject misery, and a million other mingled impressions – and they always burned with pain, but nothing had ever blazed as fiercely as the darkness he had touched a few minutes ago.

The thought of going back in there terrified him.

Yet he couldn't stay out here forever.

He needed to kick his bloody brain into gear and think of another way. Okay: the garden wall. But he couldn't see through the gloom. How high was it? Perhaps he could climb over. Or maybe he could find a way through to the front around the side of the house. Hadn't he seen a path before? When he'd been staring out of those bay windows inside the –

Screaming.

What the hell was happening now?

His stomach rolled with fear.

More screams. Deranged howls of agony, distorted through a strange, harsh crackling.

Where was the sound coming from? Not through the open door, and so not from inside the house.

Neither was it coming from the garden.

Yet the screams sounded close. How could that be?

At last, Undine made the connection. He groped at his jacket pocket and wrenched free his walkie-talkie, just as the speaker crackled again, and he heard his friends screaming for help.

* * *

Undine grabbed the wooden post at the foot of the stairs at the same time as a key scraped a lock. At the far end of the hall, the front door banged open.

The policewoman who wasn't a policewoman ran inside, throwing the door closed behind her. She too held a crackling, screaming walkie-talkie in her hand, and she sprinted towards him. The next instant, she shouldered her way past, and charged up the steps.

'Come on!' she yelled.

Undine ran after her. At the landing, a cloud of suffocating absence pushed into his head, seeking to numb his still confused thinking. He snarled, fought his way back up to a degree of alertness, and pressed on toward the bedroom.

The lights were out. Hadn't they been on earlier? He fumbled along the wallpaper, groping for the light switch until his fingers met a hard edge. He flicked the switch on. Nothing happened.

A beam of torchlight appeared ahead. It dipped as the policewoman reached to her feet, and then shone in his direction.

'Here,' she said, handing him a second torch. Undine turned it on, and the floor became a miniature mountain range of jagged shadows and broken glints.

'Where are you?' called the policewoman.

Jo. That was her name.

There was no reply, only a thick, oozing silence that stuck to Undine's skin. Even the ticking from the clock downstairs seemed muffled.

'What the hell's happened?' she asked.

Undine couldn't think of an answer.

Her torchlight reflected from the room's two bay windows, first from the one that overlooked the rear and then the one at the side of the house. The windows seemed intact, but as the beam showed more, the rest of the room looked as though a hurricane had torn through.

Undine took another step and his boot crunched on thin glass. The word 'lightbulb' popped into his head. Beside his foot he saw a microphone he had seen many times. Close by sat its metal stand, bent and crushed flat. His light swam across the scene, showing him smashed chairs and the shattered remains of various sensor probes. Dark, shiny ribbon festooned the debris like entrails, and only when Undine spotted a pair of empty plastic spools did he recognize it as tape from the recorder.

Madness hung in the metallic air, its reverberation humming at the edges of everything he saw. And below it shimmered an aura of violence. Terror leapt up at him, sharp and sudden, the glowing embers of panic only a breath away from reignition. He clenched his fists and slammed down the armoured shutters of his mind, denying his feelings as he struggled against the impulse to flee.

He made himself focus on details. The small tartan suitcase Mrs Wyndham had given to Archie. A rip in its material, and the papers detailing her late husband's family history research bleeding out of the wound. Many were shredded and almost all were crumpled. Undine began to gather them together and stuff them back inside.

Then he saw the Octopus. The box lay on its side, deep dents pummelled into its heavy grey casing. He righted it, and saw that most of the leads connecting the machine to its severed tentacles were still attached. The power cable, however, had been yanked from the wall socket. He plugged it back in. Nothing happened. The armatures on top had snapped off. The drum no longer turned.

Archie would be furious.

'Hello?' he shouted. The sound was swallowed by the watching house. 'Sunny? Archie?'

The Octopus rattled for a moment as one of the broken armatures twitched, then died.

'Where are you?'

'Oh God,' said Jo.

Undine found the disc of light made by her torch. It was on the floor, and seemed to be sitting on a shadow of a few inches' diameter, where the skirting board of the damaged wall emerged from a rumpled dust sheet. The darkness glistened.

He tried to get closer, to get a better view, but the area repelled him with a nearly physical force. He swung away, overcome by a punch of nausea. Despite his efforts to shut it out, the aura of violence was intense. It was concentrated here, concentrated in the –

Blood.

The glistening darkness was blood.

And there was Archie's pipe, caught in a fold of the dust sheet. It was about the same place he had fallen the day before yesterday and broken his arm. Undine picked up the pipe, and put it in his pocket to give back to Archie when he found him.

'There's more here.' Jo's voice, barely audible in the cloying silence, came from two or three feet further on, just past the hole in the wall.

Undine slid his torch beam across the wallpaper, searching for her. It jerked as it travelled. Part of him understood that his hand must be shaking, but another part puzzled over the way the illumination lingered on one spot for several seconds after the light moved on, and then it came to him that the silence was no longer still. The room was coming alive around him, a humming buzzing that was not quite a sound. It was in the air, but also in his head, and it was building.

The light his torch had left behind clung to the wall. No, not *to* the wall, and it was not torchlight after all but instead a peculiar opalescence rising from beneath the wallpaper, and growing stronger.

Horror burst in Jo's mind – and flashed across Undine's awareness, scything through his weakened defences with her shocked realization that she had experienced this before.

She moaned. 'No. Not again. Please.'

The buzzing rose in his head. It pushed out all clarity, and grew to a roar of anguish, of eternal hopelessness. In desperation, Undine battled to reimpose the rigidity of thought that had been his defence for years, but the torment buffeted him. It refused to be denied.

His gaze snagged on the blood by the skirting board. The pool was smaller than before. As he watched, the final traces soaked into the fabric of Lavender Edge, and the pressure pushing inside him throbbed larger until his skull seemed about to split apart.

Jo cried out. 'Get away from the walls!'

But Undine was already stumbling away. He made it to the centre of the room before his legs buckled under the weight of what was closing in on him.

Then he saw the face.

It glowered from the damaged wall, the pattern on the wallpaper impossibly warped to form glaring eyes beneath aggressive brows, an aquiline nose, a proud moustache, and a mouth that was twisted in a mocking taunt. It was the same face as before, although now it watched them with hostility and cold cunning.

A hand took his shoulder. Jo, pulling at him. Shouting at him, but centuries of accumulated suffering howled at Undine's fragile mental barriers, drowning her voice as they pleaded for entrance, desperate for respite.

The cries did not come from the demonic

visage, but pulsed from other, smaller faces manifesting around the pitch-black depths of the hole in the wall. The floral pattern of the wallpaper rippled and blurred as the secondary faces drifted into brief invisibility only to return with altered expressions, changing like the frames on a reel of motion-picture film. In frozen moments, tortured eyes raked the room until they found Undine, and mouths gaped open in pleas for help.

Archie had been wrong. Horribly wrong. What was happening at Lavender Edge had never been about 'ghoul zones' or any manner of recording of past events. And the 'faces' were *not* dead. They were aware and conscious, trapped within the gravity of this hellish house and helpless to end their own misery.

And that terrible image that Archie had identified as Ronald Wyndham? That, too, was 'alive', in a monstrous perversion of what living should mean, but the late Mr Wyndham was not alone behind that face. Something else occupied that space with him, wearing the dead man's features as a mask, and Undine frantically battered away questing tendrils as the entity he was now in touch with sought to unpick the fringes of his thoughts.

Whatever it was, was vast and powerful and ancient. It suffered too, in its own way, ravenous for release, and its cold intelligence lay behind everything taking place here.

The floor thumped into Undine. Shrieking faces writhed through the wallpaper and through the impotent lids of his eyes. They were inside his head. He saw a frightened parlour maid, hardly more than a girl; a burly soldier in a pitted metal helmet of Cromwell's army; a youth with golden stubble, cowering behind a round wooden shield. Dozens of contorted faces. Hundreds of them.

They burned, and Undine burned with them.

The pattern rippled again, and two new faces surfaced. Undine no longer knew whether he was seeing with his inner or outer vision, although their features were familiar through blurring tears of pain.

Sunny. Archie.

They stared at him, appalled and bewildered, and he stared back. Their lips moved, calling to him, screaming in silence as they failed to connect.

Their uncomprehending terror was too much.

The images dissolved. Blackness rushed towards Undine, and he collapsed into its embrace.

CHAPTER 17

'Take this.' Jo handed Undine a mug of coffee. 'Strong and black with two sugars, wasn't it?'

He nodded, his eyes failing to meet hers, and tried to hide the tremor in his hands by cradling the drink to his chest.

'Hope you're okay with cod,' she said.

Finding the food had taken a while. Once outside the Warehouse, she hadn't known which direction to try, and ended up walking across Tower Bridge to the north bank of the Thames before spotting a chippie. Afterwards, she jogged most of the way back so the newspaper-wrapped bundles wouldn't lose too much heat in the October damp. At least the activity kept her from dwelling on last night. As long as her brain was fussing over the little details like this, she could almost believe those other events had been scenes from a nightmare. A bad dream, which she should have forgotten by this morning.

She tipped tepid food onto plates she found

in a cupboard above the kettle. The scents of vinegar, fish, and warm grease filled the office. For several minutes, the only sounds were those of chewing, and the chink and squeak of Jo's fork against crockery. Undine had declined cutlery. A flake of batter became stuck to his thumbnail and she found it hard to pull her gaze from it. Shellshock, she thought. This must be what shellshock feels like. The word lodged in her mind, dull and lifeless and useless.

Undine ate no more than half before he put his plate down and wiped his fingers on a sheet of paper.

He patted his pockets. 'How late is it?'

'Almost one. I didn't want to wake you.'

He extracted a cigarette, offering her the open pack as he flicked on his lighter.

She shook her head. Now she could see Undine's eyes, as bloodshot as Christopher Lee's in those Dracula films. The shadows around them were deeper than ever, and his greying hair stood up in tufts. When they had got back to the Warehouse, there had seemed little chance of discovering a stash of proper pillows and so Jo had improvised, dragging in blankets from the lorry and tucking one under Undine's head as he lay on the sofa.

The same sofa on which she had been hypnotized a few days ago. A memory from another lifetime.

The other blankets she had lain on the floor,

before falling into a short but deep slumber atop them.

She popped another chip into her mouth, tasting nothing, thinking of her certainty that she had been about to die in that house. After Undine had blacked out, she had grabbed him under the armpits and dragged his dead mass towards the door. She remembered the dust sheets rucking up under his heels, as if the house were trying to hold on to him. Somehow, they made it to the top of the staircase. She recalled Undine groaning back to semi-consciousness, with her supporting him, letting gravity take as much of his weight as she dared as she manoeuvred him down to the hall and to the front door.

The ache in her muscles testified to the accuracy of those memories. She had collapsed against the waiting lorry; there was no way she would be able to propel Undine up and into the cab. She remembered pushing and cajoling the swaying, half-dead body until he crawled into the back, through the tarpaulin flaps; climbing in after him so she could drag him the rest of the way inside; and her belated realization that she didn't know how to drive the Institute's beast of a vehicle. So she pulled the tarp closed, tying the flaps as tight as she could. It was flimsy protection, yet she put her faith in it, believing in it as a petrified child believes in the power of the bedclothes she hides beneath. There they stayed,

Undine snoring and drooling, and she with her arms wrapped around her shaking, drawn-up knees, keeping vigil until the thin grey of dawn filtered inside.

She pushed aside her plate and sipped her tea. It was cold but that didn't seem important. Last night could not have happened. It was impossible. Yet hadn't she been the one insisting supernatural powers were at work in that house? That was the very point she had set out to prove to Professor James and his colleagues, so you might say she'd won that argument. Hooray for her.

In that early morning light, her sense of responsibility had overtaken her good judgement. She had left Undine sleeping, and gone back to the house alone. A cautious look into the hallway showed only a still normality, and a potted plant from the garden was enough to prop open the front door as she crept upstairs, into the hushed bedroom, to shovel shattered remnants of the team's equipment and papers into their holdalls, securing evidence the way she had been taught.

Her mug rattled as she placed it empty on the desk. Undine sat silent, lost in his own head, smoke curling around him.

On the way back down those stairs, she had needed all her willpower not to drop the bags and run down the final steps without them, and to keep running for as long as her lungs would allow. But she kept her composure, walked to the door one footstep at a time, and even managed to shut it behind her before she could take no more and hurried away.

On her return to the lorry, Undine had been awake, if barely. He had already moved to the cab, and she climbed in beside him, her heart racing as he turned the ignition key and the engine stalled. Then it coughed into life and Undine wrestled a gear into place, and they began the weaving, precarious journey out of Mitcham, escaping north through near-deserted Sunday-morning streets, limping home to the Warehouse to lick their wounds.

Jo watched Undine unscrew his hip flask and pour a generous glug of Scotch into his second coffee. Every movement, every sound fell into the vastness that was a warehouse with just two people inside. She walked to the office door and shut it against the emptiness. Before Undine put the flask away, she plucked it from him and tipped a large measure into her own, empty mug. She swallowed most of the contents in a single gulp, and grimaced as the liquid scraped its way down her throat.

'I need to explain,' she said after it finally released its warmth.

Undine slurped his coffee. His gaze was on the waste-paper basket, but he indicated he was listening.

'You were right,' she said. 'I did mislead you.

But, when I first met Mrs Wyndham, I really was a WPC. Then, when Archie –'

Her mind stuttered over the memory of last night.

'I needed your help,' she said. 'When I met you lot, I figured you, especially Archie, would be more interested if you knew the witnesses included police constables. That's the only reason I didn't tell you everything.'

In the end it was remarkably easy to admit the full story to the rumpled figure sitting opposite her. He showed no inclination to interrupt and, once she started, it would have taken more effort to hold the words inside.

Jo genuinely had been WPC Cross when a stranger had intercepted her and her colleague, PC Dick Condie, and urged them to hurry to Lavender Edge. Everything she had said about that first visit was the truth. What she hadn't revealed was what happened after she left Mrs Wyndham's home that late August evening. How Condie's teasing of her 'funny feelings' inside the house continued back at the police station, and how his comments grew snider and more cutting over the following days as Condie lapped up the laughter of people she had counted as friends.

A week after Jo's visit, Mrs Wyndham came to the station in person. When she asked to see Jo, her colleagues' treatment of the 'batty old cow' shocked the young policewoman. Her opinion of the force might not have been as naive as it had been before her training, but their sly, cruel mocking of a desperate woman was too much to take. Her temper snapped. That evening, after she cooled down, she returned to Lavender Edge. Condie was with her again, but Jo knew he was there only because it would give him more ammunition to use against both her and the terrified old lady.

She paused, collecting her memories: not only those that had preyed on her mind since that first evening but also those jagged new fragments that had thrust into view only last night. There was still a mouthful of Scotch in her mug. She drained it, grateful this time for the way it scorched as it went down.

'I could smell that bumper car tang. We both could. Mrs Wyndham had just been telling us about the builders running out of the house the day before.'

She shuddered. 'We were sitting downstairs, in the drawing room, and we saw that table slide out from the corner. We both saw it, plain as day. Except Dick wouldn't admit it. He stared at it, white as anything, but pretended nothing had happened.'

She looked to Undine for confirmation that she had described this before. He gave the slightest of nods.

'Then we heard that crack from the ceiling. From the room above us, I mean. Dick tried to ignore that too. The air....'

The air crackling, as if about to explode with lightning. Pressure building all around, crowding in on her!

'It was like the house was coming alive. And it was taking its energy from out of that bedroom.'

Undine leaned forward. Jo knew this was as far as her story had got under hypnosis, and she forced herself to continue, to tell him the details that had been denied to her until last night.

'I saw them,' she said. 'I looked inside that room and I saw faces in the wallpaper. Not as distinct as last night, but they were there. I practically pulled Dick into the room with me. I needed someone else there, to help me understand what was going on.'

Her tongue was dry. She moistened it with saliva.

Undine waited another second or two, then prompted her in a surprisingly gentle tone. 'What happened?'

Jo did her best to describe the hazy impressions she was able to capture, and to fight off the surging terror that sought to drown those wispy memories, to submerge them once more in the unlit depths of her subconscious: of the room seeming to distort, to shrink and expand at the same time; of the horror of feeling her own identity pulled from her; and of feeling her physical body, too, drawn out and down and under, in the invisible grip of a whirlpool or tornado that was tearing her apart from the inside out.

Of looking into Dick Condie's face as he screamed and seeing his glaring hatred, his accusation that their imminent deaths were her fault.

'I don't know how we got out,' she said. 'Except I get this idea it wasn't powerful enough to take us. Not then.'

She thought of the vanished Ray and Archie, and of blood draining into the wood of a skirting board.

It was more powerful now. No need to say that out loud. She could see Undine was thinking the same.

'He refused to go on record. Dick, I mean. He told Dave Hawkins, our sergeant, our return visit had been a waste of time. Just some hysterical old woman missing her dead husband, putting silly ideas into my suggestible female head. Made it all into a big joke.

'And poor Mrs Wyndham kept coming back to the station, asking for me, but Dave would make excuses, saying I was busy elsewhere. He warned me not to go back to the house, said that doing that would solidify the delusions of a crazy old woman. That it wasn't police business. But she had no-one else to turn to. In the end, it was a choice between the job and finding a way to help her.'

'You quit.'

'Yes.' The admission released a flood of relief. 'I'd like to say I did that solely for Mrs Wyndham's sake, but if I'm totally honest....'

'You couldn't stand the ridicule.'

Undine's insight was right on the money. He was staring at the light glinting off the black leather of his boots.

'Yeah,' he said. 'I know what you mean.'

She expected him to say more. Instead, Undine stood and walked out of the room. The door gaped open in his wake, and Jo heard him moving around inside one of the other nearby offices. She wanted to call him back. She wanted him to expand on what he had just said, and she needed him to explain last night because none of this made sense to her.

Undine reappeared, carrying a bottle she recognized. It was the same expensive whisky Archie had shared with them on.... Wednesday? She did the calculation. Only four days ago!

'I'm out,' explained Undine, re-screwing the cap of his empty hip flask and returning it to his pocket. He poured a good measure of Archie's Lagavulin into each of their mugs. 'Had to force the desk lock, but he'd understand. Tight-fisted old bastard he might be, but he wouldn't begrudge us a "wee dram". Under the circumstances.'

'What you said just then about ridicule,' said Jo. 'You were talking about you, weren't you? Your....'

She hesitated, wondering how to put it.

'Talent.'

It was a crass word. She knew that, and she regretted it the moment she said it. It provoked a snort of scornful amusement from Undine.

'Yeah. My "talent".'

He ran a hand through his uncombed hair and rubbed the back of his head.

Jo said nothing. His own need to unburden himself would do the work.

'It's not pleasant,' he said. 'If that's what you want to know.'

'How do you mean?'

Undine shook out another Embassy, stuck it between his lips, and lit up. He breathed out smoke, watching the strands curl and attenuate.

'You never know when it's going to happen. You can be walking along the street, just minding your own business, and all of a sudden....' He held up his clenched fist and abruptly opened his fingers, imitating an explosion. 'It's like you're suddenly inside someone else's pain.'

Jo took a small sip of her whisky.

'Like it was waiting there for the right person to come along,' said Undine. 'To detonate it.'

'Someone like you?'

Undine looked grim.

'Is that why you work with Archie? Those things he calls "ghoul zones" – they're what you're talking about, aren't they?'

'Among other things.'

She waited for him to elaborate, but this time Undine did not oblige.

'What does it feel like?'

Long seconds passed as Undine considered his answer.

'Emotion,' he said at last. 'But distilled. Often intense, sometimes not so much. Could be because they fade over time, I don't know.' His hand returned to the back of his head, and he blew another plume of smoke out of the side of his mouth. 'It's not always pain, or fear, or fury. It usually is, but joy can linger as well. Occasionally. Problem is, you don't know what you're getting until it's already hit you.'

Jo thought of how Undine normally seemed so closed off, so divorced from everything, reluctant to join in. 'You try to block it all out.'

The faintest of smiles ghosted his lips. 'Wouldn't you?'

'Probably. But Ray doesn't know, does he? How come?'

Instead of answering that, he asked: 'How did you find out?'

'The bus crash. It was in the papers.'

'Ah. Snooping. Once a copper, always a copper.'

'I wasn't looking for it. You happened to be in

a photograph, that's all.'

Undine focused on the glowing tip of his cigarette, but she had his attention.

'You were the one driving the bus,' she said. 'And, going by what was in the newspaper, you were unlucky enough to drive right through one of Archie's "zones". I'm guessing that's why people see a ghost in that spot from time to time. Am I right?'

He did not disagree.

'Is that how you met Archie? I presume he got in touch with you after he started investigating the report.'

'Yes, Constable.'

She ignored the sarcasm. She was starting to connect the dots, although she had no way of knowing the picture that would emerge.

'And Archie came to suspect that you're, what do they call it, "sensitive"?'

Undine flinched. Why did that description bother him so much?

'So, what happened then? He just offered you a job with the Corsi Institute?'

'Pretty much.'

She raised sceptical eyebrows.

'Well, he never came right out and said as much, but yes, you're probably right. I reckon Archie saw an opportunity to take advantage of my "talent".' He used her word with scorn. 'He would have wanted to learn about it. Maybe thought he'd be able to use me as a tool in his investigations, like some sort of bloodhound, or a canary in a cage. But he didn't tell Sunny. As far as he knows, I'm just another sceptic, open-minded enough to find the supernatural interesting without being dumb enough to believe in it. It's part of why we get on so well.'

Except she had changed that last night, hadn't she? Ripped a hole right through the heart of their friendship. Something else for her to be proud of.

'Why accept Archie's offer, though? I mean, if it hurts the way you say, I'd have thought the last thing you'd want to do is go to places where you'd be in danger.'

'What would you do?' Anger flared in Undine's reply, but died almost at once. 'You have no idea what it's like, living with this every second of the day. Always having to shield yourself against anything that might be out there. Archie's working to understand what's involved. Whatever he discovers, maybe I can use it to protect myself.'

He stubbed out his half-smoked Embassy. He appeared upset, perhaps more at himself than at her.

'Anyway, I never thanked you,' he said. 'For getting me out of there.'

'You're welcome.' Jo seized the change of subject like someone grabbing a lifebelt in a choppy sea. 'And I never said sorry, for how I acted the other evening. And last night too, I guess. I don't know what got into me. It was that place, like its madness was infecting me.'

'You could be right,' said Undine.

The way he said it sent a chill down Jo's spine. 'What do you mean?'

'The stuff I felt in there, that was a part of it. Something did get into me, and into Archie and Ray too. They've never behaved like that before, not once since I've known them. Maybe it affected Mrs Wyndham as well, and you.'

He swallowed, and Jo thought for the first time that Undine might be even more frightened than she was. Perhaps that wasn't so surprising, considering how vulnerable he must feel.

'The thing in that house,' he said. 'I don't know what it was, but that was no recording or any echo of something that happened in the past. Nothing like that. Whatever it was, it was aware of us, and it was deliberately stirring up the tensions between us. And there was something more there, like a – like a whirlwind of negative emotions.'

Jo doubted she could have put it into words herself, but Undine's phrase captured something of what she had felt. 'Why would it mess with us like that?' she asked.

'I don't know. I only know what I sensed: that the worse it affected us, the stronger it became. And as it became stronger, it was able to hurt us more.'

He stopped, although there was clearly more

on his mind.

'Just say it,' said Jo.

Undine's dark-ringed eyes were more haunted than ever. 'And not just us.' His skin seemed to tighten as he gathered his thoughts. 'Those other faces we saw. I think they were trapped inside the house, and that ... thing there, it was tormenting them the same way it was us, feeding off their suffering.'

Trapped. Did that mean Ray and Archie were trapped inside the house as well?

'I tried to find out more about it.' Undine spoke more to himself than to her. 'But it was too much for me. I couldn't handle it.'

There was a hint of slur in his speech, and the powerful whisky was affecting her too, its muzziness clouding her ability to process all this information. On top of that, her body ached. Mentally and physically, she was close to exhaustion. She could not face another night here in the Warehouse, in her blanketed nest on the cold floor, and Undine's fitful few hours on the sofa can't have been ideal either. Neither of them knew what to do next, and would be too tired to do it even if they did. They needed to get themselves home, both of them, to the security and sanity of their own beds, to let sleep heal what it could – but not before she asked one final question.

She spoke quickly, worried she would lose her nerve because she wasn't at all sure she wanted to hear his answer, whatever it was.

'Do you think they're dead?'

Unable to prevent the images rising, she pictured their faces, Ray's and Archie's, emerging through the pattern on that wall, screaming their horror before dissolving once more into ink and paper.

Undine refused to look at her.

'No,' he said. 'They're not dead. And I'm going to bring them back.'

CHAPTER 18

Undine parked next to the lorry, the dull gold of his road-worn Cortina almost shiny against the Bedford's olive drab. He spotted Jo sitting on the low wall outside the old Warehouse building: the same place she was sitting the first time he'd seen her.

What he'd told her yesterday – that he believed the people trapped inside Lavender Edge were still alive – was only half true. He hadn't described how touching their thoughts had brought a sense of their searing torment, and of the endlessly looping vortex of agony through which they whirled. They were not dead, but death might be preferable to what they were going through.

He opened the car door. Jo peered in his direction, then hopped off the wall and walked out of the shadows, through the weak morning light.

'Morning, Harry.' She cast an eye over his

car, making no comment about the dent in the passenger door.

'It's just Undine. I've never liked Harry.'

She shrugged, with the suggestion of a tired smile. 'Okay,' she said. 'That works for me.'

Undine fumbled for his wallet. He had offered to drive them both home yesterday afternoon, in the lorry, but Jo had refused to allow that, pointing out that he was drunk and exhausted, so they had shambled away together towards London Bridge Tube station. At some point, she had hailed a taxi instead; Undine dimly recalled being dropped off in Brixton, beside the bookshop in Coldharbour Lane.

'How much do I owe you?' he asked.

'Don't worry about it. I went on to my parents' place, and Dad insisted on paying. He can afford it.' She walked across the damp cobbles to the rear of the lorry and undid the tarpaulin. 'Give me a hand?'

He helped her up into the back, and climbed in after her. Inside, he saw the familiar green and navy blue canvas holdalls, bulging from their hasty stuffing, and a small, tartan fabric suitcase, ripped down one side.

'I salvaged what I could,' said Jo.

She'd done well. He wouldn't have had the guts to go back into that house, not alone. He grabbed the bags, leaving only the suitcase for Jo, and they carried everything into the vast interior of the Warehouse's ground floor.

'Just dump it here.' Undine's voice rang off the brickwork and iron columns. In the emptiness, the two-tone institutional green walls and unpainted concrete under their feet felt even more drab and dingy than usual. On the far wall, the enormous, gently arched windows he knew so well hung in the gloom like luminous panels, but the daylight struggled to penetrate their many tiny panes of smeared glass. He flicked the light switch. Bare bulbs strung from the high ceiling sputtered into begrudging life, doing little to enliven the space.

Jo unzipped a bag and poked through its contents. Twisted metal, torn scraps of paper, the cracked case of a walkie-talkie.... She dug in with both of her hands and lifted out a crinkling, rustling mass of brown magnetic tape.

It was from one of the Grundig's spools. Undine remembered setting up the tape recorder in the centre of that bedroom, working with Ray to arrange all the equipment just so, knowing full well that Archie would only 'tweak' everything a few minutes later. Closing his eyes against a sickening ache of loss, he tried not to think about what he believed to be happening to his friends right now. He let himself drift, breathing in the faint perfumes that suffused the Warehouse bricks, ghosts in their own way of the exotic spices once stored here. His sense of smell wasn't brilliant, but he imagined he could distinguish hints and spikes of cinnamon, cardamom, cumin, anise, coriander.... He could almost hear the hum of activity in the once-lively warehouse: the creak of ropes, the banging of barrels and thump of sacks, the echoing shouts of rough humour and eruptions of lost temper as –

Enough.

It was too dangerous to let his guard down like that. Even on this familiar ground where he had more than once participated in Archie's experiments into extra-sensory perception, allowing his 'gift' to expand under the big Scot's watchful gaze, never quite admitting how much he could –

'These yours?'

Jo dangled a keyring. Half a dozen keys of varying sizes, on a ring attached to a plastic tourist souvenir from Stonehenge.

He took it from her. 'Archie's,' he said. 'He used to be an archaeologist, you know. Before parapsychology took over.'

If it hadn't been for archaeology, Archie would not have discovered the work of Tom Lethbridge, tucked away on the museum shelves of Cambridge University where Lethbridge had at one time been Keeper of Anglo-Saxon Antiquities. Without those papers, Archie would never have been drawn into the study of 'ghoul zones', and would not have ended up working for the Corsi Institute. Would not have tracked down Undine after the bus crash, and would never have encouraged him to seek his own answers as part of the Institute.

Seemingly separate events linked through time and space, nodes in a great web of interconnectivity, stretching away beyond human comprehension. A slight deviation at any point and Archie's team would never come together, would never travel to Lavender Edge, and Archie and Ray would not –

Enough!

'You alright?'

Jo's mascara-heavy eyes brimmed with concern.

He peeled a key off the ring and gave it to her. 'You'd better take this. For when I'm not around. Can't have you sitting on that wall every time you get here too early.'

She nodded, a softness gentling her features. 'Thanks.'

'There's nothing worth nicking anyway.' He prodded the open holdall with the toe of his boot. 'It's all in pieces.'

'Appreciated anyway.' She hesitated, then opened her handbag and pulled out a notebook. Between the pages nestled a small, neatly folded sheet of paper. 'It occurred to me last night,' she said. 'In case you need to get in touch with me.'

She handed it to him. A telephone number, with a Richmond area code.

'Emergencies only,' she said.

'Obviously.' He gestured to her handbag. 'It's

a good idea though. You got a pen in there?'

She did. In the back of her notebook, he scribbled his name and the number of the payphone outside his bedsit.

'Best to keep the police out of this, I reckon,' he said as he passed the book back to her.

Jo zipped up her bag. 'Sod the police,' she agreed. 'What about other investigators though? There's a group I was thinking of contacting.'

Undine shook his head. 'No chance. Trust me, you'll either end up with enthusiastic amateurs who don't have a clue what they're dealing with, or, worse, scientists who'll be more interested in proving their theories and rubbishing their rivals than actually wanting to help. We're better off without the distraction.'

'Your call,' said Jo. 'You're the expert.'

No. He wasn't. Archie was the expert, but Archie wasn't here.

Jo surveyed the wreckage spread around them. 'So,' she said, 'what are we going to do?'

✻   ✻   ✻

That was the question. Undine pictured blood glistening by the skirting board, and thought about it vanishing, absorbed into the fabric of Lavender Edge. No bodies, though. A good sign? Did the absence of bodies suggest that his friends were physically 'in there'? Presumably not inside the building as such, but rather that they had been taken *through* the walls, to another place. How the hell was he going to get them back?

Follow the evidence. That's what Archie always said so maybe they should start with that.

Not that they had much to work with.

They finished emptying the bags, and Undine stared with dismay at the junk salvaged by Jo. Not a single thermometer had survived, their glass casings cracked and empty. Wiring dangled from various electronic gadgets that had once been plugged into the Octopus, and the dented grey casing of the machine's main body was in poorer condition than he had realized. Using a screwdriver, Undine released the upper half of the cover so that he could dig his fingers under the paper drum. He tugged and twisted and finally wrenched the drum free, then tore off the paper on which the probes' esoteric measurements were recorded in multicoloured spikes and troughs. He collected it into a roll, smoothing the wrinkled material as best he could. The machine had clearly registered frantic activity on almost every channel, but unfortunately, with neither Archie nor Ray present to interpret the tracings, Undine was none the wiser as to what any of it meant.

'Damn it!' Jo held up Ray's SLR camera. The lens still clung to the front, but the optics were shattered and, worse, the back panel swung wide open. 'The film's exposed. It's ruined.'

Well, that was one job to cross off the list.

Undine had intended to develop the photographs himself later, in the Institute's dark room. He scooped handfuls of the shiny brown magnetic tape into one of the holdalls instead. 'I'll see if I get anywhere with this.'

Jo settled the broken SLR back on the floor, taking what he considered unnecessary care, and picked up one of Archie's field notebooks. 'Alright if I make a start on these?'

'Take them up to one of the offices,' he suggested. 'Ray's has the most comfortable chair.'

Then, remembering she might not know where that was, he added, 'Second on the left.'

❊   ❊   ❊

Undine pulled off his headphones and drew in a shuddering breath. He wiped away cold liquid snot, pinched the bridge of his nose in a futile effort to block his tears, and angrily choked down the grief churning inside. Thank Christ he had locked the office door.

Yesterday, he had confided in Jo something of what it was like to be hit by the unexpected psychic echo of emotions. She had done her best to empathize, to try to understand why he needed to be so wary every second of every waking hour, so guarded and so apart from the moment. He hadn't shared this aspect of it, however: the shameful after-effects of that bastard sensitivity, the way it drained him and left him as vulnerable and weepy as a teenage girl.

He rummaged in his pockets for a handkerchief, and dried the stickiness from his fingers. Then he scraped the cloth across his nostrils, balled the hankie, and sniffed the hurt back inside.

Should he bother putting the headphones back on? As far as he could tell, the recording contained nothing useful. The tape was so crumpled that much of the sound was indistinguishable beneath crackling and popping, and the few audible sections had done nothing but reignite painful memories.

'Fat load of pissing good,' he grumbled. He pushed back in his chair, which protested with a loud squeak. He knew what he would have to do.

The door to the office rattled. Apparently, she hadn't expected him to lock it. There was a belated double knock.

'You okay in there?'

Undine cleared his throat and gave his eyes another quick wipe. 'Two seconds.'

He let her in.

'I thought you said something.' She looked at him with a little too much interest.

'No.' He brushed past her, into the corridor and on to Archie's office to look up what he needed. Along the way, he decided he would get the telephone number too, to warn them in advance what he was sending in.

He fished Archie's keys from his pocket, unlocked the middle desk drawer, and took out the address book. As he slid the drawer closed again, he saw the forced lock on the bottom drawer. He reached in there and took out the bottle of Lagavulin. What was left of it. They had drunk more yesterday than he'd thought.

'Guess we should keep this safe,' he said as Jo joined him. 'We can finish it with Ray and Archie after we get them back.'

Jo gave a thin smile of agreement as he transferred the bottle to one of the undamaged drawers. He took Archie's pipe from his jacket pocket, tucked it beside the whisky, and locked them both away for another day. A day to look forward to.

Then he stood, laid the address book on Archie's desk, and flicked through until he found what he was after.

'The Corsi Institute?' Jo asked, looking past his elbow and reading what was there. 'I thought *this* was the Institute.'

'Only in London. They've got teams around the world. I'm after their central office, in Rome.'

'Rome?' Jo's eyebrows pulled together. 'Is "Corsi" Italian then? What does it mean?'

'Somebody's name,' said Undine. 'I never thought to ask who.' He copied the details onto a scrap of paper.

'Why do you need their address?'

He gave an exasperated sigh. 'You never stop, do you? Because I'm going to send them everything you salvaged from the Octopus. Neither of knows how to read that stuff, do we? Maybe someone there can.'

'Are you sure?'

'No. But they're the ones who made it.' Anticipating her next question, he continued: 'And yes, Archie designed the Octopus, but he needed someone with the skills to actually build the thing. And the funds too. The Institute should have his original designs on file, or even better the final schematics. Something that will help decode the data, because right now all we've got is a load of colourful squiggles.'

She appeared to accept that.

'I'm going to send them the tape too.'

'You managed to get something from it?' She sounded impressed.

'Something. The quality's not great though. All I could do was splice the least damaged sections together. They'll probably have someone who can clean up the sound, and maybe then they'll hear something useful.' He doubted it, though. 'If nothing else, they'll want it for their archives.'

'I'd like to listen to what's there before you post it to them.'

Rather you than me, thought Undine. He didn't think he could bear hearing that again. 'Knock yourself out.' He handed the address to her. 'After you're done, you can save me a trip to the Post Office.'

She took the paper. In her other hand, she held a cardboard-backed notebook. One of the ones in which Archie liked to record his 'field observations'. She saw he had noticed.

'This is what I was coming to tell you. I've been through these. There's nothing that's much help, not as far as I can see, although I did find a bit about you.' She frowned. 'I wasn't sure whether to show you, but....'

She passed the notebook to him, her finger bookmarking a particular page.

Undine recognized Archie's deliberate handwriting, but instead of looking straight away at what Jo wanted him to see, he flipped forward and back. The book might have been through a tornado. Many pages were partly or fully torn out, and those that remained were tattered and creased. He identified sketch plans showing the layout of Lavender Edge, and phrases Archie must have jotted down during their first interview with Mrs Wyndham. There didn't seem to be anything pertaining to Saturday night, but with Archie's arm in plaster it would have been difficult for him to write anything.

At last, he looked at the page Jo had indicated, surprised to see it appeared earlier in the book than the initial Lavender Edge notes. Although some of the text had been ripped away, it was evident the observations there concerned Undine. One cryptic comment suggested that Archie intended for Undine to experiment with dowsing for psychic impressions using different types of pendulum, and that the length of string and the number of oscillations might relate to the category of information. From the context, it seemed to be a reference to their investigation of the haunted Pyramus theatre in Soho. So that's what the old Scot had been up to, offering him that pendulum.

The next sentence confirmed that this note had been written at or shortly after the Pyramus: 'U appears to exhibit intense emotional response at toilet location. Possible U can be trained to mitigate this response through use of 'flooding' technique, combining relaxation exercises with exposure to stimulus under relatively controlled conditions. Something to explore at future date? (Later:) U lies that distress was due to food poisoning!'

Lies. The word hit like a punch to the gut. A bald, unvarnished observation that could not have hurt more had Archie been standing there, accusing him in person. And that exclamation mark at the end sharpened the pain, as if the Scot were laughing in his face. All this time, and despite his suspicion the scientist understood more than he let on, Undine had believed he was in control of how Archie perceived him. But Archie had seen right through him all along.

Undine had been nothing but a guinea pig in his experiments.

And Jo had read this! Was she watching him now, enjoying his humiliation? No, her back was to him as she perused the books on Archie's shelves; she was making a show of not being interested in his reaction. Not exactly leaving the office, though, was she?

Something in the way she stood there flashed him back to the awful foreboding he had felt when they met. It seemed clear now that the dread she had aroused in him had been a premonition of their journey to Lavender Edge.

He turned the page over, covering the offending words, and found another sketch. The basement of the theatre. Where Archie had stood, observing him. Judging him.

He snapped the notebook shut and slipped it into his jacket; he didn't want Jo sticking her big nose into those pages again. Then he tried to push aside his paranoia and force his thinking onto more productive lines. He should include the Octopus tracings from the Pyramus in the package to Rome. If he didn't then that was more data that would never be deciphered; another night of pain endured for absolutely nothing.

'Oh, for Heaven's sake!'

Jo's cry pulled Undine from his introspection. She hurried past him and bent down to reach under Archie's desk.

'I completely forgot about this!' She dragged

out a holdall, grunting as she took the weight, and hoisted it onto the desktop.

'What is it?' asked Undine.

'I left this here for Archie the other morning, to see when he got back from hospital. It's what I found inside the wall.'

… They're in the walls …

Confused images bubbled to Undine's mind. Fragmented memories of the chaotic conclusion to their first night in Lavender Edge, a night which should have warned them against ever going back. Jo tearing into the plaster to expose more of that hole in the bedroom wall, and reaching in. The cramps convulsing Undine's stomach.

She unzipped the holdall.

'Don't!' he cried, but it was too late.

Jo lifted out a nodule of stone. It was about the size and approximate shape of a clenched fist, and she placed it on the desk. Despite her care, it thudded down, shaking a few grains of plaster dust from its black exterior.

Undine tensed. Any moment now, another wave of dark energy would come crashing over him.

That didn't happen.

Gingerly, he relaxed his mind a fraction, and allowed his thoughts into the space around the stone. Nothing. Only an ominous, ill-defined sense of danger, which was just as likely to be the product of his own nervousness.

'What do you reckon it is?' asked Jo.

He had no idea. 'This is what you found in the wall?'

She nodded. 'Lodged in an old wooden beam. There was a hollow in it, like a niche shaped specially to hold this.' A wrinkle formed between her eyes. 'To be honest, I'm not entirely sure why I wanted to take this out. The thing is, I was angry at how none of you seemed to be doing anything, and I wanted to prove Mrs Wyndham's story was real, that you should take it seriously.'

She stared at him, and he knew there was something more.

'I think it wanted me to find this,' she said.

'"It"?'

'Maybe the same thing you say was pretending to be Ronald Wyndham.' She bit her lip, furiously trying to understand her actions. 'It felt like I was being encouraged to reach into that hole, that there was something in there I was supposed to find.' She gazed at the stone. 'Why would it want that?'

Undine thought about the pain that had gripped him just as Jo emerged from the broken wall, clutching her prize. The way the air became taut with electricity and the lights went out, and how Archie took a tumble in the sudden darkness, fracturing his arm when he crashed to the floor.

Why had everything happened at that moment? According to Mrs Wyndham, the phenomena at Lavender Edge had been occurring for several weeks before their visit, although the house was peaceful enough when they'd arrived. He remembered Archie even suggesting the haunting had already run its course! What had changed with the discovery of this stone?

'Hey,' said Jo. 'I think there's something written on this.'

Before Undine could stop her, she blew the dust away without a thought of what might happen.

'What the hell's wrong with you?' he yelled.

She stepped back, startled but indignant.

'Look,' she said.

His nerves sparked as he examined the object. It was black, and he would have described the substance as glossy except it seemed to hold on to the light that fell against the surface. Ultimately, however, it was only a lump of stone.

A stone with a pattern carved into it.

'See?'

It wasn't writing, though. What was it? Undine blew away more of the fine plaster dust.

'Oh, so it's alright when you do that?'

He ignored her.

He had seen that pattern before.

CHAPTER 19

Reels whirred and clacked, rewinding, gathering speed with a rising whoosh until the last few inches of tape whisked free and the right-hand spool spun empty. Jo pushed the stop button, lifted off her headphones, and mussed her flattened hair back into shape.

Nothing. Listening to the recording all the way through, twice, had achieved nothing other than an intensification of the guilt gnawing at her. Her promise to help Mrs Wyndham was a mockery. Not only had that poor lady abandoned her home in despair but two men she had coerced into working with her were now missing, Christ only knew where.

What had she got them into? Undine's certainty that his friends were alive, trapped in some way inside that house, sounded ridiculous, yet hadn't she experienced something similar herself? She tried again to tease out the strand of memory she felt almost breaking the surface of her mind: she knew it involved that evening in the house with Dick Condie, that sense of being caught in a whirlwind, of an immense force stretching and pulling and dragging at her, attempting to twist her out of this world and towards a different manifestation of reality, and she did her best to capture the tantalizing sensations whispering to her – but the memory was too unsettling to hold onto and dissolved before she could grasp it.

She was out of her depth. Terrifyingly so. She knew nothing about ghosts or haunted houses or psychical research. For God's sake, she was so useless that Undine wouldn't let her go with him while he chased down some idea he'd about the stone she had found. He wouldn't even reveal what his idea concerned. She was a liability. Worse, she was dangerous to those around her.

But she couldn't just sit around. There must be something she could do. She might no longer be a policewoman but just because she didn't wear a uniform didn't mean she had forgotten her training. Let Undine go dashing off in pursuit of inspiration; she still believed in the value of good, old-fashioned police work. The dogged, methodical collation and sifting of evidence. The unglamorous back-room drudgery that was responsible for putting away more villains than any high-flying, glory-hunting detective would ever admit.

She trudged to the top of the stairs and

looked out over the mess of broken equipment and scattered papers below. Maybe they had overlooked something before. Maybe, within all that salvaged debris, still lurked some useful information.

And, now she thought about it, there might be more evidence to consider too. The team's notes from their first visit to Lavender Edge, for example, and any thoughts they might have noted down afterwards. They wouldn't have brought everything to the house with them on Saturday, so there should be other surviving material somewhere here in the Warehouse.

Jo walked back through the deserted offices, looking at the rooms afresh with the eyes of a police constable. Undine's office held nothing of interest, and nor did Archie's, but Ray's filing cabinet proved to be unlocked. She slid the drawers open, and among the records of past investigations, she saw a folder labelled 'Lavender Edge'.

Inside were photographs. Guilt again wrenched her insides, its hunger renewed by her recollection of Ray clicking away with his SLR, the camera currently lying smashed on the floor downstairs. The photos showed views in and around the house, which she recognized despite the perturbing swirls and blurs warping the images. With them was a sheaf of typewritten paper, which bore Ray's initials. It took a few seconds before she identified it as a transcript of her own words, spoken while under hypnosis. Beneath that was a cardboard carton, which, according to the label, held the tape recording of that session. The thought of hearing her hypnotized self talking was oddly disturbing; however, curiosity got the better of her. She went back to the recorder, loaded the reel, and squashed the headphones on again.

It was a strange sensation, hearing herself speak as if half-asleep, responding to Archie's warm, soothing tones, her drowsy voice murmuring sentences she did not recall uttering. Ultimately, though, it added nothing to what she had already learned since that recording was made. She returned to the folder and leafed through the final few papers it contained. More transcripts – these ones of everything Mrs Wyndham had told them during their first visit. Ray had certainly been busy, although he had seemingly run out of time to follow up on his note reminding him to try again to interview Mrs Wyndham's builders. Jo swept everything back into the folder, intending to carry it down with her in a minute, and look over it all again in conjunction with everything else down there.

Just one thing left to do here first. One of the desk drawers was stuffed full of envelopes of assorted sizes, so she found one suitable for the tape recordings and Octopus tracings Undine wanted her to send to Rome. That done, she turned to leave the office, and came face-to-face with one of Ray's hideous jackets hanging from a hook on the back of the door.

Would he ever wear that again?

The question preyed on her as she moved to the ground floor. Marching into the centre of the chaos, she sat down, cross-legged, and arranged her finds around her, including Archie's notebooks, which she intended to comb through a second time, and the notes she had made at the library concerning the area's local history. She dragged Mrs Wyndham's tartan suitcase closer and opened the catches. The lid popped up, and inside were old photographs, genealogical trees, and certificates of births, deaths and marriages – the fruits of Ronald Wyndham's years of delving into his family tree. Many of the documents were torn or crumpled: bearing the battle scars of Saturday night.

She worked through it all, scouring vast fields of haystacks for needles that might or might not exist, and she realized her efforts might be futile, but she kept her focus and pressed on methodically through every scrap of evidence surrounding her. And by the end, she had discovered precisely nothing that could help them.

When she stood, the blood rushed back to her legs in pins and needles. She collapsed against the nearest pillar, shifting her weight from foot to foot as she waited for the maddening discomfort to fade, and tried not to scream with frustration. All that work – not to mention the terror of creeping back alone into Lavender Edge to save this rubbish in the face of God knew what! How could all of that have been for nothing?

It couldn't. She wouldn't allow it.

Undine's instructions had been strict. After listening to the recording, she was to lock up the Warehouse and leave. She was absolutely not to interfere with his investigation. But Undine was no longer here. He had given her directions to a pub where they were to meet this evening to catch up on each other's progress, but there were hours to go yet before she'd need to head there. She thought about Ray's reminder about the builders. She knew how to interview people, and she'd be a damned sight better at it than the unsociable Undine. Plus somebody still needed to talk to her old 'friend', that arsehole Dick Condie, in case his memories had returned more fully than her own.

Jo gathered the papers and pictures into neat piles. She placed heavier fragments of the broken equipment on top to keep the piles in place, then she put on her jacket, took Ray's note, and picked up the envelope she'd addressed to Rome.

As she made her way towards the Warehouse door, a weird idea occurred to her. It would have seemed crazy even a few days ago, but now....

Now it seemed no more insane than

anything else she had got herself involved with.

She made up her mind. Once she finished at the Post Office, she would interview the builders, and then she would persuade Condie to see her. That would probably take the rest of the day, but when she spoke to Undine this evening she would tell him there just might be a third person they could try to contact.

She wondered how he would react.

CHAPTER 20

Undine stomped down Rivermead Path. The noise was deliberate, something to focus on, to hold in the howl of anguish that threatened to burst his chest.

He didn't want to be here, but that maze pattern drew him. Twice now he'd seen it: first on that pamphlet's cover, then carved into the stone pulled from the wall at Lavender Edge. Chances were Oldroyd knew nothing about it (why would he?) but Undine needed to know for sure. No matter that he loathed the idea of visiting the weird shopkeeper again, of enduring more of his hippy nonsense about thin places and ghosts. He sniffed, and smeared away the tears prickling his eyes.

That was the other reason. Coming here got him away from Jo for a couple of hours. He couldn't let her see him in this state.

He pounded on, concentrating on the thudding of his steps instead of the image of his friends' faces rising to the surface of that bloody wallpaper, their features shifting and coalescing into soundless screams. His emotions blazed like ripped electric cables, sparking and flashing unpredictable violence. The after-effects of Saturday night had been delayed, but they were on him now and as powerful as any he had experienced since the first time.

Undine had been 15, a few weeks shy of his sixteenth birthday, that winter of 1957 when Harry and his mates clambered through the bomb-sites that still littered the bruised streets of post-Blitz London. The ruins in front of them had been levelled, but the children who played here knew of a void under what had once been the house, and of a gap hidden beneath one particular heap of scorched planks and shattered bricks. A gap just large enough to wriggle through, and steps below, leading down into darkness.

Harry cupped his hands against the frozen air and lit a fag. Like the others in his gang, he longed to exude the effortless macho cool of American stars like Sinatra and Bogart, and he sneered at the stories younger kids swapped about those steps: that they led to the subterranean lair of a ghost.

'You ought to be careful,' warned Jack. 'Them stairs don't look so good.'

Harry flashed a grin. 'Stay up here if you're scared. I'm going to see what's down there.'

He went alone. The cellar was dark, and dank from exposure to years of rain and snow. It had never fully dried from the wartime fire hoses, and the air was thick with the stink of mildew and rot. Harry kicked aside drifts of rubble, starting as he caught a rusty tin can by accident and sent it clattering away. In the furthest shadows, small unseen feet scampered from the intruder.

'You alright?'

'Just rats,' he called up, relishing the distaste his words would provoke.

There was a heaviness to the dark down here. He flicked the end of his cigarette away, watching the glowing tip disappear into the murk, and he waited.

The thought that his prolonged absence was worrying his mates made the stench and damp worth enduring. Actually, he didn't notice the stink so much anymore: it was obscured by the scent of smoke still hanging around him. Although, now Harry was paying attention, it didn't smell much like cigarettes after all. It was more like a Guy Fawkes Night bonfire, and it was getting thicker.

His mates were smelling it too, judging by the growing commotion of voices above him. Or else they were scared by the idea of rats in here. He ignored the hubbub and walked deeper into the cellar.

The voices rose, the words indecipherable

but their tone gathering urgency. More footsteps now – human this time: the hurried clatter of high heels as a woman started to run. Who was she? There were no girls in Harry's gang, let alone grown-up women. But the question was suddenly unimportant because he could hear a mournful wail, a rising note of warning, which flooded him with an abrupt, chilling certainty: death was approaching.

The sound soared. It was far away, and it was coming from all around, and it was inside his head, rising and falling in a fearful, revolving banshee howl.

The air was vibrating! An ominous drone widened and swelled as Harry's entire existence shrank to a terror of noise and sickening dread: sensations like nothing he had felt before, yet ones he experienced now with the familiarity of untold nights of anxiety. The ground heaved to the crumping impact of falling explosives, and the dull red ember from his discarded cigarette had become an impossible lambent glow, which intensified and hardened until a crackling, flickering illumination filled the cellar. Heat scorched him, and the middle-aged woman who sheltered in this tomb with him screamed in his face.

Harry screamed too, although he had no memory of that. It's what the others told him, after they carried him up the cellar steps to the relative safety of the street-level ruins. They left him there, tears and grime streaking his ashen features. His mates, of course, had seen and heard nothing unusual apart from Harry's sudden and unexpected attack of the vapours. Jack in particular had found it hilarious how their humiliated leader had been so spooked by kids' stories that he lost his bottle and ended up blubbing like a girl.

The memory melted into the feel of brick: rough yet cool against his forehead.

Undine took a step back, groggy, and saw he had been leaning against the wall of Oldroyd's corner-shop. His heart hammered, and there was the cold of sweat on his back and in the armpits of his shirt. How long had he been standing like this?

Probably not long, because he appeared not to have attracted attention. He blew his nose and checked his reflection in the window, rubbing his eyes again and straightening his tie. Then he swallowed his pain and pushed open the door before he could change his mind.

The bell jangled above, and the last vestiges of 1957 sank back into the past. Gone for now, but Undine knew that – like ghosts – they lingered unseen, awaiting the next time something triggered them.

'Hello again.'

The elderly shopkeeper stood behind the counter, in front of the ribbon-curtained doorway and Tarot card-decorated wall. Just as last time, he might have been waiting for Undine to arrive. The lens of his wire-framed spectacles was still cracked, and the interior of the shop was still gloomy and hushed. Oldroyd even appeared to be wearing the same shabby pinstriped suit.

'How may I help you this time? Hm?' Oldroyd's eyes glittered, as hard and dark as those of a crow.

Undine saw what he wanted on the magazine rack. He pulled out another copy of the local history pamphlet.

'I bought one of these last week,' he said.

Oldroyd's gaze did not leave him.

Undine placed the pamphlet on the counter and turned it to face the older man.

'This design on the cover. The maze. None of the articles say anything about it.'

The faintest of smiles touched Oldroyd's lips.

'It's just that, the other day, you seemed to know quite a bit about this area. I was wondering whether you might know something about this maze.'

'Oh, I do, Mr Undine.' His smile was clearer now. 'Yes indeed.'

Undine was impressed the shopkeeper remembered his name. Then again, a practised habit of remembering customers' names was probably good for business.

'It's a very old pattern,' said Oldroyd in his reedy, clipped tones. 'Perhaps you have seen something similar before?'

'I'm afraid not,' Undine lied. He wanted answers first.

Oldroyd looked disappointed. 'Ah. Well, it's an old pattern, as I said. This is an old place.'

'You've said that before too.'

'Hm. Yes. I mentioned the Weall also, did I not?'

That word again, the weird-sounding name where the pronunciation of the syllable shifted halfway through, from the short 'a' of 'bat' to the longer 'ar' sound of 'path'.

'You never said what it meant.'

'You gave me little time, as I recall.'

Undine took out his notebook. 'Fair enough,' he acknowledged, unscrewing his pen. 'But I'm listening now.'

'Yes.' Oldroyd's eyes gleamed, cold and black. 'The Weall has stood here for thousands of years. Since long before the first Anglo-Saxons settled in this area. Since before the Romans.'

Undine was lost already. 'Romans?'

'Before them,' repeated Oldroyd. 'Then the Anglo-Saxons, when they arrived, gave the Weall its name, but otherwise they stayed away. Even their burial grounds stopped at the edge of this site. They knew, or learned, not to interfere with what stood here.'

'Learned what?'

Oldroyd opened his claw-like hands. 'Who knows? Their stories are lost to time, Mr Undine, but their lesson survives. They understood enough to leave the Weall alone.'

'Why? What is it?' Undine made no attempt to pronounce the peculiar word.

'Protection,' said Oldroyd. 'Hm. A barrier against The Outside. Time has worn this place thin, you see, or perhaps it always was thin.'

The conversation was veering towards Oldroyd's bloody 'thin places' again. Undine pulled it back on track. 'A barrier? Who built it?'

'A fascinating question. One I wish I were able to answer.'

Undine jabbed the pamphlet cover with his pen. 'But this maze has got some connection with your barrier, is that it? So maybe the person who drew this knows more.'

The old man's eyes glittered. 'Alas not. Local history, as you will have gathered, is something of a passion with me, but my knowledge has its limits.'

'You drew this?'

Oldroyd inclined his head modestly. 'These small publications are my own work. Written and illustrated by my hand.'

'That's terrific. But what about this pattern? Is this what the barrier looks like?'

'It is a part of its design,' said Oldroyd. 'An important part.'

The shopkeeper exhaled a heavy sigh, his poised humour evaporating without warning. 'I tried to stop her,' he said. 'I warned her not to damage the structure.'

'The structure? You mean the house? This barrier is inside Lavender Edge?'

'Mr Undine, it *is* Lavender Edge,' said Oldroyd.

The sudden intensity in the eyes behind those cracked spectacles held Undine tight as Oldroyd continued speaking, his words coming faster now.

'We have to repair what's been done. That's why you are here. I can help you. The circle has already been drawn, and we should begin right away. I have the formulae, can tell you what to do. We need to re-channel the flow before the damage –'

'Are they alive?' Undine's mind burned with the memory of Ray's face, and Archie's, screaming.

Oldroyd stared, his train of thought derailed.

'The faces that appear in the wallpaper,' said Undine. 'I asked you about them before when I was here. You never answered my question.'

'Didn't I?'

'Look,' said Undine, controlling his temper. 'I know some of the stories about the house now. A lot of them say the faces are like ghosts, like echoes of people who died on that spot.' He studied the shopkeeper. 'That's not true, is it?'

A moment ago, the old man had been raving. Now he looked almost amused again.

'Hm. Oh, they're not dead, no. Not in the sense you mean. What would be the point of that?'

Undine had no reply.

'You see,' said Oldroyd, 'it is in the nature of a thin place that some...' – he seemed to consider which word to use – '... essence, let's say, would likely remain were a person to die there. But The Outside gains far more from life than from death, hm.'

'The what?'

'Everything feeds, Mr Undine.'

Undine shuddered. Oldroyd's words reminded him of the pain and suffering he had sensed inside the house. They made him think of Saturday night, of what had happened in the hour or so before Ray and Archie disappeared. The hostility in that room, the out-of-control bickering between Undine and Jo, and between him and his friends. The way the force inside that place had grown stronger at the same time that their emotions soured and sowed discord like a disease....

Feeding?

Oldroyd nodded in response to Undine's half-formed intuition.

'I think of it as "dark emotion",' said Oldroyd. 'A crude phrase, hm, but one that conveys the point. Resentment, fear, sorrow: such feelings generate an energy of sorts. A palatable energy, it would appear.'

'Something in the house was *feeding* off our bad feelings?'

'Feeding. Manipulating you too, I expect. Whipping up arguments, conflict, terror. It has grown skilled at that.'

Oldroyd's features darkened. He looked down. For a few moments, he was silent, and Undine was about to ask for more information about the faces when the shopkeeper's head twitched up again.

'It wears the faces deliberately. I am convinced it does. A masquerade, hm, performed for no reason other than to terrify whomever happens to be present at the time.'

Undine struggled to make sense of what the shopkeeper was saying, and what the implications were for his friends. 'So the actual people – the ones whose faces appear. Are you telling me they're not really in the house? Then where are they?'

'Ah,' said Oldroyd. 'No, they are in there. In a way. But sometimes The Outside wears them.'

Undine's fists clenched. He shoved his hands into his coat pockets. This conversation was insane! And getting information out of Oldroyd was like squeezing blood from a stone.

He touched the heavy object in his pocket. Not yet, he decided.

With an effort, he kept his voice calm and asked: 'So what is it, this "outside" you keep referring to?'

Oldroyd raised his eyebrows. 'Now that may be a question beyond any of us. The nearest I have come to an answer is to consider everything human beings call "reality" to be an island. A single, isolated fragment of order surrounded by an infinity of chaos. Hm. If you can picture that, then The Outside would be everything that lies beyond such an island's shores.'

He frowned. 'Or perhaps not everything. Perhaps it is itself only a splinter of the greater chaos that exists out there.'

'What does it want?'

Oldroyd shrugged. 'To come through,' he said, as if the answer should have been obvious. 'Hm. In the same way that Nature is said to abhor a vacuum, it is compelled to go where it is not.'

'But it can't come through because of this barrier, this Wa –' Undine stumbled over the strange pronunciation.

'Weall'

'Because this thing is keeping it out?'

Oldroyd's eyes flashed. 'You must repair it.'

Undine scoffed.

'Of course,' said Oldroyd, 'the task would be easier if we had the node.' He trailed off in expectation. When Undine failed to reply, Oldroyd picked up the pamphlet and displayed the cover with its drawing of the maze.

Undine's fingers closed around the fist-sized lump in his pocket. 'You mean this?'

He pulled it out and placed it on the counter. For its size, the stone was surprisingly heavy, and it nearly crashed against the wood, Undine catching it just in time. He left his hand on top, ready to snatch the object away should Oldroyd move to grab it.

But the shopkeeper made no such attempt. Oldroyd stared at the black, faintly iridescent stone, seemingly captivated by the time-worn carving in what was currently its upper surface.

For the first time, it occurred to Undine just how difficult it must have been to carve into the incredibly dense material, and he wondered how old the object must be for the pattern to have become so worn down. He compared the design to the drawing. There was no denying they were the same. The maze resembled a stylized image of a tree, perhaps an oak, the opening at the base leading upwards like a trunk to great looping branches that spread out and around. Or maybe there was more resemblance to a brain, the entrance leading to an inner labyrinth of folded convolutions....

'I knew it had been removed,' said Oldroyd with what sounded like relieved satisfaction. He peered at Undine over the top of his cracked wire-framed spectacles. 'You shouldn't have taken it, you know.'

It wasn't me, thought Undine. His memories were hazy, but he recalled how unaccountably nervous he had been that first night, sitting with the others in the upstairs room. He thought of Jo, and re-experienced a twinge of the nausea that had overcome him as she plunged her hands into that damned hole in the wall. That was how she had found the stone – this 'node' as Oldroyd called it. What had happened next dribbled in as a confusion of pained impressions and details told to Undine afterwards by Ray during their dash to take Archie to hospital: the throbbing of heated air; the crackling ozone tang; a lightbulb smashing; and Undine's own murmured insistence that 'they' were 'in the walls'.

'You weakened the barrier.'

Undine shook his head, both in denial and to clear his thoughts. 'I don't buy it. Those builders made only one hole before they fled, which just happened to be right at this critical spot in the building? That's a hell of a coincidence.'

'The Outside influenced them. Just as it no doubt influenced the one who removed this.'

'But the faces,' said Undine. 'Stories about those go back years. Decades. Maybe even longer.'

'As I have said, The Weall has stood for a long time, and time weakens most things. Now, however, without the node in place, the barrier is on the verge of full collapse.' Oldroyd looked grim. 'The Outside has also been here a long time, trying to push through, but *it* grows stronger with the passing centuries.'

A note of deeper urgency came into Oldroyd's voice. 'You must replace the node.'

'What, just pop this stone back in and everything will be hunky dory?'

'You must put replace it,' said Oldroyd again, 'but carefully. The alignment must be correct.' He poked his bony index finger against the drawing and started to trace the winding loops through the maze. 'These,' he said. 'These channel the energy that would otherwise accumulate. The house, the structure as a whole, transforms that energy. Through the node, it redirects it. The energy can never be destroyed, hm, but the flow can be dissipated, its intensity reduced, to keep The Outside from growing strong enough to bleed through.'

Oldroyd's expression pleaded with him.

'Do you understand?'

Undine wanted to say no, but perhaps he did grasp something of Oldroyd's meaning. He thought of Archie showing off the Octopus to Jo that day in the Warehouse. How he had described the function of the printed circuit board as channelling electricity through the physical components. It was the merest tickle of understanding, and it evaporated as Undine tried to tease meaning from it, but Oldroyd had made the key point clear. Put the stone back where Jo had found it. The thought of returning to Lavender Edge sent an icy blast through Undine's gut, but if it meant saving his friends, he would go.

'Put this back?'

'Yes,' said Oldroyd. 'But you will need to take great care. Energy will have accumulated since the Weall was damaged; if it is discharged without control the structure will not survive.'

'And what about me? Would it kill me at the same time?'

Oldroyd's black crows' eyes twinkled. 'You might find that preferable to the alternative.'

Undine almost laughed. Embracing this lunacy seemed the sanest reaction left to him. 'Well then, I suppose you'd better make sure I know which way round this node of yours has to go.' He lifted it and turned it around, looking for any sign of a slot or irregularity in its shape to offer a clue. There was none. As far as he could tell, the stone would slide into the recess Jo had described just as readily one way or another.

'Don't you remember?' asked Oldroyd.

'It wasn't me who took the bloody thing out!'

Oldroyd frowned. 'But you must know who did.'

Oh, he knew that alright, although he very much doubted Jo had studied the stone's precise position while she fumbled inside the blackness of that hole. Especially if she had been under the influence of this force Oldroyd described.

'What if nobody noticed?' asked Undine.

Now Oldroyd looked troubled, as if he had not considered this possibility before. 'Describe to me the wall in which the node was found. Of what was it made?'

'Brick. Plaster over that, then wallpaper.' He thought over what else Jo had told him. 'Oh, and your "node" was embedded in a wooden beam, apparently. Like a carved-out niche.'

'The older structure,' murmured Oldroyd. 'Perhaps, if the energy left its mark over the centuries....'

He touched the pamphlet with one long finger, prodding the base of the illustration, at the maze's opening. 'The present house has existed long enough for its substance to have been affected. Any alteration of the fabric would be most visible here, at the gate. Find such a sign in the wall and you will know the direction of the node's opening. That will show you the orientation.'

'Yeah, I still don't get why you need me to do this,' protested Undine. 'Why not do it yourself if you think it's so bloody important?'

For a moment, a violent fury appeared to overcome Oldroyd. With an effort, he leaned back, allowing the shadowy interior of his shop to envelop him. The dim light mirrored the lenses of his spectacles so that his eyes were lost to view behind shining glass. His reply, when it came, was spoken in a voice suddenly full of loss and weariness.

'I am an old man, Mr Undine.'

No argument there, but Undine sensed it was a partial explanation at best.

'I have done what I can,' Oldroyd continued.

Undine examined the lump of stone in his hands. Would replacing this really free Ray and

Archie?

'If I do this, what will happen to the others? The faces. You said they're trapped: will this release them?'

Oldroyd's eyes remained hidden. 'When the node is replaced, the energy feeding The Outside will diminish. Its power will weaken, and it will lose the strength to draw on those who are held there. Their torment will end.'

The shopkeeper thrust forward from the shadows, his eyes visible once more, glittering hard and black behind the cracked glass of his spectacles. He clutched Undine with long, bony fingers.

'You have a gift, Mr Undine. It's why you were chosen.'

Chosen? What the hell was he talking about now?

'It will enable you to do what you must, but be cautious. It makes you vulnerable too. You must seal the breach without further delay, before the Outside grows more powerful.'

Undine twisted free of the man's feeble grasp – but in that moment, he grasped the full, appalling implications of what Oldroyd wanted him to do.

He backed away, aghast, pulling the heavy stone to his chest.

CHAPTER 21

To Jo's surprise, they stopped outside a sleazy bookshop on Coldharbour Lane.

'Funny looking restaurant.'

'We'll be eating soon,' said Undine. He checked his watch.

Jo held back from asking what time their reservation was for. Since turning up late at that dive of a pub to meet her, Undine had barely spoken a word. Something was bothering him, and whatever it was had pulled him so deep inside his head it intimidated her.

She watched as he fumbled a key from his pocket and unlocked a door beside the shop. When he pushed the door open, it slipped from his fingers and crashed into the interior wall. Was he drunk? Jo felt a little tipsy herself, but they hadn't had that much. Mind you, the last few days were taking their toll on her, and the impact must be worse for Undine whose friends were, at best, missing. In his present state, she didn't dare tell him she suspected they were dead.

She let Undine lead her down a short, narrow hallway to the bottom of an even narrower staircase. Somewhere close by, some lucky so-and-so was already tucking into their meal. It smelled good.

Two flights up, she found herself on a dingy landing. She took a moment to get her bearings, and decided that the landing led along the rear of the building, above the bookshop. Through a window to her right she could see an overgrown back garden below them, although it was difficult to make out detail in the meagre light. The mouth-watering aroma of food was stronger up here. For the first time in days, eating felt like more than a necessity, and her stomach rumbled.

Opposite the window were two doors. Between them, mounted in the wall, hung a payphone, while a third door stood at the far end. A small object sat on the threadbare carpet, propped up against the second door, and when she drew close enough, she saw it was a scuffed hardback book.

Undine swore. He rummaged through his pockets a second time, having apparently forgotten he'd need his keys again up here. He nodded towards the book. 'Grab that.'

Jo read the cover: 'Shamanism Around the World'. What was this all about then? She spotted a sheet of paper stuck between the pages and discovered it was a handwritten note.

'It's addressed to you,' she said. 'From someone called....' The handwriting was atrocious. 'Sid? Says he struck lucky: a mate of his owns another store and had this in stock, so he bought it off him. He hopes it's what you're after.'

Undine nodded absently.

She closed the book, relieved that at least one of them seemed to be getting somewhere. If Undine had asked for this title especially, that suggested he was pursuing a line of evidence. He might have bothered to mention that to her! Why this book though? And she wished he would tell her where he had gone this afternoon and what was preying on his mind. She fought her impulsive need to know, her instincts telling her to tread carefully, that if she pushed too hard Undine would close down completely.

He struggled to fit his key into the lock. He looked distinctly unwell. The hollows surrounding his eyes were darker than ever, and his tousled hair and unshaven chin showed more grey than she had noticed before. At last, he got the door open, and the delicious aroma of cooking instantly intensified.

Undine walked straight in – no 'ladies first' here – and made for the kitchen. Or, rather, for a small area that contained an oven, a kettle, a worktop, and a few cupboards. He grabbed a towel, opened the oven, and jerked his head back as a cloud of steam wafted up at him.

Jo followed him inside. 'This your place then?' She looked around with curiosity: a single wooden chair; a small table; a record player sitting in one corner; and in another a few dozen books piled on the floor beside a larger selection of records. The place was tiny. Working for the Corsi Institute evidently did not pay well.

'Yeah. All mine.' With a towel wrapped around his hands, Undine took a casserole dish from the oven. He placed it on a board that sat surrounded by spice jars.

Jo crossed the room to join him. It only took a couple of steps.

'You cooked?'

Undine lifted the lid. 'Surprised?'

'A little,' she admitted. 'Wow, that smells good!'

It did. Warm and rich and layered: she'd eaten curry before but this looked and smelled special. 'What's in it?'

'Goat.'

'Goat? You planned us a meal or a Black Mass?'

He almost smiled. 'Trust me.'

Undine stirred the mixture then put the dish back into the oven. He left the lid in the sink.

'Another half hour.' He rose, stretched, and walked over to what Jo had taken to be a sideboard but when he opened the door, she saw a compact foldaway bed. He undid a latch, lowered the bed, and took off his trench coat and hung it on the edge of the tired mattress. 'Make yourself at home,' he said, pulling the chair out from the table and indicating that Jo should take that for herself. 'I need a slash.'

'Make sure you wash your hands!' she called after him as he turned along the landing in the direction of the third door she had seen. Most likely a shared bathroom. She sat down and flicked through the book in her hands.

It wasn't her cup of tea. From what she could make out, shamanism was a form of folk religion involving altered states of consciousness and interaction with the spirit world. It was bizarre, and she couldn't understand the link with Lavender Edge. Perhaps there wasn't one after all.

She stopped at a striking black-and-white drawing of a man she took to be a Red Indian, or possibly an Eskimo. He wore a feathered headdress and one hand gripped a small, round drum. Both of his arms were extended, and his head was thrown back, eyes screwed in either agony or ecstasy, while distorted, wraith-like ghosts or demons howled around him.

'Lovely.' She shuddered, imagining Undine in that situation.

... *It's like you're suddenly inside someone else's pain* ...

The accompanying text documented shamanic initiation ceremonies. In restrained, academic language that somehow made the content more disturbing, the author had written about rites of passage that typically involved physical illness and psychological crisis. The book described how a prospective shaman suffered a sickness that took him to the borderlands between life and death. How he would have to journey over that frontier and into the very depths of the underworld before he could be reborn and later return with information vital to the tribe's survival....

The door snicked closed.

She looked up. Undine's hair clung to his forehead in damp strands from where he had splashed water on his face.

'Interesting reading matter,' she prompted, raising the book.

He grunted. 'Sid's my landlord. I asked him to get it for me. He owns the salubrious establishment downstairs.'

Jo smiled, hoping Undine would say more.

He avoided her gaze. 'It's not important. Just something Oldroyd said. Made me curious.'

'Who?'

For a long moment, he didn't answer. Then: 'Remember that shop across the road from Mrs Wyndham's house, on the corner?'

Jo nodded.

'That's Oldroyd's.' Undine scowled with disapproval. 'Bit of an old hippy. Lived in the area for donkey's years, he says, and knows it like the back of his hand. Thing is, he's written some pamphlets about local history, and – if he's to be believed – he knows a hell of a lot about that house.'

'That's where you went this afternoon?'

'Yes.' Undine's face clouded. What had this Oldroyd character told him?

Undine walked to the kitchen and produced a bottle of wine. 'Red alright? I thought this would work.'

He was changing the subject. Jo bit back her frustration and told herself to be patient. Sooner or later, he'd come out with it. 'Fine by me.'

Undine glugged wine into a pair of glasses and took rice from a cupboard. Jo put the book down and sipped her drink. Not bad. For all his rough edges, Undine certainly knew a thing or two about dining. She stood up to stretch her legs, and wandered around the cramped space, ending up kneeling by the records.

'Put on anything you fancy,' Undine called out.

She looked around. His back was to her as he stirred the contents of a saucepan. Returning to the LPs, she didn't particularly fancy any she saw: 'The Hit Sound of Dean Martin', 'Sammy Davis, Jr. at Town Hall', 'Moonlight Sinatra'. She would have preferred something modern to liven the mood. T. Rex would have been good, or Crystal Starcruiser, or Slade. All this Rat Pack stuff was rather dated.

Although it did suit Undine, she decided: the dark suits and ties; the smart footwear; and even the surprisingly delicate gold cufflinks he liked to wear. Maybe the booze was affecting her judgement but now that she considered these things, Undine was quite a snappy dresser.

Or would be if he carried it better and you ignored the ash stains and crumples.

She picked out the Sinatra and put it on the record player. The empty sleeve she rested against the other albums, and she began to nose through the books stacked beside them as the music expanded and warmed the ambience of the room. It was better than she had expected, and she started to sway in time with the lilting melody, melting into the –

Oh, God! What if he found her selection romantic?

She reached for the record, but halted, her hand hovering above the stylus. Swapping this album for another would only draw more attention to it. She opted to turn the volume down instead, reducing the music to a casual background noise, and when she glanced around, Undine seemed absorbed in his cooking. She relaxed, and turned back to the books.

Top of the pile was a slim hardback, titled 'The Principles of Psychic Occultism'. Its cover showed an attractive brunette perched on the edge of a black altar. Stark naked, of course – the fashion choice of all modern-day occultists, from what the papers said. Most of the other titles also focused on the supernatural, occultism, and psychical research. That made sense, given what she now knew about Undine.

What would have been more unexpected – at least until tonight – were the cookbooks, which came from all around the world. It seemed Undine had a penchant for exotic cuisine. She took another sip of wine to appease her impatient stomach, and hoped the cookbooks were a sign of good things to come.

She placed Undine's new shamanism book on the others, then carried her drink to the kitchen, where for some reason Undine was leaning half out of the window. As she watched, he slipped a small china plate of what she guessed was goat meat onto the ledge. A grey shape uncurled from the darkness and resolved into a Siamese cat, which started to eat even before the plate was down.

'Easy, Frank,' murmured Undine. He stroked the animal's silvery fur and it arched its back with pleasure, tail raised. Bright blue eyes evaluated Jo for a moment, before returning to the more important matter of dinner.

She laughed, the sudden connection catching her off-guard.

'Old Blue Eyes, right?'

Undine's reply came with something between a grimace and a smile. 'You got me.'

He closed the window, muffling the sounds

of traffic and voices from Coldharbour Lane, and rinsed his hands under the cold tap. She stood beside him as he took the casserole dish out of the oven. The mixture within now included dark-coloured beans, she noticed.

'How are you with spicy food?' he asked.

'Okay, I guess. How spicy are you talking?'

Undine dipped in a spoon and tasted it. 'Well, I'd best not add any more chilli.'

With deft skill, he chopped up some unfamiliar grassy green herb and sprinkled it into the food. As a final touch, he squeezed in some lemon juice. He was still withdrawn, although his mood seemed a little less dark than when they'd arrived.

Time to find out what he'd learned.

'I managed to get that parcel to the Post Office before it shut,' she said.

'Good.'

She waited for him to say something about his own afternoon, but Undine only hummed along with the subdued music as he served the curry on plates with rice and a strange sort of warm, flat bread.

She tried again. 'It should be on its way to Rome by now.'

Undine nodded.

Damn him. She would just have to ask outright. She took another quick sip. Okay, here goes.

'So,' said Undine, interrupting her before she

could ask. 'You going to tell me how you got on at the Warehouse or what?'

∗   ∗   ∗

She'd been dreading this. She had just given Undine her only good news – that she had posted his parcel to Rome. Nothing she had left to tell him was going to go down well.

'Not so good.'

Undine carried the plates to the table and set hers in front of the chair. His own plate he balanced on his lap after he sat on the edge of his bed.

'Actually,' Jo said as she took her seat, 'it was a complete waste of time. I went through everything I could find but got nowhere.'

Undine used his bread to scoop up some of the curry. She copied him. God, it tasted fantastic.

'Okay.' She braced herself against his anger. 'I know you told me not to do anything else, but I couldn't just sit around for the rest of the day doing nothing.'

'You surprise me,' said Undine. He licked sauce from his lip. 'Go on then. What did you do?'

His reaction was too calm. Warily, she admitted to visiting her old police station to chat with Dick Condie. Hot blood rushed to her face as she recalled the snide jibes of her ex-colleagues and told how Condie himself had laughed in her face when she saw him, and refused even to confirm the basic facts they both knew, let alone tried to think of any details he had remembered since.

'He's even more of an arsehole than before,' she muttered. She kept quiet about her angry tears as she had stormed out of the station.

'Sounds like it.'

Jo stared at her food, wondering how to broach the rest of what she needed to say.

Undine groaned. 'There's more, isn't there?'

'I found a note in Ray's files. Someone still had to talk to Mrs Wyndham's builders, the Doyle brothers, so I went to Tooting, thought I could interview them myself. They weren't there, though. The office was closed.'

Again, she waited for Undine to berate her. He said nothing. Was he listening? 'But there was a car repair place next door. I asked in there if they knew where I might find them.'

The mechanic she'd chatted to had been young – not yet 18, she guessed – and awkward, with grease stains on his face like those of a boy playing at Red Indians. According to him, the Doyles had gone away – to where and for how long, he didn't know – and he joked that the Micks had probably botched another job and were hiding out until the fuss blew over. Jo gave him a fake laugh and the Institute's telephone number, and asked him to call her when they reappeared. Her assurance that they were in no trouble allayed most of his suspicions, and a suggestive smile did the rest, and although she hated leading the blushing youngster on, she was pretty sure it worked. 'I reckon he'll phone back when he sees them.'

Undine mopped up the last of his food and chewed on the bread. His dark eyes looked inward.

'That's everything.' Jo slid her empty plate away and sat back in her chair. 'And that was delicious. I mean it. You really didn't need to go to so much effort.'

'The meat needed using. I was going to cook it the other evening, but-' A shadow crossed Undine's face. He patted his jacket. 'Anyway, I like to cook. Helps me think.'

He pulled out his Embassies and lit one. Jo shook her head at the proffered packet but helped herself to more wine.

'Think about what?'

Undine breathed out smoke. Then he reached behind him to where his trench coat lay on the bed, and from one of its inside pockets he produced a rolled-up magazine, which he handed to her without comment.

It was not a proper magazine, she saw now, but more of an amateur publication. The cover illustration featured a maze.

Her eyes widened. 'Oh, my God.'

'Yeah,' said Undine. 'It's the same.'

She glanced up, and he was holding the lump

of black stone she had found at Lavender Edge. He placed it on the table in front of her, and she looked from the stone, to the illustration, and back again. Undine was right. The pattern matched precisely.

'This is from your shopkeeper?' she asked, meaning the amateur magazine. 'He knew about this?'

'Oh, Mr Oldroyd had quite a bit to say, as it happens.' Undine tapped ash onto the edge of his plate. 'Among other things, he said that when you took this stone out you managed to make things in Mrs Wyndham's house about a million times worse.'

The statement punched into the pit of Jo's stomach. So it *was* her fault! Ray. Archie. *Her fault*.

Her head throbbed with guilt, drowning out Undine's next words: '... that I shouldn't blame you ... influences people ... affected the builders ...'

He indicated the stone squatting between them on the table.

'He reckons it compelled you to take that out.'

What was that? Was he saying she wasn't to blame after all?

Relief flooded her, but immediately came up against a torrent of questions. Competing currents of emotions and thoughts swirled and roared in a maelstrom of confusion.

'Not so fast,' she said. 'Give me a moment

here.' She lifted her glass, more to give herself breathing space than because she wanted any more wine. 'Tell me everything, but slowly.'

He did, and Jo did her best to take in the details. He told her how the maze-patterned stone was supposedly the key component in a structure called the Weall, which was some ancient barrier against what Oldroyd described as 'The Outside'. Whether that expression referred to some sort of entity or a force or something else entirely was unclear. She got the impression Undine didn't really know either.

What she did grasp was that the stone – or 'node' – was meant to control how the barrier channelled and dissipated a kind of energy that built up at sites like Lavender Edge. It reminded her of Archie and all his talk about ghoul zones. Her mind whirled. She wanted to believe what Oldroyd had told Undine, not only because she needed to understand what had happened and to know there might be a way to make things right, but also because his story absolved her of responsibility for the part she had played.

Several seconds passed before she realized Undine was no longer talking.

'And Ray and Archie?' she asked. 'What did your shopkeeper say about them?'

'He confirmed what I thought. They're not dead.'

Undine's tone held a strange edge of defiance. It put her on alert. Something more was going on, something Undine had yet to tell her.

'That's good, isn't it? And what about the other faces?'

Again, Undine summarized what Oldroyd had said – that stories about the haunting of Lavender Edge always involved faces. Even from the years before the present house existed, there were accounts of faces appearing at the site, in the arrangement of leaves on a tree, in the ripples on the surface of water, in the dust....

'Some of the older tales called them "The Devil's Faces",' said Undine. 'Nothing to do with the Devil though. They're the essences of people who died there, trapped in the energy currents.' He took a deep, troubled drag on his Embassy.

'They're alive,' he said. 'I felt that too, when we were at the house. This thing is using them. It tortures them to feed off their pain. And apparently it sometimes likes to wear their faces as a mask because that scares the shit out of people, so it can feed off their fear too. It's a fucking monster.'

He ground his cigarette into the ashtray, and blasted smoke from his mouth.

Jo leaned in and spoke quietly. 'Did he say what we can do?'

'He did.' Undine sounded bitter. 'In fact, he was quite insistent.' He nodded at the stone. ' We need to put that back where you found it.'

That seemed simple enough. Not that she looked forward to going back into that house.

'Okay,' she said, drawing the word out.

Undine reached for his packet of cigarettes again. 'But it has to go back in exactly the same position it was in or it'll just make matters worse. So, as long as you can remember which direction that pointed when you found it' – he jabbed his cigarette packet towards the bottom of the carved pattern, where the maze's single entrance opened out – 'everything will be just groovy again.'

Jo bit her tongue, stung by his sarcasm. Of course she didn't know the direction. She appreciated that Undine was hurting, but taking it out on her was not going to help.

Undine lit yet another Embassy.

She had an idea. She opened her handbag. 'I bought these with me.'

At Peel House, one of her instructors had liked to emphasize the usefulness of visualizing problems. That was why she had brought these away with her from the Warehouse, to bring along tonight. She unwrapped the parcel of photographs – the images taken by Ray during their first visit to the house – and began to spread them across the table.

Undine watched, then grunted and took their dirty plates to the sink to give her more room.

'There,' said Jo as he returned to stand beside her. She pointed at two of the photos.

Like the other images, they were fogged, but

they were the clearest views they had of the hole in the bedroom wall. In the second, the wooden pillar that had held the stone was just about visible in the shadows, and towards the top she could make out a darker blob in the wood.

'That must be it.' Jo lowered her face and squinted, hoping she would be able to see the orientation of the maze pattern. 'I can't make it out. You got a magnifying glass anywhere?'

Undine found one. He used it to look at the image himself.

'It's too blurred.' He swung away in disgust.

Jo took the glass from him and examined the photo for herself, but he was right. The fogging effect that spoiled the pictures was most pronounced over the stone itself, and the image gave nowhere near enough detail.

'What about the surrounding wall?' asked Undine.

'What about it?'

'Something Oldroyd suggested. He thought the energy might have left marks on the wall, that there might be some change in the bricks or plaster around where the maze opening went. I don't know, a scorch mark maybe. See anything?'

Jo looked, but she knew what the answer would be. 'Anything like that would have been in a part of the wall that's already been knocked down.'

She held the magnifying glass out to Undine so he could see for himself. He didn't bother taking it. She wondered briefly about the other idea she'd had this morning, but that now seemed even dafter than it had then, and she dismissed it. Undine stared at the photos, his mouth a thin, grim line.

'What about the Doyles?' asked Jo. 'They must have been surprised to discover this stone inside the wall. They might remember which way up it went.'

She knew she was clutching at straws, but Undine nodded.

'Good idea.' The emptiness of his voice was not convincing.

'Right,' said Jo uncertainly. 'Well, it's a little late now. Want to head there first thing tomorrow?'

Undine shook his head. 'You go on your own.'

He looked again at the photographs of the hole in Lavender Edge. 'I'm going back there.'

CHAPTER 22

'Don't be ridiculous,' said Jo, horrified.

Undine stood where he was. Smoke curled up and around him, and silence filled the bedsit. At some point, the Sinatra LP had come to an end, unnoticed.

'It's too dangerous,' she protested. 'At least wait until after we've spoken to the Doyles. Then we can go back to the house together. We'll work out how to put the stone in, and then we can figure out how we're going to get your friends back.'

'I'm not going to put the stone back in,' said Undine. 'Not yet.'

He tore his gaze from the photographs and turned to Jo with anguish in his eyes. 'Nobody's going to do anything to repair Oldroyd's pissing "Weall" before Ray and Archie are back from wherever the hell they are. Don't you get it? Once that barrier is fixed, that's it. They'll never be able to get back. They'll be cut off from us forever.'

So that was what had been preying on Undine's mind all evening.

'But after last time,' she said. 'You could have died!'

'I'm not going to leave them in there.'

That wasn't what she had meant. Desperately, she tried to think of alternatives.

'What about Oldroyd? Can't he help?'

Undine sneered. 'He's not interested in them. All he cares about is getting the Weall sealed as quickly as possible. He's likely to try himself if I don't do it, or else he'll find some other idiot to do his dirty work for him.' He blew smoke into the air.

'Look,' said Jo. 'I get why you want to do this. I want to help them too. Jesus, Undine, you have no idea how bad I feel about this! But if you go storming in, you're just going to get hurt. Or worse. What are you planning on doing there anyway?'

She had his attention. 'You've no clue. Have you?'

'I'm open to suggestions, love.'

But her mind was numb. Nothing in there other than the stupid idea she thought she had rejected a few moments ago.

'Exactly,' said Undine.

Stupid, but what did she have to lose?

'There might be somebody else we can ask,' she blurted out.

Undine looked puzzled. 'Who?'

'Mrs Wyndham's husband.'

Undine stared at her. 'Ronald Wyndham? As in the *late* Ronald Wyndham?'

'Why not? We saw The Outside wear his face. That means part of him is still in the house. You said so yourself.'

Undine's bemused expression shaded to amused sarcasm. Gradually, that too softened.

'It came to me this morning,' said Jo, 'while I was looking through his family history stuff. Not that there was much left of that. Nothing helpful. But if anybody knew about Lavender Edge and all its secrets, Ronald Wyndham did. So, it occurred to me: what if we were able to contact him? Like a séance or something. That's the right word, isn't it?'

Undine made a sound that might have indicated agreement.

'This morning,' she continued, 'I couldn't decide what questions we should try asking him. But maybe he knew about this stone. Or maybe one of his ancestors came across it at some point....'

She had been going to say something else, but doubts were creeping in, and she was losing the thread. She pressed on. 'If so, then he'd surely have kept a record of it. A description of the maze, made when the stone was in place. Okay, we don't have his description anymore, but if we could ask him....'

There were so many ifs in what she heard

herself suggesting: *if* they could hold a séance in the house, and *if* they could contact Ronald, and *if* he could respond, and *if* he knew what they needed. And even if the living Ronald had ever known, would what remained of him remember?

And if they tried this, how would the Outside react?

Undine's face hardened again. He shook his head. 'Wouldn't work, and even if it did, it still wouldn't help Ray and Archie.'

Jo found her thread again. 'Well, what if we didn't try contacting Mr Wyndham? What if, instead, we attempt to contact your friends? If we reach out to them, maybe *they* can help us find a way to get them back.'

Undine looked thoughtful.

'I still say we should try the Doyles first,' said Jo, 'but –'

'No,' said Undine. 'I told you, I'm not putting that stone back yet.'

'Then let's try this. At least it's not a direct confrontation with that thing.'

It still meant going back to Lavender Edge, though. Jo realized her legs were shaking, and was glad she was sitting down so Undine couldn't see that. The thought of going back to that house filled her with dread. She could only imagine how much more vulnerable Undine felt.

* * *

Undine sat slumped on his bed. As determined as his words had been, he appeared broken, as if the mere prospect of exposing himself again to the power in that house had already defeated him. Jo wished there was some way she could help him.

'Haven't you ever found any way of protecting yourself?' she asked, looking around Undine's bedsit as if a previously unnoticed suit of armour might be standing nearby.

'Apart from never leaving this room?'

She ignored the bitterness. He was scared.

'Well, what about Mr Oldroyd? He's so keen for you to go back to the house. Didn't he give you any advice about how to keep safe when you got there?'

'He must have forgotten that bit,' said Undine.

She looked at his books, stacked nearby on the floor. Undine's small personal library on the supernatural and the occult, with his new 'Shamanism Around the World' sitting on top.

'Why did Oldroyd tell you to get that particular book?'

'He didn't tell me to get it. We were talking. He wanted to know if I knew what a shaman was. That's all.'

'And that was enough for you to order a book on the subject?'

'It was the way he said it.' Undine frowned. 'Okay, yeah, I did wonder whether he might be trying to tell me something. That, perhaps, if I worked out how a shaman uses his powers....'

'Maybe he was onto something?'

'He wasn't.'

'How can you be so sure? You haven't even looked at it yet.'

Undine spat his reply out. 'Because I tried it before. It nearly bloody killed me, alright?'

Jo opened her mouth, then shut it again.

Undine puffed on his cigarette. 'Something similar anyway. On Saturday, when we all went back to the house. Just before Sunny and Archie....'

His skin was pale. Sweat dappled his forehead.

Jo passed him his glass of wine. He drained the contents.

'I'd just read a bit about shamans,' he said, 'in one of those books.' He put down the glass and rubbed his forehead. 'I was thinking about that, while we were up in that bedroom. And then I started to feel something, like there was another presence in there with us, messing with my thoughts, trying to get inside my head.'

'What happened?'

'I don't remember the details. Basically, though, I panicked. I think I got this stupid idea that what I needed to do was let go, to fight that thing's fire with my own. That if some witchdoctor was strong enough to do this stuff then so was I.'

Undine studied the carpet. His next words

were barely audible. 'I wasn't.'

Jo's own memories of Saturday evening were fragmentary, chaotic, dominated by the appearance of that face in the wall and then by the screams from Archie and Ray as she rushed back into the house. It had been horrible, yet mild compared to what Undine must have been through.

'Maybe you could learn,' she said.

She felt the feathery brush of a memory. 'What about Archie's journal? Didn't he write something about training you to handle your, you know?'

'He was thinking of something else.'

'But perhaps he –'

'See for yourself.'

Undine reached again to his trench coat and this time took out a slim notebook. Jo recognized it as the one she had given him this morning, and suppressed her surprise that he had kept it with him. He hadn't seemed interested before.

'Don't look so pleased. It wasn't any help,' said Undine.

He had bookmarked a page. She opened it and found the same entry she had persuaded him to read.

'It's from our investigation at the Pyramus,' said Undine.

'I don't –'

'The first time you came to meet us, when you had to wait outside the Warehouse, that's where we'd been: the Pyramus theatre.'

'Right.' Jo re-read Archie's jotted note: his suggestion that it might be possible to train Undine to mitigate his 'intense emotional response' by employing a technique called flooding, by 'combining relaxation exercises with exposure to stimulus under relatively controlled conditions'.

'Flooding,' she said. 'I hadn't heard of that before I read this.'

'Nor had I. I looked it up.' Undine pulled himself from the bed and crossed to his book collection. He took a hardback from the pile. One of the pages was folded down at the corner, and he opened the book there before handing it to her.

It was a dictionary of terms used in psychology. Flooding, she read, was a psychological concept beginning to arouse interest. The research was recent, dating only from the last few years, but in essence the idea maintained that a person could be trained to manage their fears through controlled exposure to whatever frightened them.

So what? It seemed to be just a clever way of saying you grow less scared of something when you know you can cope with it. Jo thought about the first time she'd had to place a stranger under arrest; a daunting prospect to begin with but with somebody to support her she had learned she was capable of handling the situation. Once you stripped away the fancy terms, the idea seemed pretty obvious.

She suspected there was more depth to it, though. Plus, Archie had clearly seen potential in this approach....

'Told you,' said Undine. 'Fat lot of use.'

Then it clicked.

'They're talking about the same thing,' she said.

It was Undine's turn to look blank.

Jo pushed her chair back a few inches until she could reach down to the pile. She picked up his new book and when she opened it the pages fell open at the half-page, black-and-white drawing she had seen earlier. She skimmed the text, and as she refreshed her memory, a small knot of excitement grew in her chest.

'Listen to this. It says here that "It is necessary for the shaman to 'die' in this way in order to understand 'death', to experience sickness in order to overcome sickness, and ultimately to return in his more powerful, reborn form as the Wounded Healer, holder of the cure that will heal all who suffer."'

She turned to him. 'You see the connection?'

'Sounds like hippy bollocks.'

'They're saying the same thing! This author and Archie. It's like the two of them are writing in different languages when really they're discussing the same type of experience.'

She showed the page to Undine. 'Your

shopkeeper was trying to tell you the same as Archie. Just from a different perspective.'

'But he doesn't know about me.'

'Maybe he heard about what happened to you at Mrs Wyndham's. Or maybe you've got some kind of aura or something he can see. From the way you describe him, it seems like he's into all this occult stuff.'

She shoved the book under Undine's nose, leaving him little choice but to stare at the drawing of the shaman wearing his feathered headdress and brandishing his round drum.

Undine's features twisted in cynicism.

'Think about it,' Jo encouraged. 'What if you tried again to do what you were just saying, except in more controlled circumstances? Not at the house. Somewhere safer, with someone with you to support you. You might be able to learn how to control your ability.'

Undine looked far from enthusiastic. She understood his reluctance, recalling how he had described the pain of coming into contact with one of those 'ghoul zones', but, for Christ's sake, how long had he been searching for an idea like this?

'I'm not wearing bloody feathers,' said Undine.

Jo smiled. 'I don't think anyone wants to see that.'

Undine drew on the remains of his cigarette then stubbed it out. His fingers were shaking.

'We'll need the right location,' said Jo. She had an inkling of a suitable venue but wanted the idea to come from Undine. She tried to convince herself that she wasn't simply protecting her conscience in case things went awry. 'Somewhere else we know has that "ghoul" energy.'

'The theatre,' said Undine.

He glanced at his wristwatch. Jo thought of Ray and Archie, trapped in an unimaginable nightmare, enduring unthinkable torment every second that ticked by.

She touched Undine's shoulder. 'I know,' she told him. 'We're going to help them. And then we're going to stop this thing from hurting anyone else. But, like I said, your charging in there on some suicide mission won't do that. We'll go back to the house as soon as we can, but not until you're ready.'

At last, Undine gave the slightest of nods.

Weariness, and the effects of all the wine, washed over Jo.

'It's late,' she said. 'Get some rest. First thing in the morning, we'll 'phone the theatre, okay? You're already investigating the place, so just tell them we need to go back to finish what you were doing. They don't have to know what's really going to happen.'

CHAPTER 23

The plastic earpiece burned his ear. His head throbbed and his eyes watered, and still the ringing on the other end of the line went unanswered. Undine threw the receiver into its cradle and pushed his chair away as he stood. It crashed into the wall of Archie's office. For the hundredth time, he checked his watch: gone ten already. What time of the bloody morning did they start work at that pissing theatre anyway?

He needed to keep busy. He stomped down the stairs to the ground floor and surveyed the mess of stacked documents. By his foot was a broken oscilloscope, currently serving as a paperweight. He bent down to pick it up, shook it, and heard the rattle of destroyed electronics. A thin lead trailed from the rear casing, dangling onto the concrete below: once a vital connecting plug into Archie's Octopus machine and now about as much use as cold spaghetti.

At least the oscilloscope's screen was intact.

Undine carried the gadget upstairs, where he added it to the few other items he had found that still looked as if they might function. They would be needed later: set dressing to fool the theatre manager.

He tried the phone again. Still no answer.

A couple of Anadin went down with a mouthful of last night's warm, leftover wine. Hair of the dog. He re-screwed the cap on his hip flask, scraped his tongue against his teeth in an attempt to remove the foul taste, and wasted a few more minutes running an electric shaver over his stubble. It did little to help his appearance but a lot to tighten the throbbing in his head.

Which was nothing compared to the pain Sunny and Archie were suffering right now.

His stomach gurgled, and he passed another ten minutes on the toilet. When he emerged, he was glad to see Jo had not yet arrived. Hopefully she wouldn't need the khazi when she did, not for an hour or two.

The shaver went back into his desk drawer. After checking his watch again, Undine walked back to Archie's office and redialled the number. The rings at the other end were harsh, distant, endless – the sound enfolding his sludgy thoughts, soothing them with the lure of sleep. Worry had kept him awake most of the night, and as he listened his eyelids slowly succumbed to the pull of gravity: drooping, closing, locking.... He daydreamed about his packet of Embassies. His headache blanketed his brain like sandpaper. Did he dare risk a cigarette yet, or would that –

'Yeah? What is it?'

Undine drew a sharp breath. 'Uh, good morning.' He cleared his throat, blinking himself into a semblance of alertness. 'I was hoping to speak to Mr ... um....'

What was the bloke's surname? Come to think of it, what the hell was his first name? Bob? Bill? His hair had been greasy, in need of cutting.... 'To Robert. He's the manager.'

'Yeah, I know what my job is, ta very much. Who's this?'

'I'm, erm, calling from the Corsi Institute,' said Undine, realizing too late that he had somehow frittered away half the morning without planning what to say. Archie had always handled these conversations. 'We met last week. We were conducting an investigation – a scientific investigation, that is, of –'

'You're one of those ghost hunters, yeah?'

'That's right,' said Undine. Archie would probably raise a gentle objection to that description, but Undine doubted he could do that himself without starting an argument.

'So what do you want?'

'Well, our results from the other night were interesting, it turns out. Very interesting. We're going to need to conduct a follow-up investigation. As soon as possible. It should only take an hour or two.'

'Yeah, see, I don't know about that.'

'It really wouldn't take long,' said Undine. He had a flash of inspiration. 'And it'll be great publicity for you when we tell the Press what we've found. Sort of story the nationals love.'

'Yeah? Right, well, I suppose we could arrange something. Just give us a moment, yeah?'

Undine heard the rustling of paper down the line.

Robert came back. 'Okay, well, we're swamped for the next few days. Auditioning new acts, you know. How about next Monday?'

That was nearly a week away!

'That's a bit late. I was hoping we could do this tonight, after you close. We wouldn't need long. You won't even know we're there. It's just that these phenomena tend to be transitory, you see, and –'

'You're one of the ones was here last week, aintcha?'

'That's right.'

'Yeah.'

A certain tone had crept into Robert's voice. Undine did not like it.

'Yeah,' Robert repeated. 'I remember you now. You're the one told me to sit on the bog in case I shat meself. Then you went and threw up all over the place.'

Undine had a horrible feeling he was losing what control he had of the conversation.

'Yeah,' continued Robert, 'I think I'd prefer to deal with your boss. The Scottish gentleman. He there?'

'He's, um, on another assignment right now.'

'Well, why don't you ask him to call me when he gets back, yeah?'

A new voice came over the line, in the background. Female, young, seductive. She spoke Robert's name.

'Professor James might be a while,' said Undine. 'If tonight is inconvenient, maybe we could arrange something for tomorrow?'

'Yeah. No, I'll sort it with your boss, thanks. Now if you don't mind, I have work to be getting on with.'

And, with that, the phone line went dead.

Undine closed his eyes, seeing Ray's and Archie's faces in the wallpaper, screaming in silence. Frustration surged in him like lava.

'Bollocks!'

He slammed the receiver and sent the phone skidding across the desk.

'Good news, I take it?'

Jo was standing in the doorway, looking pale and red-eyed. 'Jesus, Undine. It stinks in here. And you look like hell. Was that the theatre?'

Undine nodded.

'And?'

'And their manager is a twat. Says he'll only

talk to Archie, and in any case the earliest time we could go back is next week.'

'We can't wait that long!' She ran a hand through her shaggy blonde hair. 'Okay. So what's the plan?'

Undine's head pounded. The painkillers were having no effect.

'It's Tuesday today, isn't it?' asked Jo.

'So?'

'Do they do a Tuesday matinee?'

'How the hell do I know what they do on a Tuesday? Why?'

'Well, if they have a performance this afternoon, we could buy a pair of tickets and sneak away during the play. You know your way around the building, don't you? How to get to the area you need?'

Under different circumstances, Undine might have laughed. 'I don't think this is quite the sort of theatre you're thinking of.'

Jo gave him a quizzical look.

'It's more of a, let's say, private members' club.'

'Private members?' Jo stared at him for a second. He watched the penny roll into position, getting ready to drop.

'Where did you say this place was?' she asked.

'Soho.'

'Oh, for God's sake!'

'Still fancy sneaking off to the toilets? I'm sure none of the punters will follow you inside,

310

and your old mates in blue will be perfectly understanding if anyone catches us.'

'So we do it a different way. We could go there tonight, after it shuts, try to bribe our way in maybe....'

'Forget it.' Undine got to his feet, grabbed his trench coat, and strode past her, out into the corridor.

'Where are we going?'

He pulled out his cigarettes and jabbed one into his mouth. Lighting it would aggravate his pounding head, but its mere presence gave a measure of comfort.

Jo hurried down the stairs behind him. 'What's the hurry? Where are we off to?'

'Where I should have gone to begin with,' said Undine. 'I know you meant well, love, but we've wasted too much time already.'

His boots rattled the final few steps, and then he was striding across the open concrete floor.

'I'm going after Sunny and Archie,' he said. 'You don't have to come with me.'

CHAPTER 24

The high wall and hedge threw long shadows as Undine stepped through the gate. Darkness enveloped him, accompanied by a deepening of the hush that filled the street. Surely it wasn't usually this quiet in Mitcham at two o'clock on a Tuesday afternoon? They had arrived to find an air of desolation hanging over Rivermead Path, broken only by the faint sigh of traffic from the main road, and here in the front garden of Lavender Edge they were screened from even that slim lifeline to the everyday world. Undine pulled up his collar against the damp chill and lifted his gaze towards the crumbling brick wall. The house's great windows threw back nothing save reflections of gloomy October sky.

Behind him, leather creaked as Jo crept closer.

'You sure you're ready for this?' she whispered.

Undine squared his shoulders and gave a curt

nod.

They approached the portico and the concrete step that led up to the front door. Gravel crunched beneath his boots like crushed bone. He forced the sound from his thoughts, concentrating on the shutters on his mind, making sure they were tight.

Without warning, his stomach growled. The stillness seemed to magnify the liquid grumble, and Undine froze, half-expecting the house to react. Half-digested chunks of fatty steak-and-kidney pie rearranged themselves with a thin gurgle, and he swallowed a queasiness that had little to do with the questionable café food Jo had insisted they stop to eat along the way.

'Stealthy,' she muttered. Then, with a harsher hiss: 'Damn it.'

'What?'

'The lock.'

For a moment, Undine did not understand. Then he saw shining silver against the ancient wooden door: somebody had fitted a brand-new lock. He tried Mrs Wyndham's key anyway, but of course it didn't work.

'You don't think she's sold the house already, do you?' asked Jo.

Undine didn't bother to reply. They both knew he had no idea.

He pushed the door, just in case, but it was every bit as closed as it looked. He pressed his hands to the wood, wondering how he could force it open. If they had brought the lorry instead of his car, they would probably have found a crowbar stowed away in the back, but manhandling that beast through the streets would have been too much for him; his pounding head was only now beginning to respond to all the Anadin. He looked around the garden, breathing in the scents of wet earth and decaying leaves and trying not to broadcast stray thoughts.

'Can you see any heavy logs?' he asked.

'You're an idiot.' Jo swept past him. 'And you'd make a terrible burglar.'

She ran her fingers along the base of the nearest window. 'Your first lesson in crime. Burglars exploit weakness. Also, being sneaky buggers, they prefer not to take a battering ram to the front door.'

As she moved to the second window, her self-assured expression faltered, and Undine glimpsed the fear she was covering. Back at the Warehouse, she'd made it clear she considered this a mistake. Even so, she had refused to let him come alone.

She checked the remaining windows to the left of the door, then moved on to the right, swearing under her breath as each frame resisted her explorations. Then she reached the end of the wall – and vanished.

Undine hurried after her. He rounded a corner and found her examining a short stretch of wooden fence that ran from the side of the house to the garden wall.

'Bingo,' she said.

He saw that she was standing by a door in the fence, presumably a way through to the back garden, but he could see no keyhole or even a handle, and there seemed no way to open it from this side.

'Give us a leg up,' said Jo.

Except for that.

He cupped his hands, and Jo placed one booted foot in them, reaching up to the top of the fence as he boosted her. She was lighter than expected, and more agile, and was over in moments. A latch lifted with a thunk, and the door swung open. Jo beckoned him through, closing the door again behind him.

'So this is what they teach you in the police, is it?' he asked.

If she replied, he did not notice, distracted by the sudden stab of painful memories. He recognized this garden. He had fled here on Saturday evening. He almost heard again the screams crackling from his walkie-talkie, the hideous screams of Sunny and Archie, and his chest lurched as he realized that his hold had slipped: his mind had opened, and he was plunging into the psychic imprint of his own terror!

But it was a false alarm. They weren't that sort of echo. Only his own recollections.

Heart racing, Undine let Jo go forward to study first the conservatory door and then the windows along the house's back wall. Renewed dread fluttered inside him, almost claiming him, and for those few seconds he would have given anything for her to turn to him in defeat and say they would have to give up.

The moment passed. Bollocks to that. On Saturday, he had been too late to help his friends. He would not let them down again.

Jo made her way back to the conservatory door.

'No luck?'

She shook her head. 'Not yet. But this one isn't much of a lock.' She looked over her shoulder, making sure the tall trees hid them both from the neighbouring houses. 'You didn't see this, okay?'

From somewhere, she produced a small leather packet. It looked like a purse at first, but when she unzipped it and opened padded compartments, Undine saw an assortment of curiously angled metal tools.

'A souvenir,' she said, 'before you ask. You never know when it will come in handy.'

She peered at the lock, selected two of the tools, and set to work picking the mechanism. After what could have been seconds or endless minutes, Undine heard a metallic click, and Jo opened the door half an inch.

'No sign of an alarm.' She slipped into the dim

interior.

Undine took a deep breath and followed.

*　　*　　*

The air inside hung heavy and thick. Something was different from last time. Undine passed through the small conservatory and stepped nervously into the more familiar surroundings of the drawing room. Only then did he understand what had changed: he could hear no ticking from the grandfather clock out in the hallway. It was as if the house's heart had stopped beating.

'It must have run down,' whispered Jo.

Undine murmured agreement, trying not to envisage other possibilities. He needed to keep his attention focused, to keep the outer shell of his awareness hard and closed until the time came.

Jo let out a shaky breath. 'I can almost feel it myself. It's like there's something in here with us. Watching.'

'Don't let your imagination run away with you.'

He hoped that was all it was. He sensed no sign yet that The Outside was aware of their intrusion, but how could he be certain?

Jo took a step deeper inside. 'At least we don't have that stone with us.'

They had argued over whether to bring the

317

node with them. Jo worried that carrying it into the house would be like walking into a thunderstorm brandishing a metal pole, whereas Undine's gut told him that any potential weapon was better than none. In the end, however, he'd had to admit that what she said made sense, and in any case leaving it behind would remove any temptation for her to try replacing it before Sunny and Archie were safe again. So the heavy lump of carved stone was back at the Warehouse, locked away inside one of the drawers in Undine's desk.

Motes swarmed in the grey light, stirred up by their entrance. Less than three days ago, they had all been in this house together, yet it felt like the place had been abandoned for years. Scorched dust lingered on the air, and Undine coughed to clear his suddenly dry throat.

'I've just thought,' said Jo. 'Shouldn't we have brought one of those thingy boards with us?'

'A Ouija board?' He should have thought of that himself. Both Ray and Archie agreed that the boards could on occasion be useful, although they had come to that conclusion via different routes. Archie always hoped the communications came from spirits, while Sunny believed they originated in the subconscious. Whoever was right, the team usually kept a board handy in the back of the lorry, although – like the crowbar – that was a fat lot of good right now.

On the other hand, Ouija boards did have a bad reputation. Their critics claimed the boards attracted evil entities, so maybe it was for the best.

He tried to sound confident. 'We don't need one.'

'Well, you're the expert.' Jo moistened her lips. 'Where do you want to do this?'

She glanced at the ceiling, towards the upstairs room and that hole.

Undine shook his head. 'Let's not get any closer than we have to. How about here? We know there's been activity in this room.'

Jo's eyes flicked to the corner where, under hypnosis, she had described seeing an antique table move by itself. No table there now. Undine started to wonder what had happened to it, whether Mrs Wyndham had arranged for its removal, but he caught himself.

Stay focused....

Jo nodded slowly. 'Okay. But, for the record, I still think this is a bad idea.'

❊　❊　❊

Undine pulled the sofa up to the rear bay window. Sitting by the glass kept them away from the walls, as well as a little nearer to their escape route back out through the conservatory. As added insurance that they would be able to beat a hasty retreat, Jo wedged the back door open with a cushion.

They sat together on the sofa. Undine closed his eyes and tried to control his breathing, calming the rapid pounding of his heart. It seemed to take forever. He sucked in another long, deep breath, counting to seven before letting it out even more slowly. Gradually, his body settled.

Doubt flickered, playing around the edges of his thoughts. He gave it no time to crystallize. He relaxed his hold on his mind, allowing those thoughts to open, and as he sank into the calm warmth his awareness expanded.

It came to him almost at once, with a nauseating roll like sea-sickness. It was everywhere: the weight of despair and hopeless resentment he had been locking out. Its corrosive touch ebbed from the substance of this building, pulsing in waves.

He recoiled, but remained under, placing his faith in Jo. Anchored to the knowledge of her presence beside him, he waited for his conscious acceptance of their physical forms to haze away once more, and when that happened he made himself sink deeper and further, just as he had practised in secret before, in the Soho theatre, and on earlier investigations where he had known Archie and Sunny would help him if needed. Would he be able to find them now?

The pressure of trapped emotion rose around him, blackness closing in with sharp intensity as it jabbed through the now-unprotected walls of his psyche. Great swipes of soundless screaming buffeted him as he groped through the darkness, searching for anything that felt like friendship.

Something moved nearby. He detected the wake of an immense alien quality, and braced for what was there to coil back around and strike at him – but no attack came. Instead, a wash of soothing female words reminded him he was not alone. He gathered himself, and pushed out, reaching further than he had ever risked before.

After an age, he came to a place where immaterial essence boiled into flames, and imprisoned pain solidified and licked at him. As if in a dream, he shifted his awareness until he was somewhere else, somewhere where faraway fragments of memory rose and fell like voices on a breeze. From a direction impossible to classify, Undine at last sensed a soft tug of sympathetic attraction.

This was something new: a whispering lamentation that murmured with the familiarity of friendship. It was close: the barrier between it and Undine so thin it barely existed, the sheerest veil all that was keeping them separate. Was this it? Contact? Anxiety rippled through him. He cast around for the gentle current of Jo's reassurance, found it again, and drew it in like the purest mountain stream. This was the moment of decision.

Undine let go of his fear and allowed his final

veneer of resistance to slip away…

… and a hurricane of fire blew into his mind.

Flames shrieked through his brain, searing synapses and blasting away his self-identity. The savage violence poured in and in and in, and Undine cried out in agony as Jo's words disappeared into the roar and time became nothing but eternal pain.

* * *

Jo gasped as Undine's body clenched. She reached a tentative hand towards him, puzzled by his face, which remained as calm and expressionless as a sleeper's, then hesitated as his head slumped forward. His breathing stayed deep and regular, but she was alarmed to see beads of sweat on his forehead.

'It's okay,' she said, struggling to keep tension from her voice. She was supposed to be helping him to relax, but how was she meant to do that? She thought of the way Archie had spoken while guiding her into a hypnotic trance, and she tried to recall his words from the tape recording.

'Just breathe, Undine. Feel sunlight and peace spread through you, all the way out to your fingers and toes. Your muscles are relaxing.'

Undine's arm spasmed.

'It's okay. I'm here for you.'

Was he even able to hear her? Was she doing this right? And why the hell hadn't they discussed this in more detail before starting?

But how could they have prepared with no idea what to expect?

'You're safe,' she said, knowing it was a lie. Neither of them were safe here.

Her attention snagged on a glow in her peripheral vision. Her head turned before the fear of what she might see could stop her.

An area of the wallpaper was pulsing with interior light. Within the glow, the pattern's floral designs were losing distinction. Edges blurred, shifting and coalescing. Eyes and mouths formed and melted and reformed, swimming in and out of existence.

Undine's body loosened.

'It's working.' She spoke in little more than a breath, afraid the sound might disrupt what was happening. Undine looked unconscious. For a dreadful instant, Jo was convinced he had stopped breathing, but his chest continued to rise and fall, slow and deep. 'You're doing it,' she told him.

On the wall, eyes dissolved, and features re-knitted into an arrangement she began to recognize. A skinny face, a big nose....

'Oh God. Undine, I can see Ray.'

There was no doubt. The image showed Undine's mate. Except, as she watched, those welcome features trembled and changed, the face becoming that of an older man, with the memory of a pipe stem clenched between his teeth. Eyes, although sketched in nothing but dark blurs, conveyed an abyss of yawning horror.

'Archie?' Jo spoke directly to the apparition. 'Can you hear me?'

In hideous silence, Professor Archie James's image faded back into the swirling shapes. His eyes, so full of doom, were the final elements to go.

On the sofa, Undine moaned.

'Don't lose them now,' said Jo.

Undine exhaled, long and deep, and the lines in the wallpaper re-established themselves as Ray's features, clearer and more fully realized than before. But again it was the eyes that transfixed her. They were wrong. Jo remembered them as warm with humour, not creased in pain like these. They stared around the room without comprehension until they fixed on her. His mouth opened. His lips moved with inaudible pleas.

Then his image was melting.

'Hold on to him!' shouted Jo, forgetting she was meant to keep Undine calm.

Undine's head lolled from side to side. His dark hair was soaking wet.

Jo watched, helpless, as Ray sank from view, subsumed into the glow until all that was left was a boiling soup of shadows on the wall. Was that it? Was he gone for good? She wanted to reach out to where his image had been, to somehow grab hold of the young man and pull him back to the world, but that was impossible. She stared, aching with the loss of someone she had hardly known, as restless forms coiled and writhed before her.

The motion did not remain random for long. A new energy began to assert itself, pulling the patterns into its own arrangement.

The apparition forming in front of her was larger than the others had been.

The third face emerged, and Jo's stomach twisted. She had seen this image before, this man with a full moustache that bristled below a strong aquiline nose. Last time, however, he had not been in such distress. The face flickered and stuttered, but its mouth remained, open in an endless, silent scream.

It wasn't Ray, and it wasn't Archie, but Jo knew who this was. Undine had rejected her idea to try to contact him, but somehow, uncalled for, he was here now, offering them an opportunity.

'Undine, it's Ronald Wyndham! He's here. I can see him! Ask him!'

A tremor ran through Undine's body. His head snapped left, then right. Spittle bubbled from the corner of his mouth.

Ronald's face blurred.

'Don't lose him!

The features sharpened once more.

Undine's breaths quickened.

Jo felt light-headed: elated yet terrified at the same time. This was too dangerous! Undine should have listened to her. They should have waited for their chance to visit the theatre, to rehearse under those 'relatively controlled conditions' specified by Archie in his notebook.

They had rushed into this, and any control she'd once had was slipping through her fingers.

'You're doing well,' she lied, fighting the tightness that choked her voice. 'Ask him if he remembers the stone. The maze. Does he remember what it looked like? Where the opening pointed?'

Undine's breath came in ragged gasps.

Ronald Wyndham's features solidified, and Jo's skin crawled. The apparition's pain-filled eyes sought her own. Its lips dragged away from their scream and strained to shape words.

'It's okay,' she said, speaking more to herself than Undine.

Then she smelled it. That sharp ozone tang of fairground electricity. The dusty air above her head cracked, and in a moment, the room was full of a vast, intangible weight pressing down on her, throbbing through her brain.

Waves of pressure dulled her thinking. Her vision distorted, and through tears she saw Ronald's face contort in torment. His image started to disintegrate.

Undine's lips curled back. His hands clawed empty air as his back arched, almost throwing him from the sofa. Jo bent to him, placing a hand on his chest, feeling his shirt drenched with sweat and his heart pounding through her fingertips.

And as she watched Ronald Wyndham's face sink back into the flowery wallpaper, half-forgotten memories thrust into her thoughts: her own terror as she re-experienced herself being pulled into the wall upstairs. That thing hadn't been strong enough then, but its power had grown. It had wanted her before. It wanted her even more now and it knew she was here!

Her fears clamoured for attention, crying for her to abandon this futile, doomed exercise. Leave Undine! Save yourself! Get out now before it's too late!

She eased Undine back against the cushions and stroked his feverish brow.

'That's enough,' she said. 'You have to come back to me now, Undine. You hear me? We need to get out of here. It's time for you to come back.'

Undine did not respond.

CHAPTER 25

Another wave of flame crashed against Undine's mind. The vortex howled around him, icy claws wrenching at his being, trying to tear him from his precarious grip.

'Sunny! Archie!'

They were near. He felt them.

'I've come to get you out! But I need you to help me!'

Freezing fingers grabbed for his thoughts, numbing them, but Undine refused to let them take him.

'I'm here!'

Flames whirled past in a kaleidoscope of colour. Undine tensed, anticipating the lash of a brilliant, searing tongue. Instead, the colours coagulated, gathering texture and solidity, becoming a shifting overlay of mismatched clothing. The sense of familiarity swelled into hope.

'Sunny! Is that you?'

Liquid fire snatched up and coiled around Undine's waist. It tried to dislodge him, to pull him into the surrounding madness. Undine struggled from its grasp, his non-existent flesh sticking to its icy touch and ripping from him as he tore himself free.

The fiery tendril dissolved, and the wind divided. A skinny face loomed through flaming clouds.

... Oh God. Undine, I can see Ray ...

Undine stretched out his hand and Ray's face shimmered like a mirage.

'Try to reach out to me!'

Ray's image broke into a smile so wide it risked breaking his narrow face in two. His voice drifted into Undine's awareness.

... You know me and Undine are about as psychic as a pair of bricks ...

Ray's voice. But empty of meaning. Nothing but an echo.

'Can you hear me?'

The wind snarled, whipping the image away. Undine lost his grip and tumbled further into insanity.

'Sunny!'

Undine tasted the glow of whisky, and found himself becalmed in the friendly aroma of pipe smoke.

'Archie?'

He caught a glimpse of the smoke, and concentrated on its drifting feathers, watching it coalesce into an impression of Archie's face. The Professor's pipe sat clamped between his lips as he drew contented puffs, but when Undine tried to make eye contact, he found only doom-filled pits of utter darkness.

... I understand you were driving the bus, Mr Undine. It must have been an awful shock ...

'Archie! Focus on me. Hold onto –'

A dagger of ice pierced Undine's spine, a fatal strike that sent his body –

No! He had no body in this place! He squeezed the illusion from his thoughts.

'Archie, do you know where you are?'

The image frowned.

... I call it the Octopus ...

It gave a wistful smile, and faded.

'Archie!'

... Flipping hell! The Faces of Lavender Edge ...

That was Sunny's voice again, full of excitement. Undine remembered how thrilled his mate had been at the opportunity to investigate the story from his childhood. An eddying current brought Ray's face bobbing past. Undine saw his friend's daft grin.

'Sunny, over here!'

The image appeared to react, although it kept its distance. Hazy features came into sharper focus, and dismay seeped into eyes that began to dart from left to right. Undine could not tell what Ray was seeing.

'Can you hear me?'

Ray's gaze locked on to something, but not Undine. The mouth shaped words that the screaming vortex whipped away before the sound reached him.

And then the wind was carrying Ray away, and Jo was calling.

... *Hold on to him* ...

But Undine was being taken in the opposite direction. Helpless, he tumbled at the edge of a whirling storm, licked by flickering flames that froze his soul.

The sense of familiarity lay behind him now. He was entering a different aura, a new presence....

The fires cast shadows, and the shadows were really a moustache, thick and bristling beneath a proud nose. This was a face made of pain, forcing itself into being. A mouth that was an everlasting scream into the wild wind of a hurricane that dug its teeth deeper into Undine. It punched then dragged at him, wrenching him first one way then another, but a voice urged him to stay close to this new manifestation, and he fought to keep his position.

A warm ripple gave him the strength to stabilize himself. He heard Jo calling.

... *Ask him* ... *the stone* ...

Her words meant something important.

'The stone,' said Undine, remembering. 'In the wall.' He dredged up a representation of the node, visualizing the carving on its shiny black surface.

Ronald Wyndham's eyes widened.

Undine sent out a questioning thought, showing Ronald the maze, rotating it.

'Which way up?'

Undine saw recognition in those pain-filled eyes. He saw the slow solidification of the intention to form words.

'You've seen it before,' he urged. 'Haven't you? Try to remember.'

Then the vortex howled again, and ripped Ronald Wyndham's face away.

❋   ❋   ❋

Undine floated alone.

Currents shifted once more, as something vast altered direction. A shadow grew, eager for the conclusion. It drew near, and at that moment Undine knew The Outside had been toying with him. It had permitted him to see those faces because it wanted to taunt him with the truth: Undine was powerless to save them. Now it was coming to feast on the despair sown inside him, the despair that would mature once he understood. And Undine was beginning to understand.

He understood why Oldroyd referred to these locations as 'thin places'. Whatever manner of membrane separated the stuff of Undine's universe from a wider, unimaginably alien existence, was thinner here than it ought to be. Thinner, and more permeable.

He understood that when someone died in such a place, shreds of their psyche might be snatched away by the weird currents and swirling vortices that formed the immaterial substance of this strange borderland. He understood that the Faces of Lavender Edge had never been entirely dead, yet neither were they truly alive.

Not spirits, though. Not that. They were nothing but fragments of personalities: confused memories and torn scraps of vitalities that had once defined character. Unable to dissipate or 'move on', or whatever normally happens in the aftermath of bodily death, these tatters remained, unending echoes of the fear and anguish of the final moments of lives that were no more.

Ray was not here, no more than his image caught in a photograph or the imitation of his voice trapped in a spool of magnetic tape represented the 'real' him. The same held true for Archie, and for Ronald Wyndham, and for all the others whose visages appeared in the walls here.

There was nobody left to rescue. His friends were gone forever.

Undine's tortured essence sagged. The raging winds shrieked their triumph as the vortex closed around him. Any moment now, the tightening fires would burn him away, and he had been robbed of any desire to prevent that happening. Soon, all he had been would end, and the undead ashes would be for all time trapped in this terrible non-place, reduced to an infinity of tormented misery on which that thing would feed. He didn't care.

In total despair, Undine surrendered to the inevitable. He let go, relinquishing the last strands of his failing sense of self, and he invited the Outside in.

❊   ❊   ❊

Later.

Undine drifted. The hurricane of tortured emotion was gone.

Eternity came and went, and stray thoughts floated in its wake.

He had been wrong.

He should have died, but by surrendering completely he had left no obstacle to resist The Outside's onslaught. With nothing to attack, the howling fury had passed straight through, leaving Undine naked and devastated. His mind was blasted, scoured clean as if by a scorching desert wind, but he was alive.

Barely.

… Undine? …

The sound came from far above, smothered by fathoms of darkening void.

… -r me? …

It was a voice he knew.

Undine pulled the last of his dwindling existence back from the limitless expanse. He shrank into himself. With the last strand of his extended sense, he flailed upwards, reaching for the beacon represented by that voice.

... come back ...

Change. Was he moving? Or was he remembering a dream of having a physical body?

He dreamed of feet shambling. Stumbling.

The voice again, encouraging:

... this way ...

It shone, and he held fast to the gentle sound as blackness swelled around him.

Damp chill caressed his face. Then gravity was back, and he was toppling into it as the blackness expanded to swallow him.

✻   ✻   ✻

Cold. His eyes opened to a sea of flaming red.

The voice pushed against the fog that filled his mind. Insistent, it cut through the muzziness.

'-dine!'

He saw a head, silhouetted against fiery oranges and crimsons.

'We're out. You can stop now.'

Warmth enclosed his hands.

'Time to come back.'

Undine staggered, legs little more than an

abstract concept, but someone was there to hold him.

Her words continued. They were representations of concern, but he was too dazed to take in more than that.

He saw trees, and he allowed his attention to flow up the trunk of the nearest. He rippled through every gnarl and groove of its encrusted surface, absorbing the energy that radiated from deep within the living core, rising higher now as he sped along a branch, a twig, a blazing leaf, breaking through the veined skin and travelling deeper until he joined the life-force not only of this leaf-twig-branch-tree-garden but of all life on this planet, and it was glorious....

Jo slapped his face.

'Undine!'

He was in the back garden of Lavender Edge. Jo stood next to him, in the shelter of the trees and bushes that ran beside the garden wall. Some twenty feet away, the conservatory door gaped open, a cushion jammed beneath it.

'Did you see them?' she asked. 'Ray and Archie? And Ronald Wyndham?'

He should tell her, but he hadn't the strength.

'What did they tell you? Did you find out how to help them?

Or the will.

She was desperate for hope, for good news. There wasn't any. Oldroyd had been right. Ray was gone. Archie too. Nothing remained of them here but shards of broken memories.

Grief and fury raged through him, searching for an outlet. He needed to vent his anger. His mouth opened, his jaw twisting and clenching, but there was no breath and no sound. His stomach cramped. He curled over, and was suddenly and violently sick, acidic vomit spattering a tree and pooling on the wet grass.

It was too much. So much new knowledge seething through his subconscious, overwhelming his ability to process the flood of information. Rushing through it all, however, was an incandescent stream of awful truth.

He did not resist as Jo helped him to his feet. His legs were weak, shaking.

She was still talking at him, firing questions.

He reached a trembling hand inside his pocket and pulled out his cigarettes. Jo lit one for him, and he sucked down the rough smoke, staring at the house, its outline black against the darkening sunset, as he tried to reassemble his mind's defences, to pull the shutters back down. It was only a matter of time before The Outside was powerful enough to reach beyond the house, to reach out here. Maybe it already could.

Jo's hand touched his shoulder. She guided him away from the door, towards the fence, her incessant probing questions clattering uselessly against his stunned shell.

Yes, Oldroyd had been right. They should have found out how to replace the node while they still had time. Now Undine understood: it might already be too late.

CHAPTER 26

'It's all arranged.' Jo placed the telephone handset back into its cradle.

In Archie's office chair, Undine held the node in his hands, continuing to stare into the maze carved into its surface. He did not reply. His craggy features had settled into an expression of dull gloom, and his dark eyes were lost in the bruised shadows of exhaustion.

Jo tried to sound upbeat. 'You were right about that manager. Sarcastic so-and-so. But I sweet-talked him: told him Professor James will be out of the country for the next few weeks. He still wasn't keen on having *you* there, mind, but he gave in in the end. We're all set for Monday night.'

All set to do what they should have done in the first place, she thought. If Undine were to have any chance of learning how to defend himself, he would need a safer environment than Lavender Edge in which to practise. As things stood, the Pyramus theatre was their best choice, and although a week was a long time to wait, it would give Undine more opportunity to recover after this afternoon. He still looked close to collapse. His face was grey and drawn, with eyes in hollows so black he looked as if he had gone ten rounds with Joe Frazier. She wished he would tell her what he'd been through. Apart from the devastating confirmation that Ray and Archie were dead, Undine refused to share what he had learned at the house.

He turned the lump of black stone over in his blunt fingers to study its incised design from a different angle. She was reminded of a child trying to assemble a jigsaw puzzle meant for adults.

Maybe they should have taken the stone with them to the house after all. Maybe they should have just shoved it back where she had found it, jammed it in any way they could, and prayed for the best.

Maybe that's what she should do herself right now. Then there would be no need for Undine to expose himself to that thing in Lavender Edge ever again. Then the theatre could be put off until he was fully recovered and strong enough to cope with what might happen. And given enough time, they might even be able to find a more suitable venue to help him learn how to control his ability.

Should she go? But what was it Undine

had said before? He had tried to explain what Oldroyd had told him, describing the barrier at the house as like a piece of broken electrical equipment; ever since Jo had removed the node, the Weall had been accumulating energy, and that energy had been building and building with no means of discharge. The moment the stone was replaced, it would complete the circuit. Then all that energy would want to explode out at once. She hadn't understood it all, but she grasped the central problem: the slightest error at that point would be disastrous.

So, before she could do anything, she was back to needing to know exactly how the node should be fitted into its niche, in which direction the maze should open. Until then, they were stuck.

Was that what Undine was trying to figure out? As she watched, he rotated the stone again, his eyes never leaving the carved lines.

She turned, and walked out of the office to the top of the stairs. Below her, mounds of paper still covered the ground floor of the Warehouse. Every surviving scrap of information about Lavender Edge. Had she missed anything?

And could she trust Undine to wait until after Monday night? For now, he was distracted, stunned with grief at the loss of his friends, but how long would it be before he got it into his stubborn head to do something stupid?

Again.

Another thought struck her. That new lock on the door: if Mrs Wyndham had agreed to sell the house to that Mr Erskine or whatever his name was, the developer might even now be preparing to knock the building down! If that happened, there would be nothing to hold back The Outside.

With no clear course of action, Jo wandered downstairs. She might as well look through the documents again, if only to drown out the maddening doubts and fears.

Despite everything, or perhaps as a retreat from it all, she quickly became absorbed in the research, and time drifted by in a rustle of paper. She plucked out a slim notebook. It was dark blue, with an imitation leather cover that had survived the chaos of Saturday night relatively intact. She flicked through the gold-trimmed pages of what turned out to be an address book, and spotted a name: Elsie.

Why did that ring a bell?

... I'm going to stay with Elsie ...

Something Mrs Wyndham had said. It hadn't registered before; she had been looking for clues as to what was happening in the house. Now Jo remembered the once formidable old woman, in coat and headscarf and carrying a small brown suitcase, choking down tears as she hurried out of her family home.

On her way to stay with her friend Elsie.

There was no telephone number next to the

name, but there was an address. In Beddington, which wasn't far from Mitcham.

Jo's knees cracked as she got up from the concrete floor. Her legs were still stiff by the time she had walked upstairs and into Archie's office.

Into what used to be Archie's office.

Undine sat where she had left him, in Archie's chair, gazing at the stone. His posture was more alert than before, and smoke wafted up from a cigarette held between his fingers, and although his head did not move, his eyes rose to her as she entered.

'I think I've found her,' said Jo.

'Who?' Undine's gaze dropped back to the stone.

'Margaret. Mrs Wyndham. This might be the address she's staying at.'

'So?'

'So this means I can go speak to her. She might not have sold the house yet. If not, maybe I can still persuade her not to finalize anything for the moment. Buy us a bit more time. It's something, at least.'

The idea took a few moments to percolate into Undine's brain. 'Okay,' he said without enthusiasm. He lumbered to his feet and took a step towards her, and his legs gave way. Jo reached to help him. He pushed her arm aside.

'I'm alright,' he said, leaning on Archie's desk.

'No you're not. You're half-dead, you idiot. Stay here and get some rest, and let me handle this.'

Undine glared at her. At last, he said, 'Fine.'

'Good.' Jo walked to the door.

The telephone rang. Undine snatched up the receiver. 'Yeah?' He scowled. 'It's for you.' He passed the handset to Jo.

'Hello?'

The voice on the other end was male, young, and hesitant. 'Oh, er, hi. I don't know if you remember me. It's Kevin. From Triple-A Auto. You were here the other day, asking about the Doyle brothers. From Doyle Construction? You asked me to call you if I had any news.'

Kevin? Oh, right: the awkward, grease-stained mechanic at the car repair shop in Tooting. She'd asked him to keep an eye out for Mrs Wyndham's builders.

'Kevin, hi!' said Jo, injecting the words with a brightness she really didn't feel. 'Thanks so much for calling!'

Undine pulled a face. She turned her back on him.

'That's alright,' said Kevin. 'Actually, I tried to get hold of you earlier, several times, but I couldn't get an answer. I was getting worried I had the wrong number!'

Was that a hint of betrayal in those last few words? Oh, God. Please don't let him think she'd been leading him on.

'Yeah, I'm sorry about that. Something came up. What have you got for me?'

'It's cool. It's just, I saw them. This afternoon. John and Danny.'

'They're back? That's great. Are they still there now?' Jo checked her watch: it was a little after seven, so it seemed unlikely they'd still be at work.

'No. They was there this afternoon though. That's why I was ringing.'

Damn! They should never have gone back to the house this afternoon!

'Thing is, though,' said Kevin, 'I know where they might be now. If you're still interested?'

'Where?'

'Do you know the Prince of Wales in Garratt Lane? It's just down the road from us. They like a few pints in there after work most nights, after locking up.'

Jo was already pulling on her leather jacket, cradling the handset between her shoulder and neck. 'You're an angel, Kevin. Thank you so much!'

'I, uh, might be there myself later. If you're heading that way?'

'Sorry, Kevin. Everything's such a rush just now, you know how it is. But thanks again. I really appreciate this.'

She put the phone down before he could reply. She felt bad for the young man, but time was pressing and there were considerably more important matters to worry about.

'Undine, I'm off.'

The only response was a gentle snore. Undine had collapsed into Archie's chair. He was out for the count, less asleep than unconscious.

Probably the best thing for him.

She left him to rest, and picked out an 'A-Z' from one of the office bookshelves. The map gave a fairly clear idea of where the pub was, and she still had the keys to Undine's Cortina, having driven them back from Mitcham this afternoon. If she went now and headed through Clapham, she could be in Tooting within an hour.

And if she didn't spend too long there.... She turned over a few pages to check. Yes, she could head a little further south afterwards, and make a short detour via Beddington before she returned to the Warehouse: with luck, she'd have time to visit Elsie's address tonight too, and chat with Mrs Wyndham.

Jo took Undine's trench coat from the back of the office door and draped it over him. She slid the cigarette from the sleeping figure's fingers, and stubbed it into the ashtray, then she gently prised the black stone from his loose grasp. She wanted to show the node to the Doyles, in case the sight helped jog their memories.

She also wanted to ensure Undine didn't take it back to Lavender Edge himself if he happened to wake up while she was gone.

CHAPTER 27

He blazes. A fiery comet, he tumbles through the vortex of misery and loss and suffering.

He is on the far side of the wall, yet his return lies in the past.

He died in that other space, yet he exists in the present.

Alternate realities overlap, and he is an interference pattern of ripples, which coalesces to become a state that is neither, and new.

Layers of self-identity tear free as he falls. He sheds years that erupt into particles of bursting energy, and they trail behind him.

Exposed and molten, his soul-stuff flows bright and fierce.

Elsewhere, Undine's physical body twitches, and his breath carries a faint, uneasy moan. Here, he wears a feathered headdress and holds a small, round drum in one hand. He extends his arms and throws back his head, and as he screws closed his eyes, his mind explodes.

✻　　✻　　✻

The universe is in his head, and the universe is a bubble of order, defined and contained by a membrane of heart-breaking fragility.

The existence of this bubble is an outcome of chance. A product of random fluctuations within the infinity of chaos that boils on the other side of the membrane. Through the chaos seethes The Outside, and The Outside is strongest where the skin is weakest.

… Do you know what a 'thin place' is? …

The redbrick house rises around him, insubstantial as a ghost. It is one manifestation of a barrier that is itself a single threadbare stitch in a patchwork curtain stretched through time and space.

… The Anglo-Saxons, when they arrived, gave the Weall its name …

But the Weall was unimaginably old long before its naming. Nothing endures forever, and the pressure against it is relentless.

An atom of reality shears. He smells an ozone tang and hears the hum of force released. Centuries dissolve, and a crack expands.

He sees lives begin and end. He watches minds die, giving up their energies. Occasionally, those tattered thoughts catch in the currents that swirl at this damaged border, and in time those fragments of memory are glimpsed by other minds. A new energy – fear – mixes with the currents, and The Outside is drawn to this novel, seductive scent. It tastes, and finds nourishment. It is hungry for more. It experiments. It learns how these captive scraps of personality can be made to yield richer substance through misery, suffering, despair.

The Outside grows in awareness, and studies the living beings that glow just out of reach. It wears dead memories as masks, and this induces terror in the living, swelling its power, lengthening its reach.

Mrs Wyndham sees her late husband's face, and she weeps with horror.

Dust trickles from the Weall.

A man visits with plans which would demolish the house that stands here now. The Outside watches, and it listens. It has learned cunning.

Men wield tools, and smash into the barrier. The trickle becomes a landslide, and The Outside pushes further in.

It terrorizes Mrs Wyndham, wearing down her resistance to the man who plans destruction.

In a dark room, it seizes opportunity, whispering to a younger woman, coercing her into removing the barrier's heart.

The landslide becomes an avalanche.

The Weall is crumbling. Its final collapse is now inevitable. Its fall will be a puncture in the membrane, through which The Outside will bleed – and once the bleeding begins it will never end.

✸   ✸   ✸

Sweat drenches Undine's body. New understanding saturates his mind.

Lavender Edge is the Weall but the Weall has been more than only Lavender Edge.

Structures raised by human hands endure for mere heartbeats. They rise, they decay, they are replaced.

Yet the node endures.

The stone that fell to Earth in flames untold aeons before. Black and faintly iridescent. Glossy yet somehow unreflective of light. Heavy and impossibly dense.

Undine's eyes flicker behind closed lids. Images flash past, too fast to process. He pulls impressions from the blur.

Stars.

A land of fire and rock.

A world of ice.

Long-haired and bearded men carry spears and shun a henge of rough-hewn oaken tree trunks. A hollow has been scraped into the largest trunk, and a black rock nestles within.

A troop of Roundheads sets up camp in a farmhouse, on the banks of a narrow stream. Across the gentle water, wide fields of lavender fade into the horizon. A burly soldier curses, unable to calm their restless mounts.

A calico merchant takes a nervous sip of wine, gazing through the window of his new mansion. Had he, after all, been wrong to ridicule the locals' superstitious tales?

Shapes writhe beneath the solidity of a gaslit wall, and a parlour maid clutches her rosary and prays for strength.

The same location, form shifting in the flow of time.

Each new structure renews the Weall – but the correct adjustments must be made. The Weall is both the sum of its parts and more. It is its own location in its entirety: the fabric of the structure; the method of its construction; its design; its relationship to the geology of the landscape and the stars that wheel in cycles overhead; and the arrangement of angles where walls and ceilings and gables meet. It is a multidimensional architecture of almost incomprehensible complexity, with the black star-stone as its living heart.

The lines carved into its surface are the key. For each new manifestation of the Weall, the node must be precisely re-oriented. The membrane is stretched so thin at this place that the confusion of realities generates a destructive energy, yet this same energy, properly channelled, is redirected to power the Weall, which in turn holds together the integrity of the membrane. Yin is Yang, and Yang is Yin, and the serpent consumes its own tail.

A greater-than-human understanding was required to perform such a delicately balanced feat of cosmic engineering. The beings who originally carved the maze possessed this. Whoever they were and wherever they went, those beings found a way to bequeath a fraction of that understanding: just enough to ensure that the Weall would continue to be regenerated.

Since the ancestors of *Homo sapiens* were first guided to this site, there has been a guardian here. A guardian in an unending line of guardians.

But if that line breaks?

A figure stands with its back to Undine. It is a man: elderly, long-limbed, wearing a shabby pin-striped suit that might once have been brown.

Heavy stillness fills space that becomes the gloomy interior of a shop.

Undine speaks to the man.

The figure does not move.

'I'm here!' calls Undine.

The man turns, and fastens a pair of spectacles over his ears. Undine is unsurprised to see a jagged crack in the left lens.

Mr Oldroyd smiles, and speaks in a reedy voice. 'Yes. Yes, I think you must be. You took your time.'

Then the shop is gone, and Undine is rising.

He leaves below him the blasted essence of his core for he knows it will continue to forge itself anew. He rises towards the sound of screaming.

He surfaces into a shallow dream. The screams are coming from the bell tower of a church he recognizes: it is the church that stood not far from the house he grew up in.

Undine flies closer, zipping over moon-drenched rooftops, and the screams resolve into the ringing of bells....

CHAPTER 28

Jo slipped through the lights an instant before they turned red. The rain was holding off, and she'd made better time than expected as she passed a sign to the Oval. The Elephant and Castle would be coming up any moment: not long now before she was back at the Warehouse. Would Undine still be asleep?

Eighty per cent wasn't bad at all.

The traffic was light enough to risk taking her eyes off the road for a moment, and she checked her watch. In the flicker of passing streetlights, the hands were hard to distinguish, but she got the impression it was around ten p.m. She hoped Undine would be awake because the Doyles had indeed been in the Prince of Wales. The Victorian pub had been quiet, as it probably was most Tuesday evenings, and the barman had been happy to point the brothers out to her, and even happier to pour them the couple of pints she paid for.

They'd looked happy enough too, keen to chat with the young blonde leaning in with her most engaging smile. Until she mentioned Lavender Edge. That changed the mood.

No, they didn't want to talk about what happened there. They just wanted to forget everything to do with that job. The old woman could keep any tools they'd left behind, and nothing could persuade them to go back.

Then the barman brought over their drinks, and that oiled their tongues. In a thick Dublin brogue, the older Doyle – John – found he recalled how the brickwork had crumbled almost to powder at one particular spot the moment they set to work on the wall in the upstairs bedroom. As his brother, Danny, stared into the black depths of his own Guinness, closing himself to the conversation, Jo encouraged John to tell her more. Whereabouts had the wall felt weakest? Was it to the left or the right of the hole?

John mapped out the hole in the air, his rough hands describing the shape, teasing out the memory.

'About here,' he said at last, indicating a position at around two o'clock. 'I think.'

He shook his head, coming back to the present and blanching as the repressed thoughts of what had happened next began to stir.

'How sure are you?' asked Jo.

He took a deep draught of his dark pint. 'Maybe eighty per cent?'

She hadn't even needed to show him the stone.

Up ahead, a white Mini pulled out into the road. The distance between Jo and the Mini shrank faster than she'd anticipated, and she eased off the accelerator.

Eighty per cent. They could work with that. If Undine's information was correct, the node had likely affected the wall's physical structure at the point where the channelled energy had for centuries flowed out of the entrance of that maze pattern. And the wall had crumbled most readily at around the two o'clock position.

She grinned, pleased with herself and looking forward to telling Undine.

She probably wouldn't mention Kevin though. Her cheerfulness dulled as she empathized with the young mechanic's disappointment. She had spotted him watching from the far side of the bar as she spoke to the brothers, and he'd clearly wanted to say hello although he hadn't come over; she guessed he was still concerned about her motives for tracking the Doyles down and didn't want them to know who had grassed them up. But after Jo thanked the brothers and was making her way to the door, she saw Kevin take a few steps in her direction, only to lose his nerve and veer back towards the safety of the bar. She took pity on him. She owed him, after all. She walked back and tapped him on the shoulder, and regretted her impulse when his face lit up and she got a lungful of Hai Karate aftershave. He must have splashed on half a bottle of the stuff. Before he spoke, she thanked him and motioned to the barman to pour another pint of whatever Kevin was drinking. Then she dropped some money on the counter and made her escape before the blushing youngster's brain found its gear.

'Sorry, Kevin,' she murmured as the Mini ahead slowed down and its left indicator light flashed on. She pulled right to overtake, her tired vision blurring in the sudden glare of headlights coming the other way.

She made it past the Mini and, safely back in her proper lane, stretched her shoulders, wriggling to get comfortable in the unfamiliar seat of Undine's Cortina. Fresh air would help. She wound down the window a couple of inches and welcomed the invigorating chilly blast.

She had news from Beddington too. Even though she hadn't been able to speak to Mrs Wyndham directly, Jo had been right: the old lady was staying at that address with her friend Elsie. A good friend, no doubt, but a poor liar. Elsie refused to let Jo enter, claiming Margaret Wyndham was unwell and needed a peaceful night's sleep.

You're not the only one, thought Jo as she stifled a yawn.

Mrs Wyndham had definitely been awake, though. Jo saw her shadow on the carpet in the hall behind Elsie, where she was hiding behind the open door halfway down, listening to them talk. But arguing would only have made the two women close ranks against her so Jo simply left a message, imploring Mrs Wyndham to telephone her as soon as possible. She scribbled down the Institute's telephone number and, speaking loud enough to be overheard, stressed that she had urgent information and that it was vital Mrs Wyndham should under no circumstances agree to any plans which would involve further building or demolition work at Lavender Edge.

When Elsie closed the door, Jo blocked it with her foot. She took the woman's hand, looked her in the eye, and quietly urged her to make sure Margaret called soon. Elsie blinked at the unexpected intimacy of Jo's gamble, but assured Jo she would do her best.

Tower Bridge Road stretched before her. It was a straight run now until she turned off shortly before the river, and she reckoned she should be at the Warehouse in ten to fifteen minutes. She wondered again whether to wake Undine if he was sleeping when she got back.

A bus lumbered past in the opposite direction, wheels hissing through the Cortina's open window. Weary heads lolled against glowing windows: Londoners heading home to normal lives and warm beds. Jo thought of her own bed, waiting and familiar and oh-so-welcoming. This time, she couldn't hold in the yawn. It pulled her jaw wide, taking control of the muscles in her shoulders and expanding along her arms and out to the tips of her fingers. Her eyes closed –

– and she jolted awake to the blare of a horn, light exploding in the windscreen. Instinct pulled the steering wheel to the left, and a split-second of whirling images resolved into a motorcycle roaring by far too close to her window. Its angry horn dopplered past, and was gone.

Her pulse thumped in her throat. Her eyes flicked between her mirrors and the road in front as she watched the motorcyclist recede without incident. He was okay, thank God. She took several deep breaths, sat straighter, and wound the window down as far as it would go.

Just as well she would be back soon. She shivered in the cold wind, aware that at some point in the last few seconds she had made up her mind. She would leave Undine asleep – and get some kip herself before giving him the news. Home seemed suddenly and unattainably distant, and the Warehouse's ratty old sofa a luxury beyond compare.

Minutes later, the Cortina crept over the cobbles outside the Institute building. She climbed out, shut the car door as softly as she could, and clasped her keys tight to keep them from jangling as she found the one that would open the Warehouse door.

She padded to the entrance, reached for the keyhole, and the door opened.

Undine stood there, an empty blue holdall gripped in his fist.

'Where is it?'

She knew straight away what he meant. She patted her handbag, feeling the shape of the node within. 'It's safe.'

'Show me.' His dark eyes pierced the murky light.

She pulled out the heavy stone. Undine plucked it from her grasp. He thrust it into his holdall and zipped the bag shut.

'Car keys?'

Jo glared at him, but slapped the keys down into Undine's outstretched hand.

'Right. Come on then,' said Undine, pulling the Warehouse door closed. He marched past her towards the Cortina.

'What do you mean, "come on"?'

But Undine was climbing into the driver's seat. He tossed the bag onto the rear seat. 'We're going back.'

'It's late. We need to –'

'Just get your arse in here! If you hadn't taken the sodding stone with you, I could have been there by now.'

He slammed the door and twisted the ignition key. The car growled back into life.

'Hold on a moment,' said Jo, but the Cortina was already reversing into the road. 'Oh, for

God's sake!' She hurried to the passenger door, yanked it open and fell inside as Undine pulled away. 'What's the bloody rush?'

'You had a phone call,' said Undine.

Jo tugged her seatbelt around her and clicked it home. Undine hadn't bothered with his.

'What call?'

'Your Mrs Wyndham.'

'Oh.' That had come quicker than expected. 'Yeah, sorry, but I went round to see her earlier. I didn't mean for her to wake you up. But listen – I managed to speak to the Doyles too, and I've got a pretty good idea how the stone –'

Undine swung the Cortina left. Jo was pushed back into her seat as he accelerated into Tower Bridge Road.

'Slow down, for God's sake! Didn't you hear me? I know how the stone goes in. We can sort this out tomorrow morning.'

'No, we can't,' said Undine.

And he told her what Margaret Wyndham had said on the phone.

＊　　＊　　＊

'Knocking it down? Already?'

'She wasn't a happy bunny,' said Undine.

Jo listened in disbelief while Undine recounted how Mrs Wyndham, close to tears, had raged down the telephone line. She had ordered him to stay away from Lavender Edge from now on, and the same went for Jo, and for anyone else they knew: none of them was to have anything further to do with her or the house. Furthermore, she had made it blisteringly clear that Jo's message had come too late: the defeated old woman had washed her hands of the entire affair. She had already sold the property to the developer, Mr Erskine.

'I guess that explains the lock.' Jo shook her head. 'But it seems so fast. She was so intent on holding on to her home.'

Undine grunted, accelerating through the traffic lights before they could start to think about changing.

'I reckon Erskine's been itching to get his hands on that land ever since Ronald Wyndham died,' he said. 'From what I could make out, he's got plans for a whole terrace of new houses there. Maybe he pressured her into it. Maybe he upped his offer. Whatever happened, it pushed the old bat over the edge.'

'One more day can't make much difference, surely?'

'He's taking no chances. Got a demolition crew standing by to begin first thing in the morning.'

'What?!'

Undine evidently didn't see any point in replying. He stared grimly ahead, lights strobing his ashen face. There was something different about his attitude, which Jo couldn't quite put her finger on, but she feared that whatever rest he had got before the phone woke him had been nowhere near enough.

Her own body ached with tiredness. She was in no condition to do this either, but what choice did she have? She had promised to help Mrs Wyndham, and she had let the old woman down. Everything she had done to try to help had only made things worse. Christ, if it hadn't been for her, Ray and Archie would still be alive! She still didn't understand what was happening at Lavender Edge, not entirely, but she understood enough to know it had to be stopped. And that there was nobody else in a position to fight it.

Or was there?

The streets were even emptier now as the two of them sped south.

CHAPTER 29

Undine slowed as they passed the Cricket Green, and by the time they turned into Rivermead Path, the Cortina was creeping through the quiet streets. He pulled in to the pavement, and winced as the front tyre squeaked the kerb. Nearly midnight was no time to be attracting attention, not when they were about to break into the same house for the second time that day.

Jo hurried to the corner shop before he had locked the car, and looked up at the lettering over the windows. 'This one, yeah?' She spoke in a whisper. On the way here, she had got it into her head that they should consult Oldroyd before going on to the house, pointing out that the shopkeeper seemed to know more about Lavender Edge and its secrets than anybody else. Arguing with her would have been even harder work than talking to Oldroyd, and Undine supposed it was just possible the old hippy might have one final bit of advice for them. With or without his input, however, Undine understood now what he needed to do.

He drew on his Embassy, the tip glowing red with a comforting crackle. He let the smoke go, and watched through its dissipating veil as Jo pushed the shop door. Unsurprisingly, the door did not open. Shading her eyes with her hands, she leaned against the darkened glass and peered inside.

Undine reached past her, and pressed a doorbell discretely screwed into the weather-battered door-frame. Somewhere, a buzzer croaked.

They waited.

'Try again,' said Jo.

Undine pressed a second time, and again they heard the muffled buzzer and nothing else.

'Is there a side entrance?' Jo scanned the building, but the front door, on the corner of the road, was the only visible way in or out.

Undine checked his watch, angling his wrist to catch the illumination from the nearest lamppost. 'Come on. The old codger's probably dead to the world.'

Jo ignored him and pushed the bell again, holding it down for long bursts. 'Wake up!' she hissed.

Light moved in the edge of Undine's vision. He looked around, and caught the twitch of a bedroom curtain in one of the houses opposite.

'We're attracting attention.'

Jo sighed in exasperation. 'I noticed.' She gave one last look through the glass then stepped back. Suddenly, she spun around, took hold of Undine's hand, and playfully pulled him towards her.

'What the hell are you doing?'

'Just act natural.' She wheeled away from the shop, pulling Undine behind her as she strolled along the pavement. Any nosey neighbours would see a girl in love, without a care in the world. Undine endured the performance until they passed the lamppost's pool of light, then he snatched his hand free and stalked into the sheltering shadows of the high wall around Lavender Edge.

'Don't flatter yourself,' said Jo as she joined him. But she said it with a wry smile, and Undine, despite his sickening anxiety, could not help smiling back.

'We just don't seem able to keep away from this place, do we?' said Jo.

She meant it lightly, but her words brushed something deep and unremembered from Undine's recent, uneasy sleep. A few inches from his face, a spider had spun a web between the old brick wall and an overhanging branch of a tree that stood inside the garden, and Undine fleetingly wondered whether a fly could ever appreciate the intricate strands of the pattern that had ensnared it.

He took another long drag on his cigarette.

'You sure you're ready for this?' asked Jo.

'No choice.'

'No. I suppose not.'

Her hazel eyes, heavy as ever with too much mascara, shone against her pale face with a giddy cocktail of fear and excitement. Undine, too, felt the buzz of adrenaline. It cut through the fatigue that had overcome him back at the Warehouse, and mixed uneasily with his concerns. His senses felt sharpened, perhaps too sharp. Would he be able to still his thoughts for long enough to get inside the house without The Outside noticing? With enough luck, he might make it as far as the bedroom before the thing reacted to his intrusion. But what then? From the moment it became aware of him, he would be battling to keep that alien presence out of his head, to prevent it destroying his mind before he could replace the node.

He tried not to think further ahead than that.

'You should stay out here,' he told Jo. 'Keep watch.'

'Not a chance,' she whispered back, and once again he knew there would be no point arguing with her.

He took a final pull on his Embassy, and flicked it away. Exhaling smoke, he opened the front gate.

✳   ✳   ✳

They headed straight to the fence at the side of the house. Undine boosted Jo over, and she let him through. The conservatory door, when they reached it, was locked. They exchanged a glance. Neither recalled re-locking the door that afternoon.

Undine watched Jo kneel before the door with her lock-picking tools. His heart hammered at the base of his skull, punctuating the doubts that assailed him. He knew the pain waiting for him in the house. There was no question of whether it would happen, only when, and he hoped he could withstand the agony long enough to do what he had to.

What if he couldn't?

The pulse of blood in his ears was a roaring ocean. He grimaced, shaking away a rolling surge of giddiness. His legs felt faraway and useless.

He thought about the night he had stumbled helplessly out into this garden. The screams from his walkie-talkie. He remembered Sunny and Archie, and better times – and he contemplated wider concepts of time, as well as space, and the warping of both in the visions he had lived through a short while before, and in which submerged elements of his self still burned. He re-experienced the multi-layered overlapping of the Weall in all its shifting forms over the millennia, and he accepted the imminence of chaos pressing against the thin membrane of reality, and the madness that boiled beyond.

For the first time in his life, Undine truly grasped the fragility of everything he had ever known, and he centred himself on the simple fact that he knew now what he had to do. And why it had to be him that did this.

As he'd said, he had no choice. He thought again of the spider's web on the wall. Maybe he never had.

Jo pushed the conservatory door. It swung inward without a sound, and she stood.

Undine gripped his holdall, feeling the weight and solidity of its contents. He checked again that the shutters on his mind were fast. Then he straightened his tie and lifted his chin, and as he walked inside, he rolled his shoulders as if his beloved Rat Pack were marching in step beside him.

✻   ✻   ✻

Undine raised a finger to his lips. There were sounds, deeper inside.

Muffled voices. Male. Not loud, but unmistakable in the otherwise oppressive silence. The absence of ticking from the grandfather clock was an almost physical presence, pressing against his imagination. Without it, the house felt wrong.

Not that it had ever felt right.

He motioned to Jo to stay in the

conservatory, and crept across the drawing room floor, grateful for the thick carpet that swallowed the tread of his boots. The door to the hallway was ajar, and he nudged it open a fraction more to peer through the gap.

At the far end of the hall, he saw the front door. A few feet before that, light spilled under an interior door, which was shut but which must lead into a room at the front of the house. The sound of speaking died away, overtaken by a swell of orchestral music.

Somebody was listening to a radio.

'A night watchman?'

Undine jumped at Jo's whisper. She was standing right by his shoulder. Couldn't she do anything she was told?

Irritation flared. In an instant, Undine was alert to his slip, caught the emotion, and damped it – but not before a low creak groaned from the ceiling. He pulled in his thoughts, locking his mind down once more. Stillness returned, and settled on them like a shroud.

He glared a warning at Jo as he lowered his bag to the floor, and teased the zipper open. She mouthed a 'sorry' to him. Her guess was probably right though. Mrs Wyndham had likely told Erskine of the Institute's involvement, so the developer might well have hired someone to keep an eye on the property overnight. They were fortunate the watchman hadn't been here this afternoon.

It was an unwelcome detail, but they could do nothing about that now.

Undine extracted a pair of torches – solid, heavy affairs wrapped in rubber casing – and handed one to Jo. He re-closed the bag, and clicked on his light. The beam lanced through the dusty air, hitting the wall where the antique table had once stood; Mrs Wyndham must have had her valuables removed after she decided to sell up. Jo's torch beam shone across the far wall, where it found the small, framed watercolour of Lavender Edge still hanging in place. An unwanted keepsake, it seemed. The other paintings were gone, and the shelves were empty of knick-knacks.

Since the single creak, there had been no sounds from the bedroom above them. Undine pointed to the ceiling with his torch, and Jo nodded, her mouth tight with tension. They padded out into the hallway, past a discarded, rumpled dust sheet that marked the spot where the grandfather clock had stood. So Mrs Wyndham had taken that too; that explained why there was no more ticking. They reached the foot of the staircase, only a few paces separating them now from the closed door farther down the hall. From here, the music was clearer. Undine smelled a sweet, pungent aroma.

He climbed onto the first step. The music was familiar, but he was no connoisseur of classical pieces and was unable to put a name to it.

It wasn't his style, although it was far more appealing than the noise youngsters listened to these days, and –

A stab of anxiety reminded him to focus his thinking. Around them, the house crouched in hush. With one hand gripping the comforting heft of his torch and the other holding his bag close to his leg, away from either wall or banisters, Undine took the next step, and then another.

By the time he reached the top, he was out of breath from the discipline of breathing silently. Across the landing, the bedroom doorway yawned open, daring him to enter.

He adjusted his hold on the bag. The movement redistributed his weight, and a floorboard groaned beneath his left boot. His blood was suddenly ice-water as his body tensed, and he strained to keep his thinking locked down, not to broadcast alarm.

From the downstairs room, the orchestral sounds went on as before.

He lightened the load on his foot. The wood rose under his sole, moving back into its accustomed position. He moved forward, aware of Jo following him even though her movements were inaudible below the rushing in his ears.

As they entered the bedroom, the air seemed to sigh. He eased the door closed behind them, as if shutting them into their own tomb.

Dust sheets lay in drifts across much of

the floor, like sleeping ghosts in the gloom. To the left and ahead hung the two bay windows, beyond which lurked only impenetrable murk. In the wall to his right, fringed in cracked plaster and torn wallpaper, glowered the hole.

Jo's nose twitched.

Undine smelt it too. That sharp electric edge. His scalp tingled.

The seemingly empty space around them was full of an unseen presence. The pressure against his thoughts increased as something pushed a little further through an invisible barrier, displacing reality.

Jo's expression hardened. She could sense it too. That disturbed Undine even more.

He looked away from her, holding his fear in check.

Why didn't it strike?

Undine opened a tiny corner of his mind for the merest moment and tasted ... puzzlement. He detected curiosity too, glimmering at the storm-front of a vast bulk of power, a power barely contained at the point of eruption. He slammed the shutters once more.

'It can't read me,' he said. 'It knows we're here, but doesn't understand why. I think it's waiting to see what we're up to.'

He took a step closer to the hole, struggling to keep his thoughts off the stone that weighed so heavy in his bag.

Thin glass crunched beneath his boot. A

fragment of shattered lightbulb, perhaps, or debris from one of Archie's gadgets. Another long creak rolled from the shadowed depths of the hole; it fell to the skirting board, and rumbled on through the floor, warping gravity as it rippled through him. Panic took its first bite.

He tightened his grip on the bag.

'You okay?' asked Jo.

'Fine,' he lied.

He took another step, into air that was thickening, becoming harder to move through.

'Undine.' Jo's murmur was a warning.

He turned. Her eyes were wide, staring past his shoulder. He followed the shaking beam of her torch to the opposite wall, to the right of the window, momentarily confused, not comprehending how their two torches could be casting so many pools of diffused light. Then he saw that the light was not coming from their torches at all.

Ominous patches of sickly yellow illumination were rising within that wall. And as he became aware of that, so he realized the same was happening in each of the other walls around them. The glows deepened, throwing the floral shapes in the wallpaper pattern into silhouette, and intensifying the blackness inside the hole.

The first faces boiled to the surface, and Undine's composure faltered. Soundlessly, they screamed their unending deaths at him. Features melted and ran as further faces formed and reformed, and he glimpsed, among others, visages he had seen before: the Cromwellian soldier, the long-haired and bearded youth, the parlour maid – they rose and fell like a siren call of insanity.

'They're only images, Undine. They can't hurt you.'

Yet they did. They scorched his mind, and his self-control flinched from their touch.

Jo gasped, and he saw why. Sunny's face swam among them, and Archie's – churning and dissolving with all the others, and screaming their own unheard torment.

Unheard, but Undine could hear their screams in his memory. Crackling through his walkie-talkie. And he could hear them in the substance of this room too, because this was where they had been killed, pulled into the wall at this very spot. Echoes of that violence, so fresh, so personal, roared against his mind, searing him with the record of his friends' shock, their horrified disbelief, the wrenching pain of their undying deaths....

This was intended to repel him – but Undine was stronger than before.

He accepted the storm of agony and the pain of his own raging grief, and he absorbed that energy; he used it to force apart the pressing air and he took the final step that brought him to the hole.

CHAPTER 30

Undine pulled on the bag's zipper. His muscles trembled as he overcame resistance and metal teeth parted with a sizzle of electrostatic charge. His thoughts reached the lump of stone the holdall contained – and in that instant The Outside understood.

Shattering blue light cracked open the air. In the corner nearest to Undine, a hammer abandoned by the Doyles vibrated. Grains of brick and plaster dust skittered around it, and an unnatural breeze rippled the builders' sheets.

From the hole beside him came a thrumming power. The pressure in the room increased again. He felt The Outside struggle to squeeze more of itself into the house, and there was a snapping and clawing at his mind as he lifted the node from the bag.

Jo called to him, but the rising wind took away her words. He turned in time to see a dust sheet tear loose from the floor beside her, whipping up at her head and smothering her face as it was forced into her nose and mouth. With her free hand, she ripped the cloth away.

'Two o'clock!' she called.

Wind howled around the room, but Undine could not tell whether the noise existed in the real world or in his head.

He thought a man shouted, demanding to know if somebody was upstairs.

He ignored it, and examined the glossy yet unreflective black stone. His thumb caressed the grooved maze pattern that would have to face out towards the room.

Sharp-grained granules of dust and grit blasted his face, drawing blood. He screwed his eyes closed against them.

His thumb found the entrance, where the lines of the maze splayed open. Through which the energy would be redirected.

Jo fought her way to his side.

He turned the node over in his hands, rotating it until its orientation sat naturally with the understanding that was flowing through him as if in a dream.

Jo nodded. 'Yeah, that should be right!' She had to shout to make herself heard. 'That's what Doyle told me! He said the opening should be at about the two o'clock position, like that!'

Guilt crossed her face. She started to say something else but bit it back, then said it anyway, the words spilling out of their own volition.

'But he was only 80 per cent sure! What if he was wrong?'

'He's not,' said Undine. 'This is the right way. I can feel it.'

Jo's eyes filled with a question he doubted he could ever answer.

The door to the room slammed open with a crash that shook the windowpanes, and a man was yelling.

'What's going on? Who are you?'

Undine couldn't stop himself glancing towards the doorway. He took in the scene as a snapshot image: a young guy in need of a haircut; enveloped in an oversized donkey jacket, and brandishing a hardback book as if it were a weapon; it had the word 'Philosophy' in its title; his eyes bulged.

'Are you supposed to be here?'

The question pierced Undine's mental shield. His focus faltered. A chink opened in his armour – and a spear of psychic lightning stabbed through. Fire shot along its ionized path and jabbed into his mind.

He fell backwards, but Jo was there.

She steadied him, and directed the light of her torch into the hole. It showed a thick beam of wood, its ancient solidity marred by a single shadowed hollow. The socket was about the size of Undine's fist, and undoubtedly where the node was meant to sit.

'Do it,' she said.

Undine reached forward, through the wall and through the searing agony slicing into his brain. He turned his hand, aligned the opening of the maze, and jammed the stone into its niche.

✻   ✻   ✻

The howling wind fell away. Pressure left the room like a death rattle.

Night crept back into corners as the glowing patches within the walls died – and as the lights faded, so the faces disappeared.

Jo played her torch beam around the room, and it slid across the calm surface of what was nothing but old floral wallpaper, and a partially knocked-through dividing wall.

'Is that it?' she asked. 'Is it over?'

Undine was too drained to say anything.

'I've called the police.' The night watchman sounded even younger than he looked. 'They told me they'll be here any minute.'

Jo shook her head. 'You didn't call them,' she answered with a knowing smile.

Hairs tingled on the backs of Undine's hands.

There was something. A sound. He bent his head to the hole, grunting as his muscles protested. Yes, there it was: a faint humming. Like standing too close to an electricity sub-station.

He looked into the hole, and could just

make out the outline of the node, limned in an indistinct green glimmer. Fascinated, he stared, watching the gleam gather strength, fine lines of light spilling along the channels of the carven maze, filling them.

'What is it?' Jo could hear it too. The hum was clearly audible, and its pitch was rising, becoming an unsteady whine.

'What's that noise?' asked the night watchman. 'What have you done?'

Behind Undine, Jo yelped and torch bulbs popped. Darkness swallowed the room.

Undine did not look round. The sight of the node captivated him. It pulsed, as the reactivated Weall gathered and channelled the supernatural force that collected at this thin place where the membrane between realities was thin enough to tear. And now the lines of the ancient maze were ablaze, the gleam growing to a violent glare as streams of light over-spilled their grooves and trickled around the black stone in unpredictable patterns.

Jo was calling to him. 'What can you see?'

He could not reply. He watched with mounting dread. Too late. Oldroyd had warned him to seal the breach without delay, before The Outside grew too strong to be held back by the Weall, but Undine hadn't acted quickly enough. He had tried to rescue his friends, and wasted time he didn't have.

Energy coursed through the Weall. It flooded

into the node as it should, but it was too much and all at once. Unearthly currents collided and splashed and dammed their own paths, and the power pouring in was not flowing through, not completing the circuit. The maze opening remained dark, the only point on the node's curved face not yet aglow. The energy was trapped.

A shaft of emerald brilliance pierced the carved surface, stabbing out at Undine. Hairline fractures of crystal light zigzagged from the rupture.

He jerked his head away. At the same moment, a myriad cracks shattered the grooves of the maze, the building energy reached a critical mass, and the entire node exploded into a cloud of pulverized rock and powdery black dust.

❋   ❋   ❋

Undine's head rang. Seconds slipped past in a dark so profound it suffocated.

'Won't someone tell me what's going on?' The night watchman's voice was the whimper of a scared schoolboy.

A presence loomed into the room. Immaterial weight filtered into the air, and the darkness itself began to glow.

Bruised light of fluctuating, indeterminate hue spread across the flat surface of the walls, and then it was pushing out into the third dimension and was over their heads and seeping beneath their feet. All was shifting colour and the swimming residue of a pattern no longer confined to sheets of old wallpaper.

'Get out!' cried Undine. 'Get to the shop!' It was all he could think of. Oldroyd was the only person who might know what to do.

Jo stared around in panic. 'Where's the door?'

There was no door. The bay windows, too, were gone. There was only the dull glow through which the colours moved, and the only break in the unquiet substance of that glow was the jagged black rip of the hole.

Colours filled the room amid a rising susurration of low sobbing and confused pleas for release. Arrangements coalesced within the light, before dissolving and reforming. Wherever Undine turned, eyes widened in horror and mutating features twisted in the grip of torment.

He battled to keep the madness out of his own mind, all too aware of the triumphant presence groping towards his knowledge of how he had failed.

The night watchman moaned. Faces swooped past, caught in the vortex of The Outside's feeding frenzy, and everywhere was bubbling, seething motion.

Everywhere but a lone point of stillness in the burgeoning chaos.

There, a new face was forming. As the other faces swirled around it, this new apparition held its position. It surfaced through the glow, and its features hardened until they were those of an elderly man.

What did The Outside want them to see now?

Hard black spots like the eyes of a crow glared at Undine from behind the impression of thin-framed spectacles. Broken lines of shadow suggested a crack in what would have been the left lens, and Undine recognized the new face. Like a punch to the guts, he realized its significance.

It was Oldroyd.

And if Oldroyd were already dead, there was nowhere left to turn.

CHAPTER 31

Years ago, long before she ever thought of joining the police, Jo had been a passenger on a ferry when it was caught in a storm halfway across the English Channel. The memories tainted her dreams for weeks after: the rolling deck dropping away underfoot, vomit sloshing around the heaving floor, the sense of being utterly at the mercy of the elements.... The crossing had been awful. This was immeasurably worse.

Her stomach lurched as she fought to orientate herself within the luminous whirl of shifting faces. She staggered to her left, and found herself looking into the gaping darkness of the hole, which hung in a non-space, no longer defined by a surrounding wall. The void gazed back, mocking her distress, but it gave her a point of reference, a single feature that held steady amid the motion. She forced herself to think and to remember the layout of the room: if the hole was in that direction then the door had to be located a few feet past her right shoulder.

She turned slowly, keeping her bearings. The chaos of light that bubbled where the door should be repulsed her sanity, but she made herself look – really look – deep into what she saw there, forcing the confusion to reveal the world she knew should exist. The door handle *was* there. With effort, she could just make out the lines of its shape, and understand where the surface of the wall began.

'That way!' she cried, pointing. 'Get the door open!'

The night watchman was closest. His eyes were blank, his brain unaccepting of the madness engulfing them, and he still clutched his heavy book. Yet he reacted automatically to Jo's authoritative shout. He reached with his free hand to the place she indicated.

The space that contained the door rippled as if a rock had plunged into depths beyond this world.

'Oh God,' breathed Jo as the man's hand sank into the shimmering, fluid plane. His wrist vanished and then his forearm, and he arched back, moaning in terror as he strained to extricate himself.

Whispering voices responded with their own rushing cry of dismay.

Was it her imagination, or could she feel the pull from where she stood? She flashed back to when it had almost taken her before: the same sickening distortion pummelling her as space seemed simultaneously to shrink and expand in every direction. The night watchman turned his head, his eyes pleading to her to help, and she saw again Dick Condie's accusing glare as those powerful currents drew the two police constables in, sucking them down, body and soul – down and under and out of themselves. The Outside had nearly taken them then; if it had been stronger, they would have been lost forever.

It was stronger now.

She watched, paralysed by the shock of what was happening again, and the young man's shoulder disappeared.

The spell broke. Jo lunged for his remaining forearm.

'Undine! Some help here!'

She batted the hardback book from the man's fist and gripped his hand.

She pulled. It wasn't enough.

The night watchman wept as the side of his head sank into restless light.

Jo looped an arm around his waist, securing her hold before letting go of his hand and stretching her other arm around his chest. Her fingers strayed dangerously close to the formless surface.

'Undine!'

Where the hell was he?

She smelled urine. A stain spread across the crotch of the night watchman's trousers. The force pulling him from her was too much. His head went under.

'No!'

Jo dug her heels into the ground, feeling an unseen dust sheet crumple and slip beneath her, and as she battled for a foothold she found a little purchase. She heaved.

She was able to take a half-step back, and her grip was still holding firm around the man's body.

She screamed, forcing her legs into what she told herself was the floor. Throwing every pound of her small body backwards, she desperately levered the dead weight in her arms up and away, and suddenly they were free.

She fell, landing on her elbows. The night watchman's body collapsed across her shins and feet. She wriggled and rolled him away from her.

Oh, Christ, don't be dead. She fumbled at the cold flesh of his neck, seeking a pulse. Nothing. She pulled back the sleeve of his donkey jacket, and when she felt a heartbeat flutter under his skin she gasped with relief.

Shuffling backwards on her knees, Jo dragged the unconscious body into the relative safety at the centre of the room. She struggled to catch her breath, adrenaline turning to anger as she wondered why Undine hadn't helped her. Where the hell was he?

He stood nearby, just gazing into the kaleidoscopic patterns.

She clambered to her feet, bristling with the need to yell at him, but her fury caught in her throat as she grasped what he was staring at.

Alone within the rushing storm of images, one face hung composed and still.

Something about that face felt familiar. Something she could not quite place.

She tugged at his shoulder. 'Undine.'

He gave no reaction. Alarmed, she tugged harder.

Undine pulled away, refusing to respond. The image hanging before him had him captivated – and as Jo watched with growing horror, its mouth began to move.

CHAPTER 32

The shadows that were Oldroyd's lips moved. They shaped words. For a moment, Undine thought he heard the shopkeeper's voice, and he strained to listen over the suffering that roared about them.

Like a bellows breathing greater violence into a furnace, The Outside intensified the vortex of agony. It drew off the increased psychic energy blazing from those tormented faces, feeding, gathering strength in preparation for its final push through the shattered barrier and into his world.

Much of its essence was already here.

Undine struggled to keep his focus on Oldroyd's face. In some way, he understood the other man was doing the same, that each was acting as a beacon for the other, and that they were forging a connection to bridge realities. He wondered again what had happened to the old man since their last meeting, but when he sensed his concentration faltering, he pushed down such concerns.

The irritating tugging at his shoulder returned, more forceful than before. Jo's voice battered into his awareness.

'It's trying to trick you!'

Undine dragged his thoughts from her distraction.

… cannot do this alone …

There! He could 'hear' Oldroyd! Or, rather, he could distil meaning from the shapes that Oldroyd mouthed.

Abruptly, the unreality of the situation tilted, and the strangeness of what was happening crashed against Undine's mind. His rigid hold on the stream of his consciousness slipped, and panic surged. He saw anew how precariously he was poised, and the inevitability that he would at any instant be ripped away and taken by the wind that tore at him like a hurricane of red-hot knives.

Jo was screaming at him. 'It's a trap!'

Was she right? Was the image before him another of The Outside's manipulations? Was it merely that thing wearing Oldroyd's face as a mask, as it had with Ronald Wyndham's?

Undine flinched as a tongue of flame lashed over him.

… hold hard …

Oldroyd's eyes were two points of coal-black stillness.

... you have a gift ... it's why you were chosen ...
Undine recognized the glitter of those birdlike eyes. He looked past the spidery crack of the shopkeeper's memory of his spectacles, and he knew. He accepted the reality of Oldroyd being here with him, wherever 'here' might be. Barely aware of his own voice, he answered Jo. The words scraped through his throat.

'I know who this is. We need to listen to him. Trust me.'

CHAPTER 33

Jo hoped to God Undine was right. The whispered torment was a physical wind now, whipping her hair and clothes, and crackling with threads of electric blue lightning. But it wasn't as if she had a better plan to offer.

She had to shout to hear herself above the growing storm. 'What do you want me to do?'

Undine's hoarse reply was even harder to make out. '... to help Oldroyd ... you with me ... like you did this afternoon!'

She stared at the fluctuating outlines of the hauntingly familiar face. So that was Oldroyd? Was he dead? What had happened to him?

The air reeked of scorched dust.

Undine was trying to say something else.

'... -ows how to repair the Weall ...'

Undine's ash-stained black suit rippled and flapped as he stood his ground. His face looked deathly pale and, with the smudges around his exhausted eyes, skull-like in the restless light.

His mouth was locked in a rictus grin of terror and a pain Jo prayed she would never experience, but she saw his determination not to break contact with the face hanging before them.

He was no longer the same man she had met outside the warehouse by the Thames. The change reminded her of the difference between the raw recruits she had trained with at Peel House and some of the experienced front-line officers she had worked with later: men whose battle-scarred cynicism had taken them down bitter paths. She hoped Undine would not go that way – if they survived this.

Something pulled at the dust sheets she stood on. They slid below her feet, as she fought to stay upright.

'Okay, Undine! I'm not going anywhere. I'm going to be right here!'

She thought he nodded. The next moment, his legs gave way. Undine dropped to his knees, yet his head remained upright, and his attention stayed fixed on the crow-like eyes of the face in front of him. Communion, she thought. Undine was in communion with Oldroyd.

She almost laughed, unable to suppress the mad thought that Undine would be mortified to know how he appeared to her at this moment, gazing so deep into another man's eyes. He looked so camp.

*   *   *

Fierce intention burned in those cold, black eyes. In the other faces, the eyes were submerged in the madness of suffering, but Oldroyd's were different. Undine could not look away. Oldroyd's image possessed consciousness and intelligence, and it was communicating. Impressions and meaning flowed into Undine's receptive mind, telling him that Oldroyd, unlike the others, had not been brought to this hell by The Outside. In some incomprehensible manner, Oldroyd had come here of his own accord to await the node's destruction, the signal that all other hope was lost. This – what was happening now – marked the endgame, their final chance.

Undine shaped his thoughts into a question:

… *Who are you?* …

… *the one who must do this* …

… *Do what?* …

… *the Weall must be healed* …

Oldroyd's image wavered, battered by unseen forces. Undine's ghost-self grabbed for him, newborn instinct telling Undine this was his role. This was why he –

(had been chosen?)

– was needed here. His despised psychic ability, now tempered and re-forged in shamanic fire, was the means for Oldroyd to reach out from the heart of this insane maelstrom, and for Undine to anchor Oldroyd's presence while the old man attempted to repair the barrier.

Undine held their position. Sobbing moans

of despair came at him in waves. They dragged at his fears and insecurities, suffocating him and threatening to pull him under and away.

His grip on Oldroyd weakened.

Faces screamed around them, but somewhere in the eternity beyond this place, Jo was saying she was with him, and knowing that gave him strength. He clawed his way back to the surface of the vortex, and renewed his hold on Oldroyd.

❊   ❊   ❊

'I'm here,' Jo told him.

For all the good that did. Undine had been silent and motionless for more than a minute now, yet his body – still kneeling before the old man's face – radiated tension.

Her own body fizzed with adrenaline and the choking, desperate need to act, but what could she do? The room raged with light and whispering, screaming insanity, and Jo dared not step away from its centre, terrified lest she touch the walls and be pulled inside, as had so nearly happened to the young man lying unconscious beside her.

Crackling electrical discharges played around the hole. Streamers of lightning lashed at her with increasing frequency, closing the distance a little more each time.

'You're doing well,' she told Undine.

But whatever the hell it is you're doing, for God's sake do it faster!

The luminous whirlwind shimmered as a colour Jo could not name passed through it. She detected a subtle shift in the solidity of her surroundings. As she stared in horrified wonder, a cloud of a material that twisted her perception of it seeped out of the hole. It uncoiled in her direction, and reality bent and distorted within its essence as if she were looking through an ever-changing series of fisheye lenses of different magnifications.

Through the warping transparency, she saw a workman's abandoned hammer tremble. It bulged and contracted as it lay where she had once seen floor. The edge of the cloud drew nearer, and she felt the floor sink, old wooden boards stretching and giving way beneath her like a trampoline. The night watchman's body rolled against her boot, and she struggled to keep her footing on the impossibly yielding surface.

A groan of effort escaped Undine.

'Keep going,' she said, surprised at the calmness in her voice even while she watched a crack appear in what should have been the floor.

The crack grew longer. It stretched from the hole, and, as it grew, the warped substance at its edges liquefied, letting the altered reality of the room drain into its widening gap. It was strangely beautiful.

Something moved in the corner of her eye.

She turned, and glimpsed a dark shape flying towards her.

She had just enough time to interpret the shape as the hammer she had seen a moment before, and to register that her body had reacted, throwing her to the side, but not fast enough, before the hammer thudded against her hip. She gasped in shock.

Jo lost her balance. She lurched sideways, put out a foot to check her fall, and her leg sank through the nothingness where floor had been. Carried by her momentum and flailing helplessly for something solid to grab, she tumbled through the yawning chasm, too shocked even to cry out.

*   *   *

Names did not exist for the colours Undine witnessed. They sizzled through the vortex of suffering, laser beams of unearthly power. Their lethal energies were bound precariously to the will of Oldroyd, who was fighting to shape them.

Fractured visions of screaming faces hurtled around Undine. The Outside whipped them into an ever greater frenzy, drawing on the totality of their agony as it battled to breach what remained of the weakened barrier.

The colours broke apart to reveal their inner structures: enormous spinning crystals that Oldroyd cracked and reformed into patterns which, to the watching Undine, carried the meaning of pentacles, if not the strict geometry appropriate to such a concept.

The vortex shrieked, pulling at Undine. It was a deliberate attack: The Outside wanted to stop what he was enabling Oldroyd to do.

Undine fought back, but could no longer keep out the suffering. Wordless accusations of failure wrenched his innermost being. Poison bled through his defences: insidious persuasions that his sensitivity made him a joke, an over-emotional wreck. That everyone he had ever known had mocked him behind his back. That every tear he had ever shed was testimony to his weakness and made him more deserving of the cruel laughter gouging his mind.

Oldroyd paused in his work. He looked to Undine in sudden alarm.

Far away, through lifetimes of pain, Undine knew he was losing his hold on the other man.

✻　　✻　　✻

Jo fell, and the whispering, screaming storm swirled around her.

There was no ground to reach, no material world to interrupt her plunge, and falling was all that was left to her, falling forever through her shame and her failure and her guilt.

People were dead. Because of her actions and because of her failures to act.

Although.... Hadn't Undine explained why it wasn't her fault? She struggled to remember. Something about a black stone, and a trick played on her....

She thought she recalled an elderly woman, desperate, with nobody to turn to. And a time when Jo wore a uniform, driven by a desire to help those in need.

Jo burned in the certainty of mistakes made. Remorse crippled her, paralysing her will.

Yet didn't she have a duty to rectify those mistakes? At least to try?

She fell through the abyss, striving to make sense of the chaos that had swallowed her.

She felt the weight of the night watchman's body, still unconscious and still lying at her feet.

How could that be?

She tumbled over and over, head over heels, and at the same time she saw Undine kneeling close by, motionless, his back to her and the distance between them unchanged.

She screwed her eyes closed, blotting out the madness, forcing herself to think. How could they be falling together in this way?

Her senses were telling her one thing. Logic was telling her another. She could not be falling. She needed to believe she still stood in the bedroom inside Lavender Edge. The confidence of reason quietened her storm-tossed thoughts, and she knew that when she opened her eyes, she would see the room again.

She opened them, and all she saw was the howling vortex.

So she was lost. But her identity remained intact. The Outside had not taken her completely. Not yet.

Time passed and still she fell. She started to identify patterns within the motion of images rushing around and through and past her. Gradually, she discerned that several of the faces were gravitating towards her, as if drawn to the shame she radiated.

One came closer than the others, and she discovered with a start that she knew the features swimming before her. She saw in them a dignified but strong gentleman, grimacing in an eternal scream, his teeth clenched on the memory of a pipe stem.

'Professor James.' She heard herself make the words, but could not be sure they consisted of actual sounds. 'Archie?'

The image altered. A suggestion of a frown appeared. Shadows shifted in the depths of doom-filled eyes as a lifetime's ingrained curiosity rose above the horror.

'You recognize me,' said Jo. 'Don't you? Jo Cross. Remember? WPC Cross?'

The repeated lie bit into her, but she needed a memorable detail to hook into the apparition. Archie would remember the policewoman.

He gaped at her, and for the first time Jo truly understood what Undine had meant about the faces. These were not the people that had once lived. They were not even their surviving personalities. They were no more than fragments ripped from disintegrating minds, torn away at the moment of death, mere scraps of thought and emotion.

Nevertheless, the spark of recognition glinted in those eyes.

'Archie,' she said. 'I'm so sorry.'

Strange currents rushed through them both. Archie's image trembled, and Jo expected it to be dragged away but it held fast.

It held – because he was fighting against the flow. At some level, Archie – this tormented tatter of what had been Archie – was consciously aware of her! Maybe there was one final way to help him.

'Oh God, Archie. If you can hear me, you need to listen. Really listen.'

Her eyes stung with tears. She could think of only one thing that might ease his suffering.

'This place isn't real, Archie.'

She tried to remember what he had once told her.

'Focus on the sound of my voice,' she said. 'Let everything else fade away, because it's a beautiful summer's day, Archie. It's so beautiful.'

She told him he was lying on his back in a meadow, repeating herself and building description upon description to create a different reality for him to inhabit. She told him about the soft grass beneath his body, and the scent of flowers on a gentle summer breeze. About the afternoon sunlight warm against his skin as he dozed and drifted in his reverie.

She spoke, and the essence that was all that remained of Professor Archibald James accepted the hypnotic dream she wove. He slipped willingly into the peaceful harbour of her soothing words, and, as he did so, the pain and terror that held together this shallow residue of mind-stuff relaxed.

His features softened, and dissipated. They slid free of the forces that had ensnared them and, with a sigh of release, they were no more.

Jo let him go and discovered she was weeping, both with loss and with gratitude.

CHAPTER 34

Pentacles. Layers of meaning spun out of the symbols Oldroyd had unleashed. Ancient ideas spiralled out and back, far beyond human history, promising to carry Undine with them, to free him from this existence and bring him into union with the forces that once shaped the primordial cosmos.

They could piss right off. All that bloody mattered was keeping hold of Oldroyd.

Undine leaned deeper into the burning hurricane, and rode the pain. He refused to loosen his grip, even as he understood he wasn't strong enough. A fresh riptide of fire coiled around his waist, dragging him under once more, and this time would be the last.

He held on to Oldroyd anyway. Out of sheer bloody-mindedness, he was going to give the man every last moment in his power to give.

He steeled himself against the expected lash of agony, and for an instant the shrieking howl of the vortex dipped, and the pull on him slackened. Then the cacophony returned.

Somehow, however, it was no longer the same.

The lash did not reach him.

The vortex roared, and Undine sensed an eruption of puzzled rage.

Something had happened. What?

Oldroyd was calling to him. He felt so far away.

Undine strained to take in the sense.

… tell her to repeat …

What the hell did that mean?

… Tell who? Jo? …

… yes …

Unable to think clearly, Undine simply did as he was told. He re-tightened his grip on Oldroyd and called out.

'Jo! Whatever you just did, keep doing it!'

❋　❋　❋

Undine's words were indecipherable, but some of his meaning filtered through. Jo rubbed away her tears and tried to concentrate on what was happening around her. The whirling chaos had just stuttered, and although its energy was building again it had yet to resume its full intensity.

A new image drifted closer, taking advantage of the slack current but tentative in its approach, afraid to defy the power that kept it in thrall.

Jo did her best to send encouraging thoughts. Whether or not the image picked up on her sentiments, it came nearer, the lines of its features solidifying until Jo made out a female face. She was young, probably not out of her teens. A suggestion of dark hair escaped the edge of some sort of maid's cap, and her eyes were full of frozen horror, locked inside the final moments of a short life.

'It's okay,' said Jo. 'You're having a bad dream. That's all this is. Nothing but a bad dream.'

The vortex roar was building again. Heaving tides snatched at Jo, dragging her this way and that, and she tumbled – but the image stayed with her. Sublimating her own terror into a desperate effort to ease the young woman's torment, Jo babbled words of comfort and snatches of childhood prayers. The words seemed less important than soothing tone of voice.

They fell together, and Jo watched fear melt from those phantom eyes. The blur of dark hair, the outline of a cap, the hazy contours of mouth and cheeks and chin – they all relaxed, and for the merest moment Jo saw a dawning smile. Then the face blurred, like a watercolour caught in rain, and was gone.

It vanished, and the storm dipped again – and Jo made the connection. She remembered Undine saying that The Outside tortured the essences trapped within this vortex; that it did so deliberately to feed off their emotional distress. With grim satisfaction, she realized that every face she released was an interruption to that energy source. She could fight it!

Her momentary elation died as the tides captured her once more and held her helpless in their grasp. More faces approached, surrounding her and keeping their positions despite the resurgent currents. Among them, Jo spotted the aquiline nose and thick moustache of Ronald Wyndham.

✻　　✻　　✻

Undine was no longer sinking. There could be no doubt that the forces pulling him under were weaker than before, but he dared not relax his struggle against the sucking undertow.

Neither could he relax his precarious grip on Oldroyd's ghost-self. Everything that Undine was, burned – but he had passed into a state beyond anything so nonsensical as fear, where suffering was so fundamental to his fast-disintegrating being that it was all but inconsequential. Undine's sole purpose – the only vestige of his identity – was the need to anchor Oldroyd's unearthly presence in this hell.

He watched Oldroyd manipulate shapes that Undine had once comprehended as pentacles. Now, he experienced them as multi-dimensional flows, inside of which self-replicating copies surged and multiplied as they spiralled down and down into infinity.

The final shards of Undine's conscious thought absorbed the extra-sensory spectacle, watching as those spirals channelled the howling vortex, forcing it into winds like those that gusted through canyons of monolithic structures in a world he had once known.

Form emerged from the gusting currents: an immense construction in the shape of interlocking mazes that extended in more directions than Undine was able to perceive.

He attempted to follow its lines, and caught a glimpse of something greater than he could ever hope to comprehend.

He recoiled, just as the pressure of the vortex eased another fraction. The presence Undine still thought of as Oldroyd – for he had no other name to give it – was everywhere now, moving with ever-increasing speed as it wove strange energies into even stranger configurations, re-routing fundamental forces that had no place in the universe Undine remembered.

And, recalling a metaphor from that universe, Undine understood that Oldroyd was 'rewiring the circuitry' of the Weall. He was taking apart the ruins of the damaged metaphysical structure and using them to create something new.

*　　*　　*

The helmet, of a style she associated with the English Civil Wars, was little more than fog now.

'It's all over,' Jo assured the craggy, battle-scarred features before her, smiling sympathy to the soldier as his eyes gentled and the lines of his face dissolved like the dying ripples on a pond.

How many had she released now? Dozens? More?

It was good that Ronald had been among them. Margaret Wyndham would have drawn some comfort from that if there had been any way to let her know.

Jo turned in her endless freefall, aching with physical and mental exhaustion, watching with almost detached interest as further shoals of faces moved towards her through the storm, some still screaming while others mouthed silent pleas for help.

Their motion was not due to the vagaries of fluctuating currents. Jo was certain now that their own deep yearning drew them to her, that some lingering traces of their awareness sensed the possibility of escape. It drove them to swim against tides which were no longer as powerful as before.

The night watchman's body still lay incongruously at her feet, and she could still see Undine nearby. Somehow, he remained kneeling on what she had once perceived as floor, his black trench coat stretched across his unmoving back and falling around him.

'Are you still with me, Undine?' she asked.

He gave no reaction.

The outer edge of the shoal arrived. Faces crowded her, soaking in this long-denied human contact, and she spoke to them, the sounds more important than the words and coming automatically now. All around her, ghostly images slipped into dissolution in their twos and threes.

A filigree of lighting illuminated the vortex with electric blue tracery. But it was a pale imitation of the ferocity of earlier discharges, and she took it as a sign that whatever Undine was doing was having an effect. Even so, Jo wondered how much longer she could keep going.

Another image reached her, and it was the nose she recognised first. That big nose, so out of proportion in his skinny face.

Mingled happiness and regret twisted her drained emotional core.

'Ray.'

Her voice choked with affection for the unworldly scientist. They would have become good friends, she knew, if events had worked out differently. She studied the swirls that formed his blank eyes, searching for any sign of recognition. There was nothing. Whatever this essence saw did not exist in this time and space, only in scraps of memory.

A tired smile warmed her as she wondered what crazy assortment of mismatched clothes Ray's memories retained. Or perhaps he recalled himself in the stylish outfit he had bought shortly before she last saw him? In an odd way, she hoped it was the former.

Ray's features softened. The fading illusion of his mouth grew wider, cracking his narrow face open in a last broad grin, and Jo realised she had been speaking to him this whole time, unaware but comforting him, soothing him, and allowing the fear binding him to this place to die and let him go.

Then he was gone, and she found she had been crying again, sobbing tears of heartache and empathy and joy at being able to offer this merciful release.

She barely reacted to the explosion of blue electricity that temporarily blinded her. Through blobbing after-images of its arcing glare, she watched a deeper darkness bleed into the storm, and the hurricane tightened. For a long while, the roaring rush of whispered screams had been subsiding, but now the winds whipped up with rejoined ferocity. They threatened to cut her with the keenness of a thousand newly sharpened knives.

Jo smiled again. A rueful smile this time, and she regretted only that it could never be as wide or as open as Ray's had been. If this were how she died, then she would not be afraid. She refused to give it that. But first....

She gathered the remaining faces to her, welcoming them closer, and murmuring that there was nothing to be scared of.

✳   ✳   ✳

Light that was not light blazed in labyrinthine streams, coursing with primal energies. On a level of being beyond pain and beyond conscious thought, Undine persisted as a presence, an event in non-space and non-time, a living node through which sorcerous technology was worked.

Impressions washed through him – of submerged connections between house and shopkeeper, and between primordial land and the concept of guardianship.

Freezing currents of liquid fire ran around him. They shrieked to the disruption that poured through what he had become.

Powerless to act, Undine brushed against a different way in which thought could be shaped. For an instant, he experienced 'Oldroyd' as the contours of a mask, a deceiving face worn by the outer human aspect of something vast and deep and, in its own way, as alien to humanity as was The Outside. Yet whereas The Outside seethed with madness and chaos, this other was the manifestation of principles Undine could intuit only as an opposition to that which The Outside was not.

The moment passed, and the vortex still raged. Its fury, however, was diminished. Mighty rivers of power plunged into the channels being forged by Oldroyd, to be swept away. The new Weall was a dazzling superimposition of incomprehensibly intricate mazes and, as it worked its magic, Undine felt The Outside weaken. The Weall was denying it its existence here.

Then a shadow soaked through the glare.

The vortex pulled in on itself, shrinking and accelerating its spin. The whispered screams rose again, and lightning crackled through the Weall, spiking it with a spreading infection. Shadows pushed aside the light, and thickened.

Undine thought of Jo, and felt her presence, far away, associated with the release of more of the memory fragments that had been trapped here. He sensed the small lifting of pressure as each was freed, but he understood, quite suddenly, that there was no more time.

A furnace opened – and scorpion tails of psychic fire lashed out. They were everywhere, and they coiled around every one of the remaining fragments, and they constricted. Faces screamed as crushing flames squeezed the last drops of agony from their tortured memories, taking it all until the tattered scraps flared and were gone, their final energies entirely consumed by The Outside.

The vortex froze, swelled, and – abruptly – imploded. Then the collapse reversed, blasting its shockwave outward, shattering the shining, elaborate, beautiful structure Oldroyd had built, and hurling Oldroyd himself away in a shower of splinters.

Reality's veil tore, and The Outside entered.

CHAPTER 35

In the upstairs bedroom, the outline of the hole melted. Restless, protean darkness bulged through the widening space, absorbing form and matter as it came, and radiating distortion.

Jo watched it happen. It was over. They had lost.

She was no longer falling, but she had no memory of ever hitting the ground. The falling had simply ceased to be what was happening.

By her feet, the unconscious night watchman bobbed on the undulating floor. He seemed so young. No point in waking him, not when they would all be dead soon. Let his last moments be peaceful.

Had Undine's end been peaceful? She looked to where his body lay collapsed, his face crumpled against a dust sheet. Where the expanding darkness touched the far edge of the sheet, molecules gave up their cohesion, disintegrating, becoming one with the bubbling shadows.

She limped across to Undine, her leg numb where the hammer had hit, and sat beside him. She was mildly surprised to see him breathing. Not dead, but asleep in his trance, he appeared more content than she had ever seen him, and she wondered whether or not to envy the fact he would miss this spectacle. She was the only one awake to witness the beginning of the end. Even the faces were gone. While glad she had released so many, she wished she had been able to spare the rest their final, violent destruction.

The darkness oozed, and its thickening aura crept along the unsteady reality of walls and ceiling. The room's details were no longer continuously visible: the floral design of the wallpaper, the lines of skirting boards, the edges of the polystyrene ceiling tiles – all of it bloomed in and out of the shimmering murk.

There was no point in getting out of Lavender Edge, even if she could. She'd only be delaying the inevitable. The Outside would spread from this room, absorbing reality and continuing to grow. Soon it would consume the house, then the street, and who knew where it would end?

Would it end?

In any case, she had promised Undine she would not abandon him.

She draped an arm across his back. His cigarette packet had come out of his pocket, she noticed, and was trapped beneath his chest. One sharp corner dug into his chin. It looked uncomfortable. She eased it out from under him, murmuring soft words into his sleep.

'It's only me, Undine. I'm still here.'

The darkness seeped closer.

She felt, rather than heard, the first vibration of sound. Hoarse and hard to discern, it took Jo a long moment to realize it was coming from Undine.

*　　*　　*

Undine's mind throbbed. Blackness pressed against him, and he saw that it was not blackness at all but an unfolding glittering immensity in which all hues of light co-existed. They overlapped and reflected an infinity of rippling interference back into their own depths, throwing boiling shadows over eternity.

His connection with Oldroyd was fading, and his capacity for processing thought, for separating self from other, was reawakening. Emotions were stirring too. Grief ravaged him, and in its savage wake came desperate, aching, loving loss and wailing anger. He raged at his own weakness, appalled at the selfish cowardice that had kept him from acting before it was too late. Could he have stopped this?

Undine burned with the intensity of feeling. He writhed in the searing anguish from which he had hidden for so much of his life, and he drew strength from the pain.

The scattered debris of his consciousness coalesced, and the jagged borders of new, living thoughts struck sparks that flared in defiance of his surroundings.

No! This was not how he ended. He would not give in.

Undine threw himself towards the place into which Oldroyd had vanished.

Down he plunged, tasting and smelling a viscous noise, half-blinded by a turbulent discord. All sound that had ever been was replaying simultaneously, the clamour rising and rolling through forever, and although there was no possibility of being heard Undine shouted anyway.

...Jo! ...

She might be dead. But hopelessness was cowardice by another name, a self-pitying retreat from the potential of further hurt. Hope was everything. It was the most dangerous of human concepts, and it could be a weapon.

...Jo! ...

He saw someone ahead, and in that moment he was already moving in that direction.

... Can you hear me? ...

But the figure was not Jo.

Oldroyd gazed at Undine with a curious knowing smile. He floated within an eddy of strange currents, waiting for the plummeting

Undine to arrive – and then Undine was there, caught by Oldroyd's outstretched arms, and they hung together deep inside the spreading madness of The Outside.

Not Jo, yet he could hear her now.

'... only me, Undine ...'

Her voice was muffled, sinking to him through unfathomable depths.

He called again to her.

... Jo! ...

Oldroyd's hard, black eyes bore into him: *... go to her ...*

'... I'm still here ...'

... hold on to her voice ...

... Jo, I can hear you! ...

Undine rose, following the ripples of Jo's words, and Oldroyd rose with him, sharing his thoughts.

... has exhausted its energy source ... the time to act ... before it can establish another ...

The echoes of Jo's voice were stronger now. Undine held on to them, and climbed along their reverberations.

The higher he ascended, the less effort was required to keep going, and all the while he was dimly aware of Oldroyd working at his side, collecting fragmented shards of force, drawing them into strands, and weaving the results into a design that Undine's clumsy faculties of comprehension could conceptualize only as a cage – except that Oldroyd's creation was immense and immaterial. And now it assumed a life of its own. It spun itself like a spider's web through the churning chaos of space and time.

Then everything was receding, and Oldroyd was telling him it was time to let go.

... your part in this is over ...

As the dying wisps of his connection with Oldroyd faded into a dream, so the temporary heightening of Undine's supernatural senses withered.

Coarse material rubbed against his cheek, and in the last instant before Undine's physical eyes reopened, he glimpsed Oldroyd for the final time. He had shrunk to a twinkling point, at the centre of a silvery light that was crystallizing and locking in the fury of the struggling Outside as together they plunged away and out of Undine's universe.

Then the weight of a hand was on Undine's back. He tried to talk, but the effort was too much and he let his eyes close again.

CHAPTER 36

Undine opened an eyelid, and cringed from the bright, grey light. An aching strain hardened across his neck and shoulders, and he became aware of a dull pounding stuffed into the space between his skull and brain.

He tried to raise his head. Rough cloth came up with him, pressed into the flesh of his cheek. He turned away until it peeled off, and groaned.

'What's that bloody smell?'

Jo looked up. She was sitting beside him. Her eyes – shining pools in smeared and tear-streaked mascara – locked onto his for a second, then she fell across him, embracing him in a hug.

His confused thoughts struggled to make sense of what had happened. Jo was weeping. It must have been something dreadful.

The room filtered back into memory. Its atmosphere was different now. Like lying on the grassy summit of a sunlit hill, drinking in cool, fresh morning air. What was going on? He allowed his mind to reach out, just a little at first, then further, probing his surroundings as warily as a nervous patient probes a repaired tooth after coming around at the dentist. He sensed nothing. No echoes of violence, no captive despair, no tormented anguish – only peace and the glassy sheen of untroubled depths. Lavender Edge, it seemed, was no longer a 'thin place'. There would be no more need for a Weall here.

Jo was still crying, but the dominant emotion he got from her was elation. He pulled back his thoughts before her feelings overwhelmed him, and he wondered about his own physical condition. Every muscle hurt, as if he had slept on a motorway, his body battered by the wheels of an endless stream of traffic.

The extra burden clinging to him wasn't making things easier.

'Bleeding hell. How much do you weigh?'

With a surprisingly girlish giggle, Jo slid to her knees beside him.

Tears brimmed his eyes before he had a chance to blink them away. He turned his face from her, and discovered his arms were trapped under his chest; he had to tug them free before he could dig through his pockets. Blood flowed to his dead fingers and they prickled. It was with difficulty that he extricated a handkerchief.

He wiped his nose, and lumbered to his feet. When he looked around again, Jo was watching him. Sly amusement danced in her eyes, but all she said was: 'Give us a hand?'

He helped her up. She stood by him as he gazed through the nearest bay window, out over the back garden. Rosy dawn light tinged the sky, and Undine checked his watch. It was broken. He caught that faint, quiet scent in the air again, then grimaced as he spotted the night watchman's body.

'How is he?'

Jo shrugged. 'He'll be fine. Actually, he came to a couple of minutes before you did. I don't think he remembers anything that happened after he came upstairs.'

She grinned, and winced as a twinge of pain hit her. 'He had no idea where he was. I told him he'd fallen over and knocked his head on the door frame. Said I'd been walking past and heard him call out for help. I think he just wants to sleep it off.'

Undine raised an eyebrow.

'I found this in his pocket.' Jo held up a half-smoked joint and a bag of green herbal mixture. 'I guess we know what he was smoking downstairs now.'

'Bloody hippy,' said Undine. He managed a single dry chuckle before his stomach muscles clenched in protest.

'Anyway,' said Jo. 'I'm more worried about you. What happened?'

Undine drew in as deep a breath as his ribs would permit, and tried to master the competing emotions surging through him. 'Long story.' He sniffed, and wiped a hand across his eyes. 'We'd better go check on Oldroyd first.'

He pulled out his hankie again, and as they left the room, he blew his nose with a blast that almost woke the snoring night watchman. Out on the landing, he fumbled through his coat, searching for his cigarettes.

He paused. The scent was stronger out here.

'Seriously. That's not weed. What is that smell?'

Jo smiled. 'I think it's lavender.'

❋ ❋ ❋

No cars moved on Rivermead Path, but the sky was growing lighter and the breeze carried an early morning briskness.

Jo was limping.

'What happened to your leg?'

'I'll recover.' She rubbed her hip, and nodded towards the corner shop. 'What are you expecting to find?'

Undine shook his head, too drained even to try to answer that.

The 'Closed' sign still hung on the door. He tried the handle, certain he would find it locked and already wondering how they were going to get inside. Nobody seemed to be watching from the neighbouring houses, so...

He was surprised when the handle turned.

When he eased the door open, musty air sighed out into the morning. He ushered Jo in beneath the jangling bell, and closed the door behind them. They stood beside the rack of magazines and newspapers and the local history pamphlets. The interior was as still and gloomy as always, and the smell of over-boiled cabbage lingered, fainter than he remembered, and mingled now with a faded stench. Undine was no stranger to the stink of dead mice, rotting out of reach under the floorboards of his bedsit, and this was somewhat similar.

'Not exactly up-to-date with the news,' said Jo, taking a paper from the rack. The pages crinkled in the dry silence.

Undine recognized the headline from his first visit to Oldroyd's shop; it referred to the new internment laws in Northern Ireland. Reacting to Jo's comment, he searched for the date at the top of the page: 30 August. That was, what, a month and a half ago?

He frowned. 'I never noticed that.'

'The others are the same.' Jo leafed through a few publications, then turned to the empty counter. She lifted it, and her fingers left depressions in the thick layer of dust. Stepping through, she parted the curtain of ribbons to reveal the foot of a steep, narrow staircase leading up. 'Smell's stronger here.'

'Go on,' said Undine. 'I'm right behind you.'

They were both speaking in whispers.

Undine told himself it was because they didn't want the neighbours to overhear, but there was more to it than that. Something here was wrong.

On the upstairs landing, he called out softly. 'Mr Oldroyd?'

No reply came. Undine opened the nearest door and found a small room. A single wooden chair stood by the window that looked out across Rivermead Path, giving a clear view of Lavender Edge. On the floor beside it lay an antique pair of binoculars. The only other item of furniture was a wardrobe, containing nothing but a few items of greying underwear.

Across the landing, he found a tiny, spartan bathroom, and next to that a kitchen. In the cupboard were a couple of tins of baked beans and the mouldy remains of half a loaf of bread.

'In here,' said Jo.

Undine shut the cupboard and went to join her in the only room he hadn't inspected yet. It was as devoid of comfort as the others, and he wondered where Oldroyd slept – there had been no sign of a bed anywhere – but suddenly that didn't matter.

Jo was gazing down at a body. It was thin, and clad in a shabby brown pinstriped suit. Undine swallowed, and took a moment to control his still unpredictable emotions.

The figure lay splayed across the floor, at the centre of a large circle, some six feet in diameter. It had been drawn in a careful sprinkle of fine white grains, and Undine had read enough about occultism to know the grains would be salt. It was a protective magic circle, although evidently it had not been protective enough. The perimeter enclosed a five-pointed star – a pentacle – and hazy connections shifted deep inside him, stirring like the forgotten memories of an old dream.

'Is this him? Your shopkeeper?'

Jo's voice held an unsettling edge of doubt.

He focused on the body, seeing yellow skin stretched taut over bone, a mouth that gaped open, and sunken eyes behind wire-framed spectacles that bore a familiar crack in the left lens. Mercifully, the eyes were closed. He looked away.

'Yeah, that's Oldroyd. Poor old bastard.'

Jo shook her head. 'When did you see him last? Alive, I mean.'

An image flashed into Undine's mind: Oldroyd's face as it had manifested inside Lavender Edge no more than a few hours before. He pushed it down and tried to think. 'Two days ago? More like a day-and-a-half really.'

'I don't get it,' said Jo. 'I've seen dead bodies, and this man's been here for weeks, I'd say. Maybe longer. And the smell's … wrong.'

Undine took a cautious sniff. Up here, the stink of decay carried a brittle, woody note.

'He looks ancient,' said Jo, speaking almost to herself. 'Mummified almost.' She stared at

Undine. 'You're quite sure it's him?'

Undine forced himself to take a longer look at the corpse's face. There was no mistake. It was definitely Oldroyd.

He turned away, leaving a puzzled Jo to continue her study of the body. Undine concentrated instead on the circle and pentacle, wondering what could have happened. By the look of it, Oldroyd had been performing some sort of occult ritual when he died. Had he been trying to repair the Weall? Had The Outside proved too strong an opponent for him alone?

Undine's headache was getting worse.

'I've seen him before,' said Jo. 'I wasn't sure at first, but the more I look at him....'

'When?'

'That first night I went to the house. The night I told you about. When I was walking back to the police station with Dick Condie, and that man appeared for a few moments, begging us to go to the house because somebody needed help. I couldn't picture his face before, but this was him. I'm certain of it.'

Undine thought back to the afternoon – only a week ago! – when he and Ray had watched Archie hypnotize Jo to recall the details of that encounter. He thought back to Archie's comment at the time, that the old man Jo described reminded him of accounts of 'crisis apparitions', phantoms that appeared at the moment of a person's death.

The obvious question occurred to him. He didn't want to ask it, but he had to. 'How long ago was it? That night you saw him.'

'A fair few weeks,' said Jo, working it out. 'Just over a month and a half.'

Deep inside Undine, memories that were little more than uneasy flutters rolled over. Fleeting impressions came to him from a fading dream of submerged connections, and he pictured the spider's web on the wall surrounding Mrs Wyndham's garden. For an instant he trembled on the verge of wider realms of perception, where impossibly intricate patterns spun out forever in unknowable directions through space and time.

It was no coincidence that Undine had been drawn to that house, nor that he had been compelled to return, over and over again. Oldroyd – whoever or whatever he had been – had attempted to repair the Weall alone, but after the failure of his initial attempt he had needed Undine's psychic 'gift' to help him. And Jo's involvement had been deliberate too. Oldroyd had seen how to use her, and how to ensnare them both, pulling together the tenuous strands of potentiality that connected her to Undine through the telephone number Archie had left with Jo's sergeant months before.

But if Oldroyd had been dead for weeks, how could Undine have visited him here only a few days ago?

Filaments of thought evaporated as Undine reached for them, and then they were gone. Perhaps that was for the best. Leave thoughts of cosmic plans and warped realities for the hippies to drive themselves mad with, and just accept that some things were beyond the reach of human minds.

He stepped out of the room. Jo followed him onto the landing and gently pulled the door closed behind them.

'We should let the police know,' she said.

It took Undine a moment to understand she was talking about Oldroyd's body. About cold, hard reality.

'Couldn't that cause problems? I mean, your old colleagues know about your interest in the house over the road, and what Mrs Wyndham said about it. When they see what's in that room, they'll suspect a connection. They'll want to ask you questions.'

Once the police started digging, they would uncover the Institute's involvement too. How the hell was Undine going to explain what had happened to Archie and Ray? He thought about that morning not so long ago, sitting with his friends in the lorry on their way back from the sleazy Soho theatre, when everything was so much simpler, before any of this mess had started, and he again felt his eyes grow damp.

'It's okay,' said Jo. 'I'll drop by the station before I go home. Tell them I overheard some gossip about the shop, people saying they hadn't seen the owner for a while. Suggest someone takes a look.'

Undine remained unconvinced.

'Trust me,' she said. 'Once they get past the weird magic stuff, all they'll see is a dead old man. Who, as far as I can see, died of natural causes. They'll have a juicy story to tell each other in the pub, but they won't be arsed to investigate further. And if they do have any questions for me, don't worry. I can deal with them.'

She sounded confident, but her reassuring expression lingered just a beat too long.

'You're thinking of Ray, aren't you?' said Undine. 'And Archie.'

Jo didn't immediately reply. Then she gave a small nod.

In the silence that stretched between them, Undine contemplated his own grief. So much had happened, the full impact of which had been kept at bay by all the drama and was now being dulled only by exhaustion. Soon, it would hit him, and when it did it was going to hit hard.

'What about you?' asked Jo at last. 'What are you going to do now?'

'Sleep. For about a year.'

She attempted a tired laugh. 'Amen to that. But I meant afterwards.'

'I'll have to write to Rome, I suppose. Tell the Institute HQ what happened.'

'What will they do?'

Undine spread his hands. 'I don't know. Archie always dealt with them before. But I've seen reports from some of their other teams around the world. To tell the truth, I never really believed most of what I read, but now....' He cleared his throat. 'Well, I doubt this is the first time they've lost people. I expect there are procedures.'

He broke off before his welling tears could ambush him, and patted his pockets, searching again for his cigarettes.

'At least it'll be an interesting report to write.' He scowled. 'Where the bloody hell are they?'

'Here.'

Jo handed him his packet of Embassies. As she did so, she tilted her head and parted her lips, pretending the thought she was about to voice had only just occurred to her. He let her get away with the act.

'You know,' she said casually, 'I could help you if you like. One thing about police work, you get plenty of practice with paperwork.'

Undine pulled out a cigarette, relieved to find it less damaged than the crumpled, red-striped cardboard had suggested. He clamped it between his lips, considering her offer.

The past few days had changed him, but how much remained to be seen. Meanwhile, his need to learn how to control his 'gift' – and to protect himself from its effects – was, if anything, more urgent than ever. He hoped he would be able to carry on working for the Institute, using its resources to seek answers that might help him. Writing reports, however – and, more generally, the diplomacy required when dealing with other people – was hardly his strong suit.

He lit up, relishing the smoke's rough sting as it went down.

'Maybe,' he said.

AFTERWORD

And ... back to the present day. I really hope you enjoyed reading 'The Horror at Lavender Edge' and are as curious as I am about what will happen to Undine and Jo next. But before we get ahead of ourselves, a few words on where they came from.

Their story began as a response to one of those 'what if' questions that writers so enjoy toying with. For various depressing reasons that aren't important here, I needed to escape the modern world, and found myself returning to old horror paperbacks of the 1970s and 1980s: novels I had grown up with, by authors such as Graham Masterton, James Herbert, and (obviously) Stephen King. I knew those books still lurked somewhere in my attic, and an hour or so crawling through dust to discover which boxes they were stored in was a small price to pay to return them to my bookshelves. A similar impulse was drawing me to keep an eye on the television listings for repeats of films and dramas from the 1970s, a world I remembered from my early childhood but one which seemed so strange now that it proved the adage of the past being a foreign country where people did things differently. It was while watching 'The Sweeney', a rather dark and sharp-edged TV series about members of the Metropolitan Police's Flying Squad, that I caught myself wondering what would have happened to that show's lead character – the tough, hard-drinking, hard-smoking Detective Inspector Jack Regan – had he somehow ended up as a ghost hunter instead of a detective. With that, the idea of Harry Undine was conceived.

Undine did not stay that way, of course. Attractive though it was, the notion of Jack Regan one day simply deciding to investigate the supernatural seemed unlikely. What on earth would his motivation be? But Undine had taken up lodgings in the back of my brain and as the days and weeks went by, he developed. The tough guy, it turned out, was actually a lot more sensitive than he wanted to be, and he couldn't handle what that did to him. Yet neither was he prepared to reveal his supernatural weakness to anyone who might be able to help him. At the same time, his tough guy mindset was more than mere denial; it was also an effective defence mechanism because the discipline it imposed on his thoughts and emotions was the best protection he had found against the pain to which he would otherwise be exposed. In other words, the face Undine presented to the world was both protection and a prison, which was a concept I thought would be fun to play with.

He needed a companion though. And I can't help thinking of that word, companion, without thinking of Doctor Who, and when my mind combines Doctor Who and 1971, it automatically throws up the superb Third Doctor story, 'The Daemons'. The BBC broadcast that story only a few weeks before WPC Jo Cross first visits Lavender Edge, and yes, Jo's first name is a homage to the Third Doctor's companion Jo Grant. Her personality, however, is very much her own.

As for the story in which Undine and Jo become embroiled in this book, that was inspired by a creepy real-life tale from around 1962, in which ghostly faces were reported to appear on the walls of an old house in Mitcham, south London.

(You can read a summary of this in 'The Faces on the Walls: Hancock's Cottages' in 'Mysterious Mitcham': see www.shadowtimepublishing.co.uk/ mysteriousmitcham.)

Thankfully for us all, beyond that jumping-off point, the real-life tale bears little resemblance to what Undine discovers in Lavender Edge.

I did, however, decide to keep my story set in Mitcham. This was partly because Mitcham has long been associated with lavender and I had already fallen in love with the idea of a creaky old house called Lavender Edge, which I thought carried a pleasing folk-horror frisson. It was also because a lot of the reason for writing this was, as you will have gathered, to do with revisiting and reimagining my own past, and Mitcham was where I happened to grow up.

Lavender Edge itself does not exist. The description of its 18th-century redbrick exterior with all those windows does come from an old mansion which once stood in Mitcham, but the interior is that of a completely separate building from nearby Balham. Likewise, the road in which Lavender Edge stands – Rivermead Path – is fictional. In my mind, while writing, I pictured Rivermead Path as existing roughly where the real-life Tramway Path is located, because I knew that was around the edge of the real-life Anglo-Saxon cemetery that the Bidders really did excavate here, and also that there would once have been lavender fields stretching away south from this general area. It was only when looking a map some time later that I realized there is a similar-sounding Riverside Drive only a short stroll away! (I expect I had seen the name and half-forgotten it.) So, while Rivermead Path is made up, its location could be considered a strange geographical blurring of those real-life roads.

On the subject of geography, if you know Mitcham then you may be aware that the town's police station in 1971 was located beside Cricket Green, and not where I placed it, in the vicinity of Fair Green. This was not a mistake. I deliberately changed this detail for the purposes of this story to emphasize that the police officers who appear in this book are total figments of my imagination and in no way portrayals of any real members of the police force who served here at this time.

Artistic licence also provided the excuse to invent one of the bands Jo thinks about as she explores Undine's record collection. I originally intended to quote some early David Bowie lyrics in the front of this book, which I still believe would have been a lovely touch, but tracking down the copyright holder was eating so much into my writing time that I decided simply to invent Crystal Starcruiser instead. I don't know a whole lot about the band yet, but Jo clearly likes them and I'm sure she'll tell me more about them soon enough.

As for any other historical inaccuracies you may spot? Well, I expect those are mistakes and my fault.

Thank you very much indeed for reading 'The Horror at Lavender Edge'. If you liked it, please tell your friends, your family, and anyone else you can think of who might like to read it. And if you can spare a few moments, please, please, please leave a review on Amazon, Goodreads, BookBub, or anywhere else. Even if it's just a sentence or two, reviews from readers help so much in getting books noticed!

And finally, if you would like to keep in contact, I would love to hear from you! You can find my social media details and/or sign up to my mailing list at my website:
www.christopherhendersonhorror.com.

Thanks again, and my very best wishes. I hope we can meet again in the past,

Christopher

ABOUT THE AUTHOR

Christopher Henderson

Christopher Henderson was born in Streatham, south London, UK, a few months after the first man landed on the Moon. Meanwhile, just a few miles away on the other side of London, people were planning to hunt and stake a vampire in its lair in Highgate Cemetery. It was the beginning of 1970, and the birth of a very weird decade.

His childhood was steeped in the eerie, the macabre, and the uncanny. Horror and the fantastical permeated popular culture, and the supernatural was only ever a half-heard whisper away. In that heady atmosphere, he breathed deep of the vapours, and they worked their magic.

Almost half a century later, and in another life, he works in publishing and is the author (under his 'real' name) of several non-fiction books. In this incarnation, however, he writes horror. It is his escape from a world that is becoming somewhere he'd rather not be.

PRAISE FOR AUTHOR

The Horror at Lavender Edge: '... a terrific and imaginative read. Henderson's gritty, realistic characters and interesting background and lore weave together to create an immersive narrative. [...] Henderson manages to pull from a variety of genres without falling victim to the same overused plot devices so often seen. The Horror at Lavender Edge is fresh, original, and certainly worth a look.'

- HOME GROWN HORROR REVIEWS

The Horror at Lavender Edge: 'Christopher Henderson's tale manages to take all the very best things of a haunted house story then gives it an almighty twist. I'm sure the characters of this book really wished it was simply a ghost house they were investigating. But no, they're up against an even more terrifying antagonist. [...] The other-worldly descriptions and the horrors they contain is truly the stuff of nightmares.'

- MORGAN K. TANNER, AUTHOR OF AN ARMY OF SKIN

'Much more than a haunted house book ... and with rich elements of Fortean high strangeness. The characters were amazing, the plot, absolutely perfect. I cannot praise this book highly enough. Wonderfully done and actually, deeply unsettling.'

- SARAH J. HUNTINGTON, AUTHOR OF CABIN TERROR

The Horror at Lavender Edge: 'A thoroughly enjoyable read. [...] If you enjoy supernatural fiction with lots of action you can't go far wrong with this one.'

- CATHERINE MCCARTHY, AUTHOR OF IMMORTELLE

The Horror at Lavender Edge: 'Henderson does an amazing job of bringing his characters to life, they came across as really realistic which amps up the tension as from page one there's a palpable sense of foreboding. [...] This book was great fun to read. Perfect for fans of really creepy haunted houses!'

- S. J. BUDD, AUTHOR OF ENTER THE DARKNESS

UNDINE AND CROSS

Supernatural/cosmic horror thrillers set in the 1970s

The Horror At Lavender Edge

BOOKS BY THIS AUTHOR

Artemis One-Zero-Five

In the darkness between planets, a spacesuit jerks to life. Far away, a human mind has merged with the suit's robotic framework.

Nick Scott was born to explore, and the Link has given him the means to do so. Through its technology, he can be here now, charting this asteroid. Life is good – until a momentary lapse in concentration sends his consciousness tumbling into the unknown.

He survives, but a mysterious force seeps into the Link.

Soon, something dangerous is rising from the depths of Nick's mind, gathering substance, and spilling into the rain-lashed streets of south London.

As memories and dreams uncoil, imagination takes on a deadly reality, and a terrifying threat is unleashed upon the Earth.

'... a deft job of developing an ongoing sense of dread and impending terror ... a really well done, character-driven sci-fi/horror story ...' (Kendall Reviews)

Printed in Great Britain
by Amazon

37858838R00255